Just Until Dawn . . .

Steffen cupped her face with his hands and smoothed the tears away from her cheekbones with his thumbs.

"Don't cry, Jo. Everything is all right now. Nothing shall ever come between us again." He covered her face with kisses. "I never loved until I met you. You're my reason for living, my love, my heart, my darling."

All her senses were keened to the desire descending and sweeping across them with the full force of a leaping, thundering avalanche. She could almost hear the roaring in her ears. Without stirring, she felt him reaching for her as if the very air sparked and flashed with the force released between them. . . .

RD/h

This Shining Land

ROSALIND LAKER

BANTAM BOOKS
TORONTO • NEW YORK • LONDON • SYDNEY • AUCKLAND

THIS SHINING LAND

A Bantam Book / published by arrangement with
Doubleday

PRINTING HISTORY
Doubleday edition published July 1985
Bantam edition / April 1989

ISBN 0-553-27758-8

Bantam Books are published by Bantam Books, a division of
Bantam Doubleday Dell Publishing Group, Inc. Its trademark,
consisting of the words "Bantam Books" and the portrayal of a
rooster, is Registered in U.S. Patent and Trademark Office and in
other countries. Marca Registrada. Bantam Books, 666 Fifth
Avenue, New York, New York 10103

PRINTED IN THE UNITED STATES OF AMERICA
KR   0 9 8 7 6 5 4 3 2 1

To my husband Inge of 331 Squadron,
who met me at Bergen with flowers.

Chapter 1

On the morning of Monday April 8, 1940, Johanna Ryen bought her daily newspaper as usual on her way to work. After an Eastertide of sharp sunshine, which had done nothing to ease the bitter temperature, there was a strong wind blowing off Oslo Fjord and a swirl of new snow in the air. Spring was exceptionally late in coming, following a winter colder in neutral Scandinavia and war-torn Europe than had been known for many years. At the exclusive fur shop where she worked as secretary and bookkeeper, business had been brisk during the past few days with end-of-season bargains to be had, some customers wearing their purchases out of the shop to combat the weather.

Tucking the newspaper under her arm, Johanna turned in the direction of Karl Johans Gate. At twenty-one she was a tall girl with a good figure and long, beautiful legs. Her hair, which swung glossily at shoulder length, was a dark gold echoed in fine brows, her eyes a sparkling blue. Recent skiing on the slopes of Nordmarka, which cradled the city, had given a tan to her subtly expressive face, almost as if sheer good health illumined her features from within. Completely at ease with herself, she always laughed readily and honestly. Her mouth, wide and generous, had little need of the lipstick that brightened it to a red that matched the warm woollen cap hugging her head.

On her way up the wide avenue she passed some of the best shops and stores in the city. On one side lay the Parliament buildings and the Students' Park that was linked with the nearby university; on the other was the Grand Hotel, which had changed little since the time when Henrik Ibsen had drunk an aperitif there every day at noon. At the head of Karl Johans Gate the royal palace stood on a rise in neo-classical splendour, its windows looking out over the busy centre to the new City Hall, the harbour, and the long fjord-estuary that brought shipping of every kind, from liners to fishing smacks, right to Oslo's doorstep. There were no walls around the palace grounds to keep out the public. Two sentries of the royal guard in dark blue uniforms, their bowler-shaped headgear adorned by a side burst of plumage, kept a quiet eye on those walking past the royal residence and the equestrian statue of an earlier king, less well known and less liked than the respected monarch presently living there.

Johanna had seen King Haakon several times. He strolled about the city like an ordinary citizen and in May, on National Day, he stood on the palace balcony to wave to the hundreds of children and students who went past in a procession of flags to the music of their own bands. Exceptionally tall and thin, looking stick-like enough to be blown away by a strong wind, he had shown many times by his actions that he was a resolute, high-principled man.

Turning out of Karl Johans Gate, Johanna reached the fur shop. It had an elegant frontage that faced trees and the Victoria Terrasse, one of Oslo's finest buildings with cupolas and finely wrought balconies. She entered the shop by the side door, collected the mail and went straight to her office. At the end of the passageway she could hear the salon coming to life as saleswomen made ready for the day ahead. After hanging up her coat and hat, she took a quick glance at the headlines on her newspaper. There had been another big naval battle between British and German warships. Otherwise, apart from some air skirmishes, there seemed to be a curious stalemate to the war in Europe. She was thankful her country was not involved in the conflict. Norway, together with Sweden and Denmark, was resolved that Scandinavian neutrality should be maintained as it had been in the Great War, although that did not mean that she or anyone else in the three nations was indifferent to the plight of those dragged into war by the whim of a violent dictator. She had been greatly distressed by the suffering of the Polish people during the time of the blitzkrieg, when Warsaw had been reduced to ruins.

Putting aside the newspaper, she settled down at her desk to work. As always after a weekend there was a lot of mail to go through, and it included some overseas orders.

The export side of the business was of particular importance to her, for it enabled her to use her knowledge of English, which had been a normal part of her school curriculum, and French and German, which she had studied in college. Unfortunately, since the outbreak of hostilities between the Allied and Axis powers, orders had been curtailed from the countries involved, and Paris no longer received large shipments of the handsome collars, cuffs, and other fur adornments of Norse origin that had embellished its haute couture. Somehow, to Johanna, it symbolized more than anything else the shadow that had been thrown over all that was artistic and civilized by the Nazis' ruthless brutality.

Around the walls of Johanna's office were framed designs from earlier decades, the sketched figures in furs wearing the wide feathered hats of her mother's youth or the cloche hats down to the eyebrows that belonged to her own childhood. They all had a certain charm, particularly the evening furs worn with beaded headbands. These days the garments were not made on the site as they had been in the past. The making up was done in modern, fully equipped premises elsewhere in Oslo where a dedicated work force was well paid for the superb garments they created.

When some papers were ready for her employer's attention, Johanna left her desk and went through to the salon to reach his office, which opened out of that domain. Two customers were being served. Sonja Holm, the head saleswoman, who was also a friend, came across with a sales slip for her.

"I'll see to it as soon as I can, Sonja," Johanna promised. Normally she liked the chance to linger in the grey-carpeted salon with its tapestry panels, where the splendid furs were displayed. Silver fox was currently the height of fashion, as it had been for some time past, and not only for full-length garments—it being the mode to wear one or two skins, complete with head and tail, around the shoulders and fastened with a silken cord. There was also great demand among the extremely rich for ermine capes, which were the shop's speciality. Lynx and blue fox were glamorous furs, much favoured by film stars, and white fox was usually kept for evening wraps and considered a "young fur" and not for older women.

One display, which was not for sale, was a spread across one wall of polar bear skins, white and opulent. Johanna could never look at them without a feeling of sadness, thinking of a wild, lost freedom in the ice-green waters of Spitsbergen. It was the same with the other furs not specially bred for the furrier's trade. In particular she pitied the little ermine. If only it did not change colour to white with the coming of the snows, as did the Arctic fox, the hare and ptarmigan, it would have stayed in its natural habitat and never fallen victim to the trappers' snares.

Leif Moen, her employer, was not seated at his desk when she entered his office. Instead he stood by the window, examining one of several white fox skins unpacked from a box on a side table. The decor of his office complemented that of the salon in the same shaded hues. On his wide polished desk were silver-framed photographs of his wife and three children.

"Good morning, Johanna," he greeted her, replacing the skin with the rest before coming across to his chair at the desk. "What have you brought me? Ah, yes, that particular order has been delayed, and we must get the rest of these in hand immediately."

She liked working with him. He was a conscientious man who took a personal interest in each one of his employees, many of the sewing hands in the workshop having been with him since he had inherited the business from his father some years earlier. With the exception of imported Russian sable, South American chinchilla and other such furs, the skins used were of Norwegian origin, a link with his grandfather, who had been a trapper in northern Norway and whose sepia-tinted photograph showed him to have been a rough, bearded fellow—a far cry from his immaculately groomed grandson with the smooth greying hair and well-cut features.

After some time in his office Johanna returned to her own desk, collecting the queried sales slip from Sonja on the way. Working against the clock, she did not look up when her friend opened the door inquiringly a little later. Instead Johanna reached for the sales slip that had been dealt with and held it out automatically. "It's done," she said, her mind barely detached from the task in hand.

"I haven't come for that. It's lunchtime. Aren't you ready?" Sonja glanced at herself in the mirror on the wall. She had a round and lively face, and had been told more than once that she bore a resemblance to the three-time Olympic skating gold medalist and Hollywood film star, Sonja Henie. It rather amused her. She could see no likeness herself, although there was no doubt that her dimpled smiles helped her sales, and she was an excellent saleswoman. Older than Johanna by five years, she was married to an officer in the merchant fleet, and as he was away at sea for long periods at a time she was glad to keep working.

Johanna sat back in her chair with a rueful sigh. "I had completely forgotten the time. I can't join you today. I'm literally up to my eyes. I'm going to use a short lunch-break to buy some groceries that I need. My landlady and her invalid husband are on vacation, so I'm catering for myself."

"Where have the Alsteens gone?"

"To Anna Alsteen's sister and brother-in-law in Drammen. It's a complete rest for Anna there, which is what she needs. She gets very tired at times, nursing her husband night and day, although she would never admit to it."

Sonja knew Drammen well. It was a picturesque little town south-west of Oslo; flags always flew on the bridge leading into it. "Isn't Viktor Alsteen any better?"

"I'm afraid not. The stroke he suffered some years ago made a complete invalid of him. Anna's brother-in-law is in the medical profession and is the only one to whom she will entrust Viktor out of her sight for any length of time. It does both the Alsteens good to be there. Apart from Anna's getting time to herself, Viktor regains a modicum of independence in male company again. They both come back refreshed."

"When do you expect them home again this time?"

"Not for another two weeks."

Johanna did not say that she liked having the house to herself, for that would have seemed disloyal to the Alsteens, of whom she was extremely fond. When she had first arrived in Oslo, a stranger in need of accommodation, they had welcomed her into their home and within a short

time had become good friends. It was just that there was a
true sense of freedom in coming and going without having
to account to anyone, and there were times when good-
natured Anna's kindly concern bordered closely on interference. The Alsteens had no financial need to rent a room
to her, for Viktor had been a prosperous goldsmith with his
own business on Prinsens Gate before his illness. A quiet
and dignified man, small in stature, he was patient and
uncomplaining in his infirmity, comforted by the intensely
maternal attitude of his wife, to whom he had now become
child instead of husband. Had they had children, Anna
might not have cut herself off from everything else to
devote all her time to him. That was why they both liked to
have a young person in the house, bringing in the outside
world to their quiet and closeted existence.

When Johanna's exceptionally busy day came to an end
she was glad to catch the tram home, the bag of groceries
balanced on her hip as she followed other passengers on
board in time to get a seat. With a clang of its bell the tram
rattled away from Stortorvet, the large market-place,
passed the cathedral, and followed the lines that would
take it out to the terminal in the suburb of Grefsen. Large
stores gave way to hardware shops, shiningly hygienic
dairies, and bakeries with a gilded kringler bread roll suspended over the doorway. Confectioners displayed scar-
let-and-gold boxes of King Haakon chocolates, and the mil-
liners' windows were filled with fashionably wide-
brimmed hats. A black hat with a floppy brim had been
one of Johanna's first purchases after her arrival in the city.
Since then, over the past fourteen months, she had built up
a wardrobe of smart clothes which she wore with flair.

Her thoughts drifted. It was strange to remember now
that riding on an Oslo tram had once been a novelty to her.
On the farm where she was born there had been no spare
money for travel, and she had never been on a train until
the day she finally left home to take the long steamship
ride up the Romsdal Fjord to Åndalsnes at the head of it,
where the nearest railway was located. To those who lived
on the mountainous fjord-riven west coast, the ferries
were the same as trams to Oslo folk. In spite of the hard
times of the late twenties and early thirties she had had a
happy childhood in Ryendal, a valley of small farms where

the community was like one family. In summer she had
run barefoot and in winter she had always been on skis and
skates, spoiled from birth by her father and two older
brothers, but disciplined constantly and severely by her
mother. There were times now when she wondered how
two people as entirely different in character as her parents
had ever made a match together. Never once had she seen
them kiss or embrace, although her father was such an
affectionate man, always enjoying a joke and good company. Yet the two of them had provided a stable background, and she had loved life on Ryen Farm.

It had not been easy to break away from home, first of all
to attend college in the nearby fjord town of Molde and
then to come south to Oslo, but she had needed to make a
career for herself, to expand and be as independent as her
brothers and find out about living. She had learned a great
deal since coming to Oslo and was confident that there was
no situation, amorous or otherwise, that she could not handle. For a while there had been a certain man in her life
who had mattered more than the rest. It had come to
nothing. She had no regrets.

The tram had left behind the concrete blocks of modern
apartments, and older timbered buildings of mellow
charm were giving way to the suburb of Grefsen. More like
a country area than the precincts of a city, it spread out in
gentle slopes and shallow dales. Trees and orchards gave
privacy to the two-storied pastel-hued wooden houses set
amid lawns and flowerbeds where as yet only the snow-
drops had managed to defy the inclement weather.

"Grefsen!" the driver-conductor called out.

Johanna alighted in the throng of dispersing passengers
and ran across the main road to reach the gravelled lane
that would take her to the Alsteens' house. Beyond some
trees it came into sight, a sturdily built residence painted
apple-green with blossoming plants in the lace-curtained
windows which she kept watered in Anna's absence.

As she opened the front door she paused briefly on the
threshold in a moment of surprise. There was the unmistakable scent of coffee lingering in the air. Her first
thought was that her landlady and husband had cut short
their vacation and returned home. Then she immediately
dismissed the notion of their return, for the house was in

darkness. There was only one person other than herself
who would be equally at home in the Alsteens' house, and
his arrival was not welcome at the present time. Snapping
on the light in the pine-panelled hall, she called up the
stairs just in case the visitor was in his rented room.

"Anyone at home?"

There was no reply. She went through to the kitchen
and switched on more lights, the yellow and white neat-
ness there gleaming brightly. The coffee-pot on the cooker
was still warm. Two cups and saucers had been washed and
left upside down on the draining board. The visitor had
brought his own guest into the house. She picked up the
note propped against the salt cellar. The masculine writing
was strong and purposeful.

*Hello, Johanna Ryen. I'm here for a few days. I gather
the Alsteens are away. Maybe we'll meet sometime. I have
taken the spare key from under the mat. Steffen Larsen.*

With a heavy sigh she tore the note across. After her
busy day she felt particularly unsociable and not ready to
share the house with a stranger known only to her as "the
Englishman." She was newly arrived in Oslo when she first
heard the explanation for his nickname.

"I've called him 'the Englishman' " Viktor had said in his
thin, dry voice, every word an effort, "ever since he first
came here. See that photograph." He had flicked the frail,
colourless fingers of his stronger right hand in the direction
of the enlarged snapshot framed on the sitting-room wall.
"It was taken at Henley Regatta, when he was sculling for
Oxford during his university days in England. There's
nothing more English than that. Tea and cucumber sandwiches on the lawn and straw boaters and pretty hats. Oh
yes, he is 'the Englishman.' " From that day forward Viktor
had repeated his little joke countless times, always with
the same husky chuckle as if he had never recounted it
before.

Leaving the kitchen, she went into the sitting-room
where she refuelled the ashes in the wood-burning stove
with logs from a basket. The flames flared up and flickered
through the grille, touching on the fine antiques, rare
porcelains, and some eighteenth-century silver bowls that
Viktor had collected during his goldsmith days. The glow
reached the row of Anna's girlhood skiing trophies in a

display cabinet. There were few homes in Norway that did not have at least one or two of these from local, national or international contests. Not for nothing was it said that for the past four thousand years Norwegians had been born with skis on their feet. Her gaze turned to the photograph of "the Englishman." He was grinning cheerfully in anticipation of victory in the long, slender skiff, strong hands waiting on the oars, broad and muscular in shorts and a white top, dark hair blowing about his head, bare knees large as hams.

There was some foundation for Viktor's nickname since Steffen Larsen had been born of an English mother, who had wanted him educated in her own country, and a Bergen sea captain. Bilingual, favoured nephew of a rich Norwegian aunt with whom he had made his home after losing his parents, he had led a privileged existence, having one foot in England where he had made many friends, and the other foot in Norway where he had established his career and his future.

As it happened, his aunt's home was at Ålesund on the west coast, a town well known to Johanna since it was within easy reach of her own home valley of Ryendal from which her family had taken its name many generations ago. She had never to her knowledge seen him in Ålesund and neither had she met him in the Alsteens' house, although he kept a room there as a base for the times when he returned to the capital for business meetings with the company that employed him. He did not like hotels and did not want the expense of an apartment in use for only a few times a year. Anna's comfortable room to rent and her good home cooking to enjoy had been the solution. A consultant engineer, he travelled a great deal, projects keeping him to the most part in northern Norway where much was being developed. Somehow whenever he had made one of his visits to Oslo since Johanna had been living there, she had either been away for the weekend or home on holiday. Sometimes she wondered if it had been deliberate avoidance on his part, particularly since he always telephoned Anna well ahead. Anna, a veritable matchmaker, might have been the reason. Very likely he wanted to retain his freedom to come and go in the Alsteens' house without finding himself forced to be sociable with a girl in whom he had no interest. His unexpected arrival today, without forewarning, was contrary to his usual procedure. Perhaps the clue was the two cups left in the kitchen. She knew from Anna that he had a girlfriend in Oslo, an Englishwoman who worked at the British Embassy. Anna did not like her.

"Tell me exactly why you disapprove," Johanna had asked, quietly amused. She was well aware that Anna, who did not like to be thwarted, had contrived unsuccessfully to bring Steffen and her face to face. "You're usually pleased to see young couples matched up for marriage."

"For marriage, yes. Not for any other kind of liaison that falls short of it. In any case, she's not right for him. I'm hoping it will fade out. That young woman is hard and determined."

"She probably holds an extremely responsible job at the embassy. Women have to be tough to compete with men in their own field. It's still a man's world. We haven't changed that yet. What's her name?"

"Delia Richmond."

"That's a nice name."

But Anna had not been willing to concede on any point.

Johanna turned away from the snapshot and went upstairs to her room. There she changed out of her office clothes and brushed the skirt before hanging it away. Having grown up in hard times when any kind of new apparel was a special treat, it was natural for her to look after her wardrobe. During her early days in Oslo, a run in a silk stocking had been a major financial disaster. Fortunately those days were gone.

She liked the room that had been hers since first coming to the city. The painted wooden walls were a faded rose colour and there were crisp lace curtains at the window and plaited rag rugs on the pine floor. The puffy quilt on the bed was encased in a white linen embroidered cover, the pillowslips trimmed with lace.

Johanna had added some personal touches of her own to the room. A print of one of her favourite Edvard Munch paintings, that of three girls on the bridge at Åsgårdstrand on the Oslo Fjord, held pride of place. She had stood on that same bridge one hot summer day. The small silver Viking ship in the window had been a bequest from her grandmother. In the corner was an antique rocking chair that she had bought for a few kroner and piled with assorted cushions. She kept her necklaces and trinkets in an ornamental box that had been a skating prize in her school-days. Her father had carved the bookends that supported her favourite books on the chest of drawers. An enamelled frame held a family photograph of her parents standing with her two brothers outside the farmhouse, which had been built over two hundred years earlier.

She spent the evening in the sitting-room listening to the radio. It was one of Anna's most recent purchases, replacing an older model. This one had an attractive sun-ray panel and the reception was excellent. At ten-thirty Johanna went up to bed and read for a while. It was a Sigrid Undset novel and hard to put down. She finally slipped in a bookmark and put it on the bedside table before turning out the lamp.

When Steffen returned she was asleep and did not hear him park his car in the drive. Neither did she know when he entered his room, which was next to hers, although the floorboards creaked and he shut the door more loudly than he had intended. He had taken Delia to dine at Blom's, the artists' restaurant where they both liked to eat. Afterwards they had danced at a night-club and rounded off the evening on their own at her apartment, to their mutual pleasure and satisfaction. Having an important business meeting in the morning that had brought him south again, he set his alarm clock and flung himself into bed to sleep at once.

Miles from Oslo, at the mouth of the fjord, a small patrol boat was battling against a fierce sea and a rain-lashed wind. The storms around the coast had been exceptionally bad for several days. Suddenly the captain stared ahead in deep alarm, scarcely able to believe the evidence of his own eyes. Looming out of the darkness and heading into the fjord at full steam, their grey bows scything through the rough waves, were a number of alien warships of great size and power. Realisation dawned instantly. Invasion! "Good God! It's the German fleet!" he exclaimed hoarsely.

He snapped his orders in the same breath. The radio officer responded instantly by sending a signal through to

Oslo while the patrol boat's gun fired a warning shot across the leading cruiser's bow. Moments later there was the rush of a torpedo from a following German gunboat. The patrol boat was blown to pieces, filling the sea and sky with golden fire. There were no survivors.

In Oslo, upon receipt of the radio signal, the lights were extinguished throughout the city in an immediate black-out. Government ministers and high-ranking military personnel were roused from sleep or summoned from social gatherings. In the palace the King was informed that an invasion fleet was sailing up Oslo Fjord.

Complete confusion reigned at the meeting convened. Nobody was prepared for such a contingency. A call was made to London. "It appears we are at war!" One decision went unquestioned. The country would be called to arms. When the German ambassador presented himself at four A.M. his demand for capitulation under German protection was totally rejected. He drove away, secure in his expectation that at dawn Wehrmacht troops would be landing in Oslo Harbour. He believed the annexation of Norway would be completed in a matter of hours.

In the Narrows at Drøbak in the Oslo fjord the German fleet, arrogantly and fully lit as though for a naval regatta, was running into unlooked-for opposition. At the ancient Oscarsborg fortress the officer in charge ordered the two turn-of-the-century guns, never before fired in assault, to aim at the leading cruiser as she sailed past.

With a great boom that shook the old stone walls, the guns let forth across the water. The target was hit full square and began to sink rapidly, taking hundreds of sailors and soldiers down with it. An immediate change of plan was ordered by the German command to avoid further sinkings. Instead of being transported right into Oslo Harbour, the soldiers were disembarked from the troop-carrying ships below the Narrows and far south of Oslo in Vestfold, the west side of the fjord. The German fleet turned and left, leaving the battalions of the Wehrmacht to face a long and rain-swept march to the still distant capital.

It was early light when the wail of an air-raid siren and the thud-thud of anti-aircraft fire caused Johanna to awaken with a start. She sat bolt upright in bed and pushed her hair back out of her eyes with one hand. Automatically

she leaned over to press down the button on her alarm
clock before it should ring, thinking it was an unholy hour
for the routine test of a siren and for gun practice. Turning
back the bedclothes, she put her bare feet to the ground
and reached for her cream silk kimono. She drew it over
her shoulders as she ambled leisurely towards the window.
Halfway there she paused, her back stiffening as she tilted
her head slightly, listening keenly. She could hear a low
throbbing hum overhead like the approach of angry bees.

Abruptly she threw herself towards the window and
stared upwards through the glass in horrified disbelief at
the sight of German bombers with swastikas on their tails
—planes passing inland across the early morning sky.
Shock enveloped her. Her country's neutrality was being
violated and the only possible explanation was too terrible
to contemplate. She stayed as if transfixed, unaware that
she was gripping a handful of the lace curtain with a force
that drew it taut on its rings.

Suddenly there was the hammering of a fist on her bedroom door. A man's voice shouted through to her: "Are
you awake in there? You must go down to the cellar for
safety! Do you hear me?"

She heard, but in her stunned state made no move to
answer the summons. The door burst open. Startled, she
spun round. The morning light caught her hair and cast a
bloom over the curve of her barely concealed breasts in
her thin cotton nightgown. Steffen Larsen, fully dressed
himself, stared at her, drawing in his breath.

"Move!" he exploded, his expression belligerent in his
anxiety for her.

She obeyed him at once. Pulling the edges of her kimono
together she rushed from the room, he following her.
Down the stairs she ran and across to the cellar door.
Hardly had she descended the steps, he switching on the
light as they went, when she paused to look upwards at the
cellar ceiling in fear and bewilderment. A curious descending whine was coming from somewhere overhead.

"What's that?"

"Down! Get down!" Steffen shouted in warning.

He threw her with him to the floor, his body a protective
shield over hers as the bomb's huge explosion made the
whole house shift on its foundations, blasting the small

cellar window into glittering shards. All around them the
collected debris of years clattered down from the shelves
in a welter of cardboard boxes and biscuit tins and other
containers, some old magazines sliding into an avalanche.
As the vibration subsided, the single electric light bulb
continued to swing wildly on its flex, trailing a cobweb
strand.

When he felt it was safe to move, he raised her up into a
sitting position, crouching in front of her. "Are you all
right?" He peered with concern into her face, for she was
extremely pale.

She nodded. "I think so. Everything happened so fast."

"The planes have gone over now. That one bomb appears to have been all they had for us on this first occasion.
There may be another wave of aircraft to follow, so we had
better stay where we are for a while longer." He saw that
she was shivering as much from shock as from the chill of
the cellar and took off his jacket to put it round her shoulders. "Here, that should help. Don't stay sitting on that
cold stone floor. There's an old sofa by the wall."

She took his advice, tucking up into a corner of it.
"That's better. I hope we don't have to stay down here for
long."

He perched on the sofa arm. "My apologies for bel-
lowing at you in your room. I'm afraid it was necessary."

"I know that now. I was in a state of shock. I am still, for
that matter."

She was registering, without realising it, that his face had
matured since the days of the sculling snapshot. Now she
observed that he had the straight nose, square chin and
classic cheekbones that combined with the light blue eyes
to reveal his Norse ancestry. His Englishness was in the
general look of him and in the dark brown of his hair,
which was thick and well cut, rippling above his ears and at
the nape of his neck. In all he was a man of immense
physical attraction. Then her mind began to concentrate
on the crisis that had erupted and she drew her fingertips
across her forehead. "It's difficult to believe that this is
happening."

"I agree. I was downstairs getting breakfast when the
announcement came over the radio. A minute later I
heard the bombers droning overhead."

"What did the announcement say?"

"At dawn this morning, without any declaration of war, Germany launched an invasion of Norway at targets all along the coast from the south to far north of the Arctic Circle."

She was numbed by the information. It was far worse than she had supposed, her thoughts having been that the bombers must be the spearhead of an onslaught in the Oslo area. Instead, the whole country was under attack. In her mind's eye she pictured Norway spread out like a map before her. Topographically it was made up of rugged mountains, high plateaus, glacier tables, thick forests and lakes, leaving less than four percent of the land for cultivation and habitation. As for its fjord-indented coastline, that measured twenty thousand miles. It was a country impossible for a small army to defend against a great invasion force attacking at all points.

"Why?" Her face was baffled, her voice sombre.

"Well, strategically, I suppose Norway would be an excellent base from which to attack Allied shipping in the Atlantic. It's within easy range and the fjords would provide hidden shelter to German warships and submarines, giving them the advantage."

"That mustn't happen!" She was vehement.

"I agree, but the situation is bad. Extremely bad. We have practically no air defence and not a single officer or man with previous combat experience in the whole country. It's a hundred and twenty-five years since we last went to war and regained our national independence from Sweden, and now these Nazis are aiming to take it away from us again." He bunched his fingers into a fist and slammed it into the sofa arm, barely able to control his fury. "We'll see them in hell first!" Restlessly he thrust himself away. "I must report for military duty. Every minute counts and I'm doing no good down here. I'm going to take a look around." He hurried up the cellar steps into the house. She heard the cracking of glass underfoot and he reappeared, putting his head briefly through the cellar doorway to give warning. "Several windows have been shattered. Come up now, but take care." His glance went to Johanna's bare toes. "Where are your slippers?"

"By my bed."

He returned a couple of minutes later to toss in her
slippers and she caught them. After putting them on she
rose to her feet, still shivering and thinking of a hot bath to
warm her through again. In the hallway she paused by the
sitting-room door. Steffen had cleared up some of the glass
from the shattered window and was listening attentively
to the latest bulletin on the radio. She was in time to catch
the tail end of it and her heart sank still further. It was
more bad news. Denmark had been similarly invaded at
dawn on that fateful Tuesday morning of April 9 and German troops were overrunning the country.

"What of Sweden?" she inquired huskily from the doorway, removing the jacket he had lent her from her shoulders and putting it across a chair.

He glanced in her direction. "No attack there."

"Will it come later?"

"That's highly unlikely now. The Swedes' moment of
danger is past, I would say. After all, the element of surprise has gone. No, Sweden would have been included
with Denmark and us if anything had been planned
against them." He switched off the radio. "I have some
things to do here before I report to the mobilisation centre. There is a general call to arms."

Through the broken windows she could see that neighbours had gathered in the lane. From the direction in
which they were pointing it was obvious that the bomb
had dropped in a shallow dale nearby. She hoped that
nobody had been hurt. There were no military targets
anywhere in the area.

Before going upstairs she tried to call her parents on the
telephone, but without success—the lines out of the city
were jammed. She had more success in getting in touch
with a local glazier, who promised to replace the panes
during the morning. When bathed and dressed she came
downstairs, to be met by Steffen with a mug of hot coffee
for her. She drank it while clearing up the remainder of
the glass. He was working in the cellar, feeling unable to
leave until he had made it as secure against air raids as
possible for Johanna and for the Alsteens when they returned. He had already removed the bulk of hoarded rubbish and secured shutters over the cellar window, board-
ing it up on the inside. Afterwards he cleared the shelves of

anything that could inflict injury and installed a first-aid
box. In his late teens, before going to Oxford, he had
served a compulsory conscription service of a few weeks in
the Norwegian Army, but had learned little more than
how to handle a gun and look after saddle horses. There
had been nothing about bombing raids on the scale for
which the Luftwaffe had become notorious. He was simply
using his common sense in thinking of ways to turn the
cellar into a safe shelter.

When he had finished his work, Johanna called him into
the kitchen where she had made ready the breakfast he
had just begun to prepare when the bombers had come.
"This looks good," he said appreciatively, sitting down
with her to boiled eggs, cheese, cold meats, homemade
preserves and hot home-baked kringler rolls and crusty
bread. They both ate heartily, falling into a lively discussion of the present crisis and how long it might take for the
Allies to send military support and aircraft. The situation
was drawing into a companionable closeness with a speed
that could only come from the imminence of danger. They
had just finished the meal when the doorbell rang and its
sudden clangor broke in on them with an intruder's touch.

"I'll go," Johanna said.

She opened the door to a young woman she had never
seen before. Simply and smartly clad in a belted raincoat,
an emerald silk scarf lightly knotted at her throat, the girl
had anxious grey eyes. Instinctively Johanna guessed the
stranger's identity. A car with passengers and the engine
running was drawn up by the gate.

"I'm Delia Richmond." The Englishwoman's Norwegian
was flawless, any trace of a foreign accent virtually indis-
cernible. "I see you've suffered some bomb damage."

"Neither Steffen nor I were hurt," Johanna replied,
standing aside for her to enter. A mass of chestnut hair
framed Delia's triangular face with its English rose complexion, well-shaped nose and firm, full-lipped mouth. She
was, Johanna decided, extremely good-looking. "He's in
the kitchen. Come through."

"No, I'll wait here." Delia's voice was choked. "I've
come to say goodbye."

Johanna found that Steffen had begun washing up. "Delia's here," she announced.

His face tightened as if he knew the reason already and he went out into the hall, leaving the door wide open. It was impossible for Johanna not to hear what passed between them, or to avoid seeing that Delia darted to meet him.

"We're packing up at the embassy and getting out, Steffen! Those able to leave at once have been told to get into Sweden and make our way home from there. We're hoping for a ship. I've colleagues waiting outside and I can't stop a minute."

He was holding her close to him, his hands on her arms. To Johanna's eyes it was a clasp of comfortable familiarity, Delia leaning slightly towards him at the hips. "Have you heard anything at the embassy that we haven't received on the news bulletins yet?" he asked keenly.

"You'll be glad to know that the German ambassador's demand for Norway's surrender to the Third Reich was thrown back at him, much to his annoyance." Delia's lips eased in a fleeting smile before her expression tautened again, matching the seriousness of her eyes. "The King, Crown Prince Olav and the government ministers left Oslo by train a while ago to travel inland to Hamar. The Crown Princess and the royal children are already on their way into Sweden. The nation's gold has been removed from the state vaults to be secured in a secret place."

"Sensible precaution. What of the fighting?"

"All bad news, I'm sorry to say. There have been fjord battles along the west coast with the Norwegian Navy suffering a heavy toll. Bergen, Stavanger, Trondheim and Narvik are all in enemy hands. Wehrmacht soldiers were smuggled into target harbours a week or more ago in the holds of German merchant ships. In many places people woke up to find the enemy in full control of their town before anyone knew what was happening. It's thanks to the sinking of the cruiser *Blücher* in the Narrows that troops didn't land in Oslo at dawn. Thank God that splendid piece of defensive action gave the King and Crown Prince the time needed to get away." Outside there sounded a tooting of a car horn and she frowned impatiently at the interruption. "I have to go." Her voice dropped a note. "It isn't easy to leave in this way."

"I'll come with you to the car." He slipped his arm about her shoulder and they went side by side from the house.

Johanna finished clearing the table. She was thinking that her absent landlady had chosen to leave out one vital factor in her summing up of the Englishwoman. There was a definite vulnerability as far as Steffen was concerned.

When the car was gone, Steffen returned to the house and made a business telephone call, catching up with developments as if today were a day like any other, giving his apologies and reasons for being unable to attend the meeting that morning, which had been concerned with his own promotion within the company. Then he went upstairs to change out of his suit into the sturdy sportswear that was his customary clothing when he was on work sites in difficult terrain, including the stout boots he wore for cross-country skiing. He did not know where the army would send him and wanted to be prepared. Lastly he donned a warm weatherproof jacket and stuck his ski cap into his pocket. Shouldering his rucksack, he came downstairs to discover Johanna in outdoor clothes waiting for him in the hall. He raised his eyebrows at her. "Where do you think you're going?"

"To work. I gave the fur shop a phone call to say I'd been unavoidably delayed and I've arranged with a neighbour that she let the glazier into the house. I'd like a lift into town with you."

"I've decided to leave the car here and catch a tram. You drive, don't you?"

"Yes, I do."

"Well, I won't be needing my car in the army. Naturally I hope that an emergency doesn't arrive, but if one should happen you'd be able to get away. I filled the tank up yesterday."

"Thanks. Now we'll catch the tram together into town." She glanced at the hall clock. "There'll be one in a few minutes."

"Not so fast!" He reached over to hold the front door closed when she would have opened it. "You would be safer at home today."

"Everything is quiet now and I have to get to work." She was adamant. "I was told it's business as usual in the city and everything is calm. There's a basement that's safe enough if any more bombs should fall. My boss said that others would be getting in late today, too."

"I'm not surprised," he commented dryly.

He donned his peaked cap as he left the house with her. They had to run for the tram and leaped aboard just in time. There were plenty of spare seats and they were able to sit together, he swinging his rucksack into a space beside him.

"This is a crazy way to go to war," he remarked with a grin. "On a tram!"

She grinned back at him. "Let's hope you come home the same way. There's something cheerful and almost comical about trams. I like them."

"Think of me every morning when you travel on this one." His tone was joking.

"I will." For a second behind the cheerful bantering each glimpsed something deeper and more serious, as if the catastrophic events of the day were bearing down on them again all too quickly. With a swift tilt of her chin she looked out the window, trying to sustain their lighter mood. "See! All the shops are open and the banks are in operation. I told you it was business as usual."

There were also sombre signs in the grave faces of pedestrians, particularly when they paused in anxious discussion with someone they knew. Several schools were closing their doors again, sending children back home to await events.

He took his cue from her. There would be plenty of time ahead for grave thoughts and anxious moments. He had no doubt about that. With ease he began to talk of the west coast district they both knew so well. "I'd like to be told how many times I've passed by your home. I know the mountains of Ryendal as well as the back of my own hand. I've walked them many times. As for the fishing in Saeter Lake, well, that's unsurpassed anywhere."

She exclaimed in agreement. "That's my most favourite place." She had fished in that high mountain lake many times with her father and brothers. On her own she had spent countless hours on the mossy banks in which the lake was set like a pale aquamarine, the speckled trout darting in its transparent depths, its pebbles showing like a floor of pearls.

"Then when the Germans have been booted out again we'll meet there next time you're at home and I'm at Ålesund, Jo."

She smiled at his calling her "Jo." Nobody had ever shortened her name before. That was not the custom. It came from his being "the Englishman."

"That's a date," she promised.

"Not to fish," he insisted, smiling at her. "We can do that another time. To talk."

She laughed softly. "Whatever you say."

Almost imperceptibly his hand moved to tighten on hers. Their eyes held in the knowledge that present circumstances were too much with them. "Tell me why you left Ryendal for Oslo," he invited casually, his gaze on her full of interest. "Anna often spoke to me about you. I'd like to know more about you from what you have to say."

She told him of the restlessness that had made her want to leave home and talked of her work and why it interested her. Before their ride ended he made a request. "There's something I would like to ask you. A favour. It's impossible to guess at this stage how long it's going to take to clear Norway of the Nazi invaders. That means it could be quite a while before I can see my aunt in Ålesund again. I'm her only relative. I'd appreciate it very much if you would call on her whenever you're at home. Astrid is my late father's sister and a very fine person. I think the two of you should get on well together."

"Of course I'll visit her. Give me her address." She opened her purse to take out a diary and pencil. As she wrote down the address she understood what lay behind the favour he had asked of her. There was always the possibility that he would not come back from this war, however short its duration, and he wanted to ensure that Astrid Larsen would never be quite alone. As she put the diary away she felt his request had drawn them still closer together. An overwhelming sadness filled her at the imminence of their parting.

They stood to say goodbye in the market square by the statue of Christian IV with the wide hat and the Vandyke beard. The rumble of gunfire could be heard in the distance whenever there was a lull in the traffic. He looked

down into her face as if they were alone instead of in a busy
market place.

"This is it then, Jo," he said quietly. "I wish we had had
longer to get to know each other."

"I think this strange and extraordinary and dreadful day
has condensed many weeks into a few hours." It was no
time for subterfuge; only frankness would suffice. She had
always heard that war increased the pace and urgency of
life, as if it awakened in everyone a higher pitch of emotion and the need to capture briefly what might never
come again. Now she knew it was true. The whole expression on his face endorsed the truth of it, as did hers.

"Those are my feelings, too." He enfolded her in his
arms and lowered his head to kiss her fully and fervently as
if it hurt him physically to leave her. She clung to him, her
own mouth quick and responsive, nothing held back in this
poignant moment of farewell. His embrace tightened
about her.

As they drew apart he stroked the side of her face lightly
with his fingertips, a gesture of immense tenderness. His
eyes were deep and full of promise. "I'll find you again, Jo."

Her voice was a choked whisper. "I hope it's soon. Take
good care."

Classic phrases of parting in wartime. In their case everything might be ending before it had begun. She
watched him dodge the traffic across the square. At the
corner, by a store selling crystal and fine glass, he turned
and waved before going from her sight.

When she reached the fur shop she went straight to her
office and shut the door. Plenty of work awaited her and
she was thankful for it. At midmorning she managed to get
a telephone call through to her west country home. She
spoke to her mother, who assured her that all was well
there and that no German forces had reached the district,
the invasion ships for Molde and Romsdal fjords having
been sunk in one of the battles at sea.

"Don't try to come home," her mother insisted. "Your
father has heard that fighting has spread inland in some
places and you might get caught up in it."

The call was a short one, cut off by some interference on
the line. Johanna replaced the receiver much easier in her
mind now that she knew from personal contact that her

parents and her brothers were not in any immediate danger. Her thoughts returned to Steffen. Never before had someone gained such importance for her in so short a time. No use to tell herself that many other women must have been similarly attracted to him, including Delia. She was convinced that something special had occurred when he first threw wide her bedroom door, as if the magnetism between them had already brought them together, sparked off by the violence of the crisis that had overtaken their country.

It did not take Steffen long to discover that joining up with the military was going to be less easy than he had supposed. He had expected to find mobilisation centres set up at army offices and headquarters for the immediate direction of volunteers and trained men like himself reporting to the colours. But he drew a blank everywhere. The top brass and other officers alike had dispersed to battle areas and there was no one in command. When a clerk informed him that he would get his mobilisation papers in the mail, he realised exactly what a century and a quarter of peace had done to his country. Valuable time was slipping away and his temper with it. He met other men in the same dilemma as himself and eventually he and two others joined up with a fourth who had a car. The decision was made to drive to Hamar where they should find the King and a strategic centre of military command. Inwardly Steffen fumed at having to leave the city, convinced that precious time was being wasted in having to go elsewhere to join a line of defence. His hope was that they would meet advancing Norwegian troops and turn back to Oslo with them.

The journey went without incident. They drove through the gently undulating countryside where village life was normal and the farms lay peacefully, the animals still in their winter quarters, the fields patchy with snow, the slopes white. There was no sign of the troops he had hoped to see. Then suddenly, not far from Hamar, they spotted ahead sentries of a Norwegian regiment waiting at a roadblock to challenge them. Spontaneously they gave a cheer.

"Some action at last!" Steffen exclaimed forcibly. "Now we'll be able to get going."

They were taken a few kilometres eastwards to the military academy at the village of Elverum where the King and the Crown Prince and the ministers were being accommodated. After being questioned by an officer, Steffen and his companions were kitted out with uniforms, fed and armed. They were under the command of Colonel Ruge, a straight-backed man no longer young, a highly intelligent and dedicated officer who had resolved to protect the King and defeat the Germans from the moment he had been informed of the enemy approaching by sea, since when he had taken no rest. The men under his command at Elverum numbered barely a hundred, but their morale was high and their attitude fierce. The four new arrivals were welcomed by a small but determined force.

At the fur shop Johanna closed her ledgers and put them away. It was not yet lunchtime, but Leif Moen had told her and the saleswomen to finish for the day and go home. He had heard rumours that nearby Fornebu aerodrome had fallen to the enemy and whether it was true or not, he felt he should close the shop, half expecting further air raids.

Leaving the premises, Johanna stopped in Karl Johans Gate to buy a newspaper and turned when she caught the distant strains of a military band. There was something odd about the jaunty sound, instruments included that were unfamiliar to her. People were beginning to move in its direction and she followed, trying to identify the high-pitched bell-like chimes that came dancing above the drums and cornets and the rest of the booming brass. The solution came to her in the very second before she reached the edge of the pavement and looked up Karl Johans Gate towards the palace. It was a German glockenspiel!

The sight that met her shocked gaze made her stand immobile with horror. Coming down the wide avenue, headed by the German military band making up in boisterous volume for what it lacked in numbers, was a contingent of enemy soldiers in full marching procession that proclaimed occupation of the city.

"Dear God!" she breathed, clutching the folded newspaper to her breast like a shield.

Behind the band came three high-ranking officers of the Wehrmacht, leading the long line of troops marching three

abreast. Their jackbooted feet thudded in rhythm, the
skirts of their greatcoats swung in unison and in spite of the
overcast sky, the light caught the barrels of their shouldered rifles and glanced across the crowns of their brow-
deep helmets. They were alert and in good spirits, their
quick glances taking in their new surroundings. The officers actually smiled for a grim-faced photographer who
stepped into the avenue to record their arrival as they
approached.

Watching them pass in their orderly ranks, Johanna
could see that these were not men who had marched a
long distance, but troops newly landed at Fornebu aerodrome, confirming the rumour that a battle for it had been
lost. With their polished insignia and shining leather, the
soldiers could have been on parade at a festive occasion.
And they had cause for their jubilant expressions. Oslo had
fallen to them without a shot being fired in its streets.

On the pavement people were mute. Everyone was
completely stunned. A postman, coming round the corner
on his bicycle, dismounted to stare in helpless incredulity.
Nearby a well-dressed elderly man had tears of grief running unashamedly down his cheeks. He was not alone in an
open display of sorrow at the catastrophe that had befallen
an erstwhile peaceful city.

On and on the soldiers came. When a groan was uttered
by several by-standers, Johanna followed the direction of a
pointing finger. She was in time to see the national flag
with its dark blue cross of St. Olav bordered by white on a
scarlet field hauled down from a building's projecting flagpole to be replaced by the symbol of Nazi occupation. The
swastika had been unfurled over Oslo.

She hardly remembered getting home on the tram. It
was overtaken several times by local buses full of German
troops who had commandeered them to take over every
section of the city, leaving many home-going Oslo folk
without transport. Wearily she walked up the lane and
entered the house, not noticing until she was assailed by
the smell of putty that the glazier had kept his word and
replaced the window glass.

That evening she heard on the Oslo broadcasting station, now under German control, that Denmark had sur-

rendered. The Danish king and government had acqui-
esced to the German demands. Then came a fresh shock. It
was announced that Vidkun Quisling was to address the
nation.

Johanna rose from the armchair where she was sitting to
turn up the volume, which she had kept subdued during
the earlier programme. She was filled with misgivings.
Everybody knew Quisling as the leader of Norway's small
and insignificant Nazi party. In the past, its abortive attempts to gain power at election time had been something
of a national joke. It would seem to be a joke no longer.
From the sunray panel of the radio Quisling's bullying
voice boomed forth into the quiet sitting-room.

"Men and women of Norway! The German Government
has come forward with its assistance to prevent the neutrality of our country being violated by England. This protection has been rejected irresponsibly by our Norwegian
Government, who took flight after calling upon you to take
up arms."

There followed a tirade of abuse against the government, whose authority he pronounced null and void
through its own actions. Then he solemnly informed the
nation that he had appointed himself the new prime minis-
ter with his own Nazi party in full power.

"I order you to show no further resistance to the German forces," he gave out in conclusion.

In fury Johanna snapped off the radio. "Traitor!" she
exclaimed aloud. It seemed to her that the echo of her
voice remained in the room.

When it was time to go to bed, she double-locked the
front and back doors, sure it was a precaution that had
never been taken in this house before. Frequently the keys
had been left unturned; there had never been anything to
fear before. Now everything was changed.

As she went upstairs, she considered Quisling's extraordinary speech again. Although not mentioned in the evening news bulletins, which were probably already under
the pressure of German censorship, it was clear from what
he had said that the Norwegian call to arms that morning
had been obeyed by many and fighting against the invader
was widespread. She hoped Steffen was safe. It was a hope

that she would carry like a talisman through whatever dark days might lie ahead.

In the darkness of the cold night, not far from the military academy buildings, Steffen glanced at the luminous dial of his watch. It was just after midnight. Lying full-length on his stomach in the snow, he waited with his rifle for the first sign of enemy movement ahead. He and the rest of the company had received with bitter anger the information given by their commanding officer that the Germans were in Oslo. Since then Colonel Ruge had been alerted that an enemy force was on its way to compel the King back to the city, for at liberty he would continue to represent a nucleus of freedom to the nation that the Germans were determined to crush.

Around Steffen, under a row of birch trees and dug into a long snowbank, were his comrades-in-arms. They waited, tense and silent. They had a rifle each and ammunition for it, but nothing else. There had not been a single grenade or explosive or anything else vitally needed in the weapons store of the academy. All it could provide was a solitary machine-gun, which was being manned by an officer and was strategically placed. With the military buildings to the rear and right of them, they faced the expanse of snowy ground across which the enemy must come. A barricade of felled trees across the road would check the Germans' motorised advance.

Steffen looked through his sights again. He was among those detailed to give covering fire to the machine-gunner against concentrated attack. His breath hung before him in the frosty air, every nerve in his body taut. Then he swore quietly to himself in satisfaction as the distant hum of approaching vehicles could be heard, and soon the headlamps of a convoy flickered through the further-off trees.

"Stand by!"

The muttered command had been passed along. Against the pearly glow given off by the snow in the fitful moonlight, the open commercial trucks commandeered into service presented a harmless sight at first. Then the silhouettes of the passengers in the back were spotted against the lights, helmets clearly defined, rifles upright. There was no attempt at concealment. The Germans' arrogant assumption that they would take the King without opposition gave satisfaction to those waiting in ambush, geared to a reversal of surprise tactics. As the barricade caused the trucks to halt one after another, the Germans jumped out in turn and began to move across the snowy ground in the direction of the academy buildings, unaware that their dark forms made perfect targets against the whiteness. Steffen's finger tightened in readiness on the trigger of his rifle.

The Norwegian command split the snowy silence. "Fire!"

The sudden stutter of the academy machine-gun exploded into the night, taking the enemy completely by surprise. It was a company of a crack regiment of the Wehrmacht, trained to a peak of instant response, who hurled themselves fearlessly into attack, those in advance with submachine guns blazing from their hands. Shouts and screams and groans added to the nightmare noise. The scene was alive with red-gold flashes, the enemy intent on winning the fire fight in the least possible time, but Ruge's men had the tactical advantage of position and vision as well as familiarity with the ground. Some of the Germans took shelter behind a low hut, firing from there, but again and again they were picked off like coconuts at a fairground.

The German commander fought through the whole encounter in a state of disbelief. When asked if he could bring the King back to Oslo he had replied boastfully that with his men he could get the devil out of hell. Now he saw his crack soldiers falling down around him. As he emerged from a protective ridge of snow to lead a final rally, a bullet caught him and he went face down into the snow, fatally wounded.

It acted like a signal to his demoralised troops. They fell back quickly, taking their dead and wounded with them, blood left vividly on the snow. The lights and sounds of their transport disappeared into the distance.

Steffen rose slowly to his feet. Clumping down the snow-bank, he went across to the hut that had offered some protection to the Germans. There on the trampled snow he salvaged a submachine-gun that had been abandoned.

For a few moments he stood looking about him. He felt no triumph in the bloodshed, only in the routing of the enemy. That was how it had to be, and must be, until the last German was driven from Norwegian soil.

Chapter 2

Dawn brought "Panic Day" to Oslo. Within minutes of the early morning bulletin it became a phrase used by everybody. Warning had been given that a heavy bombing raid by the British was imminent with an attempted landing to follow, and immediately people began to evacuate the city. From her bedroom window Johanna could see that the road out of Oslo was already a flow of traffic and people on foot. She made ready to leave the city herself. Her plan was to take Steffen's car, drive out of the city to a safe distance and await events.

Feeling a new responsibility for the Alsteens' possessions in their absence, she quickly gathered up small antique items, including rare porcelain and silver, which she carried down to the cellar. There she packed them with newspaper wadding into boxes, which she covered over against the chance of any falling debris during an air raid. After that she took down half a dozen Astrup paintings, which she knew to be of value, and placed them in what she thought would be one of the safest corners against the wall.

When she had secured all that she knew meant most to the Alsteens, even some items of only sentimental value, she went up to her bedroom where she hastily packed a suitcase of clothes for herself. She put in what was best, having no idea when she would be able to return to the house, or if it would still be standing when she did. After closing the suitcase, there were still some evening dresses left in her wardrobe that she did not want ruined by bomb damage. Taking a large red-and-white-striped cardboard box that had originated in the fur shop, she laid the dresses in it, adding some garments out of the chest of drawers and whatever else could be snatched up in haste. Putting on the lid, she carried the box down to the cellar and looked to see what space was left. Then she noticed that Steffen had secured a heavy cupboard with bolts to the wall to prevent it from toppling, and at its base there was a narrow, curved aperture between the carved claw feet. That, she thought, would be a protective place for her clothes. Kneeling down in front of it, she slid the box underneath, pushing and pressing until it was back against the skirting, guarded from everything except a direct hit on the house.

Dusting off her hands, she went back up the steps into the hall just as there came a frenzied ringing of the door-bell. She flung it open to find Sonja, her friend from the fur shop, on the doorstep.

"Come on, Johanna! I've managed to get a taxi to take us to my mother-in-law's out in the country. Get your things. There's no time to lose."

"I have a car. You can come with me."

"Better still!" Sonja whirled about to run back to the gate and dismiss the taxi, which immediately took on a fresh load of passengers from a neighbouring house. Swiftly Johanna locked up, took her suitcase and went to Steffen's car in the garage. It was a new car, less than three months old.

"You had better not get any scratches on this," Sonja joked as they piled their luggage onto the back seat. Then, as Johanna drove out into the lane, she closed the garage door and fastened the gates before getting into the passenger seat.

"Whoever thought we should come to these straits?" Johanna remarked fiercely as they went smoothly down the lane. "We're refugees in our own country. Let's hope the British blast the Germans out of Oslo today."

Congestion on the road made driving difficult. Every kind of vehicle not commandeered by the enemy had been called into service to get people out of Oslo. Now and again a truckfull of Germans went through, a motorcycle escort cleaving a path. The soldiers themselves glanced without interest at the fleeing refugees. For them it was a familiar sight, one they had seen often enough in other lands they had occupied.

Sonja's mother-in-law lived just far enough away from Oslo to be out of range of any battle for the city. Having been telephoned by Sonja, she was on the look-out for her arrival and she made Johanna equally welcome, hurrying them both into the house out of the cold. Fru Holm was a widow and lived alone; she was small, grey-haired with a kindly face and mobile hands that danced in the air expressively.

"Thank goodness you reached here safely. I was so worried. What a dreadful calamity to have befallen our peaceful nation! I keep thinking it's a nightmare and I'm going to wake up."

Her house was neat and trim with an abundance of photographs on the walls and every other available space, each generation of the Holm family circle represented, from sepia-tinted great-grandparents to the latest babies. All three of her sons were at sea, two in the whaling fleet, while Sonja was married to her youngest. Johanna saw at once there was a good relationship between Sonja and her mother-in-law, bearing out the goodwill with which Sonja had always spoken of her.

That evening, when the three of them listened to the news, they heard that the expected British raid on Oslo had not taken place and there was no further reason to believe that it would. "Panic Day" had come to an end.

"Was it another example of German propaganda, then?" Fru Holm exclaimed indignantly. "It seems to me it was a ploy to try to make us accept Nazi 'protection' from the British. Huh! Don't they know our late Queen Maud was English and our Crown Prince was born in England? Nobody needs protection from their friends."

Sonja was turning the radio dial in an attempt to pick up a station not under German control, and by chance she tuned in to a local wavelength in time to catch a broadcast from the King. His voice came strongly over the air.

"My people . . ."

His message was short and clear. He had that day given a final and irrevocable "No!" to further German demands for capitulation. The fight would go on until Norway was free again.

During the night the German bombers went over and there was a distant rumble like thunder far away. In the morning they heard that Elverum had been flattened by bombing. The reason was obvious—it had been a deliberate attempt to kill the King. The local radio station was able to report that he and the Crown Prince and the government ministers had got safely away beforehand.

Johanna and Sonja were making ready to return to Oslo, although Fru Holm would have liked them to stay. "We must go back," Sonja said. "Johanna and I both have jobs to keep. I'll come and see you again soon."

There was plenty of traffic heading for the city again, although nothing like the amount that had been leaving the previous day. It seemed likely that many families would remain in the countryside for a few more days as a precautionary measure. When a traffic hold-up occurred on the boundaries of the city it was through a roadblock set up by the Germans.

When Johanna's turn came to drive past she was halted by the upraised hand of a corporal, rifle slung on his shoulder. He and another soldier came forward, one on either side of the car. Johanna wound down the window. The corporal lowered his head to look in at her.

"Is this your car, fräulein?" he spoke in German, roughly and rather loudly, as if he had already suffered a great deal of exasperation by not being understood.

She replied in his own language. *"Nein.* It has been loaned to me by a friend."

He looked relieved and his tone became less aggressive, more like that of a policeman giving traffic directions. "It makes no difference. I'm commandeering the vehicle in the name of the Third Reich. Drive off the road into the field there on your left. A soldier will take the keys from you."

In disbelief she stared at him. "What did you say?"

His face stiffened in anticipation of trouble. He had had abuse from every driver he had stopped so far and two had been put under arrest. The friendliness that he and the rest of his comrades-in-arms had been assured they would receive in Norway had not been evident so far. They had certainly not expected armed resistance, and least of all a defiant king who hadn't the wit to see that the Third Reich came as a benefactor and not as an enemy. Admittedly some aggression was natural from a driver being deprived of his car, but since the Norwegians had brought war onto themselves they must put up with all the inconveniences of it.

"You understand me. I'm not repeating my words. Do as I have instructed."

"I refuse! Who's in command here? I want to speak to an officer."

"I'm in command!" In annoyance he tapped the insignia of his rank and his voice rasped with warning. "I'm telling you for the last time: Park the car and get walking!"

Sonja understood most of what had been said. She had served many German customers in the past and had gained some grasp of the language. Now she plucked at Johanna's coat sleeve. "Do as he says. Please! Those other soldiers are coming forward. They'll only turn us bodily out of the car. I couldn't bear it!"

Johanna could hardly speak for rage at the German's high-handed action, which she saw as simple theft. Her teeth clenched and the temper that she dreaded within herself was reaching a white-hot pitch. "You get out, Sonja. This isn't your problem and I don't want you to be involved. Steffen has loaned me this car and I'm not giving it up."

Sonja scrambled out, retrieving both Johanna's suitcase and her own from the back seat, able to guess what would happen. She was proved right. The corporal, realising that Johanna was not going to obey, had his arm inside the car before she could wind up the window and fasten the doors. Wrenching the door open, he grabbed her with both hands and hauled her out, kicking and struggling. She was flung into a muddied snowbank where she went down heavily, sprawled across it, the breath knocked from her by the impact of her fall. Sonja ran to help her sit forward and when she had recovered her breath, assisted her to her feet and brushed the dirty snow from her coat.

"Don't say anything more," Sonja implored in a whisper, seeing how Johanna glared after the car as a soldier drove it into the field where a number of other commandeered vehicles were already parked. It was obvious that only the newest and the best were being selected. "Come on, Johanna. It's not far to walk."

To her relief Johanna responded to the plea and the gentle tugging on her arm. Without another word she picked up her suitcase and started walking, her gaze set straight ahead. She must have heard the soldiers laughing among themselves at her show of defiance but she gave no sign. When they had covered quite a distance and she still retained her burning silence, Sonja ventured a question.

"Are you wondering what Steffen will say about his car?"

"I know he'll understand." Johanna still looked ahead.

"You're so quiet. Are you angry with me, too? For getting out of the car?"

Johanna shot her a look of complete astonishment. "Angry with you? Of course not. I wanted you to do that. There was no sense in both of us getting manhandled."

"You knew what would happen then?"

"I realised I was in a difficult situation. On principle I could not give in. Since we started walking I've been wishing again and again that there was some way in which I could help get the Germans out. I loathe feeling helpless."

They trudged on along the road, drawing well to the side to avoid being splashed by slush when the traffic went by. Their suitcases were heavy, and it was a relief to reach Grefsen and take the lane up to the Alsteens' house. Indoors, they changed shoes and mud-spattered stockings. While Johanna put on the coffee-pot, Sonja went to the telephone and called the fur shop to see if it was open that day. Leif Moen was on the premises and replied. When she replaced the receiver, Sonja looked puzzled.

"The shop is closed, but he'd like us to go in for a couple of hours. He didn't say why. I said we'd get there soon."

They took a tram. As they drew near the centre of Oslo Johanna stared out of the window, scarcely able to believe that the city she knew so well should have changed its outward appearance in such a short time. The swastika was everywhere, fluttering from flagpoles or emblazoned on scarlet banners hanging like giant ribbons down the face of government buildings. Although Norwegian police directed the traffic, there were German soldiers patrolling everywhere and marching along the streets. A sense of outrage assailed Johanna with each new viewing.

As she and Sonja walked up Karl Johans Gate they saw that armed guards stood outside the Parliament buildings and every other large building of governmental importance. When they reached the fur shop the blinds were down. Leif admitted them at the side entrance and locked the door again.

"I am glad you were able to come in today. When you telephoned I had only just got here myself after taking my wife and children out of the city yesterday." He led the way, telling Johanna to bring a notebook when she and Sonja had taken off their coats.

They found him waiting for them in the salon where he had opened some of the glass display cases. His instructions were plain. He and Sonja would select the best of the furs and take them down to the storage room in the cellar where the most valuable were kept when not on display. Johanna was to list the details and attach a label to each coat-hanger that would show the furs were not for sale.

"Not for sale?" Sonja was puzzled. "Aren't the furs just going down into the basement as a protection against air raids?"

"That is one reason. The second is more important in my opinion." He looked intensely serious, almost strained. "Now that Oslo is no longer our own city we shall be getting a new kind of customer in the shop. Not the rich German tourists of the past, but the same nationals in uniform with money to spend. I do not intend to sell my choicest furs to any one of the enemy. They shall stay in the storage room until the King is back in the palace and the swastika gone forever."

Johanna felt akin to him. She understood his feelings exactly and was encouraged by the stand he was making. It was similar to her having refused to give up the car without a struggle. Neither action carried any real substance in the present crisis and yet personally to each they were of vital importance. They had both asserted themselves in the face of the enemy. She had always liked him. Now that she knew him better she liked him even more.

"Well, ladies," he said with a smile and a courteous gesture of invitation, "shall we get to work?"

For the next half an hour, sables and ermines and silver fox went swirling down the iron steps to the storage room in the basement. Those not in cotton covers, having been in the glass cases, were duly shielded and hung with room to "breathe." Finally Leif padlocked the door on what were probably the most beautiful and valuable furs in the whole country. Stock left for sale was still of high quality, for it had never been his policy to sell goods below a cer-

tain grade, but the most fabulous garments of all would not
be seen by German eyes.

Johanna and Sonja left the shop together. They parted
on the corner, Sonja to go home and unpack the suitcase
she still had with her and Johanna to search for some black-
out material for the windows of the Alsteens' house. A
complete blackout and curfew had been ordered by the
Germans throughout the city and in any area under their
control. Already there had been a run on black material
and it was in short supply. Johanna had to go into several
stores before she was lucky enough to get the final length
on the last bolt on the shelves there. She thought it should
be enough for at least four rooms in the house.

It was when she was coming out of the store again with
the heavy bundle in her arms that she saw a sight that was
to become familiar over the next few days. Three German
soldiers were dividing a block of butter between them and
eating it on slabs of chocolate. Long deprived of such luxu-
ries in Germany through Goering's policy of guns before
butter, they were seizing the chance to indulge a craving
for sweet, rich food. Later she saw others with butter
spread on cake and it became a frequent occurrence to see
soldiers coming out of grocery shops with blue paper bags
of coffee, which they opened to inhale the true fragrance,
having known nothing but *ersatz* coffee for a long time in
their own country.

That evening she hung one strip of the blackout material
over the kitchen window while she began her task of making the curtains on Anna's sewing machine. Before she
went to bed she tried to phone Ryendal, but there was no
contact.

Four days later an allied force of British, French and
Free Polish troops landed in northern Norway and at
Åndalsnes on Johanna's home fjord. By that time the whole
of the south had fallen to the Germans, and Johanna, who
had been concerned for the Alsteens in that area, now had
the further worry of how her family and friends in the
neighbourhood of Ryendal would fare now that the war
was on their doorstep. The Norwegian Army had rallied
strongly and closed ranks under the inspiring leadership of
Ruge, now promoted to general and commander-in-chief,

and bitter fighting was taking place around Bergen and
Trondheim and up the great valleys of Gudbrand and
Øster where unusually harsh winter conditions still prevailed. Her brothers were particularly in her thoughts.
Both had done their conscription service and would be in
the conflict. Erik, who was an officer on one of the coastal
steamers that plied the length of the coast from Bergen to
Kirkenes on the Finnish border, had been at home on
leave on the day of the invasion and it was unlikely he
would have been able to reach a naval fighting unit. She
fully expected to learn that he had gone with Rolf into
military service somewhere. Perhaps they were with the
King. He was still being hunted ruthlessly by the Luftwaffe, which continued to dominate the skies, and every
small village or hamlet where he took shelter was razed to
the ground in the general terror bombing aimed at killing
him and subduing the population.

Every morning Johanna had to wait to let military traffic
with its black crosses pass along the main road out of Oslo
before she could dart across to catch the tram. Armoured
vehicles and every kind of mechanised weaponry and supplies were pouring in at all the captured ports. More than
once a whole panzer division went past, the peculiarly
hollow rattle of the tanks disturbing the quiet morning like
mad, discordant music. She turned her face resolutely
away when the soldiers waved, called out to her and whistled appreciatively. Sadly one day she saw Norwegian prisoners of war being marched along. Hundreds of them.
Mostly they were youths doing their conscription service
who had been caught up in a war far beyond anything for
which they had been trained. Their faces were drawn with
misery and fatigue.

At the shop, Sonja had come to terms with the realisation that it could be a long time before she saw her husband again. Quisling's order for Norway's merchant shipping in foreign waters to hand itself over to Germany had
been defied. Not a single ship of the world's fourth-largest
merchant fleet had obeyed the order. Every one of them
had put into the nearest Allied or neutral port, a contribu-
tion of inestimable value to the cause of the Allies.

As yet there had been no German customers in the fur
shop. The officers who could have afforded to purchase

were too much engaged in military matters, either by
moving flags on a map or in the front line itself. Neither did
civilian customers come, many people being still out of the
city, either through choice or because their return had
been cut off by the Germans' advance.

Johanna observed changes taking place every day. Several of the young men who had been fellow passengers on
the bus or tram each morning had gone, some from the
first day of the call to arms. Due to the curfew, friends no
longer dropped in during the evenings and at weekends
people kept to the vicinity of their homes. In the food
shops an impromptu form of rationing had been imposed,
any deliveries shared out by the shopkeepers, who tried to
be fair with the goods at their disposal. When Johanna had
finished making the black-out curtains and had hung them,
her leisure hours settled down to a curiously lonely routine. Thoughts of Steffen were inevitably always at the
forefront of her mind.

It was as if the kiss he had given her had awakened
something tender and cherishing within her that she had
never been aware of before. She could not recognise it as
love, believing that she was too sensible and level-headed,
too much a girl of her own mind, to be caught up in romantic fancies. Yet the feeling was there, impossible to dismiss
or ignore, and at times it seemed to warm her whole heart.

In a rational way, she considered his relationship with
Delia Richmond. From what Anna had said it was obvious
there had been something between them for a considerable time. As if in proof of that was the fact that Delia had
called specially to say goodbye to him when fleeing from
the Germans, showing how much she had wanted to see
him once more. There was no reason to suppose that they
would not come together again when the war was over.

For the first time ever, Johanna experienced a virulent
twinge of a second emotion that was new to her, and she
suspected it of being what she had always despised, jeal-
ousy. She hoped it would not be her downfall, for she knew
her own faults and although she did not lose her temper
easily, it was as devastating to herself as to anybody else
when it flared.

April gave way to May and warmer weather. The seven-
teenth of May, normally an annual holiday for the rejoicing

of independence, went unmarked for the first time in a
hundred and twenty-five years. At home, Johanna ate her
supper with the national flag on the table. Made of silk and
mounted on silver, it was the only item she had retrieved
from the cellar. The house looked bare without its fine
ornaments, but she thought it best for the precious objects
to remain where they were, and her box of evening dresses
stayed in the cellar too.

When she put the flag back in a cupboard, unable to risk
leaving it on display since any show of it was banned by the
Germans, she wondered if Steffen had had a chance to give
thought to this special day. As she had so often before, she
wished that she had some idea where he might be in the
battle zone. He could be anywhere in Norway for all she
knew. She still had no contact with her family either and
her anxiety about them was constant. Mails were disrupted
and held up in the most unlikely places, some wherever
the postbags had happened to be on the day of the invasion. Telephones were likely to remain out of action in
many areas for a long time to come, many exchanges being
in the German war zone or damaged by bomb blast. The
desperate fighting and the Luftwaffe's terror bombing in
central and northern Norway continued without respite.
The Allies had failed to supply the air cover that had been
deemed necessary.

In early June when the glorious weather was making up
for the late spring, the Allies actually had some success in
northern Norway. But just when the vitally important port
of Narvik had been recaptured by the Allies, France fell
and the evacuation of the British Expeditionary Force took
place at Dunkirk. It changed the whole situation. The
Führer's most outspoken and virulent enemy, Winston
Churchill, ordered the withdrawal of the Allied forces
from Norway to strengthen Britain, which now stood alone
as a last bastion of freedom against the total might of the
Third Reich.

The first Johanna knew of this disaster for Norway was
when she was summoned by one of the younger saleswomen to Leif's office just after the day's work had begun.
When she went through the salon she saw it was deserted
and the street door had been closed against the entry of

any customers. She found all her fellow employees gathered together in front of Leif's desk while he himself stood, his face grave, on the far side of it.

"Now that we are all here," he said as she took a place beside Sonja, "I have some bad news. To prepare you, I will say that this is surely the darkest day our country has ever known. After eight weeks of fierce fighting from the very day of the invasion, which must have been far beyond anything the Germans anticipated, the battle of Norway is lost. Yesterday evening the King and the Crown Prince and the true government went aboard a British ship to sail into exile in England. They were at Narvik, the site of the victory that we hoped would prove to be the turning point, but sadly events far beyond our shores have changed our destiny."

By now most of the saleswomen were in tears; Johanna alone was dry-eyed with shock. He looked at them all compassionately. "Go home and be with your families for the rest of the day. Remember that we have been defeated in the field but not in our minds or in our hearts."

The women began to file out of the office, comforting each other. Sonja, who would have taken hold of Johanna's arm, saw she had no intention of leaving yet and went out of the office with the rest. Leif, half-heartedly sorting some papers on his desk, was surprised when he looked up and saw Johanna still standing there.

"Yes, Johanna?"

The question burst from her on a vibrating note of anguish: "What can we do?"

He understood her meaning and came around to perch his weight on the desk, facing her. "I don't know. I honestly have no idea. All I do know is that as long as there are men and women with the will to retain freedom, there is hope. Hold on to that hope. It could be the salvation of our country in time to come."

In her office, Johanna put the cover on her typewriter, her movements automatic. Then she reached out to change the date on the calendar in preparation for the next day, another part of her routine, and the significance of the date went home to her. Yesterday evening, when the King left Norwegian soil, must have been a particularly poignant departure for him in more ways than one. Long

before she was born and on the same date, June 7, the
King, born a Danish prince, had arrived in Oslo to be
enthroned, voted unanimously into his new role as monarch of Norway by a national referendum of its people. His
first words upon stepping ashore with the baby Crown
Prince in his arms, his wife beside him, had been a dedication of his life to the service of his new country. *"All for
Norway!"* Now she made the same vow herself. Anything
she could do for the return of freedom she would do. She
did not know where or what would lie within her power,
but wars could be fought in many ways and by individuals
as well as armies.

The shame of defeat caused a terrible despair to settle
over the whole population like a dank mist in the weeks
that followed. It was reflected in faces, and people found it
hard to smile. It was strange that there should be such a
sense of disgrace since everything possible had been done
in a rallying of forces to curb the enemy; nevertheless it
was there, sapping the spirit of the nation, and aided by the
new humiliations and regulations being meted out by the
German conquerors.

In the midst of it there came one bright spark of encouragement, which was to have an extraordinary aftermath,
like a tiny pebble thrown into a still pool and creating
ripples that turned into waves. The BBC began special
broadcasts in Norwegian from London, and from there the
King spoke out stirringly to his people in their hour of
despair, telling them to hold fast and that freedom would
be regained. Within a few days thousands of copies of his
speech began to flood the country, printed clandestinely in
cellars and offices and basements. Johanna found one
wound into her typewriter. She did not ask how it came
there. Instead, she simply tucked it away in her purse for
safekeeping. That evening she put it into her neighbours'
mailbox, doing her part in spreading the royal message.

Everybody had to register for a ration card and an iden-
tity card, taking a photograph along for the latter. As if to
emphasise each individual's subjugation to the Third
Reich, the identity cards were printed in German with the
Norwegian translation underneath as the minor language.
There were only about eight hundred Jews—men, women

and children—in Norway. Their cards were stamped with a red "J" and in the same week they had to surrender their radios, a harsh restriction that followed an earlier outrage in the desecration of the main synagogue in Trondheim.

Strict curfew continued to be imposed and any violation of the blackout regulations was punished with increased severity. An enterprising manufacturer began making venetian blinds of strong black paper, wood products being in plentiful supply from the vast forests, and these were in great demand by those for whom black fabric for windows had proved unobtainable. Johanna bought some and completed the black-out of the house where some rooms had remained unprotected.

All public gatherings were banned. There was to be no stopping to talk on the streets, not even if a man met his own brother; everybody was to keep moving. Listening to the BBC was strictly forbidden on pain of punishment, and the press came under the full pressure of German censorship. Travelling from place to place or changing address beyond a restricted area in any part of the country was not allowed without a special permit. Johanna began to wonder whether the Alsteens would get home again or would have to remain where they were for the time being. She had been looking forward to their return.

One relief was that the Germans had been stopped by their own high command from buying comestibles from civilian sources. The enemy forces were drawing off most of the country's food supplies in any case—meat, dairy and farm produce being diverted to military establishments. It soon became obvious to all that feeding a large army of occupation would become a heavy yoke on the rest of the population.

Tragedy struck locally in Grefsen when a youth, enraged at seeing his sister on the arm of a German soldier, tried to snatch her away and was bayoneted in the stomach. People came in great numbers to attend the funeral. His sister did not attend. She had been seized by some of his friends and had her hair shaved from her head. It was happening to girls and women elsewhere who associated with the enemy.

Another section of the population had begun to accept the German presence. The collaborators and the opportunists and those ready to take an easy chance at getting what would never have been theirs in other circumstances had begun to stand out from the rest. They were not many but they were there, and from the start they were contemptuously labelled Quislings by everybody else. It was a new name for "traitor" that had taken root in the language from the evening of April 9 and Quisling's infamous broadcast.

To Johanna, the whole regime of the Occupation was somehow associated with the ring of German metal heels in their continual marching, a sound that Norwegians everywhere had come to abhor. In a way she hated it more than their singing when they gave voice to "We March Against England," which was their favourite almost to the exclusion of anything else.

She wrote to her parents as soon as the mail began to move again, begging for all the family news, and also to her landlady, Anna Alsteen. By chance both replies came with the same post. She opened the one from home first. Her mother, thankful to have heard from her, wrote that all was as well as it could be in the present circumstances. Her brothers, as she had expected, had both been in the fighting. Rolf, who had suffered a minor wound, was helping on the farm until he received confirmation of a new teaching appointment, and Erik had been recalled to service in the coastal steamers by the Germans, who were using them for their own transport. Folding the letter, Johanna experienced a longing to see them all again in a wave of homesickness she had not experienced since leaving to work in Oslo.

Anna Alsteen's letter was a disturbing one. She was most anxious to get home again and wrote that if her dear husband had not been Jewish there would have been no problem, since they would be returning to their own residence. Unfortunately Jews were being allowed no privileges and travelling was barred to them. Her brother-in-law was hoping to get a permit for Viktor on medical grounds, but so far the German officials in that district were not considering any special cases, being too busy organising themselves into the routine running of the area. She thanked Johanna for continuing to look after the house and hoped with all her heart that she and Viktor would be returning sooner than could be expected at the present time. It was easy to read between the lines and recognise an underlying fear in Anna's carefully worded phrases that possibly Viktor might be in some special danger from the authorities. Maybe she had seen a warning in the confiscation of the Jews' radios. Johanna hoped she would be proved wrong.

By the next post she received a letter from Steffen. She was so thankful to see it that her excited fingers could hardly tear away the censor's resealing strip along the back. Spot checks were being made on the mail, presumably to ensure that no subversive plots were being hatched, and this caused some delay in delivery. She saw by the date that he had written to her on the same day as she had sent a letter to him at his aunt's address in Ålesund. He must have been wary of a chance investigation of his letter, for it was as guarded in its own way as Anna's had been, and as easy to read between the lines.

Hello, Johanna. Greetings from the west coast. After the events of recent weeks it's good to be getting back to normal. There's nothing like farm work for making one feel fit. A few aching muscles at first but that was to be expected. Now it's as if I had never been away from here. The harvest promises to be an excellent one this year. I'm looking forward to the time when you can get home for a visit. Don't forget we have a date at Saeter Lake. I went fishing there yesterday and nothing has changed. I've missed you. It's been far too long. Write to me. My regards to Anna and Viktor. Steffen.

She laughed softly. Cleverly, he had chosen not to return to engineering, which would have drawn him at once into the German work force to do their bidding. Instead he had taken up farm work within easy distance of his home, an occupation least likely to be interfered with by the enemy, who would want the land to be as productive as possible and so would leave the husbandry of it to the farmers with a minimum of interference. Could he be at her parents' farm? He had certainly been in contact with them to find out if she was still in the Alsteens' house, and from Saeter Lake he could look right into the valley below where her home lay. Her mother had given no hint, but neither

would she if it meant risking Steffen's new guise as a farm-
hand.

She wrote back to him at once. The reply came by hand
in a most unexpected manner one warm August evening
when she was sitting in the garden, still in the sundress she
had changed into after coming home from work. She saw
the silhouette of a tall man with the sun behind him coming across the lawn to her with a suitcase in his hand, and
when she shaded her eyes she recognised her elder
brother, Rolf. With a shout of joy she sprang up from her
deck chair and ran to him, laughing in her pleasure and
surprise. Lithe and lean with thick fair hair that flipped
across his forehead, peaked brows over keen greyish-blue
eyes, and a wide, energetic mouth, he was at heart the
more serious of her two brothers with feelings that ran as
deep as an underground stream. Nothing of that side of his
character showed on this occasion as he laughed with her
in their shared hug of greeting.

"I can't believe it!" she exclaimed delightedly. "However did you get here? How's everybody at home? Mother
and Father? And Erik?"

He gave her immediate assurance that everyone was
well. Then came the information that she had hardly
dared to ask. "There's a friend of yours helping out at the
farm these days. You've heard from him, I believe." He
patted the pocket of his jacket. "I've another letter from
him for you and others from Mother and friends in the
neighbourhood. You know how it is in a country valley.
Word that I had a permit to go to Oslo seemed to float
through the air and within hours everyone was wishing me
a good trip and sending greetings to you."

"Come into the house and I'll make you some supper.
The food won't be much, I'm afraid. Rationing has begun
to pinch hard and the bread is getting most peculiar in
colour and taste. White flour is only for hospitals and the
sick."

"You don't have to tell me. Already things aren't as you
remember at the farm, although nothing like as difficult as
it is for townspeople. There are Germans billeted in the
hamlet of Ryendal; they're there to keep order and ensure
that local produce gets channelled in the right direction,
which usually means to the cookhouses of the German

Army." He went with her into the house, his suitcase in his hand. "Mother has sent you some food. Butter and eggs and meat. She's always thought you were too thin and now she keeps saying she's afraid you'll waste away."

They laughed together again at the old family joke, for their mother was as thin as a little bird herself. "Butter!" Johanna said appreciatively when it was unpacked. "I haven't seen butter on the shop shelves for weeks. Now I want to hear how you were able to come and see me."

He told her he had managed to get a permit to travel to Oslo to receive confirmation of his new post at the school in the valley, for with the Germans arranging everything to their own authority, it had not been clear if the local educational board had the power to appoint him.

"Normally I would have gone farther afield to a bigger school," he said. "But when I came home after the conflict, a delegation of local people came to see me and ask if I would take over the school. They wanted someone they knew and whom they could trust to be in charge of their children. So I accepted."

"I'm glad. It means you can keep an eye on Mother and Father at the same time."

"The same thought had occurred to me."

They had a happy meal, although there were serious moments when he told her of those whom they had both known who had been killed, either in a bombing raid or on the battlefield, filling her with sadness. He told her that Steffen had been with the King's own men throughout the campaign. The parting of ways had come towards the end when the royal party had reached Molde, which was not all that far from Ryendal on the opposite side of the fjord. The Luftwaffe, following its established pattern, bombed the little Town of Roses, as it was called, to the ground. Steffen had stood near the King and the Crown Prince, who had watched the bombing in grief by a tall birch tree, with the inhabitants of the town gathered in stunned groups to gaze at their homes going up in flames. The next day, while the town still smouldered, the King and the Crown Prince and the government ministers had sailed for Narvik in the north where the last stand had been made before they were forced to leave the country. The Norwegian troops, no place for them on the ship, had been told to join other

units where they could. The men obeyed to the best of
their ability, but in a matter of days it was all over. Steffen
then went home to Ålesund to see his aunt, and afterwards
presented himself at Ryen Farm for employment.

"Steffen explained to Father that he needed time to lie
low and wait to see what should be done next. He began
work in the fields the same day and has been staying at the
farm ever since." Rolf smiled at her. "He's lost no time.
Already he has a group of men training in the mountains at
week-ends. They have no arms except those that were
buried when the Germans ordered the surrender of all
weapons, even field guns used to pot a woodcock or a deer
in the hunting season."

Her face was alight. "Do you mean that those weapons
were buried for a purpose? As a means to fight on, in spite
of what has happened?"

He nodded. "Steffen's group isn't the only one. I've
heard of others. Usually an experienced soldier from the
campaign is in charge, although sometimes it's just a gathering of men keeping fit in readiness for action in the
future. The fight isn't over, Johanna. It's just beginning." A
look of concern came into his face as he saw her eyes fill
with tears. "Hey! What's the matter?"

"I'm just so thankful to hear what you've told me.
There's been such an air of despair about everyone I meet.
The only thing any of us have had to cling to has been the
rallying call from the King in London. Now I know that
sooner or later there's bound to be a chance for me to join
in this new revival of the fight to get our freedom back
again."

He raised an eyebrow warily, his expression stern. "Hold
back there. You're my sister and I don't want you involved
in any trouble with the Germans. You remember that."

She saw she would make no headway against his broth-
erly protectiveness and decided not to protest that she was
as able as any man to learn how to fire a gun and plot an
ambush. It was as well that he did not know how she had
already defied the Germans over the matter of Steffen's
car. In her own mind she was undeterred. Somehow and
somewhere her chance would come. It was simply a matter of exercising patience for a while.

When she was alone in her bedroom she read her letters,

saving Steffen's until last. With no danger of the censor's interference, he had written freely of being at the farm and of his aunt's wish to meet her at the first chance that came along. Then he told her what receiving her letter had meant to him and of how much he missed her. His words, tender and fond, created of the sheets of writing-paper she was holding a true love-letter. A yearning to be home again swept through her with new impetus, simply because he was there.

Chapter 3

Her brother was only able to stay overnight. He telephoned her at the fur shop from the railway station before he left the city to let her know that his appointment had been given the official stamp.

"That's splendid news," she said enthusiastically. "Thanks for letting me know."

When she replaced the receiver and returned to her typing, one part of her mind seemed set on leaping ahead of him on the journey to their home far away on the west coast. With difficulty she wrenched her concentration back to the routine of the day.

German officers had begun to drift into the shop, and the saleswomen hated serving them. "They're so arrogant," Sonja had exclaimed angrily on one occasion. "They come in expecting to be served before any civilian customer who happens to be here, and they have wads of Norwegian kroner to spend on gifts to send home to their women. Not that many ordinary people can come in any more. A coat or cape, fur or otherwise, these days takes too many precious clothing coupons."

There was a German officer in the salon that morning. He was seated in one of the velvet upholstered chairs while his Norwegian girlfriend was deciding which of the coats she was trying on he should buy her. Sonja was serving with a face of stone. The officer's eyes slid down Johanna's figure to her legs and lingered there until she entered Leif's office and closed the door after her.

Leif greeted her with his customary smile. "Before we get down to work there is something I would like to discuss with you. Are you still alone in the house at Grefsen?"

"Yes." She sat down in the chair opposite his desk, resting her hands in her lap. "I've no idea when the Alsteens will return for the reason I told you the other day."

"I remember. I just wanted to make sure you hadn't rented a room to anyone since then. You said how quiet it was there on your own."

"So it is, but it's the Alsteens' house, not mine. I know they would have been pleased that my brother stayed overnight. That's a different matter entirely. I certainly wouldn't have a stranger there in their absence."

"That's what I thought. I also noticed that you kept quiet about the copy of the King's speech that you found on your desk one day."

She answered him frankly. "It was my guess you had put it there and that the Germans weren't going to be pleased about that kind of distribution. I was right about them and, I think, about you. Isn't that so?"

"Correct. Sonja was equally discreet. I consider myself to be a good judge of character and in your case and hers I've made no mistake. Do you have a good radio in your house? One that will pick up the broadcasts in Norwegian from the BBC? Not everyone can receive them, particularly in some parts of the country where reception from overseas is never satisfactory."

She was still mystified. "I listen to those broadcasts every evening."

"Then would you like to put that listening to a wider use by taking the newscasts down in shorthand and typing them up for me?"

Enlightenment dawned. "Are they to be distributed as pamphlets?"

"As news-sheets to be delivered once a week. This is not my own project, although I am behind the organisation of it. Later we hope to distribute two or three times a week, at least. Everything is still in the early stages. Some of the news-sheets will go out from here under Sonja's supervision and there will be other outlets, but that part of the operation isn't your concern."

"I'll start this evening. There is a typewriter at the house that came from Viktor Alsteen's goldsmith shop. I can use that."

"What about headphones? It's a small precaution and yet a worthwhile one. If someone hostile should overhear by an unlucky chance, everything would be lost."

"I'll do as you say."

The excitement of having been given this task was heightened by the special knowledge that here in the city certain members of the community were stirring, as they were in the forests and mountains in secret sessions of drilling and exercise. She felt her steps were lighter that day than they had been for a long time. This work would bridge the gap until something more vital came her way.

That night, and for many nights afterwards, she sat wearing her headphones, the radio on its own table in front of her, a shorthand pad in her hand, and waited for the announcement that had already become familiar to her. *"Dette er London!"* This is London. Then the inspiring burst of music, which faded as the news in Norwegian began.

She soon felt through this intense listening that she knew the announcers personally, able to tell by their regional dialects in which part of Norway they had been raised. Before long she thought of them as unseen friends.

General war news and authentic accounts of happenings in her own country went down in pencil to be typed afterwards for the underground news-sheet, which had been entitled *London Echo*. She did not know where it was printed, but she guessed it was in a cellar or warehouse. Secrecy was vital.

Through her headphones she followed in suspense the Battle of Britain. A handful of young Royal Air Force pilots were defying the might of the Luftwaffe in the skies above England. Well over a hundred enemy aircraft were brought down in a single September day. It was evident that Hitler was suffering his first defeat. To Johanna it was as if a beacon had been lit in the darkness, although it was only later she knew it was at this point that Hitler angrily jettisoned his plans to invade England, trusting that he would eventually compel surrender through heavy bombing and the cutting off of vital food supplies by sinking the Allied merchant fleets. The leading headline of the *London Echo* took Winston Churchill's own words of tribute. *Never in the field of human conflict was so much owed by so many to so few.*

Coinciding with the successful conclusion of the Battle of Britain, there was a kind of spontaneous rebirth of spirit throughout Norway that had evolved independently. It was almost as though with the coming of autumn and the crisper, invigorating days that followed, men and women had suddenly overcome the lethargy of gloom and despondency that had prevailed since the day of defeat, taking a lead from those already showing the way. Many underground news-sheets had appeared, edited and printed in secret hideouts and, like the *London Echo,* which was growing in strength, graduated to being several pages long with a thrice weekly appearance.

It had been particularly galling for the citizens of Oslo when Quisling had moved into the royal palace. Now it also housed the official headquarters of Hitler's personal representative in Norway, Reichskommissar Josef Terboven. He was an arrogant, cold-blooded Nazi, a former gauleiter, and his aim was to see that Norway, once the occupation was complete, gave the fullest strategic and economic benefits to the German war effort while a minimum number of troops were kept in the country to ensure full control. He foresaw no problems.

Then overnight, as if a silent signal had been passed from the southernmost tip of the land to the Arctic north, people were wearing paper clips on their collars and lapels as a sign of keeping together against the Germans. Invented in Norway and taken up by the rest of the world in calmer days, it was a totally Norwegian symbol that could be worn with special significance. Like the rest of the shop staff, Johanna wore one on her dress as well as her coat. The Germans soon became aggressive about this symbol. If they snatched off anyone's paper clip in the shop, Johanna had a box in her office ready with replacements. Then the men began to secure a razor blade behind their lapels, and after some painful experiences the Germans began to turn a blind eye to the eternal paper clips. Johanna saw a sergeant in the street lose the top of a finger in one such encounter.

Other movements were afoot. From the start the Lutheran state church, backed by the other churches, had spoken out fearlessly against the Gestapo and the Nazi regime. It had come as a severe setback to Reichskommissar Terboven when the judges of the Supreme Court resigned *en bloc* in protest against his interference with the

justice of the land. Sportsmen and athletes had made a
defiant gesture of their own, refusing to join the Nazi
Sports Association set up by the Germans and thus bringing competitive events to an end which, in a sports-mad
country, was a great personal sacrifice, not least to those of
Olympic standard. Fortunately every profession and trade
had its own organisation by long tradition and this gave
strength to opposition, nobody having to stand alone. Johanna, taking down the radio reports, shook her head
sometimes at the Germans' ham-fisted methods. They had
failed completely to understand the character of the people they were trying to crush. It was not for nothing that
over the centuries Norwegians had come to identify themselves with the staunchness of their own mountains.

Whenever Johanna entered or left the fur shop, she tried
to avert her eyes from the elegantly ornamented Victoria
Terrasse, which previously had been a pleasing sight to
her, reminding her of a huge white wedding cake. The
Gestapo had taken it over and established a centre from
which they were attempting to rout out patriotic activities
with bullying tactics. The police station at No. 19, Møllergaten had gained a notorious reputation, entirely at vari-
ance with its peacetime image, for what took place under
interrogation in its cells below street level. Many of those
engaged in work for the underground press had been arrested and taken there. The Germans were also building
new punishment centres. These places were called concentration camps—a name with a sinister ring to it.

Johanna's correspondence with Steffen was spasmodic,
partly because he had to guard against any inquisitive censor's checking up on him, and for that same reason he only
occasionally spoke to her on the telephone, it being known
that calls were tapped. On the day he went off to the war
he had asked her to think of him when she travelled on the
tram, covering a deeper reason for his wanting her to
remember him, and somehow she always did.

There was another diversion on the tram, a daily game
played in earnest by Oslo passengers, and it was the same
on the buses. If a German took a spare seat, those civilians
in the neighbouring seats would get up and move to another part of the transport. If there were no other seats
available they would stand, in a never-ending show of their

displeasure at the German presence. Johanna had sometimes moved half a dozen times on a single journey, particularly as soldiers liked to sit next to a pretty girl. At first this game of "musical chairs" without the music caused many scenes, the Germans retaliating by stopping the transport and ordering all civilians off. It still happened occasionally, although mostly the Germans had become resigned to it. Sometimes a soldier would shout abuse and lie back, putting his feet up, while half a dozen passengers would straphang, ignoring him as if he did not exist.

The first snows came again and the festive season drew near. That Christmas of 1940, the first under Nazi rule, promised to be a bleak time for everyone. Life was particularly wretched in Oslo, where the Gestapo was establishing a terrible hold. Students had been viciously beaten up in their own university, and arrests made after open struggles in the streets. In one part of the city two fifteen-year-old boys had been taken away for daubing "Long Live Haakon VII" on the walls of a German billet. Their parents could discover nothing about their fate, except that they had been sent to work out a penance. It could mean anything.

In the shops, stocks of Christmas decorations, tree ornaments and unsold toys from the previous festive season were bought up rapidly. Anything remotely luxurious had long since disappeared from the shelves, and basic commodities were not always available. Long lines of people waiting their turn outside the food shops were an everyday sight and often stretched the full length of a street. Sometimes German trucks passed them on the way to the harbour, shipping out Norwegian meat to Germany where nobody was to go hungry.

One afternoon when the snow was drifting down in huge flakes in the street outside, the door of Johanna's office opened and Sonja looked in, an animated expression of pleasure on her face at what she had to announce. "You have a visitor." She withdrew at once.

To Johanna's astonishment, Steffen in ski clothes appeared in the doorway, grinning seriously at her. "Hello, Jo. I thought it was high time I took a trip to see you."

She released a soft cry, rising slowly to her feet. In the midst of her joy at the unexpected sight of him she sensed

that all was not well. Inevitably, in spite of letters exchanged, they had drawn apart through individual experience over past months and there could be no immediate
return to that flow of feeling that had held them close in a
farewell embrace at the market place. She even felt a
wave of shyness, something she had not known for years.
Perhaps this was another trick that war played on people, a
cruel one that drew them together only to change and
distance them when apart.

"How are you?" she asked with a catch in her voice.
"I've never had a better surprise than seeing you today."

"I'm fighting-fit. Thanks for your letters."

"And yours. I've looked forward to every one." It was
not how she had pictured their reunion. She had always
thought they would fall into each other's arms. Instead, he
was as restrained as she. It was almost as though they were
strangers again. "What has brought you to Oslo?"

"I told you. To see you. I've already spoken to your boss.
He says you may leave now."

"Oh, good." She hoped she sounded enthusiastic as she
put the cover on her typewriter, glad of a diversion.

"I've a taxi waiting outside."

"Not the tram?" It was a brave attempt to link the past
with the present, her smile a trifle uncertain. Taking her
hat and coat from a peg, she noticed that her hands were
shaking.

"Not today." He took her coat to help her on with it. "I
can't risk a spot check on my papers."

She glanced over her shoulder at him in alarm. "Are you
here without a permit?"

"That's the situation."

She swung round to face him anxiously. "Are the Germans after you?"

"Not yet. I'll tell you everything as soon as we reach the
house. There won't be anyone else there, will there?"

"No. The Alsteens can't get permission yet to leave
Drammen."

He took her by the arm to escort her from the building.
Outside, she saw that his skis were in the rack of the taxi,
which was powered by one of the wood-burning stoves
people had begun to attach to the back of their vehicles,
petrol being strictly rationed and not available for any

vehicle not directly involved in the German war effort. He reached for her hand and held it as they were driven through the snowy streets to Grefsen. There was no telling whether the taxi-driver was patriot or quisling, and they kept conversation to a minimum.

At the house Steffen paid the fare while she hurried up the drive to open the front door. Bearing in mind the black-out regulations, she waited for him to come indoors before switching on the light. He stuck his skis in the snow outside the porch where he removed his ski boots, and as he closed the front door behind him she took the boots from his hand to set them in the hall cupboard for snowy footwear. Because of enforced economy with electricity, the bulb in the hall lamp was a small one, and when she turned to face him again they were in little more than a pale gloom from it, the silk fringe of the shade making a wall of shadows around them. His face was working and her own lips were trembling.

"Jo!" he exclaimed huskily.

She threw herself into his arms and buried her face against him. They hugged each other wordlessly, his cheek against her head. It came to her that their reunions would always be fraught and difficult for however long the war lasted, for each time they would have to find each other again. The slightest complication or turn of events could come close to parting them irrevocably, no matter how much they might wish it otherwise, for the war was their enemy in more ways than one, and inevitably he would be changed by it more than she.

He cupped her face gently and raised it, enabling his mouth to take hers in an impassioned kiss, her eyes closing on the intensity of feeling sweeping through her. He crushed her still closer to him, and when they did draw apart both knew that they had found again the promise of love that had come about at the time of their first meeting. In present circumstances it was as transient as ever, but neither could deny its immediate force.

"Hello, there," he said.

"Welcome back," she replied in perfect understanding. Then he kissed her again, slowly and still more lovingly. She was deeply stirred.

He went into the kitchen with her to unload from his

rucksack some food that her mother had sent, and passed
on greetings and good wishes to her from those at Ryendal.
While she began to prepare a simple supper he padded
upstairs in his socks to take a look at his old room and find a
pair of sandals.

"What happened to the suit I left behind?" he inquired
when he came downstairs again.

"I remembered one day it was there and carried it down
to the cellar where I had already put some things of value.
It's hanging in the old cellar cupboard."

"That was thoughtful of you. I hope it won't be long
before I need it again."

They began to talk about the previous time they had
been in the house together when the bomb had dropped
and the whole terrible nightmare of the invasion had begun. He left her only to refuel the wood stoves and bring in
fresh stocks of logs from outside after chopping a new
supply for her. By that time the meal she had prepared on
the electric cooker was almost ready.

"You haven't told me yet exactly how you travelled
here," she reminded him.

"I went by steamship up the fjord from Ryendal's nearest jetty," he told her, setting places for two at the kitchen
table. "There was no problem about that. Then, by arrangement, I made the rest of the journey in the back of a
civilian truck carrying German food supplies to Oslo, my
skis in with the same goods. The driver let me out in a side
street and I came straight to find you at the fur shop."

"Is the same driver taking you back again?"

"No." He spoke gravely. "I'm leaving for Sweden in a
few hours' time."

Her eyes widened. She came at once to stand by the
kitchen table. "Are you escaping?"

"I'm on my way to join the Free Norwegian Forces that
are being formed in England. The Underground has prepared routes to be followed on skis, mainly after dark, to
the border. With luck one should be able to avoid the
German patrols, and there is still a Royal Norwegian Lega-
tion in Stockholm from which routes to England are being
organised, sometimes through Russia and via the Mediter-
ranean."

"It will take weeks to make such a journey! Perhaps months."

He shrugged. "That's not important if I get there in the end."

With her fingers she combed her hair back in a gesture of bewilderment. "But you needn't have come south to make a get-away. It's common knowledge that people on the west coast are slipping out in boats across the North Sea. It's those in the south who have no alternative but to cross the Swedish border. You ran the risk of being picked up many times at checkpoints for being a long distance from your home district in suspicious circumstances."

He took her by the shoulder, looking strongly at her. "I told you—I had to see you again."

She comprehended the depth of his reason. In a kind of loving anger at the dangers he had faced, she shook her head at him. "You're crazy," she chided despairingly.

"As long as you're glad I'm here."

"You know I am."

Before they sat down to their meal she lit a candle and set it in a china candlestick on the table. Symbol of hospitality and welcome, it was an old Scandinavian custom never to serve food on special occasions, whatever the hour of the day or night, without candlelight. Steffen turned the kitchen lights off so that they ate in the flame's aura. Their conversation was quiet, almost intimate, and yet they did not talk any more on the subject of their own personal relationship. Mostly he gave her news from her home district and related what had been happening there.

Towards the end of the meal over coffee she told him about losing his car, leaving nothing out. He was dismayed at the stand she had taken, even though he fully understood her attitude. "You could have been arrested! Anything might have happened. I don't care a damn about the car. Your safety is all that matters to me. For God's sake don't ever take a risk like that again."

She saw she was up against the same protectiveness that she had met in her brother. Although touched by Steffen's concern for her, she could not make any rash promises, not knowing what might lie ahead for her. Instead, she merely smiled and spoke in a lighter vein. "They say confession is good for the soul. I feel better now that you know how it came about."

His face remained sombre and he reached out to hold her hand across the kitchen table. "I've something to tell you, too. Not good news, I'm afraid. It's about your father."

She felt her heart contract with dread. "What's happened?"

His clasp tightened on her hand. "In August, on the very day that Rolf was travelling back from Oslo after seeing you, your father made a courageous gesture of resistance that had a serious aftermath. He went to Ålesund on business and it happened to be the King's birthday. So he bought a carnation to wear in his buttonhole."

Her eyes widened and her lips parted on a sharp intake of breath at what might follow. The carnation was the flower of the royal house. "Go on," she urged fearfully.

"He was set upon by German soldiers. They tore the flower out of his lapel, knocked him down and kicked him into the gutter. They went on kicking him. He suffered broken ribs and other injuries. His recovery has been slow. The worst seems to be over now, although he has to rest a good deal."

"Why wasn't I told in the first place?" she burst out.

"It was decided that you should not be worried. You wouldn't have been allowed to travel home at that time and there was nothing you could do."

Her face was strained. "I'd have found a way to get there somehow."

His mouth twisted in a wry smile. "That's what your mother was afraid of. At least your father escaped arrest. You might not have been as lucky."

"Is my father able to do any work?" She found it hard to picture her parent as anything but the strong, healthy man he had always been.

"He does the paperwork and some lighter chores, although he has aged considerably and is slow in his movements. It's lucky that the schoolhouse in the valley is near enough for Rolf to continue to take on chores in his spare time and shoulder the full responsibility now that I've gone."

Johanna's expression remained thoughtful. "Now I know why my mother took on extra help in the house in August.

She wrote that a girl was coming from a fishing village near Ålesund and since then has mentioned several times that she is a willing worker. What is Karen Hallsted like?"

He grinned widely. "In one word—beautiful. Your brother Erik fell for her when he was home on leave. My guess is that he wants to marry her."

The information amused Johanna. "You must be mistaken. Erik has never been serious about any girl."

"Karen may be the exception. She's a stunner."

"So have others been before her. I suppose she fell for him. They always do."

"On the contrary. The cold shoulder was obvious."

She continued to be amused. "Perhaps for once he's met his match." Then her voice turned to a more serious note. "How does he find life on the coastal route under the Germans?"

"Difficult. The steamers still carry passengers from place to place and transport mail and cargo, but the cabins are reserved for German officer personnel. Sometimes civilians have to surrender places to German troops at a moment's notice."

"How did Ålesund look when you left?" She knew well the salty, thriving fishing port that was a departure point for the steamship he would have taken up the fjord. Ålesund was a regular stopping place for the coastal steamers going north and south. Many times she had met her brother coming ashore there.

"The cheerful atmosphere of the place has gone completely. Since the German notices went up that anyone attempting to make contact with the Allies would be shot, local people have become suspicious of strangers. Quisling infiltrators try to find out if any boats are preparing to leave secretly for England."

"How did your aunt take your leaving to rejoin the King's forces?"

"Courageously. She's that sort of person."

"I know you have already asked me to visit her when I am home again, but as you won't be able to write to her, do you think she'd like to hear from me in the meanwhile?"

"She'll appreciate that, I know."

They sat talking until it was time for Johanna to listen to the BBC newscast. He sat with her while she took down the reports. Hundreds of Italian prisoners had been captured by the Allies in North Africa, and there had been another heavy bombing raid on London in the Luftwaffe's merciless blitz.

As soon as the broadcast was over she set aside her shorthand notes to be typed up the next day. When she left her chair she saw that he had moved to stand waiting for her. She caught her breath, seeing how he was looking at her, and she went to him without hesitation. With his arm around her they went up the stairs to her room.

In the muted glow of her bedside lamp he made tender and beautiful love to her. For her it was the first time. Never before had she cared enough to share and be shared. Now she loved, her heart full to overflowing with all she felt for him. Her whole body was tremblingly aroused, responsive and receptive, ardent and giving, his nakedness silk against hers. She would never have believed that such a physically powerful man could be so sensitive in his loving. Never had she suspected the existence of such eroticism in her, waiting to be brought to light. Their physical joy in each other was a revelation to them both. Then, their passion matched, all his strength became hers. Everything was perfect between them. Everything.

She lay softly against him in his arms, their entwined limbs pale in the lamplight, and they spoke quietly. He kissed her forehead and her eyes, her temples and her ears, stroking her hair out across the pillow.

"I love you, Jo darling," he murmured again.

She curled still closer to him. "I love you, too," she breathed blissfully. He tilted her chin with his fingertips and their mouths drank each other's love once more.

"I have a gift for you." There was adoration in his eyes.

She smiled. "I didn't think there was anything left to buy."

"There isn't. It's something I made for you. A jeweller completed the work. It's my special love-gift."

She put a hand to her throat, touched deeply by the significance of what he had said. It was an old tradition, still held to in many districts, that a bride received a love-gift the morning after the wedding night. It was always a piece of jewellery. "Shouldn't it be given at dawn?"

There was regret in his low-voiced answer. "I'll not be here at dawn."

"I had forgotten that," she whispered huskily.

As he left the bed to take the gift from a pocket she sat up to clasp her hands around her updrawn knees. He returned to her side and handed her a small package. Propping himself on an elbow, he watched her unfold the tissue paper.

Her face became radiant as she gazed in a surge of delight at what she saw. It was a long string of finely shaped stones, intricately capped and linked with gold, and polished by him to a point where they were almost iridescent, the blended greys and pearly tones and tints of pink proclaiming their origin. Hours of skill and care had gone into bringing them to such a point of perfection.

"They're from Saeter Lake!" It was the mountain lake within the great range that linked his home with hers and which they had discussed on the day he had left for the war. "It's a wonderful gift."

"It should have been diamonds."

"No!" She meant it, holding the necklace to her. His thoughts of her and his love had gone into every one of those exquisite stones. Raising the necklace up entwined in her fingers, she offered it to him. "Please put it on for me."

He took it from her and slipped it over her head. It hung down to the cleavage of her breasts. She sprang from the bed to go across and admire her new necklace in a mirror on the wall. He thought he had never seen a more beautiful sight than this lovely naked girl preening before her own reflection.

She came back to him in the bed. Lying on her stomach and propping herself on her elbows, she looked down into his face, her own having become serious and intent. "I'm going to England with you."

He cupped her bare shoulders with his hands caressingly. "I've been thinking along the same lines. It was in my mind all the time on my journey here to you, but the odds are against us. Not the danger, which I know you're willing to risk with me; it's the opposition we would meet from the Norwegian diplomats in Stockholm. Passages and transport are difficult enough for them to arrange. They'll send me as a fighting machine, but they'll not give a place on the list to a woman in preference to the men waiting to get away."

Her head sank down against his shoulder in wrenching disappointment. She could not dispute his argument. Briefly she had had a dream of being with him, of being trained in England to do something worthwhile when the time of liberation came. Instead, if she went with him into Sweden she would remain as an internee, cut off as much from her family and friends as from him. She would have to let him go without her. The pain of parting shot agonisingly through her. Involuntarily her arms enclosed the back of his neck as if by some means she might prevent all distance coming between them. He responded passionately, almost violently, seized by the same despair at the imminence of separation. Their love-making was urgent and ecstatic and yet at the same time poignantly bittersweet, bringing them still closer together.

Then it was time for him to depart. When they were both dressed, he took her into his arms for a last, long kiss. Talking was over. All that was left to say to each other was in his eyes and in hers. Hand in hand they went from the room and down the stairs.

"Farewell, my love," Steffen whispered to her. They kissed for the last time. Pulling on his thick gloves, he left the house. She remained on the threshold in the unlit doorway, shivering in the icy air while he clicked on his skis. Then with a wave to her he was away, swishing across the snow, and was lost from her sight almost at once in the early morning darkness.

Quietly she closed the door and rested her forehead against it. With all her heart she wished she could have gone with him.

Chapter 4

Steffen had been gone two months. Winter still had a hard grip on the land. To Johanna, Oslo seemed to get bleaker with every passing day. Most of her spare time was spent in food queues, sometimes she and Sonja taking turns lining up with each other's ration books.

She missed the familiar blue uniform of the police, which had once been part of the city scene. Now the newly formed Quisling police and ordinary police alike wore German-style military uniforms which added their own sombre colour to the streets. She knew that many ordinary policemen hid their true patriotism in order to give advance warning to those about to be arrested by the Nazis. On police stations and all the government buildings the German eagle had appeared, moulded with great wingspans over entrances and archways as if to endorse the ever-present black swastika.

All the store windows had a hollow look. Many that had once displayed fine wares had little more to offer than handmade wooden items. The goldsmiths displayed notices that objects of precious metal were for sale only if customers could supply the same weight of those metals in exchange. She knew that Steffen had handed in his gold cuff-links in order to get the jeweller to link up with gold the stones of the necklace that she wore so often.

At the fur shop it still came as a minor shock to her eyes to see a renovated fur coat of indiscriminate origin in the window where once a sumptuous garment would have been displayed. A printed card suggested to passers-by that old furs should be repaired and restyled. In the salon itself there were only photographs of furs on the velvet-covered podiums, and the glass-fronted cupboards were almost empty.

She had no idea, when she went home one Friday after

work, that she would find the Alsteens back at Grefsen.
They had returned without advance notice. At the sound
of her door key turning in the lock, Anna came darting
across the hall to embrace her. Johanna, overjoyed at their
return, had to hide her shock at her friend's changed appearance. A plump and sturdy little woman when she had
left, she had lost a lot of weight; moreover, constant anxiety over many months had ravaged her gentle features
and streaked grey thickly into her auburn hair.

"My dear child!" Anna's tears were flowing. "Who ever
would have thought it would be so long before Viktor and I
should get home again? And how well you've looked after
everything. I'm most grateful."

Johanna, moved to tears herself, patted the woman's
shoulder. "I did nothing. It's just wonderful that you're
here at last and can be under your own roof again. Where's
Viktor?"

"In bed. The drive all the way from Drammen tired him
even though it was in an ambulance. Go up and see him.
He's not asleep."

Johanna removed her outdoor clothes as she ran up the
stairs. Throwing them over the baluster rail on the landing, she went straight to the Alsteens' bedroom. The door
was open and Viktor was propped against the pillows, his
eyes closed. Compassion choked her throat. He was not
much changed during his absence, having always been a
thin man of great presence and dignity, who had been
made frail by his stroke and general disabilities. The
thought that moved Johanna to fresh tears was that such a
harmless gentleman, in the true sense of the word, should
have been a target for Nazi vindictiveness, depriving him
for so many months from his right to be in his own home.
He must have heard her step, for he opened his eyes, his
singularly sweet smile lighting his pale, almost transparent
features.

"It's Johanna. Prettier than ever. How are you? Come
and tell me how you've been passing the time since I last
saw you." His speech was, if anything, slightly more halting
than before.

She ran forward to sit on the bed and leaned over to kiss
him on the cheek. Then she took his hand into hers. It
seemed to have no weight. "I'm still at the fur shop.

There's not much business these days due to a lack of supplies. Skins are hard to come by now. Some workshop staff have been kept on to deal with repairs and to make up whatever skins are available, but the salon staff has been reduced to Sonja on her own."

After she had talked a little longer, she made a move to get up, not wanting to add to his tiredness with too much conversation. Unexpectedly he caught at her sleeve with his stronger right hand. "Don't go yet. I have so little time in which to talk to you. We're leaving again tomorrow. My brother-in-law, Anders, has arranged everything."

She thought the strain of the journey had caused him to be confused and she smiled reassuringly. "You're home to stay now."

"No, my dear." He was quite firm. "Anna and I are going to Sweden. It's safe for me there. She wants to get me away while there's still time."

In distress she caught up the hand she held and pressed it to her cheek. "You're Norwegian born and bred, Viktor!"

"By birth, but not by race, dear child. That makes a difference to the Nazis. If Anna and I are to spend whatever time is left to us together, we must leave as arranged. Otherwise we shall be separated and never see each other again."

Then, in spite of his request that she should stay, he closed his eyes and slept, dropping off into the kind of nap indulged in by the elderly. Gently Johanna released his hand from hers and laid it on the coverlet. Then she went downstairs and faced Anna in the kitchen. She had no need to say anything. Anna sank into the nearest chair. "He's told you, I can see."

Johanna took hold of the back of another chair and swung it forward to sit facing her. "Has Viktor been threatened?"

"Many times. I can't speak of the verbal abuse we received from the Germans in the streets." Anna's restless movements and the nervous twitching about her mouth showed that she was not far from a nervous collapse from all she had been through on her husband's behalf. It would not need much more for a complete breakdown. "I had to stop taking him out in his wheelchair. What we should have done without Anders I don't know. Apart from his

personal protection as head surgeon at the local hospital,
he seems to have contact with the new movement of resistance that's growing up. I don't know how he managed it,
but he finally got a permit for us to travel. The ambulance
was a bonus for which he is totally responsible."

"How are you getting into Sweden?"

"I have papers stating I have permission to take Viktor
to a hospital not far from the Swedish border, and transport will call for us tomorrow morning." Anna became
very tense. "I have papers for you, too. I was hoping that
you would come with us."

Johanna stared at her. "Why do you want me to go with
you?"

"Viktor will have to be pulled in a sled across the snow.
I'll be on skis. We shall have a guide but it would be a great
comfort to me to have your company." Her lips trembled.
"I'm so afraid and you're so young and strong."

Leaving the chair, Johanna dropped to a knee in front of
Anna, taking hold of the woman's arms and looking up into
her face. "I'll do anything I can to help you. You've always
been good to me. I've never forgotten how kind you were
when I first came to Oslo, making your home mine. I'll
come right to the Swedish border with you and see you
across, but don't ask me to leave Norway. I couldn't do it. I
have to stay."

Anna shook her head in agitation. "I can't let you run
into danger for my sake and Viktor's, only to return here
and face the consequences of our departure. It won't be
long before the German authorities check to see if Viktor is
at the hospital or still in residence at Grefsen. Please forget
I asked you. I should never have done it."

Johanna straightened up. "It's all settled. As long as I'm
back in good time to go to work on Monday morning,
nobody need know that I've ever been away. If it should
come out I would say that I saw you to the hospital as
requested and left you there. I assume the driver of your
transport will back up whatever story I give?"

"Oh, yes. Anders told me he would be someone we
could trust completely." Again Anna began to give way to
nerves and Johanna made her calm again, insisting on having the arrangements explained carefully and clearly in

every detail. Then she examined the papers that had been
made out in her name.

An ambulance arrived the next day at the appointed
time. The driver was a young man with a cheerful freckled
face and a shock of ash-blond hair. He helped Viktor into
the back of the ambulance, saw that he was comfortable
with pillows and blankets, and then sprang out to help
Anna into it. She travelled in the back with her husband
while Johanna sat beside the driver.

"Here we go then," he announced, setting off. "I'm Kristofer Olsen."

She gave her name in turn. "Do you work for an Oslo
hospital?"

He chuckled. "I'm a medical student. I've never driven
an ambulance before. After today this ambulance will go
back to its depot and nobody will be any the wiser." He
glanced at her. "Why are you going to Sweden? Has the
Gestapo got something on you?"

"No. Nothing like that. I just promised my friends I'd see
them right to the border. I'll be coming back with you."

He looked startled. "You want me to *wait?* That could be
tricky."

She was worried. "It's important I return to Oslo
quickly. There's no other way I can do it."

He gave a thoughtful whistle under his breath. "Well, I
guess we can fix it somehow!"

"Thanks!" she exclaimed gratefully.

"That's okay."

When a roadblock loomed ahead, he shot a quick look at
her. "You're not wearing a paper clip today, are you? We
don't want any unnecessary hold-ups with the guards."

"I thought of that. I have mine in my pocket."

"Good girl." He drew up at the roadblock. A German
guard came to the window and asked for the papers. Kristofer handed over Johanna's and his own before jumping
out to go to the back of the ambulance and let the guard
see for himself that only a sick man and his wife were
inside. The guard returned the papers. They were in order; three in party, plus the driver, on an authorised journey. He signalled and the striped barrier was raised to let
the ambulance through.

Kristofer heaved a sigh of satisfaction. "That's the first hurdle behind us. Let's hope the rest will go as well."

They were stopped three more times before they reached the hospital, but there was no trouble. The early darkness of the winter afternoon closed down on them and the blacked-out headlights gave out a thin ray of light through slits, making the frosty road sparkle ahead of them. It was snowing lightly. Kristofer checked the final details with her.

"I'll go into the hospital with Viktor, you and Anna too. He has to walk. That's most important, so I must be quick to get him out of the ambulance before any stretcher bearers come out to meet us. We go to a waiting room which has two entrances. We leave the Alsteens there and you must be seen to leave with me. I'll make sure we're remembered in Reception. Anna and Viktor will leave the waiting room under their own steam by the other door which will take them to the far side of the hospital. Someone is waiting for them there. I'll show you where I'll be parked and waiting for you. Then you nip after the escaping party and catch up with them. Okay?"

She grinned at his constant use of the American slang. "Okay," she repeated.

Anna, forewarned through the communicating panel, had Viktor sitting up and ready to get out when the ambulance stopped. Kristofer ran around the doors and almost lifted him out. Then the four of them went into the hospital. Luckily the reception desk was busy and they went through to the waiting room without being questioned. Two other people were waiting there and watched as Johanna bade the Alsteens farewell, saying she was sure all would go well for Viktor at the hospital.

When she came out of the waiting room Kristofer was at the reception desk, joking with two nurses. When he saw Johanna he called out, "Ready to leave, Frøken Ryen?"

"Yes, I am," she replied.

He had a final word with the nurses which left them both convulsed in giggles, and then swaggered to her where she waited by the door. Outside they both got back into the ambulance and he swung it around the hospital perimeter, pointing out the direction she had to follow and where she would find him again. He slowed down just long enough for her to get out and then he drove off into the snowy darkness.

She ran past an outbuilding and found skis waiting for her. The falling snow would soon obliterate the tracks she had to follow so she set off at once, leaving the hospital behind her and crossing a white stretch that would be a buttercup meadow when summer returned.

There was an almost eerie beauty to the scene. The lazy pace of the descending snow created delicate patterns, and ahead the tall pines and firs of the forest stood like white inverted cones, taking on a new layer of lacy snowflakes like another coverlet. The air was colder than she had realised and was getting colder still, causing her breath to hang before her and crystallise on her lashes. At her home on the west coast, although hundreds of miles further north, the flow of the Gulf Stream gave far easier winters, temperatures never so low as in this part of the country.

She found the Alsteens and their guide waiting for her under cover of the trees. Viktor was cosily ensconced on the sled, wrapped in blankets like a cocoon, and the guide, who did not give his name, had the straps of the sled securely over his shoulders.

"Let's go," he said as soon as Johanna reached them. He began to ski effortlessly ahead and the runners of the drawn sled skimmed easily over the crisp snow. Anna followed him, all her old skills on skis revived in practise for this escape before she left Drammen. Johanna brought up the rear. She was glad she had come, knowing that she had given Anna confidence to face this dreadful time of suspense and danger.

There was no sound except the swish of skis and the sometimes ghostly creaking of a bough bending under the weight of snow. The guide stopped at certain intervals to allow a rest out of consideration for Anna who, in her midfifties, could not be expected to keep up the pace that he and Johanna could share. Anna was feeling the strain but she would not admit to it, unaware that the patchy colour of her face gave her away. Once the guide produced a vacuum flask of hot coffee, and she stooped down to hold a cup solicitously to Viktor's lips in order that he should not bring his good hand out into the intense cold.

"Are you warm enough?" she asked him anxiously.

"Oh, yes," he replied in his gentle manner, having taken obedient sips of the coffee.

"It won't be long now," she said, tucking the covers closer about his face. "Try to sleep. Then when you wake up we'll be in Sweden."

They were not far from the border when the guide halted, catching the sounds of some disturbance in the forest. Suddenly in the distance a rifle cracked and then another. More shots followed. Almost in the same instant, a Norwegian skier was upon them. He did not halt, although he took in their situation at a glance and gave warning as he went rushing by.

"Get the hell out of here! The patrol is moving in." Then he was gone.

The Alsteens' guide turned quickly to Johanna. "You and I must create a diversion. This woman with us is too exhausted to make enough speed." He turned to Anna, slipping the straps of the sled off his shoulders and onto hers. "Listen to me. You have no more than a kilometre to go. You can do it easily if you take your time. Here's a flashlight and a compass if you should need them. Keep going west. Don't worry about the Germans. We'll draw them away from you. Good luck!"

There was no time for farewells. Johanna could only echo the guide's words as she sped away with him. She had never thought she would end this expedition by encouraging enemy pursuit. The guide gave her instructions over his shoulder and they created a zigzag route, parting to cross and recross again, giving the illusion of moving in several directions and taking advantage of every dip and hollow. The patrol was drawn away from the escapees. Shots rang out, sometimes zinging perilously close, or so it seemed, but the firing was blind. Eventually the sounds of pursuit diminished and after a while she realised the hospital could not be far away. Then, stopping, the guide whose name she was never to know indicated the way she should take and parted from her without looking back.

Johanna left her skis by the outbuilding, guessing that someone in the chain would find them and take them away. At a run she passed the hospital and went to the far side of it where Kristofer was waiting in the ambulance.

He saw her coming and swung open the door on her side to haul her in. As she collapsed in exhaustion on the seat, the engine leapt into life and he swung the ambulance around to go belting out of the hospital gates.

In the snow, Anna knew she had lost the way. At some point in her tiredness she had dropped the compass without realising it until the time came to consult it again. The straps of the sled had worn her shoulders sore through her ski jacket and her legs dragged as if weighted down. Mercifully Viktor slept, and she was thankful that in the warmth of his covers he was being spared too much discomfort. Doggedly she pressed forward, sustained only by her will and determination to get her husband to the border. Her whole body was full of pain, every muscle and sinew creating its individual and agonising ache. Then abruptly her own strength went from her and she crumpled, falling awkwardly across her skis with her face going down into the snow. Some instinct to crawl to Viktor made her lift her head and as she blinked through the icy crystals on her eyelids, she focused in total shock on looming military ski boots. She had gone straight into an enemy patrol! As she gave out a long, thin wail of utter desolation, one of the soldiers stooped down. His clean-shaven, boyish face came close to hers.

"You're safe, frue," he said quickly in Swedish. "You entered Sweden three kilometres back."

She reached out and clung to him speechlessly. He helped her to sit up against him. When he looked over her shoulder he compressed his lips in a grimace of pity. Two of his comrades had gone to the passenger on the sled. He saw one shake his head while the other drew a blanket up over the old man's peaceful face.

When it became known to the German authorities that Viktor Alsteen had not been admitted to the hospital on the date set and that his whereabouts appeared to be unknown, rapid moves were taken. Since his wife, although not Jewish, appeared to have vanished with him on the same night, it was a likely guess that persons unknown had aided the couple across the border into Sweden. The evidence of witnesses pointed to it being a fact. Johanna was taken for questioning at No. 19 Møllergaten by the Quis-

ling police. These were hated even more than the German
soldiers. An army, after all, had to go where it was sent, but
traitors made a free choice to betray the lives of their
countrymen and side with the enemy.

Johanna was confident of the story she had prepared,
although a qualm quaked in her stomach as she mounted
the stone steps of the police station and entered the large
entrance hall, a quisling policeman as escort. In a side
room she answered all the questions without hesitation.
Firstly those about herself and then the Alsteens. Yes, she
had accompanied them to the hospital. Why? Anna Alsteen had been worried about her husband's condition and
had wanted female company for moral support. No, she
had not seen the couple since that night or known of their
plans. She had returned with the ambulance to Grefsen.
No, she had no idea from which depot the ambulance had
come and the driver had not given his name, as far as she
could remember. She had not been much interested in
him; her concern had been for getting the patient into
hospital.

The sergeant gathered the papers of her statement together and summoned a policeman forward. "The prelimi-
naries are done. Take her along for further questioning."
He snapped his right arm up in the Nazi salute. "Heil
Hitler!"

Johanna had whitened with apprehension. His order
meant that she was to face German interrogation, something she had expected to avoid with her straightforward
account. She was taken up to the next floor and along a
corridor. There she was ushered into a well-equipped office. In a comfortable leather-upholstered swivel chair
turned sideways to the desk, an officer sat reading the
statement that had preceded her, his brown shirt and
black uniform that of the S.S., the death's head insignia on
the collar, the scarlet armband with the swastika on his left
arm. One jackbooted leg was crossed over the other and he
swung himself slightly to and fro as he read. Without looking at her where she stood waiting, he indicated with a
flick of his hand that she might occupy the hard wooden
chair set directly in front of the desk. She sat down, her
back very straight, her hands folded in her lap. The statement rustled as he turned one page over another to con-

tinue reading the section underneath. His profile was stern, arrogance in the thin mouth and heavy chin, the short clipped hair a tawny colour. Still with his eyes on the statement, he addressed her in fluent, but gutturally accented Norwegian.

"You deny all knowledge of the Jew Alsteen's flagrant disobedience of the law, I see. Yet you lived with him and his wife for over a year from the time you took up work in Oslo. You must have known them well enough to have had some inkling of what they intended."

"Had I still been living with them on a day-to-day basis that might have been so, but they kept their arrangements to themselves."

"Then the first you knew of their disappearance was when you were taken in for questioning by the police?"

"I didn't know what was wanted until the cross-questioning revealed to me that my friends seem to have disappeared during the night. I left them at the hospital."

"They were not alone. There was a guide." Abruptly he swivelled around in his chair to face her. There was something sly in the calculating manner in which he studied her, his eyes a steely grey. "What would you say if I told you that you were seen in the forest near the Swedish border that night?"

A great quaking fear swept through her, but she did not flinch and kept her voice steady, her gaze coldly alert and direct. "I would say it was a lie. In any case, how could I be a guide? I'm not a native of that district. The forest there is not known to me as the forests of home would be."

He continued to scrutinise her while she fought against the fear that was high in her. It seemed an eternity before he gave a laboured sigh and tossed the statement contemptuously down onto the desk blotter in front of him. "I must say that knowing the country as I do, I had already given that point some thought." Sitting back, he set his elbows on the polished wooden arms of his chair and placed the fingertips of both hands together in an arc. "Had it been Ryen Valley instead of that area, I would not have let the allegations rest. I have decided that nothing more shall be said about this case as far as you are concerned."

She was hard put not to close her eyes in her relief. To

her surprise he held out a gold cigarette case and offered it to her. She shook her head. "No, thank you. I don't smoke."

He put a cigarette between his lips and lit it from a pocket lighter. "Neither did you when we first met," he said, "but at that time you were too young. Only four years old and I was a boy of twelve when I last saw you." Seeing how she drew her head back, staring at him, he gave a nod. "Yes, I'm Axel Werner. Your parents took me into their home under the Fridtjof Nansen plan after the last war, in fact the year you were born." He tapped the statement on the desk. "When I saw your name and your home address I took over your interrogation. With anyone else you would not have had such an easy time."

Nansen, one of her country's most famous polar explorers, had instigated a plan after the 1914–18 war to bring hundreds of hungry and often destitute German children into Norwegian homes where they had been cared for as members of the family, restored to health and eventually repatriated. Johanna knew Axel Werner's name and had one particularly vivid memory of him. He and Rolf had had a fight, rolling down the grassy slope in front of the farm into the summer dust of the lane, clouds going up all around them, both ending up with cut lips and black eyes.

Axel had spent most of his time with her brothers, helping on the farm and climbing with them in the mountains. He had attended the local schoolhouse where now Rolf was trying to protect his twenty-two pupils of all ages from the Nazi philosophy that the Germans were attempting to impose. In her state of tension she had failed to detect the dialect of her own home valley beneath his guttural accent. She voiced what had come into her thoughts the moment he revealed his past association with her family.

"At any other time you would have been welcomed back into my home and there could have been a renewal of friendship, but never in the uniform you are wearing."

His face tightened, yet he did not lose his temper and his tone remained even. "It is time you and others like you accepted our presence here in full understanding of the benefits that living under the Third Reich will bring you. In the first place we came to protect you from the English who, during their war against us, were laying mines in

Norwegian waters to sink your shipping in preparation for their imperialistic occupation of your country."

"Those mines were laid against the German Navy a day or two before your invasion came and when your troops were already hidden in the holds of merchant ships in our harbours!"

He regarded her almost pityingly. "For a seemingly intelligent girl you are being remarkedly stupid. We came in friendship and found ourselves rejected by a king who, with his government, cared nothing for the bloodshed of his people, which could have been avoided. Look at Denmark. King Christian accepted our presence in the spirit in which we came and no lives were lost. Do you know what our troops call a posting there? The 'Whipped Cream Front'!" He laughed at that, well pleased. The smoke curled up from his cigarette as he pressed it out in an onyx ashtray.

She swallowed. "From what I've heard many Danes have not accepted your regime."

He leaned forward and linked his fingers to set his arms on the desk, thrusting his face forward, his eyes narrowed. "Now where would you hear a false report like that, Johanna?" he inquired silkily.

It was still a cat-and-mouse game. She had almost gone too far on the strength of their previous acquaintance. It was a mistake. Nothing had relaxed between them. He was still as watchful as ever and she must be as wary. "News of all kinds travels fast by word of mouth these days."

He jerked his chin contemptuously, sitting back again. "Don't be misled by idle talk. Much rubbish is circulated through lies and mangled facts to derogate our presence here." He picked up a pencil and wagged it admonishingly at her. "You can best serve your country by becoming reconciled yourself and reconciling others to a thousand years of glorious rule." A glint of fanaticism showed in his eyes. "Norway is remarkably homogeneous. Pure Norse blood down through the centuries bringing forth the fair skin and hair and blue eyes that are the mark of the true Aryan. You Norwegians and we Germans are fellow Aryans, the same type of people in every way, dedicated to a fit body and a sound mind. You shall be with us in creating a perfect race to populate the world and rid it forever of its scum."

She regarded him incredulously. Here was a man who had spent some boyhood years in her country, who had lived for a while a Norwegian life, had come to know a people who cared exceptionally for their mentally sick and their handicapped and to whom race, colour and creed presented no divisions, and yet inherent arrogance and later indoctrination had made him a rabid Nazi. He had been blinkered to the truth and blinded to his own experience.

"May I go now?" she requested, keeping her voice under control.

He considered, reversing the pencil with his fingers on the desk. "You'll remember everything I've said to you today?"

She gave a nod. He was no fool and knew she still opposed him but he chose to let the issue rest, inwardly convinced that the simplified summary of the facts he had given her would eventually take root. Until her meeting with him today she had been a victim of outdated attitudes, and his arguments would have been given impetus through his having known her family and her home. This in itself would arouse her trust. He did not entirely agree with the Führer's attitude to women, believing they had potential for more than merely the kitchen and the bed, and he would include Johanna there. It was no fault of hers that her country had been too long on the outside of world affairs, which had made its people soft in their outlook. That could be remedied when the right men and women among them took up cudgels to stand with the Third Reich and make Norway of a like mind. He would like to see this girl among their number. Leisurely he picked up the statement again, tore it across and threw the pieces into the wastepaper basket.

"There's my absolute gesture of goodwill." His smile was benign. He had not expected thanks and neither were they forthcoming. She remained silent. He was unperturbed. Everything was in its early stages for her as yet. He continued conversationally, "How are your parents these days? Well, I hope. I saw from your statement the careers your brothers are following."

She gave her reply succinctly. "My mother and brothers are well. My father was beaten up by your soldiers last summer and is still suffering from the after-effects."

He took her information unblinkingly. "I wish your father a speedy recovery from the effects of whatever trouble he brought upon himself. Please give your family my kindest regards when you are next writing to them. Edvard and Gina were most hospitable to me and I was a poor sight when I arrived at Ryen Farm in rags and suffering from malnutrition. Those conditions will never come to Germany again now that we have the New Order under our Führer. I must talk more about it to you sometime." He rose to come around the desk and escort her to the door. There he clicked his heels together and bowed to her. "Until our next meeting, Johanna. *Auf Wiedersehen.*"

She wanted to run from the building, breathing in the pure, uncontaminated air. Instead she walked quickly, keeping her gaze ahead until she was well away from Møllergaten.

In March the Germans were put on alert all over the country. There had been a British and Norwegian raid on the Lofotens Islands off the coast. The Norwegians involved were British-trained under a Norwegian officer, Martin Linge, after whom the Linge Company was named. Made up of men who had already risked their lives to reach England, they were a powerful and courageous force. Other commando raids followed on the mainland. The jubilation felt by the population was stemmed by the savage reprisals of arrests and shootings meted out by the Germans on local people.

Johanna's days at the fur shop were coming to an end. She had applied for, and been granted, a permit to travel home. A letter from her mother, enclosing a doctor's endorsement that her father's health had deteriorated over the past months, the original cause not being stated in order to avoid prejudice, had gained her, after considerable delay, the necessary permission to travel.

Sonja was sorry to see her go. Leif's wife was going to take over the book-keeping, so there would be no new girl to replace Johanna. Leif wanted it that way, having become deeply involved in the nationwide resistance move-

ment that was evolving with some shape and form, with a
hard military core known as the Milorg directing all major
subversive activities. After telling Johanna she could have
her secretarial post back at any time, Leif asked her if she
would like her name put forward for resistance work in the
Ålesund area.

"Yes," she had said with enthusiasm. "I want to do anything I can."

Then it was time to leave. At the Alsteens' house she
locked up everything securely and took a taxi to Østbane
railway station. She hoped no harm would come to her
friends' home now that it was to be left unoccupied, and
she had asked the neighbour to keep an eye on it. Unfortunately some Jewish property was being confiscated and the
house's future was uncertain. When she arrived at the
railway station she had to take her place in a long line of
waiting passengers. The military had priority in going
aboard. Although it began to look as if there would be no
room, she managed to get a seat, for which she was grateful. The journey ahead was a long one, and due to the
inevitable joining and alighting of troops en route it would
take several more hours than in peacetime.

The train left on the stroke of seven o'clock. Due to the
black-out regulations, the blinds had to be kept down over
the windows and there was reduced lighting, making it
difficult to read. There was no refreshment car and whenever the train stopped people jumped out and rushed to
platform buffet rooms where unrationed hot soup was
available. It was not that the mild evening demanded it,
but food coupons had to be surrendered for any other
victuals. Johanna did get out now and again for fresh air
and a turn up and down the platform, but she had brought
food and a flask of coffee with her and had no need to join
the crush at the counters.

The night seemed endless. She dozed more than slept. It
was a relief when dawn came and the blinds went up, re-
vealing views so dramatically different from those left
behind in the South that it was as if magic had been
wrought during the night hours. On either side of the track
the great mountain ranges of the West rose against the
cloudless morning sky, the snow-caps tinted in the sun's
first rays. Waterfalls fed by the melting snows formed huge

cascades, thundering down in their own spray in which rainbows danced, and every steep slope was alive with rivulets that shone like liquid silver in the spring sunshine but would dry up when the summer came. The high pastures above the tree line had lost most of their winter covering, the green grass lush and vivid enough to sting the eye. Below came the thick forests that blanketed the main slopes with fir and pine and spruce and silver birch until giving way at a lower level to a natural abundance of ferns and wild flowers; then the valleys themselves took full possession with cultivated fields and spreading meadows. Fruit trees in full bloom seemed to cradle the scattered farmsteads in pink-and-white clouds. Only the oldest farmhouses and buildings stood in their natural timber, the log walls darkened by pitch and looking much as they had for four hundred years or more. Houses of a later date were painted white or ochre or saxe-blue or amber, the barns always a strong rust red, and they blended harmoniously with the rich and powerful landscape as if the colours had been evolved by nature itself.

With smoke from the locomotive drifting past the windows, the train rattled along through the vast Roms gorge, keeping pace with the wide river that was bounding over rocks and boulders in full spate in the direction of the fjord that lay ahead. Johanna strained her neck to look up at the jagged and unclimbed peaks of the range rightly named Trolls' Teeth, not wanting to miss anything in her return to this part of the country that was home territory to her. She had not fully known how much she had missed in the South these mountains of vast proportions, and her heart was reopening to everything she saw in the happiness of home-coming.

At the busy station of Åndalsnes at the head of Romsdal Fjord she left the train, which would continue northwards. It was almost noon and gloriously warm. Carrying her possessions, she made her way along the platform and without knowing why, she found her gaze fastened on a man ahead of her in the crowd of dispersing passengers. He was tall and dressed in nondescript clothes, a cloth cap pulled down on his dark head, and he carried a small brown battered suitcase. Something about him struck her as familiar. She thought he must be someone from her own

district whom she had not seen for a long time. Increasing
her pace, she hurried forward to try to catch a glimpse of
his face from the side, thinking that if she knew him they
might travel the rest of the way together and she could
catch up with the news of all that had been happening in
her absence. But his face remained turned away from her
as he threaded his way purposefully through the crowd,
and there were too many people thronging between them
for her to get nearer. When she came outside the station
there was no sign of him.

Thinking no more about the incident, Johanna followed
the sloping street that wound picturesquely down through
the little town to the quayside where a steamboat waited.
It would take her on the last lap of her journey along many
miles of fjord to her home. On board she stood at the rails
to gaze at the sparkling water that was as deep as the peaks
were high all the way from Åndalsnes to the sea. To her no
photograph ever seemed to capture the breath-taking
width and height and splendour of the fjord country to
which she was returning after being so long away.

The last passengers were coming aboard, the time of
departure imminent. German armed guards stood on the
quayside, watching everything and breaking up any gathering of more than two people that formed anywhere.
Then she saw the man from the railway station again. He
was showing his pass to the guard at the foot of the gangway just as she and every other civilian had done before
being allowed on board. The guard gave a nod and returned the pass to him. He tucked it into an inside breast
pocket with his free hand as he came up the gangway. By
chance he happened to glance up and see her at the rails in
the moment before he stepped aboard. Without the slightest sign of recognition, he turned and went to another part
of the deck.

She knew then that he had seen her on the railway
platform as she had seen him, and he had been prepared
for her presence on the ship. Remaining where she was,
she watched the casting off and the churning of the widen-
ing strip of emerald water as the steamship drew out into
the fjord. Excitement was racing through her. It was a

strange kind of reunion that had taken place in which neither could acknowledge the other. Steffen was on board. His single piercing glance at her had been one of warning and of love.

Chapter 5

It was a peaceful voyage of several hours down the fjord, calling in at many jetties along the way. The great mountains on either side were clear as cut-outs and there was barely a ripple on the glassy green water. By chance Johanna discovered that her father's cousin, Tom Ryen, was on board. He greeted her heartily.

"What a pleasant surprise to see you!" He was a large, bulkily built man with sandy colouring and a broad, affable face. A widower of some years, he had been a major in the regular army and had served at Narvik during the fighting. She was pleased to see him again, having always enjoyed his company, and noted that he was as well dressed as ever, his suit and well-cut overcoat obviously new, which was a rare sight these days. He fetched coffee for them both in the saloon. There was no cream or sugar even if they had wanted it, and if anything the ersatz coffee tasted worse than usual. They both made a face over it and then laughed. Laughter helped everything. It was no wonder that there was always a new joke about Quisling and Terboven going the rounds.

"So what are you doing these days?" Tom asked her, folding his arms on the table between them. "Still in secretarial work? The last I heard you were in Oslo."

"I left there yesterday morning." She told him briefly how it had all come about, although she made no mention of the reports she had made for the underground press or her part in the Alsteens' escape. Even if there had been no chance of being overheard by other passengers, she would have retained the same discretion. It was a hard lesson being learned that her fellow countrymen and women, never having been used to a lack of openness, too often let a word slip in all innocence that resulted in others being picked up by the Gestapo.

"How long is it since you've been to Ryen Farm?" she asked him.

"Some months now. I've been extremely busy since putting my uniform away and now I've taken on some administrative work. The wheels have to be kept turning in everyday matters. I'll drive out to Ryendal one day and have a talk with your father. I've fixed my car up with a wood-burning stove. It doesn't go far before one has to get out and refuel from a stack of logs on the roof, but it's better than being without any transport at all."

They remained together for the rest of the voyage before her destination was reached. Once, while strolling around the deck, they passed Steffen leaning on the rails and studying the passing view, the vista of mountains going on and on as far as the eye could see. If he turned his head to look after her she did not know it, for she did not glance back or do the slightest thing that would bring any attention to him. Yet it seemed to her that an electric current passed between them and she was momentarily distracted in the conversation she was having with Tom.

When her destination was reached, she parted from her relative. He was going on to Ålesund, the place she now knew must be Steffen's port of call since it was the last one on the route and he was still on board.

"Give my good wishes to Gina and Edvard and your brothers. I'll not forget my promise to visit before long. I'm truly sorry to hear that Edvard is still far from well."

"Why not come ashore and have a word with Rolf? He's sure to be there to meet me and the ship always takes a little while to load and unload."

Tom became quite reserved in his manner, more military and stiff-shouldered. "No, I'll not intrude on your reunion. You go to the rails now and see if he's in sight yet. Take care of yourself. I'll see you again one day."

She thought the change in his attitude somewhat odd, but forgot all about it when she saw Rolf waving to her from the jetty.

"Hello! How are you?" he called out as the steamship came alongside.

"Fine!" she replied excitedly from the rails.

"Is it good to be back to the mountains?"

"Oh, yes!" Good to see him, too. When she stepped from

the gangway he came forward to greet her fondly and take
her luggage. "How's Father?" she asked him at once.

Her brother was reassuring. "He'll be all the better for
seeing you. Mother is well and everything is all right at the
farm." He carried her suitcases across to the waiting wagonette, and she ran ahead of him to make a fuss over the
old farm horse in the shafts, giving him a sandwich she had
saved specially. Named Nils-Arne, he was the creamy colour with the distinctive black streak through the mane and
down the tail that characterised the pure west coast breed.
This was the horse the Vikings had bred—sturdy, hard-
working and patient, the present-day mainstay of small
farms where machinery was at a minimum. Many horses
had been taken by the Germans, and since farming families had a deep affection for their horses it had been a sad
day in many homes all over the country when the animals
had been led away.

"I'm so glad Nils-Arne hasn't been commandeered," she
said, climbing up onto the driving seat beside her brother.

"Luckily his age was against him. The Germans inspected each one and took the best."

"Well, whatever his age he's the best to me." She looked
back at the steamship as Rolf drove off along the road that
ran through farmland at the edge of the fjord. There was
no sign of Steffen or Tom Ryen. She mentioned seeing
their father's cousin to Rolf, whose brows drew together.

"We've heard rumours about him that we don't like. It's
said that he's in charge of an office recruiting workers for
the building of aerodromes and defences for the Germans."

"Surely not Tom, of all people!"

"I'm afraid that these days we're discovering the difference between the wheat and the chaff as never before."
Then, as if not wanting to dampen down the pleasure of
her home-coming, he distracted her thoughts by drawing
up on the brow of a bend in the road to allow her time at a
look-out spot, a favourite place where any member of the
family always paused at a time of home-coming. From the
octagonal white wooden church at the water's edge, a
nearby cluster of houses and three shops made up the
hamlet of Ryendal. She could trace with her gaze the road
ahead as it forked past the church and out of sight to meet

up with the way into Ålesund, which was only walking distance compared with the long detour the steamship had to take around a promontory of mountainous terrain to reach the harbour there.

The fork of the lane that led up the valley was her homeward route, wandering up the great cul-de-sac of mountains to the prime site where Ryen Farm stood, commanding the best view all the way down to the inlet, a view enriched by the huge waterfall that cascaded down the slope opposite Ryen farmhouse, its tumult increased by the melting of the snows that had silenced it to ice in winter.

"Let's go on now," she said contentedly.

They drove up the valley in the early evening sunlight. While they were talking together, Johanna took in the sights and sounds and scents of home. The wagonette carried them past farmsteads she knew as well as her own, having grown up with the children of the households. Some of the older houses and most of the barns had picturesque turf roofs from which spring flowers were sprouting like blooms on a bonnet. Then ahead, at the side of the road, the schoolhouse came into sight, painted pine green. Rolf gave a nod towards it.

"Come and visit me when class is in session. The children are all ages and they're fun, several exceptionally bright ones among them. Did you know the teaching of English has been banned? German is to become Norway's second language."

"I had heard that. It must be difficult for you to have the Germans breathing down your neck. The domain of your classroom should be your own."

"I'm one of thousands of teachers in the same boat. Our own association has already had one severe clash with the German administration and there's more trouble to come. Dictates for Nazification have been laid down that are the same as those used with success on the young in Germany." His voice tightened. "It's not enough to steal our country and our freedom; now they want to steal the minds of our children wherein the whole future lies. The entire teaching profession is consolidating itself into a powerful section of the Resistance to counteract Nazi educational policy on all sides."

It was not only the teachers who were taking action as a group. Doctors, dentists, farmers, fishermen and others who had always had their own closely knit associations had made mass resignations from their organisations, leaving empty frameworks for the Germans to control, while the groups themselves continued to operate as before at a subversive level and in resistance activities. So far the trade unions, separate from the other organisations, had escaped direct interference from Reichskommissar Terboven. It was possible he feared a general strike throughout the country if a move was made against them. Johanna glanced sideways at Rolf.

"I'm hoping to get an early chance to do my share of local resistance."

"Such as?"

She shrugged. "Whatever is available. Surely you can give me some idea of how I could be of use."

He shook his head firmly. "Take it easy for a while, Johanna. The Germans have been like hornets in this district recently. One of their patrol boats was sabotaged in the fjord and they have made a number of arrests."

She refrained from saying any more. From what Leif had told her before she left, she believed someone would be contacting her before long. It would be her decision what she would do when the time came.

The road climbed towards the head of the valley. When an arm of forest drew back before them, the white farmhouse came into view with its roof of curved dove-grey shingles and filigreed woodwork painted blue to ornament the window frames, the lintels and the porch. Farther ahead lay the rust-red barn with its turf roof matching that of the smoke-house, the wood-shed and other outbuildings. Their arrival had been glimpsed from a sitting-room window and Gina Ryen appeared in the porch. She was a small woman with silky grey hair worn in a knot, her body so thin as to be almost bird-like, her face lined beyond her age by years of hard work. Her cautious smile had never lost its childlike shyness. As Rolf drew the horse to a halt, Johanna sprang down from the wagonette and rushed up the porch to embrace her mother.

"I'm so glad to be here again!"

"Welcome home, child."

Gina remained stiff-backed and withdrawn in her daughter's arms. Her upbringing in a remote valley far from Ryendal had conditioned her from early childhood to an intense reserve that kept her from any outward show of feeling, and nothing in her composed exterior, except a heightened spot of colour in her cheeks, revealed what it meant to her to have her daughter home again. She was released from the embrace she could not return, beyond a pat on the girl's shoulder, when Edvard appeared in the doorway. With something close to envy Gina watched the exuberantly affectionate reunion between father and daughter, their arms around each other.

"I've brought you home on false pretences," he joked easily when Johanna drew back to take a longer look at him, holding one of his hands in both of hers. Although prepared for a change in him, she had been unable to visualise how wasted he would be or how drawn. The ruddy colour of an outdoor man had faded from his broad-boned face and his hair had turned quite white, yet she answered him cheerily in the same vein.

"I can see that, but no matter. I couldn't have stayed away longer in any case. You need me on the farm with summer coming and Steffen not here to help any longer."

They had lapsed into the happy bantering that always made Gina feel shut out, simply because it was never possible for her to respond to any attempts on their part to draw her into it with them. She loved her daughter as she loved her sons. They were more to her than life itself. Edvard had soon realised after the arrival of their first-born that he was always to be relegated to second place in her affections, and in his big, generous nature, which had matched his appearance before his injuries, he had never held it against her. Yet the matter lay on her conscience, no matter how often she reminded herself that she did her best to be a good wife and partner in all else. She had been at his side in any crisis, fought with him in all weathers to save a crop and rescue a sheep or cow that had strayed from the mountain pastures, and struggled and connived to save every kroner to keep debt at bay and make the farm secure. Her calloused hands bore witness to that effort. In the past she had believed sometimes he would have sacrificed everything for one spontaneous gesture of love from her, but those days had gone.

In the farmhouse kitchen, Karen Hallsted was waiting by the table she had laid for supper. She was, Johanna thought as they were introduced, as strikingly beautiful as Steffen had described her. Yet there was character and strength of will in her lovely, symmetrical face with the lustrous violet eyes and flawless complexion. Her hair was literally her crowning glory, being a platinum colour full of shining lights and dressed from a middle part into a braided coil at the back of her head. Her smile was natural and sunny.

"I've been looking forward to your coming home, Johanna. Now I can say I've met all the family."

"You've been a great help to my mother, I've been told. I'm most grateful."

Karen gave a self-deprecating little shrug of her shoulders. "I've done no more than anyone else would have done. Getting your father back on his feet has been teamwork, and if we can reverse the process of his ebbing strength with some new medicine the doctor is trying out on him, then we'll have nothing more to worry about as far as his health is concerned."

If asked what her position was in the household, Karen would have replied that she was the maid, but there was nothing servile in the title. She was a farmer's daughter in her own right, and in coming to give domestic aid to the Ryen household she was following an old custom by which farm girls left their own homes to work elsewhere, the times for arrival and departure being April and October, unless they were snapped up into marriage in the meantime, a most likely event. The tradition had evolved in past centuries to prevent intermarriage in remote valleys, and until the enemy invasion it had still been carried on by those girls with no interest in a city career and who wanted a man of the land for a husband. German restrictions on travel had finally broken the custom, and Karen had only been granted a permit to leave her own home and reside at Ryen Farm through the special reason of there being illness in the house.

Gina, ushering everybody into places at the supper table, had come as a maid herself to Ryen Farm. It was not as large in those days as the farm on which she had been born, and she had been a trifle superior towards it and to Edvard, the eldest son who was to inherit the property eventually.

Gina had had no intention of remaining longer than the obligatory six months, but she had not counted on the passion of the large, bearlike man who had made her lose her head for the first and only time in her life, making her believe she was in love with him. It had not taken long for her to realise the marriage had been a mistake. Intellectually they had nothing in common and the physical side of their marriage became no more than a duty to her. She suffered much from the biting tongue of her mother-in-law until she became mistress of the farmhouse herself. By that time Rolf had been born and Erik was on the way.

Johanna went through habit to the place at the table that had been hers since childhood. Rolf did the same, sitting on the left hand side of Edvard, who was at the head of the table. Gina sat at the other end, and Karen, her status being that of family, took a seat beside Johanna. It was of necessity a simple supper. There was black bread to eat, for the farmers had to account for their grain and received no concessions, being rationed to rough flour with its strange ingredients, including seaweed, with everyone else. There was a little homemade butter, milk to drink, and a dishful of cold veal and lamb. Although the amount of meat was sparse in comparison with the days before the invasion, it was a marvellous sight for Johanna. Meat had disappeared from the shops throughout the country, and it was a long time since she had eaten anything except fish as a main course. As for butter, she could not remember when she had last tasted it. The lack of sugar on the table went without comment, for it was rarely available.

"After the lambing," Rolf told Johanna, "we hid some of the flock up in the summer byre and we have cattle there, too. Our neighbours are doing the same. It's not much we can keep back, but at least not everything we produce is going into German stomachs. When somebody slaughters secretly, we receive a joint and so do the other farms. Then when it's our turn, we reciprocate."

"Suppose the Germans should hear the cattle lowing?"

"No chance. The byre is out of earshot from the valley

and in any case the waterfall's roar masks everything. Even if the Germans suspected something, I doubt if they would care to investigate except *en masse* and we'd have plenty of warning of that sort of approach—time to hide the animals higher up. The soldiers are scared of going into the mountains. There they're completely vulnerable. A local marksman could pick them off in turn and their bodies would never be found."

"Then the high terrain is still ours? One is free to come and go there?"

"Except where there are hairpin roads or tracks wide enough for them to drive their armoured vehicles in some strength. Luckily for us, there's nowhere around here like that."

She found it inspiring to know she could wander the mountain slopes above her home with no fear of meeting the enemy in her path.

Throughout the rest of the meal there was plenty of conversation. Johanna noticed that Rolf and Karen were on good terms, quick to laugh together and liking each other, but there was no more to it than that. She believed her brother had never really recovered from being turned down by a girl he had been in love with since his schooldays. Unlike Erik, he was not transient in his affairs.

Next morning she wrote to Steffen's aunt to ask when she might call to see her. Ålesund was in the allotted radius of locally permitted travel and there would be no problem about getting there. She put the letter in the mail-box at the side of the road and then went for a long walk, covering old tracks through the woods and across the bridge that spanned the river where the salmon would come leaping up on Midsummer Eve as promptly as if they had a calendar somewhere in the green depths of the oceans from which they came. Leaning her arms on the timber top-rail, she looked down into the clear and rushing water, able to glimpse the darting of speckled trout between the boulders. She could discern the small, pale-tinted stones similar to those that Steffen had gathered from a lake-shore to make into the necklace that she treasured. A yearning filled her for his mouth, his arms and his body. When would they meet again? Surely he would get in touch with her as soon as it was safe. Perhaps his aunt would be able to give her some news of him.

Restlessly she moved away from the bridge and continued her walk. The air was sweetly scented by the lilies-of-the-valley that covered the floor of the forest and clung to the banks of every brook and stream that flashed back the sunlight in a gushing down to join the river's flow. She climbed a mountain path to a point where she could sit on a rocky ledge near the thundering waterfall and look down at the farmhouse and the spread of the valleys with their sharp new greens, and ploughed land dark and rich as plum cake where sowing had taken place.

In the clear air she could see neighbours working around the other farmsteads. Last night not a light had shown in any of the windows due to the black-out regulations, and she had missed the twinkling clusters that previously had spread down to join those of the hamlet at the inlet's edge. Her sense of restlessness increased, the very tranquility of the scene making her want to take some immediate active part against the dark threat that lay over everybody there. The passive waiting that Rolf had advised for the time being was not for her. Again she hoped it would not be too long before one of Leif's contacts made himself known with some resistance work, however small the task, that she might do.

Johanna received a prompt reply from Steffen's aunt. Frøken Astrid Larsen wrote with an invitation to lunch. Gina made up a package of some homemade beef sausages and a small block of butter for Johanna to take, a gift that would be more welcome than gold. A neighbour gave her a lift into Ålesund in his horse-drawn trap. She alighted near the towering rock in the centre of the town where hundreds of sea gulls nested, their screeching and wheeling overhead a part of the everyday scene in the salty, busy port. Johanna had always liked Ålesund. It was built on three islands linked by bridges, the buildings so crammed together that the pastel-coloured warehouses rose up sheer from the sea water which lapped the banks at every turn in a street, the masts of tied-up fishing boats as thick as fences through which to view the passing sea traffic.

Once, in the past, she had been there when the annual cry had gone up across the harbour and through the town.

The herrings are coming! Then hundreds of single diesel
engines had started up with their distinctive tonk-tonk
sound, and the whole fleet of fishing boats had put to sea
with nets for the great shoals that turned the water for
miles around into molten silver. Now there was a three-
mile fishing limit and any boat that ventured beyond was
liable to be shot at by the patrolling Luftwaffe or vessels
keeping guard. It was the route that escapees took from
the west coast, and the number of German soldiers at the
quayside and on duty throughout the town showed how
alert a vigil was kept as a preventative measure. On walls
and posts everywhere was the now more than familiar
warning: *Any person attempting to leave the country will
be shot.* Many people had been caught and executed,
mostly young men, often still in their teens. There was a
bereaved family in Johanna's own valley.

Astrid Larsen's house occupied a choice site on a
wooded slope that looked out across the islands and harbour to the open sea. A winding road led up to it through a
residential area where many fine houses stood amid flower
gardens and blossoming orchards. Johanna picked it out
before she reached it from the description that Frøken
Larsen had written her. It was a sizeable mansion, its
paintwork a pale amber with filigreed white woodwork
that reached into simplified dragon heads at the four corners of the roof, giving it the graceful look of a Viking ship.

When she reached the side lane that led to it from the
winding road she came to a halt, hesitating as to what she
should do next, for half a dozen German vehicles were
parked outside the gate in a naturally formed forecourt
bordered by bushes and trees. At first she thought it was an
inspection raid; then she noticed there were at least two
large staff cars of the type used by high-ranking Gestapo
and the Wehrmacht. The military drivers of these and the
other cars lounged about, chatting together and smoking
cigarettes. Then she saw an elderly, distinguished-looking
woman with softly waved white hair beckoning to her
from the gate. Johanna went to her, ignoring the whistles
and remarks of the German drivers.

"Take no notice of them," Astrid Larsen said firmly,
ushering her through the gate. "This way. Follow me."

She did not take Johanna up to the main entrance, out of

which a lieutenant was emerging, pulling on his gloves and
talking over his shoulder to someone inside the hallway.
Instead they went to the side of the long, two-storied building and entered by a verandah door into a large and airy
room. Astrid stood back to appraise Johanna in a friendly
manner.

"Welcome to the small section of my home in which I'm
still permitted to reside."

"Thank you." Johanna could not hold back the question
that was uppermost in her mind. "Do you have any news
of Steffen?"

The woman put a finger to her lips immediately and
indicated that danger lurked behind some double doors
which were padlocked on her side. Her whisper came
close to Johanna's ear. "Yes, he's safe and well. No more
now, please." Then in a normal voice she added, "Take off
your jacket. I'll hang it up for you."

Johanna obeyed, finding it hard to contain her impatient
longing to question further. It did seem as if Astrid Larsen
might have had contact with Steffen.

She handed over the package she had brought with her.
"This is a gift from my mother. Living on a farm means
there is a little to spare sometimes."

It was gratefully accepted. "I must apologise for my
haste in bringing you into the house, but I wanted to get
you away from those soldiers outside as quickly as possible.
Not many of my visitors these days are as young and pretty
as you, and I was afraid of the reception you would get."

From the direction of the padlocked double doors there
came some distinctive, although muffled sounds. Astrid
noticed Johanna's startled glance and gave a restrained
sigh. "I thought you might have guessed, but obviously you
haven't. That part of the house has become an officers'
brothel. I think my home was selected because of the parking facilities outside." A look of weary forbearance showed
in her eyes. "I'm afraid it gets very noisy on the other side
of those doors at times."

Johanna was momentarily at a loss for words. She knew
of the German brothel ships that went from harbour to
harbour along the fjords and up the long coast to serve the
widely distributed troops, but she had not known before
that probably the best houses in many places were being

taken over for this usage. That this should have happened
to this quiet, dignified woman seemed particularly cruel.
"I suppose I should have guessed from some of the remarks
that the drivers made. It was naïve of me not to have
realised at once."

"So you understand German? So do I, but I pretend
otherwise. It saves being drawn into conversation when
the girls shout at me from the windows. They think me a
doddery old woman and that suits my purpose."

"How long has your home been commandeered?"

"Four months. It came as a great shock to me. I was
given an hour's notice in which to remove whatever I
needed into this part of the house. I have this room, which
was used for parties when Steffen was growing up, and
there's a small pantry across the hallway that I've made
into a kitchenette. A stairway gives me access to a bedroom and bathroom above. So here I stay, an outcast in my
own property."

"Is the rest of the house just as you left it?"

"Yes. I keep remembering pieces of china and certain
books and other things I wished I'd brought in here, but I
was in an upset state when I was being turned out and now
I couldn't bear to go back in there with the Germans in
possession." She became brisk in her attitude as if shaking
off a distress she did not want to show. "Now I'm sure you
would like to freshen up after your journey. I'll take your
mother's kind gift into the kitchen and put it in a cool
place."

Upstairs, on the way to the bathroom, Johanna saw that
access from the main part of the house had been solidly
boarded up and Astrid had drawn a chest of drawers across
it on her side. Downstairs again, Johanna wandered on her
own around the large and gracious room. Its cool greens
with white seemed a fitting setting for Steffen's aunt, who
was an elegant woman, her casual touch of a floating scarf
giving a style that Johanna recognised as an inborn knowledge of how to dress, even though her dress and hair-style
belonged to a previous decade. The house must have been
furnished when Astrid was still youngish, for everything on
view in this section was of the *art nouveau* period. The
silver objects included a pair of magnificent candelabra,
each one a draped female figure holding aloft the curving

stems of lilies in which the candle-holders were cradled.
Most spectacular of all were three paintings by Edvard
Munch that dominated one wall. Two were sunset scenes
radiating in reds and oranges the heat of a fading day,
while the third was a sensitive portrait of a girl in a white
frock, who was unmistakably a young Astrid with the long-
ish nose, wide mouth and dark eyes shadowed by shining
tawny hair. Johanna drew in her breath, turning as the
woman came back into the room.

"You know Munch!"

"I knew him. A long time ago . . ."

"Was he truly as handsome as I've always heard?"

A smile twitched Astrid's lined lips. "He was reputed to
be the finest-looking man in all Scandinavia, and rightly so.
He was more handsome than you could imagine possible."

"It's a marvellous painting of you."

"He painted it under the apple trees at his beloved red
house at Åsgårdstrand. I was spending the summer there
by the fjord with friends. My father would never have
allowed me to go to that house if he had known. Munch
had made himself notorious with women and the local
residents peeped behind their lace curtains when he went
by. For me it was the happiest summer of my life." Her
scarf wafted as she went to touch the signature in the
corner of one of the sunset paintings. "He would never
have parted with any one of my three paintings nowadays.
Did you know that he will not let any of his work out of his
possession any more? He lives like a recluse near Oslo,
painting his life away. I'm fortunate to have these to remind me of the time when I knew him well."

Johanna, looking at the portrait painted in a long ago
summer, wondered about the young, impressionable girl
and her relationship with the older, experienced artist.
Was that why Astrid had never married? Had a brief summer love made everything else pale before it? Maybe
Munch should not have given her the paintings. They had
kept the spell alive. Instinctively she folded her fingers
around the necklace she wore. It was as evocative for her
as any painting, perhaps more now than at any other time,
being as she was in Steffen's childhood home.

"Tell me about Steffen, Frøken Larsen. It must have
disrupted your life to have a young boy come to live here."

Astrid laughed merrily. "It did indeed. But once he had recovered from his initial bereavement he was my brother all over again—boisterous, good-humoured and, in time, sports-crazy. He and his mother had stayed with me many times when he was very young, so it was not as strange as it might have been for him to make his home with me while his father was at sea. Then, when my brother died on a voyage, I had to become both mother and father to him and I did my best to follow his parents' wishes with regard to his English education and so forth." She went to a rosewood cabinet and took out a large photograph album. "I'm sure you'd like to look through these while I make final preparations for lunch."

Johanna sat down and took the album onto her lap. Turning the pages, she followed Steffen from boyhood through adolescence and into young manhood. Girls figured prominently in many of the later snapshots and during his educational days; whether in England or in Norway, the inevitable pretty female company was usually present. Astrid must have thought about this afterwards, for during lunch she made a point of emphasising the fact that she had never known her nephew to be so keen that she and a girl he knew should become friends.

"You may call me Astrid," she invited as if to completely weigh the balance. "Steffen has done so since he became grown-up. I must say it makes me feel younger." Then she glanced at the gold locket-watch she wore on a chain. "It's time. He will be here now."

"Here?" In spite of her joyful astonishment Johanna kept her voice low.

Vigorously Astrid rose to her feet. "There's a small doorway in the cupboard under the stairs that you'll have to get through. You'll find yourself in a cellar that is completely detached from the larger one that runs under the rest of the house. It belonged to a farm building that once stood at right angles to this site and the Germans completely overlooked it when they inspected the place. Steffen used to make it a pirates' cave and a Viking den and so forth in his boyhood. It really is an ideal hideout."

"But here?" Johanna said again. "Under the noses of the Germans!"

"All the better. It's the last place they'd search in any

emergency. Now come along. I've locked the verandah door and the lace curtain will keep out prying eyes. If I give the alarm signal that Steffen has fixed up, you must come back into the house at once."

Johanna held her breath, partly through excitement and partly through trepidation as to how it would be when she was with Steffen again, remembering the initial restraint between them at their last meeting. Creeping under the stairs, she went through the small doorway into the cellar. Chill air and blackness met her. Then the sudden up-turning of a lamp-wick threw out a limited radiance, showing her the man she had waited so long to see again.

"You're really here," she exclaimed spontaneously.

He darted forward even as she tripped on the unexpected steepness of the steps, and she half fell into his arms. With a gasp she flung her own arms about his neck, caught on a surge of love that almost frightened her by its force, and became lost in her mouth's reunion with his. Not until he set her back on her feet again was it possible for her to draw back a pace, her fingers linked in his, to study how he looked, the two of them held in the nimbus of the lamp's glow. It gave her a pang to see at close quarters that he looked older and sterner, as if whatever he had been through on his escape to England had left its mark on him. Had he become a stranger to her again? She thought his kiss had belied that, but she could not be sure. Nothing was sure any more.

"You look well, Jo," he said approvingly. "Thinner, but well."

She gave a rueful little smile. "Everyone is thinner in Norway these days, except the enemy."

"I've been anxious about you."

That warmed her. "I wanted so much to speak to you when you came aboard the steamship."

"In my case, I had to resist the temptation to share the same compartment with you on the train from Oslo."

"Were you on it for the whole journey, then?"

"I boarded just after you."

"How long have you been back in Norway?"

"Only a couple of weeks." He put an arm about her waist and they sat together on a bench drawn up to the old table on which the lamp stood. "There are some things I can tell you and some I can't, simply because I have to obey certain security rules, and one of them is not to disclose how I reached England, for that escape route is still open. When I got there, I was lucky enough to be picked out by the late Captain Linge for special training with the Linge Company under the British Special Operations Executive, known as S.O.E., an organisation set up by Winston Churchill to direct subversive activities in occupied countries."

"Then you're here to stay."

He gave a half smile. "Let's say I'll be coming and going. My immediate task is to recruit and train agents and help to organise resistance in this area."

"What sort of resistance work?"

"Sabotage, espionage, the gathering of vital information about naval movements and much more. Normally you wouldn't be hearing anything of this from me, one of our orders being to stay away from the women and families in our lives."

"That's too severe a rule," she protested.

"Not when so much is at stake. A thoughtless word in a small community or a remark simply overheard could destroy a whole carefully planned operation. In Britain people have become remarkably reticent and security-conscious, which is what we want in Norway. There's a poster on buses and walls and in the London underground trains that says, 'Careless Talk Costs Lives.' The Milorg here can't put up posters, but we can work individually to impress the importance of silence on all aspects of resistance."

"Why have you made me an exception to this order?"

"Two reasons. Firstly, when I decided to make this secret cellar a refuge I knew it couldn't be done without Astrid's knowledge, and since I hope you are going to be a frequent visitor, sooner or later you might have suspected something. It was better to give you the full facts."

She glanced about her from where she sat. The lamp could not reach into the far depths. Rough rock walls showed how it had been cleaved out of the mountainside. "It's an enormous cellar. I've never seen anything like it before."

"It has the advantage of two secret outlets, impossible to discover from outside since they pass through piled boulders from some ancient avalanche into a thickly forested area. The entrance to the house could hardly be used for escape except with firearms, which is something that must never happen. Astrid's only protection is to feign ignorance of her cellar's being used by the Resistance if ever suspicion should fall on her."

"She's courageous."

He nodded. "The best."

"How are you able to move around freely? Aren't you afraid of being recognised by people who know you in the town?"

"I've haven't been home enough since my school and university days in England to be well known around here, and I'm careful not to frequent haunts where I might run into old acquaintances. In my pocket there's a ring of master keys that could get me into any building if I had to go into hiding quickly, and if I'm stopped for papers I frequently show a card that states I'm a member of the Quisling secret police." He grinned over that. "It gets me out of anything, even being in an area normally forbidden to civilians."

"You seem to have thought of everything."

"It comes with training. Anyone would have thought you had been similarly trained after the way you acquitted yourself in Oslo."

"What do you mean?"

"Leif Moen sent a report on you to one of my local contacts, who knows all about your getting the Alsteens into Sweden."

"Are they all right?" she questioned swiftly. "Have you heard from them?"

"No, I haven't, but you've no need to worry. No sign was ever found of them this side of the border and in Sweden they would be cared for. All that was received was an account of your part in getting them away and how you kept a cool head under interrogation. That's the second reason why I'm able to confide in you. You're in the Milorg's good books."

She seized the opportunity that had presented itself. "Then surely I qualify to be one of your secret agents!"

He regarded her steadily before giving his reply. "I'm recruiting men."

Her swift retort was full of anger. "Aren't women involved in this war, then? Aren't we being bombed and starved or imprisoned in every war zone?"

"It's not that. You don't understand what's required. The role for the agents that I'll be recruiting would be beyond your physical strength. These men may have to live for months in the mountains, surviving on whatever natural resources are available. They'll be saboteurs and arms experts and leaders of clandestine fighting groups, trained in psychological warfare, able to kill an enemy with bare hands should the need arise. This is Milorg work. There are plenty of other roles that a brave and intelligent woman can play. I know you would be invaluable to me in this area."

"How? Tell me?" She leaned towards him in her eagerness.

"By giving Astrid all the support you can. She's elderly and this will be a great strain on her."

She drew back and her anger flared white-hot. "How dare you delegate such a nonsensical task to me! Astrid wouldn't want me fussing over her as if she were half-way to senility. Leif didn't put my name forward for you to turn me into a nursemaid!"

Her temper had ignited his and he hauled her to her feet with him. "Damn it! You're in danger enough just by knowing I'm here! Do you think I'm going to throw you into greater risks?"

With a sharp thrust she pulled away to face him challengingly. "Have you learned nothing about me? Maybe making love when we did was a mistake. Too much happened too soon and we're still strangers to each other."

His eyes glittered. "Is that what you believe?"

"I've no choice. If you really knew me you'd accept that I want only to have a part in the struggle for freedom, whatever the cost. You have no more understanding of me than the Sturmbannführer who interrogated me!"

He went pale with anger and seized her by the shoulders, the shaking of his temper passing through his hands into her body. "All right! You'll get an assignment. I promise you it will be a tough one whenever it comes and you'll stand or fall by it."

She thought he would thrust her from him. Instead he jerked her back against the rock wall and crushed his mouth down on hers, hurting her with the violence of his kiss and covering her whole body with his. She was pinioned and helpless and as highly aroused as he, clinging to him with a wild elation that seemed to come from beyond herself, the excitement she always felt in his presence sweeping her away. When they broke apart breathlessly, it was as though they had abruptly become antagonists despite the magnetism between them, while their strained faces acknowledged that each had created pain and turmoil for the other. He swallowed and ran the fingers of one hand through his hair.

"That's settled then." His voice was hard and his attitude cold. "You'll have to be patient. It may be weeks before you hear from me again, but don't think I've forgotten my promise to you. The whole resistance movement is in the throes of forming into a full communicating network and there's still a lot of organisation to be done that's quite apart from my particular sphere. The Milorg wants every undertaking to be carefully planned to the last detail. Reprisals against innocent people must not be risked." He glanced at his watch and made a restless gesture of dismissal towards her. "Go back to the house again. I have to leave now. I'll wait to switch off the lamp until you're safely up those steps."

As she remounted the steps she saw they were hewn out of the rock, worn smooth in centuries gone by, and there was no handrail to give support. Emotionally, she felt torn apart. Had any woman in the distant past ever left this place in such a mood of wrath and triumph and heated desire? As she slid aside the panel that covered the aperture into the house she paused to look back over her shoulder, but she was too late. The lamp switched off at the same moment to leave total darkness, and she heard the faint thud of a secret door closing after him. In the house she dropped into a chair and held her head in her hands despairingly.

"Whatever is the matter?" Astrid asked anxiously.

Johanna's voice was muffled. "We quarrelled. In the midst of a war when we don't know when we'll see each other again, we lost our tempers."

"Oh, is that all." Astrid sighed with relief, sinking down languidly against cushions on the neighbouring sofa. "I

daresay it was Steffen's fault. Men always want their own
way, even in a war. It does them good to be opposed."

Johanna raised her head, her expression remorseful.
"For all I know the Germans could have him in their gun-
sights at this very second, and five minutes ago I shouted at
him."

"I think you can rest assured that he can look after himself as far as the Germans are concerned." Astrid tilted her
head wisely. "I've lived long enough to know that love is
not perfection. It would be a dull affair if it were. No, it's
the flaws that give it meaning and make it worth the struggle. I wouldn't say that you and Steffen are ideally
matched. You're both too strong-willed. Nevertheless, I'd
like to see the two of you spending the rest of your lives
together. I think you'd never lack interest in each other
and that's the lasting source of love."

It was logic that appealed to Johanna's way of thinking.
To have failed to fight for a principle she felt strongly about
simply because of extenuating circumstances would have
been to belittle what she and Steffen felt for each other. It
was his love for her that had made him over-protective,
the natural reaction of any caring man towards a woman
dear to him. Now she could share danger with him and
their relationship would be the stronger for it. If she should
be killed through whatever resistance work came her way,
it would still be proof that she had loved him to the ultimate depths of her being.

Chapter 6

Johanna did not intend to waste her time while waiting for her first assignment. Already fit, she kept trim with plenty of extra exercise which included hard physical work on the farm, climbing mountain paths and swimming in a shallow cove when the warm weather came. Summer was still a good time of year in spite of the Occupation, for this was when marvellously hot days compensated for the winter and the sun gave twenty-four hours of daylight, making it possible to read a newspaper at midnight. In her district the sun reappeared over the peaks at two in the morning. Farther north it merely brushed the horizon of the sea and rose again.

She made a point of running regularly in the mountains, almost as if she were training for a sports event. It was in her mind that there might come a time when she would have to run for her life as once she had had to ski for it.

In June Germany invaded Russia, crossing the frontier at three points and sweeping forward in a further stage of their blitzkrieg tactics that took no account of lives in their path. The occupation forces in Norway were jubilant. Locally they celebrated by marching up the valleys in turn, metal heels crunching the gravel of roads and lanes.

School broke up in the same month for the summer vacation, giving Rolf the chance to take over full time the work on his father's farm. As was customary, the sheep and cattle were moved to the lush and green high pastures to graze there freely until autumn. The summer byre belonging to Ryen Farm, as with others on the upper slopes, came into use again for the morning and evening milking, which Rolf and Johanna did together. It was a long climb up and down twice a day, but both of them took it in their stride.

Sometimes when the milking was done Johanna would pull the protective kerchief from her head, shake her hair

105

free and gaze down at the valley where the farmsteads were set in miniature. With the cowbells clanking and the towering peaks above her crowned with perpetual snows, she felt centuries away from the fur shop where once she had pivoted on high heels and tried on some of the most beautiful coats ever made. In a way she felt she was being given a second chance to appreciate to the full the environs from which she had come, and she was haunted by the unswerving conviction that this present phase of her life would soon be at an end and that these days of country living would never come again. Because she did not know what form the end of all this might take, she savoured every minute of every day as never before, loving all she saw in nature with a renewed intensity and observing everything, from the swallows nesting in the rafters of the barn to the increasing abundance of harebells and wild pansies that covered the banks of the lane like an azure mist. When it was hay-making time, the scene changed again, becoming sun-baked under a cloudless azure sky, the inlet glittering in the distance and the hay itself, strung out to dry on wires between poles, resembling hundreds of golden necklaces strung out across the valley. The very air was hazy with its flower-dried scent and the flicker of butterflies.

If her father had been making progress she would have been comparatively at ease during this period of marking time, but he was getting weaker and spent more time in bed again, which was a bad sign. The doctor who attended him was past retirement age, but stayed on to help the community in the absence of a successor, who would necessarily have had to submit to the new German regulations regarding the medical profession, an action the doctors were resisting.

Her father's cousin Tom Ryen kept his word about coming to visit Edvard. He arrived by car on a Sunday when Johanna was walking with Rolf and Karen in the mountains, and he had left again by the time they returned. Gina had helped him load a fresh supply of logs from the wood-shed to get him back to Ålesund and she reported the car had puffed smoke like a chimney. Edvard would have enjoyed the visit more if he had not had doubts about Tom's loyalties. There had been nothing pro-Nazi in his cousin's conversation, but Tom had admitted being in charge of recruiting workers for various projects planned by the Germans and had quoted possible new roads.

"He was cagey when I asked what other projects were in hand." Edvard shook his head uncertainly.

Tom had left a message for Johanna, inviting her to call at his office whenever she was in Ålesund. She knew now where his office was, as she passed it on her way to Astrid's house. It was in a block where the Germans had a minor branch of their headquarters, and even if she had wished to see him she would have been deterred by the sight of the guards at the door and the number of military going in and out. She thought it was as well that her father did not know how deeply his cousin was embedded in the Nazi regime.

Local friends visited Edvard regularly, fellow farmers who had been born in the valley as he had been, and their talk of crops and cattle and old times was a great pleasure to him, but the visits he appreciated most were those his younger son made briefly and without announcement. The days when Erik was granted regular leave from the coastal steamer service had ended when the Germans took control, and he never received more than a couple of days ashore on the rare occasions when he could get home.

It was now a long while since he had had the chance. Johanna had yet to see him again, and recently there had been two days of terrible anxiety when it was broadcast that a coastal steamer had been torpedoed by the British Navy, who had mistaken it for a troop carrier. A large number of soldiers had been on board, but there were civilian passengers as well. After Erik had telephoned to let everyone know he was safe, the sadness for the other families remained. Johanna wondered how Karen would feel towards him when he came home again. Her reaction to the torpedoing and the resulting period of suspense had been anything but indifferent.

In late August, when the evenings were drawing in again, Edvard began to talk of having the cattle brought down to their winter quarters. The sheep, which had roamed freely the whole summer, had begun to come back over the mountain slopes, each flock making its way slowly in the direction of its own farm, some homing instinct alerted by the changing season. It was frustrating for Edvard not to be able to carry out any chores himself and on bad days when he was confined to his bed he tossed on his pillow, stiff in his bones and ever chill no matter how warm the room. With school in session again the time Rolf could give to the farm was curtailed, but he still came morning and evening for the milking. It was early September and the last evening at the summer byre when he and Johanna arrived there to find a man they both knew, a schoolteacher from the next village, waiting for them.

"Hello, Nesheim." Rolf went to speak to him while Johanna made ready for the milking. The bell-cow had led the rest of the herd into the byre and a few needed a push to get them into their own stalls.

"Johanna."

"Yes?" She turned, the milking stool in her hands. Her brother had dipped his head to come through the low doorway and when he straightened up there was a frown across his eyes, his expression severe.

"Nesheim wants to speak to you. I thought you had taken my advice to keep out of trouble."

Puzzled, she went out of the byre. "You wanted to see me?"

The schoolteacher drew near. "I have special instructions for you. Be here tomorrow evening after dark at nine o'clock and bring a pocket flashlight with you. A parachutist will be landing not far from here with a cache of arms. I'll have someone with me to deal with the container and Rolf will dispose of both parachutes. Your task will be to guide the parachutist to the disused cabin by Troll Lake. There you'll receive further instructions that have not been revealed to me. Is all that clear?"

"Perfectly." Her face was taut. "I've been waiting for a chance like this."

"So I was told." He gave a grim nod. "Good. Until tomorrow."

When she returned to the byre she went to put a hand on her brother's shoulder where he sat milking. "Don't be angry. I'm not the type to spend my time knitting."

He looked up at her. "I know that. Just don't take chances, that's all."

She thought it was as well he did not know of the risks

she had taken in getting the Alsteens into Sweden. They were very much in her thoughts these days. Jews in northern Norway had all been arrested and sent to labour camps, men, women and children. Anna had been right in her decision to get Viktor away when she had. The situation had been perilous at that time, but it was far more so now.

The following night was rainy and black as pitch. Gina was sitting at her husband's bedside and Karen was in her room writing letters. Johanna left the farmhouse unquestioned and met Rolf as he came up the lane from the schoolhouse. Together they went up to the summer byre where Nesheim and another man, whose name neither of them was ever to know, were waiting for them. Almost without a word the four of them set off together, Rolf collecting a spade from the byre to dig the parachutes into the ground. He led the way, using a shaded flashlight when it was necessary to leap across a stream, many of which were full from the heavy rainfall that day, or when traversing a rocky patch. Within half an hour they had reached the appointed place, an area of plateau that by day revealed ferns and grasses with a distant lake set into a wide hollow where the deep water mirrored the peaks above. The four of them spread out in a wide circle to wait. There would have been no danger of talking together here, but each was too far from the next and it was a strangely isolated waiting period. When the allotted time arrived, Rolf lit a bonfire as a guide to the aircraft, and the bright flames danced high.

Johanna suddenly grew tense. Above the patter of rain on leaf and grass there came the distant drone of a plane. When it sounded as if it was directly overhead, she strained her eyes through the blackness but could see nothing. At a far distance she saw Rolf's light blink in signal to be on the alert.

Desperately she strained her ears. When nothing happened she began to be afraid the drop had been misjudged. If it went completely wide the parachutist could be dashed against the mountainside or drown in the far lake without a trace. Then she heard a swishing sound, and as if the sky had suddenly bloomed overhead, she saw the vastness of the parachute and watched it swoop down to be lost in the blackness again somewhere behind her. Now it was she who flashed her light to let the others know that the parachutist had landed, her Morse signal being that of V for victory, which had become symbolic of the Allied resolve to win through. With her flashlight beam to aid her, she hurried towards the direction in which the parachutist had disappeared. She found him in a mossy dell where the plateau dipped as if under the weight of a blanket of heather. To reassure him she kept the beam on the ground and gave the password quickly. He had released the catches that held the parachute to his harness and knotted the straps, pulling in the rigging lines of the great mass that, in spite of a lack of any breeze, rose and billowed like captive foam. A young woman's voice spoke out from the struggle.

"Thank God I didn't land on top of a tree!"

Then Johanna saw her face and recognised her as the Englishwoman to whom Steffen had said goodbye on the day of the invasion. The parachutist was Delia Richmond.

Johanna sped down the dell to give her a helping hand with the rigging. "Are you all right? You didn't hurt yourself?"

It was Delia's turn to be surprised. "Hi! I didn't expect to find another woman in this spot. I have a few bruises, that's all. Everything went as smoothly as during my parachute training. Thanks to the pilot and navigator, of course. I only jumped."

Rolf arrived then. After a brief greeting he dealt with gathering in the parachute and bringing it under control as if it were a routine occurrence that a woman descended out of the night sky. The container had landed at almost the same time in the opposite direction, and after taking possession of the parachute Rolf paused only to speak to his sister.

"You take over now. There's a hole dug already to bury this silk. I'll join you in a minute or two."

Johanna led the way with her light. It was not an easy walk to the cabin with obstacles of rocks and hillocks and bubbling streams all the way. Delia followed quickly and calmly without complaint, showing she had become used to mountain walks during her time at the embassy. With her eyes accustomed to the darkness, she saw the cabin ahead at the same time as Johanna. There was something instantly familiar to both of them about the man coming down the steps to meet them. Delia darted ahead of Johanna and threw herself into Steffen's arms. Johanna came to a standstill some little distance away, able to see by the blended shadowy shapes that they embraced. What they said she did not know or want to hear. As he took Delia into the cabin, a ray of candlelight showing briefly as the door opened and closed, she thought he must have forgotten that Delia had had a guide to the cabin. She was wrong. He had not entered himself but loomed again from the shadows, keeping a look-out. When she might have gone forward she was passed a second time as Rolf came from behind her and went ahead to reach Steffen first. They spoke for a few minutes, old friends from the days when Steffen had worked on the farm; then she heard her brother say impatiently, "Come on, Johanna. What's keeping you?"

They both stood on the steps to see her into the candlelight. Steffen looked searchingly into her face, as aware as she that the last time they had been together they had parted in anger. "You all right, Jo?"

"Fine," she replied easily, going through the doorway and giving him no chance to take hold of her. When amends were made it should not be in front of her brother or the woman who had so recently been in his arms. Their relationship was still at far too brittle a stage and, for all she knew, in his case might have been strained beyond recall. He had not had the benefit of Astrid's counselling.

Delia had produced a hip-flask of brandy which she set down on the table in the cabin beside her gloves and flying helmet, which had helped to keep her warm during her descent. Her parachuting overall was of British military issue; she had divested herself of it and cast it into the wood-burning stove that made the whole cabin like a warm oven. Later the flying helmet was also consigned to the flames. She had brought some English coffee and cigarettes which she produced out of the pockets of the blue anorak she had worn, together with a thick sweater and ski slacks, beneath the overall. In all she was dressed like Jo-

hanna, and would have passed without notice in any street
or place throughout the country.

"Let's celebrate my arrival." Delia handed around the
flask as the two men sat down at the table with her, a
candle stuck in a bottle the only illumination. "This was all
I was allowed to bring, supposedly for medicinal purposes
in case I broke a leg or an arm upon landing. Somebody
filled it for me from a long-hoarded bottle. It's from Paris at
a time when, as the song says, the heart was young and
gay." She tilted back her chair to hold the flask out to
Johanna, who had volunteered to make the coffee. "You
first."

Johanna took the flask and raised it. *"Skål!"*

Delia was next. "Cheers!" she toasted in English.

"Down the hatch!" said Steffen in the same language as
if back in a British pub.

From Rolf it was *"Bonne santé,"* in honour of Paris. The
gathering was fast becoming a merry one.

Standing by the stove, the warmth of the gulp of brandy
in her throat, Johanna inhaled the aroma of the coffee as
once she had seen the Germans do shortly after the invasion. Everybody had scorned their greed then in eating
butter on chocolate, but it had become a national joke
among Norwegians that now they would do it themselves
if the chance presented itself and if only they could remember what butter and chocolate tasted like!

Johanna found four enamel cups in the cupboard. The
men who had been with them on the plateau would be
halfway down the mountainside by now with the container. As she waited for the coffee she listened to, but did
not join in, the conversation around the table. It was becoming abundantly clear to her that Steffen had seen Delia
frequently when he was in England after making his escape there. There seemed to be a possibility that they had
done some training together. Delia was giving him news of
mutual friends and acquaintances and there were refer-
ences to parties that both had attended. As on a previous
occasion, Johanna observed the completely relaxed attitude between them, the glance of understanding, the
quick smile of anticipation as if each knew what the other
would say. She did not have the least doubt that they had
been lovers. She felt composed and curiously detached.

Perhaps the brandy helped and maybe it was that which was tuning her in to Steffen and Delia's reactions to each other in such a way that she did not seem to miss a crinkle at the corner of smiling eyes or a suppressed chuckle at a reference to something known only to them. It was not that they cut Rolf or her out of their general talk, it was simply that they had their own private line of communication in the midst of company.

She had not realised the three of them were waiting for her until she had poured the coffee into the cups for them and taken the remaining chair at the table.

"Now to business," Steffen said briskly. "Where's the important dispatch you brought with you?" He held out a hand to Delia across the table, palm uppermost.

Delia grinned and took a slim package from an inner pocket. "Here it is."

He put it down on the table in front of him. Then he took an envelope from his own pocket which he laid down and pushed towards Johanna.

"This is the assignment I promised you. Meeting our newcomer and guiding her to this cabin was just the preliminary. The package she has brought is to be delivered by you to an address in Oslo. This envelope contains a travel pass bearing the official German stamp authorising your journey. It's not a forgery, although the indecipherable German signature is. A blank stack of these passes and a rubber stamp were acquired by a resourceful resistance worker who unexpectedly found himself with access to them. You'll find enough money to cover your expenses and overnight accommodation if you should need it, but I want you to try to get the overnight train back again. Your return tickets for the fjord steamship and the railway journey are also there." He was regarding her steadily and assessingly as he spoke.

"Does Johanna have to do this?" Rolf demanded. Steffen gave him a hard glance.

"Your sister is in the Resistance by her own choice. This is scarcely her initiation into danger, although I doubt if you've heard about her part in the escape of two people into Sweden."

Johanna ignored her brother's startled inquiring stare and took up the envelope. "It all sounds perfectly clear.

What pretext do I use for being in Oslo if I'm stopped by the Germans for questioning?"

"You'll say you're going to see your former employer at the fur shop who has offered to keep your old job there open for you."

She raised an eyebrow. "How do you know he said that? I don't remember telling you."

"I have constant contact with Leif Moen in the Resistance." A smile lifted the corner of Steffen's mouth. "You'd be surprised at how much seemingly unimportant information can prove to be extremely useful at a later date." He returned to the matter in hand. "If through any unexpected turn of events you're unable to deliver the package to the address I shall give you to memorise, he will take it from you, but it's preferred that it should go direct to the person awaiting it. Any diversion increases the risk of discovery." His voice took on a stern note of warning. "Remember always to behave as routinely as possible. Never do anything to draw attention to yourself, and that includes making your appearance as inconspicuous as possible, a hard task for someone who looks like you in the first place." It was a curious compliment, for he was intensely serious. "Leave your smart clothes at home. Don't wear anything you yourself would normally have worn for a trip to Oslo and yet, at all costs, avoid looking countrified. You know the city and you know how the average Oslo woman dresses. Aim to blend into the background. Do you have any questions?"

When she shook her head he proceeded to give her the address, which was simply Number 7 on the third floor of a block of apartments in a street she knew. She repeated it three times for him. Then he gave her the password, which would only be given after a reply, especially phrased, to her question as to the whereabouts of the previous occupant of the apartment. It was very straightforward, but again she had to go through the procedure three times with him. Lastly he pushed the package across to her.

"Put it somewhere next to your body. If you carried it in your purse it could be seen when you were asked to show your papers. In a coat pocket it might be pulled out accidently or stolen. Whatever happens, you don't allow it to fall into enemy hands. That's an order."

She fully understood. "I'll obey it."

He gave her a look that told her plainly he approved of her intelligent attitude. "There's only one possible complication. As you will have heard from the radio, the trade unions in the factories have finally called a strike. The latest information I have received is that there have been mass arrests by the Gestapo in Oslo. Two unionists have been sentenced to death already. More executions are likely. If you see any kind of demonstration in the streets, keep away from it. When the Gestapo make a sweep of the streets for questioning, they take in everybody and sort matters out afterwards."

Beside her Rolf seemed on the point of protest again, and then apparently thought better of it. He lit another English cigarette and drew on it fiercely. It was indicative of his anxiety about her. Steffen appeared to have none.

"Am I to notify you when I get back?" she asked him.

"There's no need. I'll hear when the package has been delivered before you are home again. Just carry on as usual afterwards at the farm. If family or friends ask you about your visit to the fur shop, say you're thinking the offer over. We may want to send you to Oslo again." He glanced at his watch. "You had better get home now. You've a busy time ahead of you."

No kiss or embrace to send her on her way. She accepted that was due as much to her own attitude when she entered the cabin as to the state of hostility in which they had last parted. Even worse for her was the realisation that Steffen and Delia were preparing to leave together, talking as they zipped up anoraks and donned woolly caps. They were surely bound for some mutual Resistance work about which she knew nothing, for she could not believe the parachute jump had been made simply to bring the package she was to deliver. She took it up from the table, not wanting to think about them alone in the private renewal of their long association.

"Ready to go?" Rolf asked her, waiting to leave.

"Yes, I am." She made to head for the door. Simultaneously Steffen and Delia turned towards her. The Englishwoman jerked up a thumb cheerily as a sign of confidence that all would go well in Oslo.

"The best of British luck, as we say, just to strengthen

the Norwegian variety. Thanks again for being on the spot
to meet me." It had been a nerve-racking experience for
her, being the first time she had been dropped behind
enemy lines. She had been selected at a moment's notice,
there being great urgency about the package she had carried with her. It had come from British Intelligence, its
coded contents sealed tight. She hoped this Norwegian girl
with the beautiful, resolute face would seal the success of
the mission. It was her guess that its importance was beyond anything that could be envisaged by the four of them
in this mountain cabin.

Her gaze followed Steffen as he went across to the girl.
Only he had known by a coded transmitted message that
she would be coming. For a while during their S.O.E. British military-based training she had hoped they might work
together in occupied Norway, but their courses had di-
verged, his being of prime importance and highly specialised, and the emphasis from the start had been on individual effort and survival. In a way it reflected their own
relationship. Lovers and friends and yet essentially apart.
There had never been anyone else quite like him in her
life. He meant more to her than he knew. Maybe she
should let him know during this coming short time to
gether. Love-words had never passed between them. It
could have been her mistake. She would take the chance
to right it.

In the doorway Steffen and Johanna faced each other,
she poised to go out into the night. "Good luck, Jo," he said
evenly.

Briefly their gaze held, each able to see how greatly the
gap had widened between them.

With flashlights to show the way home, brother and sister hurried back across the plateau and began the descent
to the valley. Steffen would be guiding Delia down another
route in the direction of Ålesund. At the farmhouse, everyone else was asleep. Although tired, Johanna had to make
preparations for the morning, packing an overnight case
and going through her wardrobe to decide what would
match up with the general attire of the women of Oslo. It
was enabling her to keep thoughts of Steffen at bay. Her
whole concentration had settled on her assignment as if it
were an anchor to steady her.

Eventually she chose a dark blue suit that was neat and trim, teaming it with a polka-dotted scarf. In spite of hardships, Oslo women were maintaining their standards, and if stockings were almost entirely darns, gloves mended and shoes patched, it did not detract from their general appearance. There were more ways than one in which to defy the German attempts to demoralise.

In the morning she had to contend with questions from her mother as to why she had made this plan to go to Oslo without mentioning it. She made an excuse that she had become so used to living her own life away from home that she did not always think about explaining her movements. In this case she was going to visit her former employer to talk over the future. Gina said no more. She could always tell when her children had affairs of their own that they wished to conduct privately and she had suffered too much from the inquisitiveness and domination of her late mother-in-law not to allow them their independence.

Johanna got a lift from home on the milk truck. Ryen Farm was the last call the driver made for the churns left on small platforms at the side of the lane, and she rode with him to the dairy, which was located near the jetty. The steamship from Ålesund came in on time. On board, as she sailed up the fjord to Åndalsnes, she was reminded of seeing Steffen when she had made the voyage in reverse at her home-coming. Their relationship had become complicated and stressful and yet a new bond had been formed through their Resistance comradeship that had nothing to do with personal feelings.

She disembarked at Åndalsnes in good time to catch the overnight train, which had not yet come in from the north. When she bought a newspaper she was dismayed to read of the extent of the arrests in Oslo. It was as if the strike had been a long-awaited signal for the Gestapo to run amok. People from all walks of life had been taken from their homes and their places of work. It was as if Reichskommissar Terboven had decided that this should be a final crushing, an example to bring the rest of the nation to heel at last.

The train was crowded with military and she did not get a seat. She sat on her overnight suitcase all the way. Under emergency restrictions in view of the strike crisis, civilians were not allowed to leave the train at any stop unless it was their place of destination.

The conductor, looking harassed, had to face armed guards coming aboard at each halt, and during the journey Johanna had to show her papers nine times, sometimes snapped out of a doze by a barked order from grim-faced, helmeted men relishing their authority. Not for the first time she thought the general harassment and constant interference in the normal and mundane run of life was as heavy a burden as anything that could have been deliberately contrived to lower and debilitate the stamina of a people.

When the train drew into the platform at Oslo, she felt alarm at the number of armed guards who stood watching the carriages slowing to a halt. She had never seen so many there before. Among them were some of the dreaded *Hird,* Quisling's Norwegian Nazi stormtroopers who were hated as much as the collaborators and informers frequently responsible for delivering people into their clutches.

The train halted with a hiss and a jerk. Johanna lined up to get off with a wedge of passengers before and behind her. When her turn came to go through the open door she saw that some of the stormtroopers had closed into a semicircle through which she would have to pass. Concealing the great leap of fear that had sent her heart hurtling against her ribs, she made to alight. In the same instant a quietly dressed man behind her, who had been her neighbour throughout the journey, gave her a huge thrust in the back that sent her flying forward to fall against the nearest stormtrooper. He pushed her from him with an angry exclamation, sending her crashing down on her knees. Amid the noise and uproar that followed she saw her fellow passenger making a run for it, guards and stormtroopers in pursuit. Full of pity for him, she bore him no grudge for the bruises she had received. He did not get far. As he was dragged away the rest of the guards returned to their surveillance of the passengers as if nothing had happened.

She tidied herself up in the women's room. Both her knees were grazed and her carefully darned stockings ruined beyond further repair. Fortunately she had another

pair in her suitcase. They were thick lisle and irreplace-
able, a far cry from the silk stockings that had once enhanced her long legs and slim ankles. After brushing the
dust from her coat and adjusting the brim of her hat, she
felt ready to emerge.

She checked her suitcase in the depot and left the railway station. It had been little more than three months
since she was last in Oslo. In spite of the bright autumn day
the city looked gloomy to her. If anything, there seemed to
be more German eagles vying with the swastika for space
on the buildings. There was also a new flag, with the sun
cross of Quisling's Nazi party, and these were in abundance around a building she had to pass to reach the stop
where she would catch a tram. A rally of Norwegian Nazis
was being held there. A banner outside bore the slogan:
Forward with Quisling for Norway, and there were colourful recruiting posters on display. The officials at the
door, as well as many of those entering the doors, were
wearing the brown shirt, black tie and cross-strap that had
been adopted as the uniform of Quisling's own party. It
was a fact that he was drawing people of a certain type and
character to him, and although they were a minority of the
population, it was a dangerous one. Propaganda leaflets
were being thrust into the hands of passers-by, and she
managed to avoid taking one.

Otherwise the paper clip was everywhere, worn in some
cases more discreetly than before, due to the heavy fines
that had been imposed for wearing it. On the tram the
same bitter game of moving seats away from any German
passenger was still in force. Johanna had no need to change
seats, being between an elderly woman and a postman off
duty.

She alighted from the tram at a stop not far from the
entrance to Vigeland Park. Without hesitation she turned
into the tree-lined street where the apartment block was
to be found. It proved to be a plain building with a balcony
to each apartment, planted boxes nodding blossoms over
the edge of every one. She pushed open the glass door and
went up the stone stairs. There was no lift. On the third
floor she found the door of Number 7. The name in the slot
was commonplace. She rang the bell. There was no response.

She was about to ring it a second time when there came
the sound of cars squealing to a halt outside. A gasp of
fright escaped her. Nobody except the enemy had vehicles
to treat like that. As the entrance doors crashed open at
street level, there came the noise of booted feet ascending
the stairs. Johanna darted away from the apartment and
up the next flight to the floor above. There she paused to
listen, her pulse racing. She had been just in time. The
door she had just left was being pounded by heavy fists and
the bell pressed urgently.

"Open up!"

Those demanding admission were not prepared to wait.
A sharp order brought a lunge of shoulders to burst open
the door. In a once peaceful city where locks had not been
designed for that kind of forced entry, it was a matter of
seconds before it gave. Johanna peeped cautiously over
the balusters to see if there was any chance of slipping past
unnoticed, but those who had entered the apartment had
left two of their number outside. There would be more at
the street level entrance. They were Gestapo S.S. As she
drew back, a sergeant returned briefly to give further instructions to the two men at the door.

"He's got away. Check every apartment and see if you
can find someone able to give us information. Take the
upper floors first."

Johanna instinctively spun around and went up another
flight. She must not let them question her presence in the
building. In the mood that prevailed she could be taken
into custody simply for failing to satisfy them as to her
reason for being in a place where subversive activity had
been uncovered. As she reached the landing she saw that
one of the apartment doors stood open and a child aged
about four, quaint and button-nosed, was waiting in outdoor clothes, holding a rubber ball.

"Are you going to play in the park?" Johanna asked her
quickly.

The child nodded. "Mama is coming too."

At that moment the young mother came out of the
apartment and pulled the door shut behind her. At the
sight of a stranger on the landing she raised her eyebrows
inquiringly. "Were you looking for someone?" Then, attracted by the commotion two floors below and the door-

thumping of the men at the apartment doors, she leaned over the railings to take a look. "Do you know what's going on down there?" she asked in almost the same breath.

"The Gestapo has broken into one of the apartments."

"Oh dear." The woman blanched, drawing back.

Johanna took a desperate chance. "Would you let me walk to the park with you and your daughter?" she requested urgently. "What's her name?"

There came an even deeper look of alarmed comprehension, but almost automatically the mother gave the child a pat. "Tell the lady your name."

The reply came shyly with hung head. "Margit."

Johanna stooped down to her. "May I hold your hand when we go downstairs? That would make me feel like one of the family."

"Yes." There was a nodding that made the woollen bobble on the child's knitted hat dance up and down. "You can hold the ball as well if you like." It was held out.

Johanna took it between both her hands and, still crouched down, looked up at the parent in silent appeal. For an agonisingly suspenseful moment the woman poised on the point of snatching up the child and disappearing behind a closed door. It might have gone that way if little Margit, impatient to get out, had not darted to the head of the steep flight. Maternally protective, the woman rushed to take the child by the arm. Facing Johanna, she gulped and nodded.

"Very well. Don't tell me your name or why you're here. I don't want to know. When we reach the park please go away."

"I will."

Johanna talked with the child as they went hand in hand down the stairs, the mother following behind. The two S.S. men, jackbooted and black-uniformed, were turning away from an apartment door being closed by an occupant.

"Wait! Which apartment are you from?"

The mother answered, drawing level with Johanna. "Number 12."

"Do you know the man Hansen who lives at Number 7?"

"No. The apartment only changed hands a short while ago. I don't think I've ever set eyes on him."

The questioner switched to Johanna. "What about you?"

"I've never seen him either."

The man's eyes went from her to the mother and back again. Then a curt nod permitted them to pass. A glance in the doorway of Number 7 as the three of them went by showed that it was being ransacked. In the entrance hall an S.S. man posted by the glass door watched them come down the stairs. Vehicles parked outside were similarly attended. The mother had become increasingly nervous and to hide the shaking of her hands she thrust them into the pockets of her coat. Johanna opened the door for her and Margit to go through.

"Achtung!" It was the guard in the hallway, who had stepped forward to halt them on the very threshold of getting outside. Johanna and the woman froze. Then they turned. The man's leather-gloved finger was pointing to a child's mitten dropped on the marble floor. With a gulp of acknowledgement, the mother went back to snatch it up. As they went outside she pushed it back onto her daughter's hand, not far from tears in the release of emotional tension. Stifled choking sounds came from her throat as the three of them walked hand in hand to the park, Margit dancing along in the middle.

Inside the park, Johanna played ball with the child for a few minutes, dropping out as the mother took over. She knew how glad the woman would be to see her go, but for her part she would always be grateful for a kindness shown in an hour of great need. Leisurely she wandered on through the park, needing a respite to recover from the traumatic experience she had been through. The park was familiar to her. Peopled by statues created by Gustav Vigeland depicting every age and emotion of mankind, it was as yet unfinished, and in his Oslo studio not far away the sculptor worked with the same dedication as Munch, with whom he had once shared a mistress. By the tall white granite monolith that dominated the park, Johanna sat down on a seat. Her next move must be to go to the fur shop and surrender the package to Leif Moen. She felt intense disappointment that she had not been able to fulfil her assignment directly. A man had taken a seat on the same park bench and opened a newspaper. A page slipped and fell to the ground almost at her feet.

"Excuse me, frøken," he said, leaning down to pick it up. "Everything has become mixed up today."

Her gaze sharpened on him. He was youngish with an Oslo intonation. "Is that so?" she remarked cautiously.

He nodded, folding the newspaper together again. "Due to an unexpected change of plan, I had to leave my apartment to meet someone off the night train at Østbane station, but I missed her."

"Oh? Where was she coming from?" She had to be certain this was not a mere fluke of conversation.

"Åndalsnes, but she doesn't live there."

Now she was convinced this was her contact. Casually she launched into what she would have said if he had opened the door of the apartment to her. "I'm looking for the Hauge family. I wonder if you could tell me where I might find them?"

He gave her word for word the reply rehearsed by Steffen. "Do you mean Frederik and Solveig Hauge by any chance?"

"No, I don't. My friends are Rolf and Jenny of the same surname."

At this point he would have invited her to step into the apartment and look up their names in a directory. He slid the neatly folded newspaper into his pocket. "Jenny, eh?" he said, repeating the special password. Then he added quietly, "Put the package by the Vigeland sculpture of the mother with the braided hair playing with her child. I'll be watching to pick it up. One more thing. As a precautionary measure, avoid going to the fur shop. The Gestapo, aided by informers and collaborators, have launched an all-out campaign to break up our Resistance network. We don't know yet whose names are on their suspect lists, except," he added on a wry note, "it is more than apparent that mine is included. I must get away as soon as I have the package. Good day to you, frøken." He got up from the bench and strolled away.

After remaining seated for another minute or two, she stood up in her turn. There was only one place where she could unobtrusively remove the package from its seclusion inside her clothing. Behind a locked door in the women's public lavatory she unfastened the buttons of her blouse and drew out the package, which she had sewn into a piece of cotton and suspended from a tape around her neck. This time she kept the package in her hand, tucked behind her purse, when she went out into the autumnal sunshine again. As it was a weekday, there were few adults in the park. Most of those were elderly folk and women with young children. Her unknown contact was the only male adult in sight when she mounted the steps of the monolith to slide the package in the allotted place. By the time she had wandered right round the monolith, looking up at the hundreds of sculptured figures that made it curiously alive, he and the package were gone.

Back in the street she walked until she came to a telephone kiosk, having decided to ring Leif Moen, which seemed a suitable compromise. If a strange voice answered she would hang up. It was a relief when he came at once onto the line. In case his telephone was being tapped, she spoke evasively, saying she wouldn't be coming in that day.

"I understand," he replied evenly. "I'm relieved to know that all is well with you."

"Please give my regards to your wife."

"Thank you, I will."

Neither could risk saying anything more to the other.

When she had replaced the receiver, she looked at her watch. There was the whole afternoon left before she need go to the railway station for the overnight train. She would ride out to Grefsen, take a look at the Alsteens' house, and check that all inside was in order. Afterwards she would catch the tram back into the city again with plenty of time to spare.

She did not have long to wait for a tram to come along. As it took her down Karl Johans Gate she saw arrests being made as people were bundled into trucks and driven away. When she came level with the side street where the fur shop was located, she was relieved to see that all was quiet and there was no sign of Gestapo activity there.

It was strange riding out to Grefsen again. As she left the terminal she could see the roof of the house showing through the distant trees. She set off up the lane as she had done so many times in the past. When she came near she slowed her quick pace, dismayed to see a military car parked in the driveway, and an open window showed that someone was in the house.

"Johanna!"

She turned to see a neighbour descending a ladder from picking apples in the orchard that flanked the Alsteens' fence. Opening the gate, Johanna went through to her. "Hello, Fru Kringstad. Can you tell me what's happening next door?"

"I can indeed. Come indoors with me."

Johanna was made welcome with a glass of carefully hoarded homemade wine that dated back to the summer before the invasion. Over it she learned that the Alsteens' house had been confiscated as Jewish property. A high-ranking Wehrmacht officer had moved in a month ago and made it his living quarters.

"He's always having drinking parties," the neighbour said indignantly. "Russian vodka, Norwegian aquavit, Danish spirits, and the finest French wines, including vintage champagne!" She shook her head vigorously. "All loot from occupied countries. I've seen the empties being taken away. With our sugar ration of just a few grams, if and when there's any in the shops, I can't sweeten anything enough, let alone make a bottle of simple homemade wine, which used to be my hobby. I would like to keep bees. I already have a pig, a goat and some chickens."

Johanna had noticed from the tram that the whole area of Grefsen, once a suburb of fine lawns and flower gardens, had been dug up for vegetables and had mushroomed with hen-coops and pigsties in the everlasting struggle to get enough to eat. Even Astrid, Steffen's aunt, had begun to keep chickens, for with eggs at the exorbitant price of twenty kroner each when available on the black market, it was more than worthwhile. When she left the neighbour's house, Johanna looked over the dividing fences and saw that the Alsteens' grounds were in pristine condition with roses blooming in well-kept beds. The German officer employed a gardener to keep the place in trim. No need for him to scratch for whatever the earth would bring forth.

The day after she arrived back at the farm a contact checked in code by telephone that she was home safely. After that she heard no more. There was something else to

think about. A new German restriction had been imposed
upon the population. All civilians, except those belonging
to Quisling's Nazi party, were to hand in their radios.
When the Jews had had to surrender their radios it had
been in vindictiveness against them; this new development was for another reason. More than anything else the
Third Reich feared people knowing the truth; since severe
punishments and heavy fines had failed to deter Norwegians from listening to broadcasts from London, they
should be deprived altogether of the chance. On the allotted September day, in cities, hamlets and valleys, people
angrily and reluctantly handed in their radios.

With Teutonic thoroughness, every radio was labelled
with the owner's name and a storehouse was found for all
of them. In the hamlet of Ryendal, as well as in many other
places, the storehouse was broken into on the first night by
daring individuals who took their own property back or
grabbed whatever they could in a flashlight's beam without bringing a stack down noisily around them. It was not
long before most homes had access to the BBC again, radios being concealed in everything from a thermos bottle
and a cut-out telephone book to a hollowed-out log of
firewood and household tins. Rolf, who had always been an
enthusiastic wireless expert, made one for the farmhouse
that was concealed by day in a bird's nesting box on the
outside wall.

The Nazi reign of terror gathered momentum. In the
same month the radios were collected, hundreds more
patriots were shot in savage reprisals. Arrests were whole-
sale. It was said that even greater numbers were crammed
into the cells of No. 19 Møllergaten under interrogation
and torture. In the midst of all this alarming news there
was a brighter moment at Ryen farm for Edvard and Gina
when their younger son came home on shore leave. Without prior announcement, he suddenly threw open the
door of the kitchen where Johanna and her mother and
Karen were engaged in domestic tasks.

"Hey there! I'm home!"

Tall and lean in his dark steamship uniform and grinning
with pleasure at the surprise he had given them, Erik
seemed to bring a breath of the outside world with him
into the quietly mundane scene. His face was a chiselled

one with a thin nose and a cleft chin, his narrow eyes alert and observant, a clear grey in colour, and his mouth was wide with a smile full of charm. His hair, clipped short in naval style, was stubbornly curly. He looked what he was, an easy-going, virile and mercurial man who through his wits and training was well able to cope with any situation that came his way.

While his sister and mother welcomed him, Johanna with open affection and Gina with her customary restraint, Karen paused only briefly in bread-making to give him a nod and a conventional word of greeting. Yet she blushed, a hint if anyone around her needed it that she was heart, soul and body in love with him. It seemed to Johanna that Erik was the only one in the family who had not guessed the truth and Karen wanted to keep it that way, for he would be the first to take advantage of it.

From the start their relationship had been a difficult one. He was too used to his smooth ways working for him as far as women were concerned, and she had been forewarned about him by well-meaning friends before coming to join the Ryen household. Her wariness of him had, perversely, made him all the more persistent. He appeared unable to grasp that for once he had met someone able to resist him after a few heady kisses and caresses, at which he was demonically expert.

She was aware that apart from the hated presence of the Germans on board, the career he had chosen to follow suited him admirably, sailing as he did along his home coast in some of the most spectacular waters in the world, a constant coming and going of new passengers at every port of call. In the days before Hitler had invaded Poland, among the many tourists taking the round trip from Bergen to North Cape to see the midnight sun there had been women to whom a handsome young officer had made an attractive diversion. There had been one Englishwoman, according to his sister, with whom he had formed an attachment that had meant more to him than anything before or since, and it had left its mark on him. But she had returned home to her own commitments at the end of the voyage and, as far as anyone knew, that had been the end of the affair. Since then he had carried on as before.

Karen was shaping the loaves ready for the oven. They

would be like stone, for yeast had suddenly become impossible to obtain. She glanced up as Erik came to set both hands wide on the opposite side of the table, leaning his weight on them and grinning at her as she dusted off her floury palms, not a grain to be wasted.

"How have you been spending your time then?"

He had a habit of compelling answers from her, making her meet the dancing look in his eyes, showing that in no way had he been dissuaded from his original aim towards her and about which she had no illusions. The danger was that this time she was far more vulnerable. In that span of forty-eight hours when the coastal steamer had been torpedoed and before his telephone call of reassurance had come through, she had been tormented. When she knew he was safe, the force of relief had almost made her faint, something she had never experienced before. Johanna, who had come running to tell her of his phone call, had saved her from falling and seated her down on a boulder in the field where she was helping with the harvesting.

"I made the most of the last days of summer." She listed an account on her fingers. "Johanna and I had a final swim. Then there were picnics when we went to pick cloudberries, blueberries and wild cranberries. Three weeks ago I managed to get a pass to travel home where I stayed for a few days."

"What about a fishing trip up to the lake with me? I need some high mountain air. You and I shall go tomorrow and take a picnic."

He gave her no chance of excuse, swinging away to leave the kitchen and go to his father's bedside where he sat with the invalid for a long time.

Johanna saw the two of them off to the mountains next morning. It was fine and mild with no sign of the rain that Karen had predicted over breakfast, as if seeking a reason to postpone the outing. She carried one fishing rod and Erik another, the rucksack on his back holding their picnic. Johanna hoped the two of them would draw closer together in the day ahead, for she believed her brother held genuine feelings for the girl and she had seen for herself how Karen felt about him.

Past Ryen farm the lane became a cart-track and at this time of year the blueberry plants had turned crimson and many of the grasses on either side of the track had also taken on a pinkish hue as if reflecting the flaming autumn colours of the trees. Erik opened the last cattle gate and then they were on a winding path that began to ascend the mountainside through the forest and within sight, through the dark trees, of the thundering waterfall with its white spray rising high. They spoke only occasionally, keeping to the rule of saving breath for the climb, and since both of them had been born to the mountains, neither needed to stop and rest. Above the dwindling tree-line they came onto the high pastures near a cluster of *saeter* cabins at the side of the lake.

In past decades the daughters of the valley farms had stayed in these ancient turf-roofed log cabins during the summer months to tend the cattle on the high pastures. Now the cabins were used by those skiing there at Easter-time, or staying on walking or fishing trips on that part of the mountain. Leaving her rod propped outside the low-lintelled door with Erik's, Karen took the key from a ledge and led the way into the cabin belonging to Ryen Farm. Inside there was a doll's-house look to the room with its small windows and primitive furniture, some of which had been there for a hundred years or more. Beyond a closed inner door, which bore a rose painting faded by time, was a bedroom with two beds. She opened a window, chased out a few sleepy flies that had settled in for the winter and took the frying pan from a cupboard in readiness for the trout they would catch. When she turned to leave the cabin and begin fishing, Erik barred her way, a tall silhouette against the open doorway with the shimmering lake beyond.

"It's time we had a talk. That's why I wanted to be on my own with you today."

She regarded him steadily. He had had his own way all his life. Although probably neither he nor anyone else in the household realised it, he was his mother's favourite child. Gina tried to be meticulously fair in her dealings with the family, but he had benefitted more than the others and all the signs were there to an outside observer who was herself tuned to a pitch of sensitivity just by being in the same room with him. At this moment she did not intend to let him know how threatened she felt by his aroused presence in the confines of the cabin.

"There'll be plenty of time to talk when we've fished for a while." She made a move to go past him.

He gripped her arm. "You're wrong. We've little time left and a whole lifetime to discuss."

She raised startled eyes and jerked away from him. As she went out of the cabin he looked after her for a moment or two as if he would fetch her back. Then, on a muttered expletive, he followed her, snatching his rod as he went from its place by the door and feeling more like hurling it into the lake than waiting patiently for the fish to bite.

She had already cast out her line. He followed suit a little distance from her. She was wearing her hair loose today, caught by a large tortoiseshell barrette at the back of her head, and all the autumn sunshine was in the wafting strands. From the first sight of her installed at his home, he had earmarked her, his intentions normal to any young seaman ashore. At that time, through some fluke in the early stages of the German administration, he had had five full weeks off duty. Everything should have gone as planned, for he could tell she was as attracted to him as he was to her, but somehow matters had gone wrong between them and he had returned to his ship in a state of disappointment and frustration. It was a new experience for him. He was not used to being rejected and found he could not stop thinking about her. She had got into his blood and into his bones, and it was as if he needed her in order to live. On subsequent visits home he had attempted to regain ground with her. Now time had dwindled down to less than she or anyone else at home realised, and he was being compelled to waste precious minutes in fishing. It was even more galling that she should catch three trout of a good size while he only hooked a small one that he threw back. Deciding that enough was enough, he stuck his rod in the cleft of a rock to let the bait continue to drift and went around to where she stood. The three trout lay on the bank threaded onto a birch twig. He glared down at them, hands on his hips, elbows jutting.

"Surely that's plenty, for God's sake!"

She wound in her line, a frown drawing her fine brows together. "Why are you so angry?"

"I'm not angry with you." He shook his head vigorously in emphasis. "Never with you. It's knowing that I'm home for such a short while this time instead of having days and weeks and months to tell you that I love you. Do you hear what I say? I love you."

He had not raised his voice. On the contrary he had spoken quietly if vehemently. In the silence that followed it was as if his words still remained like an echoing shout in the air, reverberating against the high peaks around them. Colour gushed into her cheeks and there was confusion in her expression. She nipped her lower lip hard.

He took the rod from her and threw it aside. Then he put his arms around her, her whole body tense and defensive. Gently he drew her to him and laid her face against his shoulder, talking softly to her. Lovingly he stroked her hair, threading his fingers through its luxuriance. Gradually she raised her face to his. As their lips met, she began to respond to his kissing and caressing. Then he said what she had never expected to hear from him.

"I want you to be my wife, Karen. I'm not trying to tie you to any promises yet. I'm just asking you to remember what I've said. I love you. I'll always love you. God knows when I'll be home again, but when I do return it's my hope that you'll be ready to marry me."

She felt the last trace of restraint melt from her. Her expression was tear-stained and rapturous. With a sudden move she kissed him tempestuously.

He made love to her in the cabin all the afternoon. It was a time of sweetness and tenderness and discovery that neither would forget, he lost in her beauty and her swift passion, she loving him totally. When the time came to lock up the cabin and leave, she felt she was turning the key on the most perfect moments of her life.

They remembered to take the rods back home with them but not the fish, which still lay on the bank. When they were half-way down the mountainside she realised she had also left her tortoiseshell barrette behind in the cabin and her hair was still flowing free. They laughed at how forgetful love had made them, stopping in their descent down the path to kiss again and again.

Johanna saw by the way they looked at each other upon their return and by the linking of their hands and fingers whenever they were close that there was a new understanding between them and she was glad. Karen, tolerant and gentle and warm-hearted, would be ideal for her brother, and well able to cope with the flaws in his otherwise generous nature. Throughout the evening she expected there would be some announcement of an engagement. When nothing was forthcoming she concluded they had decided to wait until they exchanged rings the next time he came home. The love in their eyes exacerbated an ever-present ache in her.

Erik went to Karen's room that night. It was the first time he had found her door unlocked, and he smiled over past disappointments as he went to her. Her arms were waiting for him as if it had been years instead of hours since they were last together. For the first time in his life he was moved to tears in the emotion of loving and leaving, holding her close with his face buried in her hair in order that she should not see. Never before had he known such sweet loving as he shared with her.

At five o'clock, while she still slept, he slid from the rumpled warmth of the bed. It was time for him to leave and he wanted no goodbyes. She lay deep in the pillow, her gleaming hair a silken tumble and her lovely breasts uncovered. He looked back at her before he closed the door silently after him.

In his own room he dressed in practical mountain wear. Lastly he took an anorak from the closet where his uniform hung on hangers, his cap with the shining peak on the shelf above. A whole new phase of his life must pass before he would get the chance to wear it again. Taking up a rucksack, which he had packed the day before in readiness, he crept quietly down the stairs, hoping the creaking of the treads would not disturb anyone in the house. He had thought to help himself to a snack in the kitchen but there was a sliver of light showing under the door. When he opened it, his mother was at the stove and breakfast was laid.

"What are you doing up so early?" he asked her in surprise, putting down the jacket across the rucksack dropped to the floor.

"I couldn't sleep. Somehow I don't seem to need as many hours these days." No mention of wanting to see him once more before he left. No indication of the anxieties she had harboured of the chance of another torpedo destroying his ship, or how his father's health made her fear the worst, or that Rolf's struggle against the Nazification of his pupils was bringing him into the greatest danger. Even Johanna had retreated into some existence of her own, the excuse for going to Oslo having been flimsy and improbable. "Sit down at the table. Everything is ready."

She ate with him. Her talk was mostly of the farm. When he rose from the table it was with the customary thanks for food received.

"Takk for mat. I must get going now."

"I've made a packet of sandwiches for you." She took it from the sideboard and handed it to him. As he packed it away she went ahead to open the front door. The chill morning air flowed into the warm house and the whole valley was bathed in dawn. On the opposite slope the rising columns of spray from the waterfall were full of golden sparks. She stepped out onto the porch with him.

"It's a wonderful morning," he said, shouldering his rucksack. "Look after yourself, Mother."

Unexpectedly she stifled a moan in her throat and clung to him in an embrace such as he had not received from her since childhood. "Don't let the Germans get you!" she cried brokenly.

Then he knew that with some deep maternal instinct she had sensed throughout his short visit that it was likely to be the last for a long time. "Don't worry," he reassured her gently. "I'll be all right."

Quickly he broke from her, hurrying away down the porch steps to reach the lane. He walked at a swift pace. Before the trees hid the farmhouse from sight, he turned and looked back. She was still on the porch and returned his last wave. Then he set his face forward again and went on down the lane.

When Johanna came downstairs an hour later the table had been cleared, the used crockery and cutlery had been washed and put away. Gina, feeding the cat, exchanged morning greetings with her daughter, who went through the back door to an outbuilding where milking clothes and gumboots were kept. As yet Gina was unable to tell of Erik's going to anyone. Her stoicism was being tested to the full. She would not speak until she could be sure of not breaking down.

The moment of disclosure came when Karen, who was up later than usual, set a place for Erik at the breakfast table. Johanna, bathed and changed out of her milking clothes, had just come into the kitchen and was in time to see her mother lay a hand gently across Karen's to still the placing of a knife.

"Erik has already left."

Karen showed disbelief, shaking her head with a half smile. "That's not possible. I expect he's overslept and that's why he hasn't come down yet. I'll give him a call." As she went towards the door Gina moved to block her way.

"I saw him off. He's escaping. He did not say, but I'm certain he's going to England."

Karen stared and then her anguished cry came as if torn from her. "Dear God! I would have gone with him!"

"No, no. The danger!"

"I don't care about that!" Karen became frantic. "How long has he been gone? Did he say which way he was taking from here?"

"He said nothing at all." Gina's face was full of compassion.

"I must go after him!" In her distraught state Karen looked as if she was prepared to rush from the house without further thought. Johanna darted to her.

"Go and get your coat. Grab a few things. I'll hitch Nils-Arne to the wagonette. I expect Erik will start his journey by taking the ferry along to one of the fishing coves. We'll catch up with him at the jetty if we don't overtake him on the way."

They set off a few minutes later. The horse was driven at a speed to which he was not accustomed. Johanna slowed him down when they went through the hamlet where a number of soldiers were billeted, not wanting to draw any unwelcome attention. Once through it and past the church, she urged the horse on again. When they approached the brow of the road they could see the ferry from across the fjord drawing near the distant jetty.

"That must be the one he's catching!" Karen exclaimed as they went bowling over the brow and down the other side in the direction of the jetty. "There's no other leaving earlier than this one. We've about a minute left. Oh, be quick!"

As the road levelled out they were brought within a few metres of the jetty just as the ferry lowered a ramp to allow two army trucks and a dispatch rider on a motor-bike ashore. Only three people were waiting to go on board and Erik was not among them. Johanna, aware of Karen's shudder of disappointment, gave her arm an encouraging press.

"Get out of the wagonette now. There are two sentries there, but they don't usually check identification papers at local ferries unless there's any kind of alert on. Go past them and wait on the jetty ready to go aboard in case Erik is planning to make a dash to the ferry at the last second."

Karen obeyed. She took the step down from the wagonette and strolled forward while a few passengers disembarked in the wake of the vehicles. The sentries eyed her and one ventured a smile. She turned her gaze away. The three people who had been waiting went past her to embark. A ferry hand, ready to manipulate the mechanism for raising the ramp again, looked at her inquiringly. "Are you coming aboard, frøken?"

He saw her turn a frantically searching gaze back at the road and the hillside before she looked again at him, her eyes such wells of despair that he could guess something had gone seriously amiss for her.

"No," she said with stiff lips as if keeping tears at bay. "Not now."

When she returned to the wagonette, Johanna asked her if she wanted to wait for two hours until the next ferry came in, but Karen shook her head. She knew as Johanna did that Erik would never have left home at such an hour except for a specially early start which would not have included hanging around pointlessly at a ferry point. "I should think he's gone over the mountains," Johanna concluded.

Karen said nothing. She spoke only once on the drive home and then fervently. "I hope I'm pregnant. I want to have Erik's child."

Erik had not gone to the ferry. Before reaching the hamlet he had branched away to one of the farmsteads lower down the valley. A young man of his own age, a friend with whom he had grown up, was waiting by the

water-mill. They greeted each other quietly and enthusiastically.

"Hey, there! Ingvar!"

"What a day to set off for England, eh, Erik?"

Falling into step they reached a narrow bridge and
crossed the river. On the other side they were joined by
twin brothers, bakers by trade with a good supply of bread
in their rucksacks. Named Oivind and Olav, they were as
thin as rakes and the best ski-jumpers in the county.

"This is like a school reunion," Olav joked. "Ryendal is
on the march."

His brother raised a fist in the sportsmen's gesture of
triumph. "Winston Churchill, your troubles are over! Here
we come!"

The four of them laughed and continued on together
into the mountains that each knew like the back of his own
hand. Towards noon they came down in sight of a small
town on the fjord where a large number of fishing boats
were moored. While the others settled down to wait, Erik
went into the town and made for an address. One of his
fellow officers, clothed similarly to himself, opened the
door and let him in. They grinned at each other. "You're
right on time, Erik."

"You know me, Jon. Never late for duty."

It was the apartment of Jon's girl-friend, who was away.
In the sitting-room Erik was introduced to Jon's brother,
Martin, who was seventeen and escaping with them.
There was another youth, Arvid, who was the same age
and three others who, like the rest of the group that was
gathering, were in their early twenties. A map was spread
out on the table and Jon took him to it.

"It's a cod-fishing trawler we're taking. It's moored con-
veniently at the west end of the quay, which means we are
out of the town and have nothing to fear until we reach
this island where there are searchlights." From the site of
the trawler his fingertip moved to tap the point of danger.
"After that we'll go through the mouth of the fjord into the
open sea."

"Why hasn't the trawler left with the deep-sea fishing
fleet for Arctic waters?"

"The owner has been arrested, poor devil. Nobody
knows what has happened to him and we're taking the

chance to get the boat before it's requisitioned. As soon as it's dark your party will come down the mountainside to meet us by these warehouses where the oil drums are stored. Luckily for us we have a locksmith among our number." He nodded across to one of the men who gestured a circle of finger and thumb to show the padlocks would present no barrier to him.

"What about sentries?"

"There are two of them on the quay. They patrol once every hour. Martin and Arvid will be look-outs. You and I will be helping to get the oil drums on board."

Erik returned to his companions in the mountains. It seemed a long wait until nightfall. It was a moonless night and a windy one, for the weather had changed during the afternoon and there had been some rain. With eyes accustomed to the dark, they made their way easily to the meeting place. Each knew his allotted task and they worked in silence, heaving the drums on board and stowing them. When they were almost finished there came a sharp clatter, not from the direction in which the sentries might be expected to come, but from the rear. Everyone froze, hearts beating, each fearing a German ambush. Then a Norwegian voice came from the darkness, "It's all right. I only dropped my tooth-mug. We're coming with you."

"The hell you are!"

They moved in a body to seize the three youths who had come upon them unawares, threatening their plans and their safety. Erik, jerking one by the neck, judged him to be no more than sixteen. "What right have you to come demanding a passage with us?"

The lad glared. "Every damn right! You're stealing our father's boat!"

With difficulty they all stifled their laughter. The three brothers, whose surname was Berge, became nicknamed from that moment as Berge One, Two and Three, the third being the youngest whom Erik had seized. They showed their willingness to be active members of the crew by helping to load the last of the oil drums. Then the padlocks were clicked back into place on the shed doors and everyone went on board. The engine was started up. This was a moment of suspense, but the rough wind was their friend, carrying the sound away. Without lights the trawler moved out from the quayside. Erik was on his own in the wheelhouse, everyone else out of sight in the cabin obeying the rule of silence imposed on them until they were out to sea.

The island with the German bunkers appeared ahead. At present it was in darkness but searchlights spasmodically fanned the surrounding waters if anything alerted the guards. When Erik judged the moment was right, the engine was switched off. Silently they drifted while the island loomed up on the portside and seemed to keep level with them like some ship of the night. In the cabin, Berge Three doubled over with stomach pains caused by nerves. Then gradually the island drew away. When the engine came to life again those in the cabin cheered.

Ahead was the open sea.

The Germans allowed an allotted fishing limit. This applied to the entire coast from the south of Norway to the deep-sea fishing grounds in the Arctic Circle. Beyond that limit any fishing vessel was assumed to be attempting to make contact with Britain and was open to attack from the Luftwaffe and the German Navy. Under cover of night, Erik aimed to take the trawler as far out from the limit as was possible. When dawn came they had to trust that their luck would hold and they would achieve their aim of reaching the Shetland Islands where a British refuge would await them. He and Jon would be automatically accepted into the Free Norwegian Navy and the three friends who had left the valley with him that morning planned to join the Free Norwegian Air Force as air crew, the twins having shared an interest in flying since boyhood.

Jon came in sou'wester and waterproofs to relieve Erik at the wheel near midnight. "What do you think of the weather?" Jon asked, peering ahead through the rain-lashed glass.

Erik gave his opinion. "It's going to get worse, no doubt of that, but this trawler is used to some of the roughest waters in the world, as we are."

Jon chuckled. The Arctic waters in winter caused many a hazardous moment, but the coastal steamers kept to a close schedule and were rarely delayed. They were both confident the trawler could be handled in the same way. "Get to the cabin. They have some hot soup there for you."

The scalding soup was welcome. As Erik sat sipping it, the mug cupped between his hands, he took a mental count of the numbers on board: some sleeping, four violently seasick, two playing cards and another placidly rolling some cigarettes out of home-grown tobacco, a pungent and quite peculiar aroma coming from the one he was smoking. Since tobacco had disappeared from the shops, several farmers had planted a crop. Then Erik hoped for the sake of general morale that no one else had done a reckoning. With Jon in the wheelhouse they were thirteen altogether. Thirteen. Normally he was not in the least superstitious but at this particular time some primitive, atavistic sense of warning stirred and troubled him.

The morning brought low clouds, giving protection from aircraft sightings as well as a much rougher sea. The waves carried the trawler high onto their crests and then smacked her down into deep, running troughs while walls of dark green water surged by. Erik and Jon, being the only seamen on board, took turns at the wheel with Berge One, who was a fisherman like his brothers and experienced enough to share the duty as he had done with his father. Before long the westerly wind had reached gale force, howling as it lashed spray from the waves, which were gaining mountainous proportions. Water poured over the bow and gushed past the wheelhouse to drain away as once again the trawler rose on a swell. It was no longer safe to cook anything in the galley. Those still able to eat made do with bread and cheese or whatever else was available. The night brought no respite. When Erik was off duty he slept before his head reached the pillow.

He did not see the wave that hit them in the early morning light. The first he knew was that he had been thrown to the floor from his bunk and there was a roar past the portholes and overhead as if the whole trawler were being swallowed by the sea. In the cabin there were shouts and groans, somebody obviously having suffered an injury. He threw on his waterproofs and fought his way along to the wheelhouse, clambering over rigging from a broken mizzen-mast, Berge One following him. Jon, white-faced and grim, shouted at them as they entered.

"The engine has cut out! We're drifting!"

When Erik and Berge One reached the engine room they saw the worst had happened. The huge sea had broken through and the place was awash with its own tossing waves. Berge One swore violently. "The bilge pump won't work until we get the engine going!"

There followed a nightmare time with everyone bailing out, only Arvid with a fractured arm remaining in the cabin, while the drifting trawler, perilously low in the water, was battered without respite. When finally hand pumping and bailing were lifted, the storm had eased, but neither Erik nor Berge One could get the engine going again. It had completely seized. The danger of sinking had been eliminated only to be replaced by another danger. The lessening sea showed them the grey line of the Shetlands on the horizon while the still forcible wind was beginning to carry them back to Norway. With no engine power and snapped masts, they were completely helpless.

For five days they drifted. Miraculously they escaped enemy observation from the air and when their homeland loomed into sight again they were many miles south of the place from which they had left. They held a conference in the cabin; it was decided that they should scatter, those who wished going in trios or pairs, and it was the natural choice of the twins that they should be together. They had all been long enough away from Norway for the Germans to have discovered that the trawler was missing and to have received a report that two officers of the coastal service had failed to return to their ships. Local inquiries would have established who else was missing from work in the area. By now a list would have been compiled of those most likely to be on board. The storm would have put the Germans on special alert. It would not be the first time that a boat of escapees had been beaten back by bad weather and those aboard taken into custody and shot.

In hope of gaining more time in which to get away, Erik organised the hanging out of the nets over the smashed bulwarks to make it appear as if they had been on a fishing trip. Close to the shore they were overtaken by a fishing boat whose skipper gave them a tow into a small cove and provided vital information about the terrain and the defences there.

"Get going as quickly as you can," he urged. "The Germans in town were asking about a missing trawler like yours only yesterday. From here you'll have a better chance of getting unnoticed into the countryside."

Erik and his friend Ingvar had decided to get back to their own district, a decision that the others had also made, for on familiar ground there was a better chance of getting another boat and they would know whom to trust. In a strange place it was a different matter. Only the Berge brothers decided to remain in the area, having relatives there who would shelter them. They were taking Arvid with them since he was in no state for a long walk, suspected broken ribs being added to his other injury.

They all bade each other good luck. When Erik and Ingvar had helped the injured youth ashore and into the care of the Berge brothers, who hastened him away, they joined those who had leaped from the boat onto the rocks and sped off into the woods like fleeing hares. Once there, they scattered in different directions. Luckily daylight was fading. Once Erik and Ingvar thought they heard submachine-gun fire in the distance but could not be sure. It was midnight by the time they reached the slopes. When they had climbed high enough to be safe, they flung themselves down on dry leaves and slept.

It took them two days to get back to Ryendal. When they arrived they remained on the high pastures, at the *saeter* cabin where not long before Erik had been with Karen. In the same cabin the two escapees took shelter. Erik found Karen's tortoiseshell barrette and pocketed it as a keepsake for luck. After resting for twenty-four hours, they ate the last of the food they had been given at an isolated mountain farm they had passed the day before. In the clear air, Erik saw Karen from the distance several times. It was almost as if she sensed his presence, for each time she came out of the farmhouse she paused to look up in the direction of the *saeter*, making him wish he could call her to him, but he would not risk involving her in any danger. It gave him peace of mind to know no harm could come to her at the farm.

At the conference on the trawler it had been arranged that the twins should meet up with Erik and Ingvar at the *saeter*, but if they did not come at the specified time it was

to be concluded they had been delayed or caught and
there was to be no waiting. When there was no sign of
them just before dawn, the cabin was closed and the key
replaced above the door. Both men were remembering
the gunfire they had heard, but neither mentioned it, each
keeping his despondency to himself. They descended to
the hamlet taking a route that bypassed Ingvar's home, for
he had no wish to be sighted by anyone there. Their new
escape plan was without organisation and based on taking
one hazardous chance. Some of the Ryendal fishing boats
went out at dawn and some at night. They were going to
take one already home and unloaded. Once on board they
would follow in the wake of those setting out for the day
with their nets, which should get them out to sea without
being challenged. The danger of being sighted by the Luftwaffe would be greater this time, for they would be heading for the fishing limits by daylight whereas previously
they had been protected by the night.

In the dawn light, catches of fish were being loaded onto
the jetty and carted away. Farther on were three boats tied
up for the day, their owners and the night's catch already
gone. Nobody took any notice of the two men as they
strolled towards it. Sentries had just changed and had no
reason to be suspicious when they went past or took notice
when the twin brothers caught up with them and went on
board the same boat, explaining quietly they had been
forced to make a detour by seeing a truckload of German
soldiers parked on their road.

The engine started up its tonk-tonk sound and Erik was
at the wheel. There was no need for the other three to
conceal themselves this time since to all intents and purposes they were the crew preparing their nets for the
fishing ahead. Erik's face was grief-stricken at the news the
brothers had brought. Berge One and Two, seeing Germans coming out of the woods, had remained with their
injured friend and had been arrested. They had urged
Berge Three to run for it. The lad had been gunned down.
The twins had seen it all, hiding in the undergrowth. That
night a farmer had hidden them in his barn, but before
they left he brought the news that five more escapees had
been shot by the Germans. Local information was that
they had come from a wrecked trawler. It was a terrible

toll: six deaths and three arrests with the same fate awaiting. A great groan broke from Erik's throat.

He did not know that the owner of the fishing boat he was steering had returned for a forgotten pipe and tobacco pouch and was standing on the shore, watching his means of livelihood depart. The man guessed where his property was bound. It never entered his mind to shout or raise any alarm that would have brought patrol boats out to intercept the errant vessel. If he had been twenty years younger he would have escaped too. Two thoughts came to him. One was that he hoped the insurance against loss wouldn't keep him shore-bound for too long, the companies often tardy in these cases since they had the Germans looking over their shoulders. The second thought was that he wished he had been in time to get his tobacco pouch. There had been some real tobacco in it.

Thirty-six hours later, after a relatively trouble-free crossing, Erik sailed the boat into the harbour of Lerwick in the Shetland Islands. British soldiers came on board and escorted the four of them to a public building where they were interrogated by British and Norwegian officials. It was a stiff cross-examination, for the Germans were attempting to pass spies in by the North Sea escape route. It was some time before they were accepted as genuine escapees and issued identity cards, their German-issued papers already surrendered to the British authorities.

The next day, still under escort, although it was a policeman in plainclothes this time, they were taken by ferry to the mainland and then by train to London, which gave them a glimpse of the country that had become a gathering place for so many of their countrymen. They arrived at night in an air raid, the sky blasted by flames from burning buildings, with the droning of enemy aircraft overhead and the exploding of bombs shaking the ground like an earthquake.

For two weeks the four of them kicked their heels in a camp where there was more interrogation in the hopes of gleaning any scraps of information that might prove to be helpful to the Allied cause. After that had taken place, Erik's three companions were enrolled in the Free Norwegian Air Force, Ingvar to be flown to Canada for pilot training at the "Little Norway" centre established there,

the twins posted to a destination in England to train as air
gunners. More time of increasingly impatient waiting
passed for Erik before he was called for an interview. It
was not to complete finalities before posting him to a Norwegian ship as he had expected. One of his fellow countrymen in naval uniform with a stern countenance and gimlet
eyes faced him across a polished table.

"I'm offering you the chance to volunteer for special
work. We need men who know every inlet and cove in
their own west coast district of Norway where special
agents and supplies can be landed secretly and others
brought away. This service means winter crossings from
the Shetland Islands in small fishing boats that will blend in
with the local shipping upon arrival. What do you say?"

"When do I start?"

Erik left the office well pleased. He was to leave London
by train that night to reach the centre from which operations took place. The special branch he was to join had
already earned its own highly respected nickname for its
regular and undaunted secret crossings: the Shetland Bus.

On his way into Kings Cross station some dramatic plac-
ards caught his eye. *Japanese planes bomb Pearl Harbour.*
He bought a newspaper and scanned the details. The
United States had entered the war.

At Scalloway in the Shetlands that Christmas of 1941,
Erik's name had already been listed with every other serviceman in the Free Norwegian Forces to receive an annual gift from King Haakon with whom they were sharing
exile from their homeland. Included with the King's personal letter of greetings, the warm socks, knitted scarf,
cigarettes and chocolate bars, there was an additional gift
for the woman in the serviceman's life. It was labelled "For
her." This year it was a lipstick. Erik smiled, tossing it
lightly in his hand. He would save it for Karen. His decision
was like a vow of faithfulness. Oddly for him, he intended
to keep it.

Chapter 7

Johanna went up the stairs to the café above a grocery shop. The windows looked out over the cobbled street below and the wintry Ålesund waters to the bridged island opposite where the wooden warehouses stood shoulder to shoulder in their sea-faded hues, the roofs thick with snow. Most of the tables were occupied. Some soldiers were present and four sailors from a U-boat in the harbour were making a cloud of cigarette smoke at a window table. She made her way to a wall seat at a table in the least popular section of the café to wait for Steffen. The message to meet him had come the day before. She had not seen him since the night of the parachute jump or had any word from him about further Resistance work, but there had been plenty to keep her occupied at home. Not long after Erik's departure her father had had a complete collapse. It was just as if all strength had finally evaporated from his body. The old doctor had come to see him willingly enough, had prescribed whatever was still available in the chemist's shop for his patient's heart trouble brought on by the brutal German attack, and left again, grumbling about his own aches and pains and saying he would not be able to turn out when the snows came.

Edvard was still mentally aware of what was going on, able to take some nourishment and to receive visitors, but nursing was constant. Karen, who was a born nurse, took on the duties tirelessly, and reluctantly let Gina and Johanna take turns relieving her while still determinedly shouldering the main portion of the tasks. Johanna believed Karen had dedicated herself to compelling Edvard back to health against all odds. Previously his condition had not warranted full-time attention, and the girl had been kept at bay by Gina's solicitous care of him. But now fate, as if to compensate for dashing her hopes of being pregnant, had given her a chance to do something worthwhile in Erik's absence. If it lay in her power she would get Edvard back on his feet to see his son come home again.

It had been a bleak Christmas with Edvard in bed and all of them anxious about Erik and wondering where he might be. They had heard King Haakon speak on the BBC and Johanna knew a little more than the others about the monarch's Christmas in London. During a routine delivery of underground news-sheets, which she had taken on in the valley, she had met again the schoolteacher who had organised her being in the mountains for Delia's drop by parachute.

"This year," he had told her, "as with the first Christmas of the Occupation, the King will have a tree from Norway. When our secret agents returned to England from a recent sortie here, a small fir tree was dug up and taken back with them as a link for the King from his own land."

The story had touched Johanna. A Norwegian Christmas tree going all the way to London in the midst of war.

Apart from her father's illness, there had been other things to keep her busy. The Third Reich, engaged in a winter campaign in Russia, must have found itself short of essentials. Demands were issued for all Norwegians except farmers and fishermen to hand in adults' gum-boots, blankets, tents, rucksacks and men's warm clothing of every description. She and some of the women in the valley had been called in by the Germans to help sort the goods that came in from Ryendal. Everybody had to find what they could, or else face three years' imprisonment or a fine up to one hundred thousand kroner.

The New Year of 1942 had come in with a comical situation to ease the tension. Not that the Germans thought it funny. With the savage suppression of the paper clip with heavy fines and imprisonment, people had found another way to demonstrate. Suddenly everyone—men, women and children—had begun to wear scarlet knitted caps, the colour of the forbidden national flag. From the south to far north of the Arctic Circle the whole land had bobbed with scarlet pompons and tassels like a virulent outbreak of measles. It had taken the Germans a while to see what was happening. Then the inevitable notices appeared solemnly on billboards and in the press. *Warning! Red knitted*

caps. The wearing of this headgear is strictly forbidden
under pain of severe punishment . . .

Watching the door for Steffen to arrive, Johanna felt sick
with anxiety as to how it would be when she saw him again.
She had tried to reconcile herself to the rift between them,
to accept that what had begun so gloriously had been no
more than a brief affair given momentum by the hazards
of war. Yet the truth was that her love was totally un-
changed. She had loved him from the moment he had
kissed her in Oslo's market square and she would go on
loving him. There seemed no cure for it.

The café door opened again to admit another customer.
A woman. It was Delia. For a few angry and painful seconds Johanna thought that Steffen had sent Delia in his
place, but she took a seat in another part of the café without so much as a glance around.

Almost immediately afterwards Steffen entered. Upon
seeing Johanna he went to the counter to collect two cups
of coffee and brought them across to where she was seated.
His expression was taut and guarded, not against the presence of enemy soldiers and sailors at the other tables, but
against her. She realised it was a reflection of her own
expression as she looked across the table at him.

"Sorry I'm late." He had his back to the rest of the
L-shaped room.

"You chose a busy place to meet."

He glanced over his shoulder before returning his gaze
to her where she sat at his right. Nobody could read anything from his lips or hers at that angle. "That's why. I
knew it would be possible to talk here in low voices without being overheard. I have to keep an eye on Delia at the
same time."

"Has she been here ever since I last saw you?" It was a
question she could not hold back.

He nodded. "Transmitter work. She's leaving tonight
under cover of darkness. There's a chance the Gestapo are
following up information that might lead to her. We can't
take the risk. She won't be back."

Was it her imagination or had he put special emphasis on
his final words? Either way it was of no consequence now.
"I wish her a safe journey."

He had taken a swig of the ersatz coffee and grimaced

over it. "This stuff gets worse!" Leaning both arms on the table, he thrust his face towards her. "How are you? What's been happening?"

She told him about Erik's going to England. Then she talked of Rolf. With the reopening of the schools after the Christmas vacation he, together with teachers throughout the country, had become extremely anxious over rumours that Quisling was working on plans to interfere with their freedom.

"I heard about that," he said grimly. "It could be an explosive situation. I haven't told you yet what a good job you did in Oslo. Congratulations." His nod was approving and he studied her keenly. "I heard most of the details, but not how you managed to avoid questioning by the Gestapo who had entered the apartment block before you could be forewarned." When she told him what took place, he nodded again. "Luck was certainly with you that day and that's not to belittle your initiative in any way. You had a couple of narrow escapes."

"I did? A couple? How?"

"The first came when you were in a batch of train passengers about to be siphoned off at random by the *Hird* stormtroopers in a general rounding up for a spot check. It was just one of the risks of the business. Our contact deliberately created a diversion by pushing you off the train and making a dash away himself."

"He was caught and arrested," she exclaimed. "What happened to him?"

"Not much, thank God. He pleaded panic at having mislaid his travel pass and it was discovered in his coat lining after supposedly slipping through a hole in his pocket. They weren't pleased with him, but he got away with a month in a labour camp." He saw how distressed she looked. "Don't worry about it. He was on the train for that sole purpose. What you were carrying was far too important for you to be alone, and it was not because it was your first sortie. We would have done the same for an experienced courier."

She inclined her head in acceptance of his reassurance on that point. "When shall I be sent again?"

"The time will come for more assignments. In the meanwhile you will stop delivering underground news-sheets.

We can't risk your being picked up for doing that. There is much more important work ahead for you."

She was no longer surprised by the Resistance's extensive knowledge of what went on in its name and who played a part. "I'll look forward to that."

"There's something special I have to tell you now," he continued sombrely. "Not good news, I'm afraid. I took this chance of meeting you today while I'm back in Ålesund to see Delia on her way. First of all, the truth is that things have gone tragically wrong for the Resistance since that general onslaught by the Gestapo at the time of the trade union strike. What's more, Reichskommissar Terboven is not going to give up until he thinks the entire underground movement has been eliminated. The German invasion of Russia brought Norway that much nearer the battle area and he dare not risk losing his grip in any way."

"How wrong did things go?"

He shook his head to show how bad it had been. "All the networks were virtually smashed. Contacts that had been carefully built up were almost completely wiped out."

"How did it happen?"

"Terrible tortures were inflicted on Resistance members betrayed by quisling informers. Inevitably secret information was extracted which led to more arrests and more torture. It carried on and on like ripples in a pool, each disclosure bringing in more victims. After torture, for many there was also the firing squad." His face showed the strain of what he was telling her. "There's a small courtyard that the Germans have set aside at Akershus Castle as a permanent site where executions of patriots are carried out."

She received what she was being told with anguish. He guessed that she, knowing Oslo well, would be remembering the picturesque castle as a peaceful place of interest with cobbled courtyards and ancient cannons and grassy lawns from which a wide view of the busy harbour could be enjoyed on warm summer days.

"What else have you to tell me?" she asked with apprehension in her eyes.

He thought she looked pale. "Shall we get out of here first?"

"What about Delia?"

"She'll follow us after a minute or two."

Together they left the café. Outside, snowflakes were swirling lightly in the air. He raised his arm as if to put it about her, but thought better of it. Side by side they walked along until they came to some railings looking out to sea, lapping silver and grey between the buildings like a canal through a wooden Venice, the colours mellow even on this winter's day. Sea gulls hovered and screeched and the moored fishing boats bobbed gently, some with layers of snow on the wheelhouse roofs not yet brushed away, each one bright with the green glass balls that kept the nets afloat. The breathing space Steffen had given her after preparing her through the general bad news of the Resistance had helped her to summon up courage for whatever was linked with it. She spoke what she feared to be most likely.

"Has Leif Moen been arrested?" Her arms were resting on the top rail, as were his.

He turned his head to look at her. "No. It concerns your friend at the fur shop. Sonja Holm. There was a Gestapo raid on a secret printing press. She and others who were there made an attempt to get away. In the melee she was mortally wounded."

She covered her face with her hands in deepest grief. He drew her to him and held her. His act of comfort was interrupted almost at once by the harsh voice of a sentry who had just stamped into view.

"*Achtung!* Get moving. You know it's not allowed for anyone to stand about in conversation. Keep walking. *Schnell! Schnell!*" He gestured fiercely with his bayoneted rifle.

This time Steffen did put an arm around her as they moved on, having no choice, for the guards were often nervous and trigger-happy. She was crying silently. At a distance from them Delia followed. Keeping them within sight, she sauntered slowly until they stopped to say good-bye within the shelter of an archway, momentarily out of the sight of any guards.

"We'll part here, Jo," he said to her, his hands cupping her shoulders. "You can go one way and I'll go the other. I wish I hadn't had to be the bearer of such sad news for you."

Johanna's eyes flooded again and she wiped them quickly. "I had to know and it helped to hear it from you." Her glance went to Delia on the opposite side of the road before she looked back at him. "I mustn't keep you any longer. It's not safe. Goodbye."

She hurried away through the snowflakes. Her grief renewed itself. It was rare for her to shed tears and these tore out of her. She wept for Sonja and for everything that had been lost through the enemy occupation.

It was a week later when, from the farmhouse, Johanna sighted a German army truck coming up the valley between the banks of snow on either side of the lane. She was filled with trepidation when it stopped outside the farmhouse. The helmeted soldiers jumped out, some peeling off to guard the rear of the house against any escape, the rest approaching the front door. Her mother was upstairs at her father's bedside and Karen had gone to call on a neighbour at the next farm. As the hammering of a fist came on the door, she opened it reluctantly. A sergeant stood there, backed by three soldiers with rifles. He had a young, bold face with jutting cheekbones, his expression stern, a truculent set to his mouth.

"I want to see Edvard Ryen," he said in Norwegian, crossing the threshold.

"He's ill in bed."

His dark brown eyes narrowed cynically. "How convenient. Where? Upstairs?"

She moved quickly to block the foot of the stairs. "I tell you he's ill. Really ill. Please don't go up. What is it you want? I'm his daughter. I'll answer for him."

"That's impossible. He is to be arrested as a hostage."

She stared at him, baffled and appalled. "A hostage! Whatever for?"

"You have a brother named Erik Ryen," he stated with heavy impatience. "He has broken the law by leaving the country to make contact with the enemies of the Third Reich. Since he can't be brought to justice at the present time, your father must stand assurance for him until he is."

Johanna was frantic. "But my brother is over twenty-one. My father is not responsible for anything he does."

"A new ruling has been recently introduced. As a result your brother's age no longer comes into this. Don't delay me, frøken!" With his elbow bent at his side, he made a sideways movement of his straight-angled hand to indicate she should step aside. Then he looked up as hurrying footsteps brought Gina to the head of the stairs.

"What do you want here?" she exclaimed anxiously. "My husband is a sick man. He's asleep and I don't want him awakened."

"You and your daughter certainly have co-ordinated your attempt at protection," he replied uncompromisingly to her complete bewilderment. Putting his hand on the baluster rail he began to mount the flight, the soldiers crowding Johanna out of the way as they followed him while he continued to address Gina. "No hysterics, frue. I'm here to collect your husband. He will not be alone. The fathers from the other two farms in the valley have already been taken as hostages for the men who accompanied your son across the North Sea."

Gina, to whose nature hysterics were as far removed as they could be, put a hand to the base of her throat, her pupils dilating with comprehension of what this visit meant. She remained resolutely at the head of the stairs to bar any access past her. "Take me instead. I'll go in my husband's place."

Johanna cried out from the bottom of the stairs. "No, Mother! I'll go."

The sergeant was unmoved. He merely took Gina by the shoulders and moved her forcibly aside. "I'm here for Edvard Ryen, frue. Nobody else."

She rushed after him as he went into the bedroom and took a place defensively by her husband's bedside. The sergeant checked his pace and came to a standstill. He had fully expected to find his quarry well able to be jerked out of bed, but the sick man opening his eyes from sleep appeared to be at death's door, his face white and sunken, his eyes dark-rimmed.

"What is the matter?" Edvard asked weakly, looking to his wife. "What does this soldier want? Is it cattle numbers?"

She took his thin hand between hers. "I think he wants to ask you your name, Edvard," she said falteringly.

For the first time in his military life Sergeant Müller was at a loss. This was an unexpected change of situation that he considered to be beyond his jurisdiction. He even felt a loss of personal prestige at finding himself embroiled in it. Son of a veteran of the Great War, he had had instilled into him by his father some of the values and standards of the old school of the German Army, qualities he respected in certain of the older officers. He was a soldier first and foremost, his blooding having come during the blitzkrieg in Poland. It had been a bitter blow to him when he had been posted to annexed territory instead of to the Russian Front. His greatest regret was that he had once filled in an army form with the information that he spoke fluent Norwegian, having been one of the children of the Fridtjof Nansen plan. As a result he found himself doing little more than policing a persistently hostile people, a task that was unpleasant and tedious to him, something that anyone far less highly trained than he was could do. Taking prisoners in war was vastly different from dragging thick-headed farmers out of their homes and off the land to shove them into labour camps. He accepted that examples had to be made to subdue subversive activities of any kind, but he could not bring himself to drag a desperately sick man from his bed. These tactics were better suited to the Gestapo, for whom he had no liking. He glanced sideways at the wife. She had not shrieked or pleaded, merely offered herself as a substitute. He liked her courage. He admired courage above all else.

"I can see the circumstances here have not been exaggerated," he said to her. "Therefore I must get a final decision from our medical officer. I'll be back."

The three soldiers were waiting on the landing. He detailed one to remain there and went back down the stairs and out to the truck, those on duty outside rejoining them. There was little doubt in his mind as to what the ultimate decision would be. With the order reinforced he would carry it out, but he would not like it any better. However, that was nobody's business but his own. He made a check in the back of the truck where the two farmers—big, healthy fellows—who had already been taken into custody

were being kept under guard. They sat with their hands
tied behind their backs, glaring at him with impotent rage.
Going to the front of the vehicle, he swung himself up into
the seat beside the driver, "Back to Ålesund. Let's go."

An hour later the truck returned, emptied of its previous
passengers with the exception of Sergeant Müller beside
the driver and two soldiers in the back to carry the
stretcher propped between them. The truck followed in
the wake of a grey military car carrying the medical officer
in style. He was a lean, gaunt-faced man in horn-rimmed
spectacles who had gained a reputation among the troops
of being a skilled doctor while being merciless with malin-
gerers. When the car stopped at Ryen Farm, his driver was
quick to leap out to open the door for him. His mood was
not amicable. He did not appreciate being brought from
Ålesund on what he fully expected to be a wild goose
chase. Experience had taught him that illness frequently
appeared to be more drastic to a layman than it actually
was, and he intended to make sure that Sergeant Müller
thought twice before taking similar action in the future.
He glanced sideways as the sergeant came running to him
from the truck.

"Lead the way, Sergeant," he ordered.

Upstairs in the house, Gina and Johanna awaited them at
Edvard's bedside. He was still awake and had been prepared for the medical officer's coming. Ill though he was,
he knew something was seriously wrong and was half prepared for the worst.

"They're entering the house," Johanna said huskily from
the window. She moved to stand by Gina and put her
hands supportively on her mother's shoulders as she sat in
a bedside chair. They heard two pairs of jackbooted feet
ascending the stairs. The medical officer gave them no
more than a glance, shrugging off the leather coat he wore
slung across his shoulders and tossing it to the sergeant.
Sitting down in the chair placed ready for him, he leaned
forward to pull down the lower lid of Edvard's eyes in turn
and then take his pulse. After initial questioning, he took a
particular line of inquiry.

"Pain in your bones? Depression? Legs heavy and seized
up? Always cold? When did all this start?" He had to lower
his head to catch Edvard's answers and he shook his head

dismissively. "Those injuries may have aggravated your condition, but it would have been already under way. How long have you been bedridden? As long as that? Hmm." Rising from the chair again, he swept up his coat once more to swing it around his shoulders. "You did right to call me, Sergeant," he admitted with a change of attitude. "To have taken this man would have landed you with a corpse on your hands in no time at all."

"Then he is to be left, sir?"

The reply came with a callous indifference to the other three listeners. "Yes. He is going to die soon. It's simply a matter of a steady deterioration."

He went from the room followed by the sergeant. Edvard gazed after them from his pillows. He felt no surprise at what he had heard, but he wished Gina could have had the news broken to her less brutally. As she bent over him he saw there were tears running down her cheeks. He could not remember seeing her cry since the early days of their marriage when she had been homesick for her valley and her own people and the bleakness of their relationship had first opened up between them. With effort he lifted his hand and cupped the side of her face. She covered it with her own.

Karen, coming from the neighbour's home, was in time to see the army car and truck leaving Ryen Farm. She drew back into the edge of the snowbank as the car shot past her and she waited for the truck to do the same. It came at a similar pace. She could see there was a sergeant seated next to the driver and as the truck thundered past he leaned out and looked full into her face. A stare of open recognition passed between them, their astonishment mutual. He leaned farther out to look back at her, only to see that she was running in the direction of the farmhouse and did not turn her head.

She burst into the house. "What has been happening?" she cried out in agitation.

Johanna, who had been on her own in the sitting room, needing some moments of quiet in which to gather her thoughts, rose to fetch her in there. "Come and sit down. I'll tell you all about it."

Karen, her expressive face reacting to every shade of the

account, heard her through before springing up from the chair with fists clenched. "He's not going to die. I won't let him. For Erik's sake I'll make him hold on to life."

She would have gone flying up to the sickroom if Johanna had not reached forward in time to grab her by the wrist. "Wait! Don't go up there yet. My mother is with him."

Although some of the vibrating tenseness went from the girl's body, she remained straight-backed as she sat down again, her fingers entwining nervously. "I used to know the sergeant who was here today."

"You did?"

"His name is Carl Müller. He came out to our village under the Nansen plan and stayed longer than most. I don't think he would have left his foster home if his widowed father hadn't remarried and made a home for him in Munich. He went back and joined the Hitler Youth when it was formed. For a while he wrote to me." She gave a little shrug. "There was nothing romantic in his letters as I had hoped. Instead he gave long accounts of doing what the Führer wished for the greatness of Germany. Yet each letter had been opened and bore the censor's sticker on the back. Those Nazis didn't even trust their own people."

"How old were you when you last saw him?"

"We were both fifteen."

"Did he recognise you?"

"Yes. I've no doubt at all." She pushed the flat of her hands to the ends of the chair arms and gripped them. "I hope he's stationed far from here and I never have to see him again. I was fond of him once. Now I hate him for his uniform and all he represents."

Johanna had never heard Karen speak of hatred before. She shared the girl's hope that they had seen the last of the sergeant. There was enough trouble in the house already without inciting more by antagonising any overtures of friendship on his part.

Three days later, Carl Müller returned on a dispatch rider's motorbike. Gina turned ashen when she discovered him on the threshold.

"I'm not here on duty, frue," he said quickly. "Is Karen at home?"

"As you are not on duty you may not come into the

house," she replied. "If Karen agrees to speak to you, then it must be outside."

His expression hardened. "If Karen should refuse to see me, I would have to exert my authority after all."

Gina thought with despair that the enemy had power over everything and she was fearful for the girl's well-being. "I'll tell her you're here."

He waited where he was in the porch, stamping his feet. It had been a cold ride from Ålesund and it would be an even colder one back in an hour or two in the already fading January daylight. In the past he would never have been kept waiting on any Norwegian doorstep. He had been one of the community in Karen's village, going to school with her and knowing her home as well as his own foster home. But all the time he had wanted to go back to Germany. That was his place of birth, and it had come to mean more to him through his being away from it than it might have if he had remained there to see his mother die during the dire conditions and mad inflation of those terrible days. Maybe then he would have wanted to emigrate as so many others had done, particularly before the Führer changed everything and made Germany a great nation again, capable of making the rest of the world tremble. He was proud of the Third Reich and of the Nazi crusade to end all wars by bringing every nation, either by justifiable coercion or by force, under the Führer's inspired leadership. As a soldier he held reverence for such an aim.

He turned his head sharply as Karen appeared from the house, warmly wrapped against the cold. A pinched look to her face suggested she was chilled inwardly for a reason that had nothing to do with the weather, and her lustrous eyes were wary and watchful. Yet nothing could detract from her beauty.

"You haven't changed, Karen. I knew you at once."

Her expression remained stony. "What do you want?"

He could have replied simply that he was lonely, that he was wearied of almost unrelieved barracks companionship, and that he wanted agreeable female company that he did not have to purchase by some means or another. To renew a relationship with her would be the answer to everything, for in her he would find a woman to welcome and value him for his own sake. "I only want a chance to talk to you again."

"What about?"

"Old times would do for a starting point. We used to be good friends. Surely that's reason enough for wanting to ask how you are and about everyone I knew in the village."

"You could have written to your foster parents after you left if you had wanted information."

"I did write a few times, but life became fairly exciting for me when I got back to Germany. There never seemed to be any time." He held out a hand as if to take hers. "Shall we walk? You'll get cold standing there." When she ignored his hand and went on down the porch steps he followed quickly to catch up. As they began to walk side by side, he leaned forward to see her profile that was half hidden by her turned-up collar and the muffler into which she had buried her chin. "There's no need for you to be annoyed. I wrote to you."

She stopped and faced him with blazing eyes. "Annoyed? Do you think I care anything about what you did or did not do all that time ago? It's what you and your kind are doing here now that makes me hate you as I do!"

A sick disappointment filled him. He had come full of pleasurable anticipation, believing that the friendship that had been between them in the past would bridge any present differences. He had also expected in his own mind to find her grateful for what he had done for the old farmer in the house where she was living, especially since he had not known about her connection with the family until afterwards when he had consulted the civilian files. "Are you crazy?" he retorted indignantly, pushing his face towards her. "I've done you no harm, nor am I likely to. You should know that. I tell you that if anyone else had come in my place the other day, the old farmer in that house would have died in the back of an army truck." He flung a pointing finger in the direction of the farmhouse and then closed his hand to prod his thumb against his chest, still thrusting towards her. "You have me to thank for that!"

He saw by the fleeting change in her expression, subtle and sensitive as a cloud-blown sky on a windy day, that he had scored in his own favour. Always fair-minded, she could not reject the truth of what he had said, even though her attitude did not change.

"No one should have come for him in the first place. For a man with such a bad heart condition the upset of your suddenly appearing might have been too great a shock for him to withstand."

He answered impatiently, almost without thinking. "There's nothing wrong with his heart! You can't throw everything at me."

She had become very still, her head tilting to one side as she scrutinised his face. "Why did you say that? About his heart I mean."

"I should know what's wrong with him. I had to fill it in on my report." His eyes narrowed at her. "Do you have some doubt about it?"

"I've had doubts all along about his doctor, who is old and should have given up years ago. Would you tell me what was written on the report?"

He saw he had suddenly gained an advantage. She was appealing to him for information that she could never get from any other source. "It would make no difference to the outcome," he warned her.

"I realise that, but maybe Edvard could be given some different medication to ease his pains. The old doctor is too stubborn to listen to me or anyone else in the family, but he might take notice of the district nurse if I could pass on whatever it is you know and we don't."

Hope had returned to him. In her eagerness to discover what he knew, her face had lost its look of hostility. The temptation to bargain with her was great, but he decided he would gain more simply by telling her outright what she wanted to know. "All right. He's suffering from pernicious anemia. Maybe that's affecting his heart."

It was not what she had expected and it was a disease she knew nothing about. "I appreciate your telling me. I don't suppose it will change anything, but I'll still tell the district nurse."

"Where does she live?"

"Farther down the valley."

"Shall we walk there now?" He said it before he remembered what he was asking her. She had led him up the valley away from any other habitations, and to go in the other direction would be for her to be seen by friends and neighbours in the company of a German soldier. Quickly he tried to recapture the earlier advantage he had gained, seeing she was about to refuse him. "I only asked on the basis of having proved I have complete goodwill towards you and the family with whom you are living." He took a step away from her, lifting his hands and then letting them drop again. "But naturally I understand. I think you're misguided, but I understand."

He moved as if to walk away from her. As he had hoped, she called him back. "I'll go down the road with you."

The pleasure that suffused his face dismayed her. She did not want him to put so much importance on what was still against her own true wishes. He was looking at her as he had done in the days gone by when they had met by chance or she had arrived late when he had been waiting for her. A flicker of the old fondness she had once felt for him stirred within her and she was afraid he would perceive it. They had both been mature for their years and although it had been a relatively innocent boy-girl relationship, tender and caring and vulnerable, what they had felt for each other had gone deeper for both of them than might have been expected from their ages.

As they went down the valley lane together, their talk, which he kept flowing, turned inevitably to people and incidents and events they both recalled. It was impossible for her not to smile with him now and again. He felt nothing of the traumatic yearnings he had had for her in adolescence. For him it was an entirely new beginning, its only links with the past being in the foundation of having known her before, which in itself was invaluable, for her whole warm-hearted, gentle character held no surprises to hinder his pursuit of her.

He waited for her at the roadside when she went into the house of the district nurse. She was indoors for about ten minutes and when she emerged again her face was radiant. She ran back to him down the snow-banked path.

"Pernicious anemia can be treated. It may not be too late. The district nurse is getting ready now to go and see the doctor. If he agrees, she'll be able to give Edvard injections and he's to have a diet of liver, which is easy enough on a farm. She was outraged to hear the old doctor hadn't taken any blood tests. Just think! He could be cured!"

He said nothing, his face set, looking hard at her. Suddenly the boy she had known had vanished, the enemy soldier taking his place. "That's good news," he said without expression.

The excitement drained from her face. "You would have your hostage then, wouldn't you?" she exclaimed bitterly, facing him in the middle of the snowy lane.

He had succeeded in frightening her more than he had intended. It gave him no satisfaction and he would have liked to tell her to forget all about it, but there was too much at stake as far as he was concerned. If she had nothing to fear from him, then she could shut the farmhouse door on him again and that would be the end of any friendship.

"Not necessarily," he replied as if weighing his words. "Come on. Let's walk back." At his side she was anxious and silent, glancing at him continually while he looked ahead, keeping her in suspense. "Nothing is going to happen overnight. Edvard Ryen may be too far gone for any kind of recovery. I'm prepared to wait and see. As I said to you before, I'm your friend and if the people of Ryen Farm matter to you, then naturally my attitude is the same towards them. I repeat: You know me, Karen. I think you should try to trust me. You always did."

She did not quite know how to take what he had said. He had made no promise not to carry out his duty if Edvard should recover, and yet his attempt at reassurance had been clear enough and it was only fair to remember he would be forced to obey orders from higher ranks. She thought she had the key to it all. He wanted a renewal of their friendship without reservations. Perhaps he even hoped for more. She almost pitied him.

"I might trust you, but I can't trust your uniform."

"We're one and the same."

If she needed confirmation that she should not relax her guard, it came at that moment, although he had intended the reverse. At the farm he said goodbye to her, sat on his motorbike to pull the goggles down over his eyes and with a roar of the machine he sped away. She had no idea when

she would see him again, but suspected he would return
when he judged the time to be right.

Although the district nurse was permitted to carry out
the new treatment on Edvard, the old doctor let it be
known that he would not call willingly on the patient
again. He was thoroughly offended, both as a patriot and a
doctor, that a German diagnosis had superseded his. Johanna was not quite sure what the district nurse had said to
him, and she half suspected it had been put forward as a
German order to prevent procrastination. By the middle
of February, there were the first faint signs of improvement in Edvard's condition.

Johanna, returning from shopping for rations in the
hamlet, called in at the schoolhouse on the way home as
she had done ever since her return to the farm. Since
Edvard had taken a turn for the better, Rolf did not come
daily to visit any more, and for quite a while a hired man
on the farm had replaced him, for Rolf had too much to do
at the school during and after educational hours. He held
secret meetings with other teachers who had their own
network of communication within the Resistance.

Recently their situation had taken a grave turn. Quisling
had had a law passed making membership to his new
Teachers' Nazi Association compulsory for all in the teaching profession. At the same time every pupil was compelled to join his new youth movement for full indoctrination in Nazi ideology. The teachers, backed by the Church
and parents, had rejected both ultimatums. Nobody knew
what would happen next. It was an impasse.

In the hallway the familiar aroma of chalk and ink and
blackboard met Johanna. The schoolroom took up the left
side of the building and Rolf's living quarters were to the
right of the entrance hall with a staircase leading to the
bedrooms above. Up there a radio was hidden, more securely concealed than the one the local barber had hidden
in the seat of his barber's chair: a German soldier, coming
in unexpectedly at closing time for a haircut, had been
astounded when beneath his seat a voice announced, "This
is London!"

As Johanna opened the door into the schoolroom, all
twenty-two of the pupils stood up with a scraping of chair

legs, the big ribbon bows bobbing on the heads of the little girls. She greeted them.

Rolf, who was writing on the blackboard, signalled for the children to sit down again and gave her a nod. "Wait awhile," he invited. "Class will soon be over."

It was an arithmetic lesson that was in progress. Johanna walked down between the rows of desks to glance at the work being done. She knew every one of the children, for they were all from the valley farms or the hamlet. By the time she reached the last row of desks, school had finished for the day. She stood, her arms folded, at the back of the room and listened with the children to the announcement Rolf made before letting them depart.

"Today is the last day of school for a month. As you know, four weeks' vacation has been given to ease the fuel shortage. Do the home tasks I have set you. If any of you have problems, you know where to find me. That's all, children. Dismissed."

He kept good discipline and they filed out. At once in the hall there was a burst of chatter and scurrying to put on their coats and get home. Still with her arms folded, Johanna strolled to the desk and leaned her hip against the edge of it. Rolf was wiping the blackboard clean with a chalk duster.

"What's all this about a fuel shortage?" she inquired dryly, nodding her head towards the stove, which reached from floor to ceiling and gave an even warmth to the room. He looked over his shoulder at her.

"Most of the country schools have all the wood they need. It's a problem in the cities where other forms of heating are used, I believe." He replaced the duster on a hook and brushed off his hands. "But that's not the reason for closing the schools. Far from it! Quisling is in a dilemma. Twelve thousand out of the fourteen thousand teachers in this country have flatly refused to join his new Teachers' Nazi Association." He grinned widely. "He can't dismiss all of us, and this month is to give him time to think over what to do next. Inside information has told us that not only is Terboven angry with his handling of the situation, but Hitler himself is fed up with him."

She laughed, running a hand backwards through her

silky hair, her face tilted. "That's the best news since Father took a turn for the better."

"Has Karen seen any more of that German?"

"No, thank goodness, although she's as nervous as a cat every time she hears a motorbike. She's about the best thing that ever happened to our family. What Mother and I would have done without her, I don't know. All along Father tried his best to be encouraged by her faith that he would get better, and now for her he will do the simple exercises that the district nurse devised, in spite of the discomfort it causes him." She swung herself away from the desk. "I must be getting home. We'll be seeing more of you at the farm now that you'll have some time on your hands."

"You will," he said, walking to the door with her. "There are plenty of overdue chores I'll be able to deal with before school reopens."

Johanna gave him a wave as she left. She was never again to see him with his class in the schoolhouse. Before the four-week vacation was up, a neighbour came rushing into the farmhouse as she was coming down the stairs. "Your brother is being arrested! They're rounding up hundreds of the teachers!"

Without stopping for a coat Johanna ran as she was, in her blouse and skirt and house shoes, out through the front door and down the lane. When she came in sight of the schoolhouse a canvas-topped army truck was being fastened at the rear. Rolf must have been watching the lane for he suddenly pushed himself forward into the canvas opening.

"Take care of everything, Johanna!" he shouted to her. Then he was knocked backwards by the butt of a rifle swung by one of the guards inside with the prisoners.

"I will!" Her cry was lost in the starting up of the truck and the accompanying roar of the motorbikes of two outriders. At least he knew that she had heard him and would carry out the underlying message in his shout of appeal.

Other people had gathered silently and seemed too stunned by what had occurred to disperse even when the truck was no longer in sight. Against the snowy background aglitter with the midday sun, they looked like so many dark-clothed chessmen. Dejected chessmen, Johanna thought to herself, for every one of them knew and liked Rolf, who had taken up his appointment at the special request of these local folk. Their sympathy reached out to her and she nodded to each one in turn, seeing that several of the women were wiping their eyes, before she went up the steps into the schoolhouse. One of the men followed her.

"Shall I help you lock up, Johanna?"

She thanked him. They checked windows, rattled the hot ashes from the stoves to let the fires out, and made sure everything was secure. In the study she righted a chair that had been overturned during Rolf's arrest and picked up a pen from the floor to restore it to the inkstand. When everything was done she turned the key in the main door after herself and her helper. As he was on the community council, he took charge of the key. Walking home in her brother's ski-jacket, which she had taken from a peg in the schoolhouse hallway, Johanna closed her hand over another key in the pocket. It was the one she had removed from the back door when she was certain of being unobserved.

That night she returned to the schoolhouse to carry out what Rolf had wanted of her. There had been no recent falls of snow to give away her footsteps, and once inside the building the black-out blinds, which she had pulled down earlier in the day in the closing-up process, hid the landing light as she switched it on. There she set down the carrier she had brought with her to take away the radio. It was too important an item to be left there unused, and Rolf had told her once where it was concealed. She went to a framed print in the dimmest part of the landing where the eaves sloped and removed it from its nail. Had she not known, she might still have missed the panel that had been skilfully cut into the wooden wall beneath. Carefully she prised it out. There was the radio. After lifting it down onto the floor, she was about to replace the concealing board when she thought it would be wise to check that nothing else of importance was there. The wood at the back moved slightly under the accidental pressure of her fingers. She pressed again and managed to push it to one side. Deeper under the eaves was an old attaché case, which she eased forward and into the light. It held a transmitter. This was something she had known nothing about. No wonder Rolf had shouted to her from the truck with such urgency.

She admired his ingenuity. He had chosen to hide it there in the hope that in the event of an enemy search only the radio would have been seized, appearing to be all that was there. Suddenly she froze, convinced she had heard a sound somewhere in the building. Yet she had fastened the door after her and it was surely her imagination that was playing tricks. Who would come here anyway? With the honesty of the country-bred, nobody would break in to pilfer, and the Germans would have searched at the time of Rolf's arrest if they had suspected him of having a transmitter in the house. Dismissing her fears, she returned her attention to the cavity. Surely there should be some aerial wire? Her fingers found it, metres and metres of it neatly coiled together. She marvelled at the risks her brother must have taken. Probably he had had to move the transmitter continually from place to place, setting it up in a cabin or under a rock shelter on the slopes, for the Germans had detectors sweeping whole areas in tracking down subversive transmitting.

Downstairs a board creaked in the region of the kitchen. Now she was convinced someone was in the house. It could only be a German soldier who had returned on his own to loot whatever was available. Instantly she snapped off the light. There was no time to refit the wooden panel she had removed. Swiftly she picked up the radio and pushed it back into the cavity, knocking the corner in her haste. Then she found the picture in the darkness and rehung it over the aperture, her fingers fumbling to get the cord hooked onto the nail. In the hallway the door from the kitchen opened with a whine of hinges.

She held her breath, her fear intense. Somewhere on the floor beside her was the wooden wall panel that she had set down and which must be concealed. On her knees, she felt for it and encountered its smoothed edge. Catching it up, she clutched it to her. The intruder had switched on a flashlight. Its rays danced up the stairs and threw shadows from the banisters on the sloping ceiling above her head. Like a snake she went flat and when the rays moved back to the hallway she crawled through the half-opened bedroom door and pushed it closed behind her. Leaping to her feet, she half fell against the bed in the blackness. Lifting up the mattress, she thrust the wooden panel underneath it. She was just in time.

The door was kicked open with a crash. In the light that blazed into her eyes she caught the gleam and ominous click of a revolver being pointed at her by the figure that whammed into the room. Her scream was an automatic reaction and she hurled herself across the bed onto the floor to take cover.

"Good God!" exclaimed Steffen's voice harshly. "It's you! I thought it was a bloody Kraut!"

He found the light switch and snapped it on. A cream-shaded lamp flooded the room with a soft glow. There were several pieces of simple furniture and a blue-painted bed which had a high downy quilt in a checked cotton cover. At first he could not see her. She had slithered down between the wall and the bed.

"Jo?" He slid the revolver back into the holster strapped to his body and returned the flashlight to the pocket of his padded jacket. Word of Rolf's arrest had made the speedy retrieving of the transmitter essential, for the Resistance was reeling under a new spate of discovered hideouts, arms and equipment caches, arrests, interrogations and torture. His nerves were shaken by the unexpected encounter with Johanna. Believing a trap had been set, he had been primed to kill, his finger tight on the trigger.

She heard him come across the floor and still she stayed where she was, sitting with her forehead sunk into the side of the bed, the fingers of both hands dug deep enough into the quilt for her nails to pierce the cover. Rage had come with a trembling, muscle-quivering relief, an inexplicable tempest of fury that consumed her and made her shake as if with ague, although it was beyond her comprehension. All that was stormy and hot-headed within her had erupted volcanically. The bed moved at a slight angle away from her as he pulled the foot aside, the wooden legs scraping the floor. Her head dropped between her arms while she continued to grip the quilt as though clinging to a life raft. He came into the triangular space between the bed and the wall to bend down beside her.

"For God's sake, look at me," he urged, his voice sounding tight and strained.

She knew he had come within seconds of killing her. It
added to her wrath that her teeth had begun to chatter
from shock, taking away the last shred of control over
herself. She wanted to yell at him not to touch her, to leave
as quickly as he had come, to let her emerge from this
personal trauma on her own. He spoke her name again,
shifting nearer and she could smell the outdoor chill of his
clothes, his skin, his hair. All her senses were keened to the
bludgeoning desire descending and sweeping across them
with the full force of a leaping, thundering avalanche. She
could almost hear the roaring in her ears. Without stirring,
she felt him reaching for her as if the very air sparked and
flashed with the force released between them.

As his hand clasped her arm she shuddered violently,
her head jerking upwards, her eyes enormous in her white
face, her hair swinging wildly like frayed silk, her lips
drawn back over her teeth. His face was as pale as hers, his
jaw clenched. Even as he wrenched her to him she hurled
herself forward and in the impact they fell across the bed.
Their actions were frantic and frenzied, for both were in
thick outer garments and as bundled in their love-making
as polar bears. Then in the midst of all the snatching and
pulling he was suddenly warm and strong and powerful
within her, an oasis of their bodies meeting amid the ham-
pering of their twisted clothing. Her sharp cry was both
anticipative and abandoned before his mouth seemed to
cover half her face, shutting her into a silence broken only
by the screeching of the bed beneath their battling. It was
only seconds before they came together in a great explosion of passion that blazed through her loins and left her
gasping, dazed and drenched in sweat. He collapsed across
her, spent and breathless. She shut her eyes as if to block
out what had happened, exhilarated and appalled and anguished.

He rolled away from her to yank off his fur-collared
jacket and flung it aside as if it were on fire. The rest of his
clothes followed with equal speed. With hers he took his
time. She kept her eyes closed, feeling herself swallowed
up by his ardour and her own, and large tears escaped one
by one from her eyes to trickle down into the pillow. He

cupped her face with his hands and smoothed the tears away from her cheekbones with his thumbs.

"Don't cry, Jo. Everything is all right now. Nothing shall ever come between us again." He covered her face with kisses. "I never loved until I met you. You're my reason for living, my love, my heart, my darling."

The vibrating tenderness in his voice and in his caresses was a foretaste of what was to come during the night hours that they were to spend together until dawn came.

Chapter 8

Packed into cattle cars, Rolf and his fellow teachers dozed and slept on the train's journey north. Thirteen hundred of them had been arrested and distributed into concentration camps where the treatment had been unremittingly harsh. Only a small number had succumbed to the bullying tactics and obtained release by signing enrolment papers to the Teachers' Nazi Association and those were mostly people with asthma or some other disability to whom the alternative was a complete breakdown of health.

The train began to slow down. In the cattle cars the men stirred and yawned, getting to their feet to stamp circulation into cramped limbs, stomachs rumbling with hunger. Rolf tried to peer out through a crack of light at the suburbs of Trondheim. When he had left the city at the end of his student days, he had never expected to return in this fashion. With a jolt and crashing of bumpers the train came to a halt in a siding. There was a rattle as the bolts were pulled out of the door and it went sliding back, the bright light pouring in making people blink and shade their eyes.

"Out! Out!" the guards shouted, rifles in their hands.

Rolf leaped to the ground. Those who were slow were thumped with rifle butts. He took his place in the long line that was forming two abreast as men continued to pour out of the train. These were five hundred teachers who had been numbered off from the rest in captivity for transport by ship to a labour camp far north of the Arctic Circle. There had been no deference to age in the selection. An elderly headmaster, who had not been far from his retirement, took the place next to him in the line.

"How are you today?" Rolf put the question to him in a mutter, for conversation was forbidden now as it had been during the punishing treatment in the camps.

"Somewhat bruised, but otherwise unharmed, I'm

170

thankful to say. Fortunately I slept all the way on some straw and that helped me to recoup my strength. It is most kind of you to enquire." The older man spoke with dignity, as if the two of them were in his own study, from which, during his arrest, he had been ignominiously dragged in view of his terrified pupils. The previous day he had been among those ordered to run round and round the camp until they dropped, only to be kicked to their feet again.

During the waiting, while the rest of the men continued to lengthen the line, Rolf thought about his sister and hoped once again that she had found the radio transmitter. The need for secrecy in the transmitting of specialised information had prevented him from giving her as much as a hint as to its existence. It had been essential that the Germans should not discover it during a routine search of his school. That was why he had trusted her to use her wits by shouting at her from the truck, committing her at last by his own will into subversive work that would endanger her. It would be her task to get in touch with someone in the Resistance about the transmitter, for although the hiding place was known to a few people, it was doubtful when or if any one of them would be able to collect it.

At the head of the line came the barked command. "Forward march!"

Rolf and his colleague moved forward with the rest. At the time of their arrest they had been issued with prison camp uniforms, drab garments of coarse cloth that flapped about their legs and bodies, and a kind of forage cap that unbuttoned to protect the ears in cold weather. That protection would be needed when they reached Kirkenes, which was located only a stone's throw from the Finnish border. Spring would not reach there for another four or five weeks yet and polar conditions would prevail. Rolf's only consolation was that at least they were being sent to another part of their own country and not to Germany, the fate of many Norwegians arrested on other charges. On the first day of captivity, a half-Jewish teacher had been pulled out of line, his identity card having shown the stamped *J*, and through the grapevine that springs up in any imprisoned gathering it was said that he had been sent to join a boatload of Norwegian Jews being shipped out of Oslo for a camp in Poland called Auschwitz.

On the march to the harbour Rolf absorbed the sight of the mellow-hued city of Trondheim with its eighteenth-century houses like iced wedding cakes and the spire of Nidaros Cathedral dominating the skyline. Every broad and narrow alley was familiar to him from the days when he had charged about on a bicycle, sometimes with Solveig perched on the crossbar, her unruly hair tickling his face, her nearness arousing him as it always did. It had been sheer good luck that the girl he was in love with at the *gymnasium* throughout his higher education should have gained a place at the same college. Solveig was as ambitious as he, and they had worked hard, played hard and they had loved hard.

The abortion ended everything. He had known nothing about it. Solveig came back to college after the last vacation before they took their finals and it had taken place during the short time they were apart. It had changed her completely—all the laughter and the fun and her exuberance for life snuffed out through an action she had taken on her own initiative without a word to him. He hated her as much for what she had done to herself as for making him feel shut out, rejected and humiliated. Their quarrels had been bitter and vituperative.

"Stop saying we could have married!" she had screeched at him, her curly mop dancing about her enraged, tear-stained face. "I don't want to marry you. I've never wanted to marry you. It could never have lasted the way it was. Why can't you see that?"

He had not been able to see it. They had taken their finals side by side without an exchanged glance either before or after the examinations, their silence towards each other cruel and stony. The last he saw of her had been at Trondheim railway station when they were all going home. Somebody else had his arm about her waist. She looked dull and dejected. The hurt she had inflicted was still too painful for him to speak the few words to her that might have mended at least friendship between them. Her train went in the opposite direction from his and after it had steamed out of the station, giving him a last glimpse of the pale oval of her face at one of the windows, misted by raindrops, he had never seen her again. She emigrated to the States that same summer, going first to stay with relatives in North Dakota. He was glad she had escaped the Occupation.

At the quay a small wooden ship lay alongside. In its heyday it had been on the coastal line, but was long since out of service. Rolf recognised the name, *Skjaerstad*. Erik had done some of his cadet training aboard. In her coastal days she had taken a complement of one hundred and fifty passengers. Now she had to accommodate five hundred, and in addition, fifty guards.

"I think we're in for a rough trip," Rolf commented wryly to his colleague. It was not a reference to the weather.

It was worse than anything he could have imagined possible. Prisoners were crowded in together until it became impossible for those in the hold to move in any direction. Within a matter of hours the clean-scrubbed ship stank like a cesspit. Rolf was wedged into a part of the dark hold where there was not enough room to stand up or lie down, the blackness unrelieved except by a glimmer of light showing around the hatches overhead. He was not seasick but many were, for the wintry seas had been gale-lashed from the moment the steamer had nosed out of the harbour. At one port of call a local quisling doctor came aboard. A look of helpless incredulity stamped itself on his face as he made a perfunctory round of the ship and viewed the scene with the groaning sick in the hold. He threw up his hands at the uselessness of attempting anything while such a lack of hygiene was allowed to prevail and left again to send an angry report on this treatment of professional men to headquarters in Oslo. It was ignored. The ship continued on her way with a steady deterioration of weather, rations and treatment by the guards, many of whom were seasick themselves. It took thirteen days for the vessel to make a journey that normally took four, and when the hold was opened in Kirkenes harbour Rolf thought the stench must be rising as it had done from the old prison ships arriving in Botany Bay.

The arctic air, sharply clean and cold, met his face like a benediction as he disembarked, helping ashore his elderly colleague from the original line-up, who was barely able to walk. Rolf had never been to the little mining and fishing town of Kirkenes before and, after the dim light of the

hold, it looked as bright as an Astrup painting, its colours
stark against the snow hiding the great fertile valley that
yielded forth so much in its brief summer. In peacetime
tourists who voyaged north to see the midnight sun were
welcomed ashore here from the coastal steamers, a point
of return for the voyage back to Bergen. Today the townspeople stopped to stare in shock and sympathy at the bedraggled procession of men coming from the steamer,
those too weak to walk alone supported by others.

Near a corner, a woman darted forward and dropped a
winter-stored apple into Rolf's pocket before scurrying
away at a soldier's angry shout and raised rifle. Somebody
else received a rolled cigarette of home-grown tobacco
and another a piece of dried fish. The townsfolk had little
to spare, but they wanted to share what they had. To Rolf it
was a forewarning. These people knew what awaited them
and wanted to give some aid while the chance was available.

His misgivings proved to be right. In spite of what had
already been inflicted on them during the voyage north,
he would never have believed such hell could have been
created in his own land. Everything about the camp was
grey, from the guards' look-out posts to the bleak com-
pounds and electrified wire fencing that kept them
penned by night in long huts where they were crowded
together in fetid conditions, sanitary arrangements being
totally inadequate. Some found themselves housed in cardboard tents due to overcrowding, which were poor protection against the bitter arctic chill. By day they were put to
heavy manual labour that was often beyond the strength of
the older men—road-building and cleaving out rock for
concrete pillboxes and shoving mining wagons down to
the harbour. The food was often no more than a bowl of
watery soup and a slab of stone-hard black bread. Yet, bad
as it was for the teachers, it was still worse for the Russians
and East Prussian prisoners-of-war they worked alongside.
With less food and harsher punishment, some were little
more than walking skeletons, their faces cadaverous and
covered with sores. While road-building, one was shot for
breaking away to catch a yellowed cabbage leaf drifting
along in a ditch, starvation overcoming all other fear. Rolf
and a fellow teacher carried the emaciated body back to

camp for burial. The man's compatriots showed no emotion. Death had become too commonplace.

At Ryendal in the spring sunshine, Gina walked slowly home from Sunday service. She wore her church-going clothes—an unfashionably long black coat over one of her best dresses with a lace collar. Her hat was black straw, slightly misshapen through age. It had not suited her when it was new and it suited her still less now; the fact she had made a mistake with her purchase did not mean that a perfectly good hat should be discarded. Her appearance had ceased to be important to her long ago, except that everything she wore must be spotlessly clean, well pressed, and neatly mended. She carried a small bunch of lilies-of-the-valley which she had picked at the wayside. They powdered the valley like a new fall of snow, the delicate scent rising in the still air. There had been some in a glass vase on the altar that morning. Although the clergy had been denied all authority by Quisling since their resignation *en bloc* in protest against the Nazi regime, people still filled the churches when services were held. It was only where dubious Nazi replacements had been appointed that the pews stayed empty, only one or two collaborators attending.

Her prayers that day had been for her absent sons and her thanksgiving for the signs in Edvard of a slow and steady recovery to better health, if not to the ox of a man he had once been.

She looked about her as she wandered along, savouring this quiet time to herself and observing everything. Being country-bred and country-raised, she took as keen an interest in the fertile state of her neighbours' fields as she did in her own. Apart from feeding the animals and milking, no other chores of husbandry were carried out on the day of rest and the Sunday peace lay over the valley, almost tangible in the stillness broken only by the sea gulls wheeling in from the fjord. She wished the tranquility could reach out to the many in need of it in the heat of war.

Ahead of her she saw Johanna coming from the farmhouse, swinging along with her long-legged stride as if the ground had springs beneath the surface. So much vibrant youth and energy made her feel dry and withered, worn out by the years, and yet at the same time she drew warmth from the sight of the young, as from the sun. She had been expecting to meet Johanna on the way, for the girl was off to see Astrid Larsen on an afternoon visit. At the service, Gina had prayed for her daughter as well as her sons. Since the day of Rolf's arrest, Johanna had been preoccupied and at times quite absent-minded, only half listening when others spoke to her. It would do her good to have a pleasant outing in her elderly friend's company.

"You're off then," Gina said to her as they came within earshot.

"That's right. I don't expect to be late home."

"Give Frøken Larsen my kindest regards." There was no relaxation in the severe expression that was normal to Gina. Nothing to show that she was as much concerned for her daughter as for her sons.

"I will. 'Bye, Mother."

As Johanna went to walk on, Gina reached out unexpectedly and caught her sleeve between black-gloved fingers. "Here," she said brusquely, pushing the lilies-of-the-valley into her daughter's hand. "I know these are your favourite flowers. Wear them today." She turned back her own coat revers to remove a pin and hold it out.

"Thank you." Johanna gave her a speculative sideways glance as she pinned on the flowers. It was always impossible to define how much her mother knew intuitively or guessed.

"Get along with you then." Abruptly Gina stepped forward up the slope to the farmhouse, the encounter closed.

Johanna inhaled the scent of the tiny blooms as she went on down the lane, every one of them a blessing to take with her to what might be the most important meeting of her life. The Resistance had summoned her. At last she was to be absorbed into full-time work for them.

Gina, with her hand on the farmhouse door, was seized by a hollow quake of premonition and she struggled against a longing to call back the disappearing figure of her daughter. Straightening her shoulders and stifling the anxiety she had experienced in the lane, she refrained even from looking back. Weakness did nobody any good.

Sunday afternoon was quiet in Ålesund. Couples strolled along pushing baby carriages. There were fathers out

alone with their children, carrying fishing-rods and bait.
Outside Astrid's house there was the usual complement of
parked cars and yawning drivers. Some of them knew
Johanna by sight now and had told newcomers that she
was not one of the inhabitants of the officers' section of the
house, as had been at first supposed. This meant she was
spared the previous lewdness. Some bade her a polite
Guten Tag. On principle she could not return the greeting
and at the same time, in the midst of hatred for their alien
presence, she pitied them. So many were ordinary men
starved for friendship beyond that of their own kind.

Astrid, her silvery-grey hair dressed as always in immaculate waves, her dress a silk print with the pleated inlets of
a mode belonging to the early thirties, opened the door.
"Come in," she invited serenely. Her composure was
completely genuine. The fact that she was virtually living
on a time bomb did not disturb her sleep at night on her
own behalf. She was grateful for the riches life had given
her, not least for being of some use to her country in her
old age when she might have been expected to resign
herself to the pastimes of dotage. When she worried it was
for younger lives put in jeopardy, and it was her earnest
hope that nothing she ever said or did would give any clue
to their whereabouts. With the Gestapo's sustained onslaught against the Resistance in an attempt to eliminate it
once and for all, many secret meeting-places had been
given away by informers and those under severe torture.
At times there had been days of agonising suspense. Fortunately the very site of her living quarters was insurance
against suspicion falling on her property unless deliberately betrayed. The fact that her cellar was kept exclu-
sively for the most secret meetings of the highest leaders of
the Resistance reduced its chances of discovery, while at
the same time making it a prize the Germans would be
glad to seize. At the present moment she had two of the
Resistance fighters most wanted by the Gestapo in that
area in her underground retreat. "Keep your jacket on
until after the meeting," she advised Johanna, who had
been about to remove it. "It's always chilly in that cellar."

"Am I to go down straightaway?"

"Yes. They're waiting for you."

She knew Steffen would be there since it was he who had

summoned her by a coded message. "Who is with your nephew?" she asked. "Do you know?" Although she no longer saw Delia as a threat, it was her hope that their paths would not cross.

"You'll know when you get there." The lines of Astrid's upper lip became fan-shaped as she compressed her mouth briefly. "I've learned not to ask him anything any more, although in this case I happen to know it's one of Steffen's engineering colleagues in this area. Hurry along now. I mustn't delay you. Those were my instructions."

Under the stairs Johanna tapped the Morse signal of V for victory on the panel. Contrary to her expectations it was not Steffen who drew it back to admit her. She was helped through by a large man in his late twenties with rough brown hair, thick brows and a tanned, good-natured face. When he greeted her with a hearty handshake his clasp inadvertently crushed her ring into her finger, making it difficult not to wince.

"Glad to know you." His strong voice came deeply from his broad chest. "In the Resistance I'm known as Gunnar."

She smiled back at him, an instant liking mutual between them. Here was someone whom she felt she could trust. "Are we to be comrades?" she asked.

"You'll probably see quite a lot of me from now on, but our friend here, known as 'the Englishman,' is in charge." He jerked a thumb over his shoulder to where Steffen sat awaiting her at the table in the lamplight. "He says 'we' sometimes instead of 'I' when he's referring to the Resistance in general, but I tell you, everybody jumps to his orders in this region."

It was the first time she had heard Steffen's alias, and she liked his choice, understanding that it was a play on Viktor Alsteen's little joke. As she went across to the chair that stood ready for her, she thought it curious that a man who loved her as much as Steffen did should be able to regard her with such a glittering and uncompromising eye. She knew why. He had explained it to her on their night together at the school house. Until he became accustomed to her facing danger through his directions in the Resistance, he had to divorce himself entirely from his feelings for her. Otherwise he would not yet be able to find the will-power to commit her to an assignment. It was why his attitude had been so distant from her in the cabin on the night of Delia's arrival by parachute, quite apart from the strained relations between them at that time.

When she was seated in front of him, Gunnar having settled his big frame on the bench, Steffen went straight to the business in hand. "I've been waiting for something special to come up for you, Jo. Now it has. There's an important post being advertised locally and I want you to get it. You would be working for your father's cousin, Tom Ryen."

She was astonished. "He's a quisling."

"That's why I want you in his office." There was a newspaper with some writing materials at his right hand. He picked it up to hand it over to her. The advertisement was ringed in pencil. She read it through. Her qualifications would cover every requirement, including a stipulation on being able to read, write and converse in fluent German. He prompted her. "Well?"

"I'd stand a good chance if I could manage to stay civil to him," she declared frankly. "When I met him in the fjord steamship I didn't know then that he was a collaborator and I haven't seen him since."

"You'll stay civil," Steffen stated flatly. "Anything else?"

"Tom won't show favouritism just because we're distantly related. He would hold it against me that I have one brother escaped to England and another somewhere in a concentration camp. Surely in Tom's eyes that would make me a bad security risk, particularly since his department is in the German headquarters."

Steffen waved this point aside impatiently. "There are few people these days without a member of the family in the Germans' bad books for one reason or another. In any case, collaborators don't trust their own kind. If Tom Ryen thinks you want the job for its own sake, everything should be straightforward." He surveyed her intently as he gave her warning. "I have to say you couldn't be taking on the job at a more dangerous time. Last week nineteen Resistance fighters, no older than you or me, were executed by the Gestapo's firing squad for less than what we're expecting you to do for us."

She was aware of the other man's scrutiny. If he was watching for any cracks in her resolve, he was wasting his time. Deliberately she tapped the pencil-ringed advertisement with her forefinger. "I'll write my application from home this evening."

Satisfaction snapped in Steffen's penetrating gaze and he exchanged a glance with Gunnar. She sensed a faint relaxation in the atmosphere and realised how much importance they were placing on her securing a position in Tom's office. "That's right," he endorsed, sitting back in the chair. "No delays. Now Gunnar will tell you what's involved."

Gunnar shifted his chair forward and leaned towards her with a forearm across the corner of the table. "Basically you are to keep your eyes and ears open for anything that might be of use to us, however trivial it may appear. Listen to any snatches of conversation in your hearing. Watch constantly. Let no letter or document or any other official paper, even a simple work enrolment form, go through your hands without a second glance. Find out where certain classified material is filed in Ryen's office or elsewhere."

He paused to let Steffen, his face without expression, continue the instructions in a hard voice. "In order to make communication easier, we shall want you to leave the farm and move in with Astrid. She has already agreed to this arrangement."

"What should I be looking for?"

"First and foremost, for any connection, however remote, with chemical factories, laboratories, or depots, including the shipment out of an end product, or the lack of it, which is equally important."

Gunnar gave the explanation. "As you know, Tom Ryen recruits workers for every type of building erected by the Germans from power plants to gun bunkers, and transfers some of this work force from place to place according to where they are needed. These movements can reveal a great deal to Intelligence, particularly when a new building goes up with some mystery about its purpose. That's the kind of specialised information we are sending to London. That's what we want from you."

Steffen commanded her attention again. "You see, Jo, some of us have begun to believe that something especially sinister and dangerous has begun to develop."

"What is that?" She could sense the intense gravity in both men. It made a chill run down her spine.

"It's the making of a new bomb by the Germans that has yet to be tested. All that is known is that its effect will be devastating."

"Is there a name for this terrible weapon?"

"Not yet."

She shivered and rubbed her arms from an inner chill of trepidation. "Is it being made in our country?"

"No, but a vital moderator essential to its construction, known as heavy water, is being produced in the district of Telemark at the Norsk Hydro Electric Company plant."

"That's at Vemork. I remember that Rolf went there once on an instructional tour during his student days."

"I was there myself quite often in more peaceful times. Now German secrecy and security surrounds it." His next words came harshly, not sparing her. "If Germany should gain the advantage of this monstrous weapon, then it could be the end of freedom for a thousand years. Maybe forever."

She stared at him incredulously, assimilating the horrific threat looming on the horizon. Now she knew why they had given her the test sortie to Oslo and why she had been forbidden to distribute the underground newspapers. They had been waiting for a chance like this one to come their way and were plunging her into it. She had wanted to become a full-time Resistance fighter and here she had landed a task that would make her a cog in the wheel of such gathering momentum that she was almost dazed by it. Her pulse began to quicken with excitement.

"To whom shall I report?"

"To Gunnar or to me, according to which of us can get through to you." His face remained expressionless. "A replacement will always be sent by the S.O.E. if the Gestapo catches up with either of us. You'll have a code word for that contingency."

He scraped back his chair and stood up. "I'm leaving now. Gunnar will see you back into the house. I'll be in touch again with the finalised details about the delivery of your reports when you've secured that position as Ryen's secretary."

She wrote and posted her application that same eve-

ning. For a suspenseful week she heard nothing. Then a
standard reply came, giving her the date and time of her
interview.

When the day came she gave careful consideration to
what she should wear. Tom was a man who loved women
for being women and he would appreciate her presenting
an extremely smart appearance. It would flatter his ego to
have a secretary who gave presence to his office, particularly when matched by her secretarial abilities. There was
certainly an advantage in knowing the character of a pro-
spective employer. Too much was at stake for her not to
use whatever means were available to gain that post.

She settled on a smart black costume which had not
been worn since her Oslo days. It had the widely padded
shoulders, long jacket and shorter skirt that had been coming into fashion when Hitler invaded Poland. The silhouette had been oddly prophetic, almost foreshadowing the
uniforms that were soon to become the daily garb of so
many. With it she wore a treasured, impossible to replace,
white chiffon blouse with a softly gathered collar that billowed around her neck, and she topped the outfit with a
beret of crocheted black silk that had a Paris label and had
cost her almost a week's salary, an extravagance she had
never regretted.

A pair of high-heeled shoes, again not worn since her
employment at the fur shop, awaited her decision as to
what she should wear on her legs. Her last pair of silk
stockings had disintegrated while she was still in Oslo. The
choice lay in home-knitted stockings, a pair of lisle ones
with darned heels or another in a new lacy pattern that
everyone was knitting since it saved wool, which was often
unpicked and unravelled from an earlier garment, and was
more flattering to the legs. She decided on a black pair of
these. The effect was not comparable to silk with her costume, but the appearance was quite svelte on her legs,
which had not lost their tan from the hay-making and
harvesting of the preceding summer.

In his office, Tom Ryen took a break with a cigarette
before interviewing the next applicant. It was a German
cigarette. No rolling his own for him out of tough, home-

grown leaves. Having access to German supplies was one of the perks in the job he did, and in a cupboard here, and in his cellar at home, he had a good supply of wines and spirits with the exception of scotch whisky, which he missed. He had not gone hungry or thirsty since the days of the fighting when he had been prepared to die for his country, but when the Germans took command and the ultimate sacrifice had passed him by, he had decided to make the best of the situation and had had no cause to regret that decision. He prided himself on being a realist.

He pushed his bulk out of the chair and went across to the window of his roomy, comfortable office with its teak furniture and hand-woven curtains in rich, dark colours that had been designed and made at a pre-war art centre. The sunshine had a strong warmth through the glass, stinging into the back of his freckled hand holding the cigarette. Outside, a wind off the sea, blowing across the harbour, flapped the long coats of the sentries on guard outside the gates of the fortifications that the Germans had burrowed into the solid rock. It was a section of the slope that banked the town and up which the houses climbed, spreading out into lawns and orchards. Leisurely he drew on his cigarette and unbuttoned his well-tailored jacket for greater comfort. He was aware of having put on some weight, particularly since military discipline had become a thing of the past. He kept his army uniform hanging in a wardrobe, although he doubted he would be able to do up the buttons again, for he believed his paunch had expanded beyond recall. The Germans, respectful of all things military, always addressed him by his rank of major, which gratified him, although his rank was all that remained of the career he had known before.

Born in Bergen with the good humour natural to Bergensers, but without their appetite for hard work, he was the youngest son of a well-to-do branch of the family. After travelling abroad and seeing something of the world, he had returned home to settle on a career in the army. It appealed to him for its social aspect, its lack of tedious overseas commitments and the fact that it was a far from arduous existence once the training was over. Since he could work when it suited his own ends, he did exert himself until he reached the rank of major quicker than most,

whereupon he took events as easily as possible. Although
his wife, whom he had married after a brief courtship, had
bequeathed him a handsome amount of money and property, theirs had been a love match. She had been a lively,
happy woman, almost as pleasure-loving as himself, and
neither of them had wanted children to interfere with
their lives. The ten years since she died had dulled the
edge of an untimely bereavement and he had been about
to marry a Swedish woman when the invasion had come,
keeping her within the boundaries of her country as it kept
him within his. When everything had settled down and the
Allies had been defeated, he hoped for a revival of their
relationship.

In spite of how the situation might appear to outsiders,
he was not in favour of the Nazis. He would have preferred
conditions to be as they had been before the invasion, but
since that was not possible he saw no harm in being an
opportunist, particularly when nothing could change the
rule of the Third Reich which had come to stay. As a result
of his philosophical attitude he was well liked by the Germans. They appreciated the services of an intelligent collaborator who had their best interests at heart, while at the
same time wanting the fairest deals that could be arranged
for his own countrymen. Had he been a complete traitor
they would have despised him. He knew they despised
Quisling. They had their own jokes about the portly minister-president, mostly about his incompetence and big-
headedness. It had become apparent that the Reichskommissar had finally lost patience with the blunders perpetu-
ated by the man, considering it a current disgrace that
Quisling's ham-fisted methods had resulted in the
churches being left as empty of administration as the
schools.

Tom stubbed out his cigarette in a silver ashtray. He
frequented the officers' mess, able to come and go as he
pleased, and it was there that he had heard that Hitler
himself had expressed great displeasure with Quisling,
wanting to hear of no more trouble in Norway. Had this
been related to him directly he would have had difficulty
in restraining his amusement at such a faint hope, but
fortunately he had merely overheard it at a neighbouring
table while having a drink at the bar. The Germans' Achil-

les heel was their complete failure to understand the Norwegian temperament. Until they came to terms with the average Norwegian's iron will as far as his rights to freedom were concerned, they would never succeed in establishing their New Order in any shape or form. He was not particularly proud of his own method of gaining personal independence, but hardship, pursuit and torture were not experiences he cared to invite.

Returning to the chair at his desk, he flicked a switch and asked for the next applicant to be shown in. If he had wished, he could have been allotted an army clerk, but he tried to keep military personnel out of his own realm, not an easy matter when they occupied every other set of rooms on all three floors. Anyway he liked female company and considered an office bereft without the shimmer of a blouse over soft breasts, the click of high heels and the gleam of silk-stockinged legs. His former secretary had been married to a German officer, which meant she was better dressed than other Norwegian women these days, and she had brightened the office for him until she became pregnant, distorting her face and her figure. He had been thankful to receive her notice. The door from the outer office opened.

"Frøken Ryen," the temporary army clerk announced, showing Johanna into the room.

Tom rose to his feet, a broad smile creasing his face, and extended his right hand, a gold ring shining on his little finger. "Good morning, Johanna. This is a pleasure. I haven't seen you since we met on the steamship. Sit down."

She shook hands with him. His palm was like silk, his nails manicured, his grip firm. She noticed at once that he had put on a considerable amount of weight, not an easy thing to do in Norway these days, and it was like a final confirmation of all she had heard about him.

Sitting down in the proffered chair, she found herself subject to his old charm. In view of their surroundings she could no longer accept him as the friend he had always been, but that did not mean she could switch to disliking him. Although he was weak, self-indulgent and everything she abhorred as far as his collaboration was concerned, she could not dismiss his many kindnesses in the past, the

occasions of laughter in happier times and the encouragement she had received from him when she had first
wanted to go to Oslo to work and her parents had been set
against it.

"You're looking well, Tom," she said as an opening.

"Never been better." He was still beaming at her, his
sandy-lashed eyes narrowed into fat folds. Her beauty
washed over him. She was, as the old adage says, a sight for
sore eyes with her bandbox appearance and the nifty angle
of the beret on her golden hair. Only her stockings met
with his disapproval. Admittedly she even imbued those
with style. It was simply that home-knitting had no place
on legs such as hers. With his sense of humour coming to
the surface, he thought that if he had any influence with
the Führer he would have ensured supplies of silk stockings in all the shops. Personally he felt deprived of the sight
of straight seams rising forever and fancy clocks on the
sides of trim ankles. The Germans had no sense of priority
in such matters. The twinkle in his gaze reflected something of what was passing through his mind. "I was most
interested to receive your letter of application to become
my secretary, Johanna. Have you had enough of life on the
farm? It must have been tough having to return to it
again."

His own home, outside of Ålesund, had once been the
house to a large farm. His wife had inherited it upon their
marriage and from the first day they had rented the land
out for others to farm. They could have lived elsewhere,
except that the house itself was a treasure with large rooms
for parties, its own shallow bay for swimming, access to the
fjord for sailing and some of the best ski slopes in the
district. He still gave parties, his guests high-ranking officers of the Wehrmacht who appreciated the surroundings and liked to stay there instead of in military quarters
when visiting the area. Many privileges had come his way
in return for his hospitality, including the use of a splendid
car with a generous petrol ration to replace his wood-
burning model, which he had sold for treble the price he
had given for it.

She answered him easily. "I went home because I was
needed there. Now that a German doctor has diagnosed
his complaint correctly, Father is in better health and

things have changed. Help is well organised in the house and on the land, which leaves me free to take up my secretarial career again."

"I heard Edvard was showing signs of improvement when I telephoned Gina one day to inquire after him. I always expected you would go back to Oslo as soon as you had the chance."

"I'd like to, later on. At the present time the city is too unsettled."

He let her remark pass without comment, aware she was referring to the wave after wave of arrests sweeping through the capital. The activities of the Gestapo sickened him. He preferred to ignore the happenings they brought about. "Then we'd better get down to brass tacks and discuss the job I'm offering. What's your shorthand speed these days?"

When the routine questions had been duly asked and answered, he told her what the office hours were and explained how he liked the place run, concluding with an introduction to his filing system. He was impressed by her knowledge of German and could see that she would deal with everything in a competent manner, for it was echoed already in her attitude towards him during the business part of the interview, showing she did not intend to take advantage of the fact that they were distant cousins and bore the same surname. She was by far the best qualified of the interviewees, quite apart from being the best looker, and her attractive appearance would add prestige to his office. There only remained one matter to settle.

"Now, about your brothers," he said heavily, moving his bulk to one side of his chair and playing his fingers on one of the chair-arms.

She realised the moment had come when everything was hanging in the balance, and tightened her hands in her lap. "Yes?"

"They would have been an embarrassment to me if anyone in this place had chosen to link our joint surnames. As it happened, nobody did. I prefer matters to remain that way. Do you understand?"

"Perfectly."

"Then you have no objection to my wish to safeguard

completely my position on all counts, however slight the connection?"

"None at all. I'd be here to do a job to the best of my ability. That's all that would matter to me."

He was satisfied. It was easy to guess that she had private loyalties that were as strong as ever, but she had made it clear that her work would be all-important to her and would be divorced from anything else in her life. It was good enough for him. He was aware that many whom he recruited into work for the Germans did so through the necessity of supporting their families and not through choice, but the end result was the same. So it would be with his new secretary and her eagerness to resume her career. He had decided to appoint her, able to visualise many a mundane task delegated into her capable hands.

"If you should be appointed, would you continue to live at the farm?" He had a good reason for finding out about that. The kernel of an idea was forming at the back of his mind, although it was too early to make any reference to it.

"No, I have an elderly friend in Ålesund, Astrid Larsen, who would be willing to let me have a room and live with her."

"That would be an excellent arrangement." When his own selfish requirements were not to the fore he could be a generous man and he wanted to show Johanna she would lose nothing by her business association with him. "I'm sure you and your parents have been anxious about your brothers. I've heard nothing more about Erik since his disappearance, but I can tell you what has happened to Rolf."

"Where is he?" There was a catch in her throat. "We've heard nothing. All we know is that he's in a camp some-where."

Taking a pair of horn-rimmed spectacles up from the desk, he put them on as he went across to one of the filing cabinets and pulled out a drawer. Taking out a sheaf clipped together, he glanced down the names until he found what he was looking for. "He was taken to Grini after his arrest."

"Grini?" She whitened. It was the concentration camp that struck dread into everyone, for it had become notorious as being the worst camp in the whole country.

"Since then he's been moved to a labour camp near Kirkenes and there he'll stay until the teachers in prison, and out of it, break down this united front against joining the minister-president's Teachers' Nazi Association."

"They won't do that."

"I'm inclined to agree with you." He replaced the sheaf of papers and closed the drawer.

"Why do you have that list?"

"I get copies in a case like this one where a large number of prisoners have been formed into a new labour force. Even though I have nothing to do with the military movement of compulsory labour, I'm kept informed about them." Linking his hands behind his back, he regarded her from over the top of his spectacles from where he stood. "Do you still want to work for me?"

Her head jerked up. "More than ever. I think I'd go mad if I had to return to domestic chores after getting back into an office today."

"Good. Then the job is yours. Can you start on Monday?"

A rush of relief was followed by a heady exultancy. "Yes, Tom. I'll be here."

He saw her to the door and then went to the window to watch her go down the cobbled street. The sentries turned their heads to follow her with their gaze. Not even those stockings could disguise her beautiful legs. The idea that had come into his mind earlier returned to formulate itself a little more.

As Johanna walked through the town bound for the winding road that would take her up to Astrid's house where she would deliver the good news, she did not notice a heavily bearded fisherman turn aside casually to study some deep-sea tackle displayed in a shop window. He watched her reflection go past on the opposite side of the street. Erik, who had landed a fellow countryman, a secret agent, in a neighbouring cove the night before from his "Shetland Bus," wondered where his sister had been and where she was going. She looked well, which was a good sign. Although he had made many trips across the North Sea, this was his first experience of seeing a member of his own family and having to avoid recognition. It had happened to others serving with him, some seeing their own

wives and children and still having to turn away. The rules
laid down were strict. Too many lives were involved and
too much was at stake for the slightest risk to be taken.
Whenever someone had erred, invariably the results had
been tragic, often not because of anybody's wish, only
through a family's natural jubilation at a reunion that could
not be kept secret in a tight-knit community and frequently reaching German ears. Reprisals against local people were savage. The fishing village of Telavågen near
Bergen had been wiped off the map after two Resistance
fighters had been found sheltering there. The villagers saw
their homes burned down, their fishing boats sunk and
their cattle confiscated before they themselves were
carted off, all the men over sixteen to concentration camps
in Germany, all the women and children to labour camps
in Norway. If it had been Karen passing by instead of
Johanna, he would still have kept his face averted.

When evening came he would be sailing back to the
Shetlands with a secret agent going to consult with the
Norwegian Government in London and two people forced
to flee the Nazis. This was his last trip until autumn came
again, for the return of everlasting daylight to the night
hours made it virtually impossible to cross without being
sighted by enemy ships or planes. He ended his apparent
scrutiny of the window's display when his sister's reflection
vanished from the glass.

In the far north the snow retreated daily from the
Kirkenes area to settle in the heights. The hardships of
everyone in the camp had been made worse by the bitter
cold, a torment to the poorly clad, and many were suffering from the after-effects of frostbite. Now the brown
earth, left naked by the snow, was leaping forth in green
growth and tender northern flowers in the full glory of the
arctic spring. Rolf in his patched prison uniform, bearded
and with his hair rough cut, turned his face to the returning sun, absorbing it into himself as those in other
lands rejoice in rain after a lengthy drought. There was
news to cheer him and his colleagues. It had just been
passed to him by a local tradesman delivering goods to the
camp commandant. In the absence of letters, which were
not allowed to be written or received, any scrap of news

from the outside world was welcome and the information given to him would be a tonic to everyone.

He made the announcement in the compound from an upturned crate. All those who were not bedridden through injury or sickness gathered in front of him, looking much like a motley school assembly. Rolf grinned at them, a breeze flicking his shaggy hair.

"My friends! I have great news! Although our imprisonment is to continue, all our colleagues left behind at Grini and other concentration camps are to be released. The majority of teachers in this country are to be allowed to return to their schools, all of which will be reopened after the long closure. Do you realise what this means? Quisling has given in! The official cover-up says there was a general misunderstanding by those in our profession as to what was intended. In other words, the Teachers' Nazi Association is virtually eliminated and the Hitler Youth movement planned for our pupils has fallen through." His voice gained momentum. "We've won our cause!"

There was a tremendous burst of cheering. They clapped each other on the back and shook hands and shouted their jubilation with the sportsmen's fist of victory. Some wept, overcome by knowing that everything they had suffered had brought a reward which at times had seemed as remote as the Holy Grail. All knew that by standing together they had stopped the Nazi advance where it mattered most. If freedom of thought had been broken down, then the whole Resistance movement would have been without a future.

Rolf, who had jumped down from the crate, was joining in the hand-shaking and jubilation. This success would strengthen those in other fields, and the switch in the situation give him more authority as the camp spokesman. He would work now to get the sick released. For the rest of them nothing would be as hard as it had been before.

Chapter 9

It took several days before Johanna became used to her new surroundings. Her desk was in the outer office, which was well appointed with a sizeable window that looked down into the street, boldly patterned curtains and a lacquered floor that shone like a mirror. A cleaning crew of local women kept everything spotless, which was at least in the tradition of all things Scandinavian. There was nothing difficult about her work to make her feel uncomfortable—it was being in close proximity to so many uniformed Germans that she found unnerving. At first she could not get over an instinctive pang of apprehension every time the door opened and a soldier entered. It was the same when she showed her identity card at the entrance each morning. As for the constant barrage of "Heil Hitler" with every coming and going, she thought it was like a form of demonic worship and was thankful that at least her office and Tom's were spared a photograph of the Führer on the wall.

It had not been easy letting her parents know that she was to become Tom's secretary. "I can't stay at home indefinitely," she had replied to her father's strongly voiced objections. "As for working for a collaborator, that is unfortunate, but even people who are not quislings have to answer to the Nazis in some way or other. There's no way of avoiding German authority."

Gina, who had appeared more puzzled than angry, probed her reasons. "You could have gone back to the fur shop."

"Maybe I will, later on. Meanwhile I'll be near at hand if you want me at any time."

Her father had continued to be upset until her mother calmed him down with her reassurances. Not for the first time Johanna thought her mother to be an extraordinarily perceptive woman. There were many parents these days who suspected their adult offspring of being involved with the Resistance and some were equally involved themselves. On the other side there were families unaware that one of their members was working for the Germans. Sometimes when the truth came out it brought about rifts that would never be healed. At least her parents knew that wherever her employment took her and however they might object to it, she would not be influenced by Nazism.

In preparation for whatever might come during her employment, she had devised her own code for recording information that might be of use, keeping a notebook in her purse in which to jot down in shorthand as mundane shopping notes anything of the slightest interest, for she had to be ready for a spot check of her belongings at any time.

She met Gunnar by arrangement to clear all points that had arisen now that she knew the office and its layout. There were to be various signals by which she could let it be known that she had information to pass on, the most sophisticated a coded telephone call, the simplest and safest a stick left in a certain cleft tree.

In the office, she soon saw that Tom's inclination towards an easy life would be to her advantage. Within a couple of weeks of her becoming his secretary, she saw how he was shuffling work over to her that should have been his responsibility. She took it willingly, hoping eventually to glean something of use from much that was mundane and routine. She saw her task as passing on minuscule pieces of a jigsaw puzzle which might or might not prove to be a vital link when the whole picture was put together by Intelligence.

The first time a German officer tried to date her she was not unprepared. She had had attention from all ranks in the corridors and on the stairways from the day she started to work there and since she was there, none of them would suspect she wasn't as much a collaborator as her employer. The lieutenant who strolled into the office was a tall young man who wore his uniform well and knew it, a medal ribbon on his chest for valour in one of the blitzkrieg campaigns. She was typing a letter and had looked up with a faint smile of greeting since he was within her province.

"Guten Tag," she said. "Do you have an appointment with Major Ryen?"

He shook his head, coming to stand in front of her desk. *"Nein, fräulein.* It's you I want to see. I'm in the office on the next floor up. I thought I'd like to introduce myself. I'm Kurt Scheidt. If I may be of assistance to you in any way, please don't hesitate to let me know."

"Well, thank you," she said easily. "I'll remember that."

"Is it correct that you are related to Major Ryen?"

"We're first cousins once removed." She indicated the letter in the typewriter. "I am rather busy at the moment."

"My apologies. Would you be free this evening? There's a dance at the officers' mess in the garrison headquarters and I would very much like to take you there."

"Sorry," she replied brightly. "I have a date already."

"Then tomorrow? There's a hotel that's allowed special catering facilities for officers' entertainment. We could dine there."

The connecting door into the main office opened and Tom came out, large and affable. He did not look anything like a white knight and yet he had come to her rescue, raising his eyebrows inquiringly at the officer as if he had not caught snatches of the conversation through the opaque glass panel. "Ah. Are you waiting to see me, Oberleutenant Scheidt?"

"Er—no, Major. I was talking to Fräulein Ryen."

"Oh, yes?" Tom commented nonchalantly. Turning to Johanna, he pushed back his cuff to study his gold watch. "Better make it a quarter to six instead of six o'clock this evening," he said as if confirming an arrangement with her. "I've two more letters to dictate. Come into the office now."

The lieutenant left and she followed Tom into the office. "I could have managed that myself," she said to him with amusement, "and better than you did."

"I know that, but I don't want you pestered," he replied, sitting down at his desk. "These small fry must be kept at bay."

"What do you mean?" She seated herself in the chair from which she took dictation, her shorthand pad and pencil ready on her knee.

"It's not important now. We'll talk about it another

time." He proceeded with the dictation and she thought
no more about the incident.

On the day that Edvard came downstairs for the first
time it was Karen who guided him. Gina stood waiting at
the foot of the flight. She had long since come to accept
Karen's obsessive care for her husband, understanding its
roots, and it had relieved her of many chores and sleepless
nights. The girl was pink with excitement, her silver-fair
hair caught up in a ribboned topknot that added colour
and gave her the innocent look of a child at a party. She
cajoled Edvard briskly, not diminishing his dignity by her
encouragement.

"That's it. Well done! Now another step. And another."

Gina could have completed the girl's inducements as if
they had been part of a nursery rhyme. Now another step
for Erik. And another for Erik. She supposed everybody
found his own way of getting through the trial of separation, or any other crisis. Karen's was more unusual than
most.

By the end of the week Edvard had progressed to sitting
on the porch in the sunshine. Karen had just seen him into
the house again and had returned to collect a plaid shawl
from the chair when her name was spoken. She turned
around, the shawl in her hands, and caught her breath in
dread. Carl Müller stood on the grassy slope leading up to
the house, feet apart, thumbs in his belt. He was without
his helmet this day, his forage cap at an angle on his dark,
short-cropped head. Her eyes narrowed against the sun.

"How long have you been there?" she exclaimed, re-
vealing involuntarily the anxiety that had seized her.

"Long enough to see that Edvard Ryen is back on his
feet."

"Stop spying on him! It's ghoulish. Why can't you go
away and forget all about us?"

He came slowly across to the stone steps, looking up at
her. "I told you before, I mean nobody here any harm. I
can see for myself that the listed hostage is still convalescent. I didn't take him when he was sick in bed and I'll not
take him while he is still obviously far from well."

She clutched the shawl to her in desperation. "Why do
you have to take him at all?"

"That depends on you. Let's talk about it, shall we?" He held out a hand as if to take hers.

Frightened and distressed, she returned the shawl to the chair and went down the steps. When he offered his hand the last time they met she had ignored it. This time he did not intend to be rejected. He kept his hand thrust out to her like a threat, compelling her to fall in with his wishes, and because she saw this stubborn change of attitude in him, she reluctantly gave him hers. He seized it with pleasure, closing their palms together with fingers linked. Again he exerted his advantage over her when he diverted her steps from the head of the valley where there were no farmsteads.

"We'll go in the other direction today, I think." He was beaming at her. "I'm proud to be seen with you, Karen. I'd like the whole world to know that we're friends."

Her face was stark. "You wanted to talk. I'd like to get it over as quickly as possible."

"There's no hurry. I got a lift on a truck coming to the hamlet and I don't have to go back with it again for a couple of hours. I thought we could have something to eat together in the café by the inlet. I managed to get hold of some civilian ration coupons for you."

"I don't want them!"

"Are there no shortages at Ryen Farm then?"

She halted, jerking her hand from his clasp. "I won't be mocked, bribed or blackmailed into being friendly with you! Say what you have to say and be done with it!"

He realised he had pressured her too hard and too soon. His aim to show his power from the start had misfired. "Calm down," he said affably. "Don't misconstrue everything I say. I'm here for one reason only and I'll be completely honest with you. Seeing you again a while ago meant a great deal to me. I know we've both changed since the days when we were kids and in love. Naturally I don't expect you to feel anything for me from that time, but as the weeks have gone by I haven't been able to stop thinking about you. I'm not claiming anything from the past. I'm just telling you that you've begun to mean something new and important to me." Because there was truth in what he said with regard to his feelings for her, it came through in his voice and in his expression. "If I have to bargain my silence about Edvard Ryen's recovery against your going out with me, I'll do it. Then, with time, I hope you'll come of your own free will."

Dismay spasmed her face. She looked as if she would have run from him if there had been anywhere she might escape the ultimatum he had put to her. He stood watching her, waiting for her to break. Her eyes went dark, reaching sapphire depths, and every vestige of colour drained from her face. Then the moment came. Her gaze shattered as if life had gone from her.

"I'll go out with you." She scarcely recognised the hollow voice as her own.

He was triumphant and full of hope. With time he'd win her around. Once more he held out his hand to her and received her limp fingers fondly. "It will be like it used to be between us before long. We'll both forget differences caused by others. This is the happiest day for me in this country since I was last here."

As they walked down the lane she saw people pause in their work to look towards her in disbelief. They had heard with censure that Johanna had gone to work for a quisling cousin, and now there was a second girl from the same household parading with an enemy soldier.

To Karen the lane had never seemed longer. In the hamlet the same astonished looks followed her. To her relief Carl did not try to push his luck by taking her into the café where other soldiers were to be seen, perhaps because he was not entirely certain yet that she wouldn't bolt from him. Instead he took her to the grassy slope overlooking the fjord. It was the kind of day she loved best, when the balmy air was so still that the water reflected the rising banks of the fjord like a mirror, every house and tree inverted, every rowing boat and anchored fishing boat floating on its own image. They sat down side by side, he with his arms resting on updrawn knees, she with her legs tucked under her. She pulled a buttercup from the grass and twisted it between her fingers, saying nothing. He did all the talking, telling her news from his home and where he had been and what he had done since the time he had last seen her. It was not until she saw he was becoming irritated by her lack of response that she made an effort to overcome her choking despair and began to utter a com-

ment now and again. There was little chance that he
would keep his side of the bargain if he failed to get any
pleasure from her company.

"I don't want anyone else to know about the bond we've
made," he impressed upon her. "Will you promise me
that?"

"I think Gina Ryen will guess."

"Then let her guess, but don't confirm it. This is only an
intermediary time for us, Karen. The day will come when
we'll look back on it and laugh."

She saw he really believed what he was saying. In spite
of what he had said about not expecting her to have retained the love she had had for him in the past, he was
confident that much of what there had been before would
revive to aid the new beginning he had conjured up. She
considered, and rejected, the idea of telling him she was in
love with Erik, who was the indirect cause of their meeting
again in the first place. If he became jealous he might
revert to arresting Edvard. The authority he had gained
since their adolescent days had changed him completely.
She saw him as being dangerously unpredictable.

Fortunately for her they stayed by the fjord too long for
him to have time to walk her home again. She accompanied him to the truck where he climbed in beside the
driver and looped an elbow over the lowered window to
say goodbye to her, his grin happy, his ego boosted by
other soldiers nearby seeing this lovely girl looking up at
him.

"We'll go to the cinema on Friday then. It's a German
film. Plenty of action. *Auf Wiedersehen!*"

When she re-entered the farmhouse Gina was waiting, a
thin hand spread across her chest as though anxiety had
become a physical pain centred there. "Has he come back
for Edvard?"

Karen swallowed. "No. It's my company he wants. I
suppose it's not surprising. We were friends not so long
ago."

Gina stared at her wordlessly, comprehension dawning.
It was as if once again the solid ground shifted beneath her
feet. Her family—and she thought of Karen as a future
daughter-in-law—was disintegrating: her sons scattered,
her daughter employed by a quisling and her husband still

on a knife-edge of life or death, for he could not exist without the necessary medication that would be denied him in a camp. She stood motionless as the desolate girl went past her up the stairs to shut herself away in her room.

Johanna liked living in Astrid's house. They had their meals together, sometimes played cards in the evening and generally shared much of their time. Yet there was a freedom to come and go that made it different from living at home where normal family conditions of farm life almost compelled an accounting of one's time. She was enjoying the same companionship with Astrid that she had known with the Alsteens, whom she often thought about, praying they had made the last few kilometres into Sweden, particularly since it had become apparent that the Nazis intended to remove every Jew from Norway into the concentration camps in Poland and Germany. Many had been shipped out already and protests from the Church had been ignored, one of the factors that had led to the clergy's final break with the Quisling government. The only good news regarding prisoners was that the sick among the teachers still held captive in the Arctic were being allowed to come home. Rolf was not among them, which at least meant he was well.

Her bedroom on the upper floor was little more than a box-room. Astrid had taken out the items stored there from the commandeered part of the house to let Johanna have whatever space was available. Its size did not bother her, for the window gave light and air as well as a view out over the sea where the distant islands lay like half-submerged giants and from where a Viking warrior had once left to found a dynasty in Normandy. It was lucky she was a good sleeper, for at times the noises from the neighbouring room on the other side of the division would have disturbed her rest. Astrid, who slept lightly and had been subjected to the indignity of this intrusion upon her hearing since the violation of her home, had somehow made herself deaf to it all. It was only when a party was in progress that she sometimes paled at the drunken roistering that penetrated the walls.

"I don't care what goes on in there," she stated with

dignity, twisting her graceful hands together. "That's their
business. It's my dear house I worry about. I'm afraid it will
never be the same."

Johanna was sympathetic. She did not think it would be.
"We can be thankful that this part of it has escaped damage."

"I console myself with that thought." Astrid moved
about her beautiful room like an exotic goldfish in her
floating silk skirt, touching her treasures with delicate fingertips, her gaze lingering on her Munch paintings.

In spite of Tom's inherent laziness, Johanna found him
an easy man to work for, he being thoroughly even-tempered and jovial. It was rare for him to be out of sorts with
anyone. He liked the good things of life, but whereas Astrid appreciated the aesthetic side, his taste was more basic. He was subject to the authority of the German gauleiter, who occupied a suite of offices in another building,
and every now and again he had to report there on various
matters. Johanna typed all the material to be discussed and
felt she had her finger on everything that was going in and
out of the office. Whenever she came across an item she
thought would be of use to the Resistance, she made contact and delivered what she had noted at the appointed
time and place. Gunnar was the one she met, Steffen being
absent again. The Resistance was still suffering from being
decimated by the Gestapo some months before, and those
leaders who were free and active were shouldering far
more than they would otherwise have been expected to
do. Venues for meeting Gunnar, and occasionally Steffen,
were changed constantly, varying from a cellar to crowded
cafés and to the cabin by the lake, the place where Delia
had landed by parachute. There was a specially coded
message for when she had something of urgent importance in hand. As yet she had had no cause to use it.

After a few weeks Johanna went home for a weekend. It
was harvest time and as she walked up the lane with an
overnight bag slung over one shoulder everyone was busy
in the fields, the valley having a rich look as if the corn had
absorbed the colour of the sun itself. At the first farmstead
she had waved to those she knew there. When there was
no answering wave she thought they were too busy and
slightly too far away to have spotted her. When the same

thing happened at the next farmstead on the other side of the lane, she felt the first chill of ostracism reach her. It was the only time in her life that she had walked the paths of home without a friendly word or a smile from someone. Neighbours she had visited since childhood, almost as one of the family, did not appear to see her go by. Some of Rolf's pupils, climbing over a stationary wagon, silenced a younger child who answered her greeting. When she had gone past, one of the boys sprang down to shout after her, "We don't want collaborators here in Ryendal!"

So that was it. Everybody knew now that she was working at the German headquarters and had drawn their own conclusions. She did not blame them. Their hostility was hard to bear and it would get worse as time went on. As she continued up the lane she sensed cold stares, and when she passed the schoolhouse where another teacher had been appointed in Rolf's enforced absence, she guessed that the fact she had two brothers who had risked their lives for freedom made all in the valley more bitter towards her.

Edvard, leaning heavily on his walking-stick, came unaided onto the porch to meet her. She flew up the steps and they hugged each other. "You're looking so well!" she exclaimed, standing back as she held him by the arms. His face, weathered over the years, had had its tan revived by hours of sitting in the sun, giving him a far healthier look than his general condition warranted.

"Only through being lazy, I'm afraid. As yet I can only do some paperwork. Your mother runs everything like clockwork, and young Karen is her right hand." He moved with some difficulty to sink down weakly on the slatted porch seat, and she sat beside him. "That doesn't mean things are fine here. Far from it." After the initial pleasure of seeing her again he was becoming once again the querulous convalescent, which her mother had warned her about on the telephone. "I should be out in the fields, not skulking here uselessly. Your mother is out there in my place, and as if that were not enough a German is helping to bring in the harvest. My harvest!" He thumped his chest in outrage. "I've forbidden it, but neither she nor Karen will listen to me."

Johanna raised her eyebrows. "I didn't know about that. Is it the sergeant Karen knew in her schooldays?"

"That's him. They're walking out together—have been all the summer. I always thought she and Erik would make a match of it one day, but that's gone by the board." He shook his head irritably. "It's come to a poor state of affairs when a young woman can't keep true any more. When I was young the women waited years while their men established themselves in America before sending for them, and there was never a case of one breaking faith."

She turned her head to look down the valley. "I had a cold reception on my way up here. Now I know why. Karen has been stamped as a collaborator, too. I can see it hasn't been easy for you and Mother to have two of the household tainted in everyone's eyes."

"It damn well isn't," he agreed forcibly, "particularly when you could give up your job tomorrow and Karen has the power to send that German packing."

She could see there was going to be a strain throughout the weekend. As she stood up she patted his shoulder, almost in a reflex action of reassurance, trusting it would be hint enough that she had good reason. Maybe Karen had an equal cause. "I think I'll change my clothes and go out into the fields to give a hand."

Edvard attempted to shake off his angry despondency. "Try to make your mother and Karen see sense about letting an enemy onto my land. Apart from my personal feelings about it, there's the danger involved that if he should suspect I've more cattle and sheep in the high pastures than I've listed, then the whole farm could be confiscated."

"I should think they're being very wary. Don't worry. I'll talk to them both later."

In her room she found a thin cotton dress in the clothes closet and put it on. From a drawer she took a flowered kerchief and put it over her hair to keep out the corn dust, knotting it at the back of her neck. Downstairs again, she went out the back door to avoid a further confrontation with her father and set off across the bridged stream to where she could see the others working. On the way she passed a German army jacket hanging on a post, and with the forage cap stuck on the top it looked like a curious scarecrow. It was the third harvest of the Occupation—to which there was no end in sight. She wondered how many

more summers must go by before those uniforms were
swept into the sea.

Drawing near, she saw Carl Müller in his shirtsleeves
working at a fast pace, taking sheaves from the ropes on
which they had dried and tossing them into the wagon
where a hired hand was stacking it. Karen and Gina were
wielding rakes over the ground, drawing together the
dropped and scattered blades in a gleaning against the
winter ahead. They all looked in her direction and greeted
her as she came within hailing distance. Only Carl paused
in his work, wiping his brow with his forearm, his hair
fronded by sweat. He looked totally happy and appeared
to be as much at home as if he had been born amid the
peaks and crags that soared up around him on all sides.

"We meet again," he said amiably to her, leaning on his
pitchfork. "I've made myself one of the work force."

"So I heard from my father." She noticed Gina avert her
eyes and seemingly concentrate even more on the task in
hand.

Over the weekend Johanna had plenty of chances to
assess the situation. Karen had changed more than anyone.
She had lost weight and there was a brittle look to her as if
she might easily snap. Outwardly, at least, she was her
usual calm and gentle self, helpful and capable and quick
to run any errand for Edvard, who once again sat for meals
in his place at the head of the table. On Saturday evening,
Carl returned to take Karen to a dance somewhere. She
left the house in a light-coloured dress, almost sprite-like
with her pale hair aswirl and her bone-slim figure. From
the window Johanna saw Carl put his arm around her waist
possessively. Karen neither responded nor drew away. She
seemed resigned.

Johanna turned away from the window, pushing her
hands into the pockets of her skirt. "Why do you allow that
sergeant to come here?" she asked Gina, who was darning
a sock on a wooden mushroom. Edvard had fallen asleep
while reading a newspaper and was breathing heavily, his
head back against a velvet cushion.

Her mother did not look up. "He doesn't come into the
house."

"That's not the point. You must be inviting trouble from
friends and neighbours by appearing to condone the liai-

son. I've discovered I'm out of favour with them, but at least you can't be blamed for the work I do away from here."

"We've been asked to send Karen back to her own village. I told them our home is her home for as long as she pleases."

"I'm glad to hear it." Johanna perched on the arm of a chair, looking at her mother's head bent over the darning. "What is this collusion between you and Karen? You're in it together, I can tell. What hold has that German gained over the two of you?"

Gina dropped the darning into her lap, her startled eyes meeting her daughter's gaze. Quickly she glanced in her husband's direction to make sure he was still sleeping and had not overheard. Then she straightened her back, once more in control of herself. "I can honestly say that Karen and I have not discussed the matter at all. There's no need. Her poor little face gave her away after she had spoken to Sergeant Müller the day he returned. In exchange for her friendship he's prepared to keep word of your father's recovery from the military authorities."

"Oh, my God!" Johanna's whispered exclamation sprang from the depth of her compassion for Karen, not through consideration for the sleeper in the room. "Father doesn't know that? Why haven't you told him?"

"He might do something foolish."

"Give himself up, you mean?"

"I prefer not to think about it." Gina squared her shoulders as if there were an almost unbearably heavy yoke across them, her face hardening until the skin strained over her cheekbones. "Karen's virtue is expendable. Your father's life is not."

Johanna was at a loss for words. There seemed nothing to say in reply to the primly expressed and utterly ruthless statement that had been made.

When Karen returned from the dance in the early hours, she found Johanna waiting up in Chinese cotton pyjamas, the faded rose colour showing that they had been bought in pre-war days. "Why aren't you sleeping? It's late."

"I wanted to talk to you. Let's sit outside."

They went out to the slatted seat where earlier that day

Johanna had sat beside Edvard, the only perpetual sound that of the cascading waterfall. Karen sank back on the seat wearily. "I suppose you've guessed."

"It wasn't difficult. We're all in your debt—my parents, my brothers and I."

Karen's voice was without expression. "I don't want anyone's gratitude. Carl is not Hitler. Underneath his Nazism there are still traces of the boy I once knew, and at times I manage to forget his uniform. It could have been worse. Much worse. I let him kiss me. I even let him fondle me since he seems to consider that's a fair part of the bargain." She appeared quite detached from what she was relating, as if she had found a means of shutting herself away in her own mind from it all. "That's as far as it's gone between us. He cares for me—not seriously, but enough to hope that with time we'll mean more to each other. I also feel sorry for him. The war has made as much of a mess of his life as it has of mine, except that he doesn't realise it."

"Is there any chance of his being posted to northern or southern Norway—anywhere away from here?"

"Not at the present time. Anyway, I'm glad you know the truth of it. I couldn't talk to anyone else as I'm talking to you. I love your younger brother. I'll always love Erik. I'm waiting for him to come back. If he loves me as I love him he won't listen to others. The chance that he might turn against me doesn't make any difference. Edvard is not going to be taken as a hostage as long as I can prevent it."

For the first time Johanna saw that, in some ways, her mother and Karen were much alike. In spite of their frail, almost delicate appearance, each was possessed of an intractable will and out of it came their strength.

It was a relief when the weekend was over. Gina, perhaps fearful that a slip of the tongue from Johanna might give Edvard an inkling of the true situation, was edgy and sharp-tongued, sparing nobody. As Johanna left she decided it would be a long time before she came home again. A weekly telephone call would have to suffice.

"How did you enjoy your weekend?" Tom asked her on Monday morning.

"Not much," she replied, seizing the chance he had given her. "Thanks to you I'm in everybody's bad books."

"What do you mean?"

She told him of the hostility she had encountered in the valley and of her own parents' attitude towards her without giving any background details beyond her position as his secretary being unpopular. For some time she had thought it would be prudent to ensure that if she was arrested at any time, Tom could report there was an estrangement between her family and her, which should absolve them from any suspicion. She had not expected to have some minor family friction on which to base the exaggerated estrangement, and that was all to the good.

"So you won't be going home for a while?" He was facing her across his desk and the letters from the morning mail she had put in front of him.

"That's right."

"Sit down a moment."

She obeyed, wondering what was coming. Always spruce in his appearance, he smoothed his already smooth hair back over his ears with the palms of his hands and then cleared his throat. "There's something I've been mulling over for quite a while. Well, ever since you came to work for me, in fact. I'd like you to hear me out before you give a decision either way on what I'm about to put to you."

"I'm listening." She was puzzled.

"I've put aside my employer's hat now and I'm speaking to you as family and as a friend. You remember my wife, don't you? After all, you must have been twelve or thirteen when she died ten years ago."

"I was thirteen and I remember Ingrid well. She was so vivacious, always fun to be with. Naturally we didn't see her often."

"That's just how she was. A wonderful hostess at the parties we used to give. I still miss her, particularly out at my home when I entertain at weekends. Would you be prepared to act as my hostess? You're young and beautiful and it would make all the difference to my guests to have you there. You'd not be bothered by any of them, I promise you. You'd be under my cousinly wing, as the saying goes. I'd make that clear."

She had heard that he entertained high-ranking Nazi personnel and her first reaction would have been to give an outright refusal if she had not remembered in the nick of time what it might lead to on behalf of the Resistance.

Deliberately she played for time, wanting to be entirely sure of the situation. "I'm not certain I understand about the cousinly wing. Are you saying you would let your guests think there was something between us in order to give me protection?"

"Something like that."

She laughed protestingly. "Tom! You're remarkably old-fashioned. I haven't come straight from the farm. I did work in Oslo and I can look after myself."

"As you wish." His smile was amused and indulgent. "It's simply that I have your well-being at heart. I spoke from the highest motives, I do assure you."

"I didn't think otherwise. What would you want me to do? Arrange menus? Organise your household? Book a band for dancing? I'm sure you have a list of women to invite when the occasion demands."

His eyes narrowed between his sandy lashes. "You have the hang of it exactly. An excellent housekeeper, whom I'd had since Ingrid's last illness, left as soon as German officers began coming to the house. Her replacement has been far from satisfactory. You could reorganise everything and appoint whom you liked."

"Give me a few days to think it over." She needed to consult the Resistance.

"Naturally." He appeared to think that he must add extra inducements. "I'd see my way clear to let you have time off whenever you needed it. We'd arrange the work to let you leave early when necessary. Sometimes there's only one or two officers at the weekends. At others a whole crowd will come for a party."

She shook her head firmly. "You mustn't get the idea I'd be prepared to get caught up in your domestic arrangements on a grand scale. I'm a secretary first and foremost, but as your cousin I'd get the house in running order for you and then things would go smoothly anyway. Once that was done, I'd only be at the house for social occasions."

He was satisfied, convinced that what he wanted of her was as good as accepted. There had not been a day yet when he hadn't been pleased with her secretarial work and attractive appearance. Moreover, from the moment the weather had permitted, her beautifully tanned legs had come bare of all hideous coverings, adding to her

charming appearance. He was always being asked about
her by the officers in the building, for she had not been
many weeks in his office before she gained a reputation of
being impossible to date. One or two had even become a
trifle too curious, not exactly suspecting her of being disloyal to the Third Reich, but wanting to know about her
background to a degree that he did not welcome since his
own was linked to hers. To bring her into his social life
would quash any speculations about her. "It's going to do a
lot for me if you will do all this." He chose to become more
confidential. "I'll tell you now that you'd be helping me
towards a special goal. I hope to get into government eventually. That's why the contacts I make now will be exceptionally useful later on."

"But you'd have to join Quisling's Nazi party for that,"
she said without thinking. Then she realised instantly from
the way he was regarding her that he was already a member and she was angry with herself. It showed her how she
had been lulled into forgetting briefly that in spite of their
thoroughly agreeable business partnership, he was totally
linked to the enemy.

"I joined when I put my old life behind me," he said with
a shrug of his thick shoulders. "That's how I got the position I hold here. It wouldn't have been mine otherwise. I'll
not press you towards membership yet, because my guess
is that you're not quite ready. I understand the pull of old
loyalties, because I went through all that myself." He felt
he was cementing the goodwill between them as never
before. "It's good that we can be frank like this with each
other. I want you to stick with me, Johanna. You could
move to Oslo with me later on. How would you like to be
secretary to Quisling's successor at some time in the future?"

She managed a little laugh. "Ask me again at a later date.
I think you have a long way to go yet."

"I have indeed." He had one more thing to ask her and
gestured her to remain seated when she would have made
a return to work. "I'd appreciate it very much if you would
accompany me to a party in the officers' mess this evening.
We need only make a brief appearance, staying for about
an hour or two, but it would be a beginning for occasions to

come. You see, it has been noticed that you definitely discourage German company."

She was startled, realising her blunder. That was an aspect of her position she had not considered. Her smile came as quickly as her answer. "I'm choosy, Tom. I don't go out with small fry."

He chuckled at the echo of his own words. "Wise girl. Then you'll come with me this evening? Good." He made the arrangements about picking her up in the car.

Back at her desk, she gazed unseeingly at her typewriter and released a long breath. Things were starting to move at a fast pace and in a direction she had not anticipated.

Astrid, who never showed surprise at anything, taking events completely in her stride, asked the vital question. "What are you going to wear?"

"That's the problem. Tom said the women dress up and the only evening wear I've ever possessed was left behind in Oslo. I'll have to do what I can with a white dress and a spray of roses from the garden."

"I think I may be able to help you. Let's go to my bedroom."

Johanna followed her upstairs. Astrid opened the door of a clothes closet and rummaged towards the back of it. "You may find something here." She pulled forward the skirts of several evening dresses in shades of coral and pink and grey and green, threads of silver shining and gold beadwork glistening. "What about these? They should fit you and we're both about the same beanpole height."

"They look fantastic. Let me try them on." Johanna was already pulling off her dress over her head. Astrid took out a dozen evening dresses from a larger number in the closet. Each one was in a cotton cover that fastened with snaps and all were immaculate. She uncovered chiffon, crêpe de Chine, georgette, raw silk and metallic fabrics. "Clothes have always been my extravagance," she admitted, "and until the Occupation I went regularly to Oslo and Bergen, attending the theatre and banquets held by a number of associations to which I belonged."

Johanna could easily have decided to wear the first one she put on, but the excitement of seeing so many pretty gowns after three years of deprivation was intoxicating. She paraded in each one as though she were modelling along a catwalk in a Parisian *haute couture* salon. Astrid, sitting on the side of the bed, applauded like a potential customer. They thoroughly enjoyed themselves and it was only lack of time that prevented Johanna from going through the whole of Astrid's collection.

Tom drew up outside the house on time. He had, on occasion, attended parties in the commandeered section and was familiar with the address. He got out of the car and had reached the gate when Johanna came down the path from the side entrance, having glimpsed his arrival. Afterwards he thought that if he had been a youth again he would have gaped at the delicious sight of his cousin. She was wearing a simple but superbly cut dress of crêpe de Chine in a colour that reminded him of cool, ripe pears and which showed off her slender, small-breasted figure. Her hair, newly washed, swung like golden silk and was fastened back at the right temple by an ivory barrette. She wore no jewellery and carried a filmy shawl that trailed from one hand.

"Hello, Tom. I knew you'd be punctual. Is this your car? Splendid, isn't it?"

He dashed to open the door for her and she slid into the seat. As yet he had said nothing to her. Getting in behind the wheel he found his voice. "It's a nice evening."

"Grand."

As he reversed and drove back towards the road, he anticipated the effect she would have on the gathering they were to attend. A broad grin spread across his face.

The party was being held at the headquarters of the garrison, a large mansion on the outskirts of the town. Johanna paused with Tom on the threshold of the long room where once civic occasions had taken place. The buzz of cheerful sounds, the clink of glasses being refilled by white-coated stewards and the background music supplied by army musicians on a dais, accordions predominating, did nothing to quell the surge of revulsion that rose within her. She thought she had become accustomed in her comings and goings in the office to the ever-present uniforms and swastika flags, but somehow in a festive setting she was seeing those gathered there with fresh eyes and renewed fury at their uninvited and unwanted presence in her land. As a result her expression closed, giving her an unconsciously distant look that in no way detracted from her allure to those who turned their heads and saw her standing there.

As the first of the officers broke away to come forward, she thought ironically of the praise Astrid had given her appearance. "You look fine enough to meet the King, Johanna."

She had replied, laughing and appreciative, "I wish that were possible. And I mean here, with the Germans gone forever."

Now she was about to meet a captain of the Waffen S.S. She had already spotted several others in the same field-grey uniform with the blue-green collars in the room. As he bowed to her, clicking his heels, one part of her mind snapped into the query as to why a crack regiment had been posted to the coastal region of an annexed territory when they were surely most needed at the Russian Front. She accounted it later as a life-saving thought, for it enabled her to raise her face with a dazzling smile. His own showed extremely good teeth.

"Fräulein. Such a pleasure. What may I get you to drink? Would you like to dance?"

She danced with many of them, sharing her smiles among them. Deliberately she displayed no interest in discussing anything remotely connected with the Wehrmacht, changing the subject if any one of her partners brought in any reference to his routine, however mundane. She knew that an important rule laid down to men in the Resistance, apart from remaining inconspicuous at all times and never contacting their families, was never to trust women they did not know. It seemed a likely guess that officers of the Wehrmacht had been given the same warning. It was her hope that she could establish herself as part of Tom's social circle to the point where conversations would be carried on without any special thought to her being present. She did not expect to unravel any great military secrets, but she did hope to add to the pieces of the jigsaw puzzle that she was able to pass on from her office papers.

Tom knew several of the other women at the party, but he did not dance, preferring to concentrate on the amount of liquor available and in talking affably to those he knew, or those whom he wanted to know better. When supper was served he sought out Johanna, wanting to make sure she was all right and not bored. She was no ordinary girl to be excited and swayed by attention. Sometimes he felt she saw through him with a devastating clarity, although if that was the case she would also discern that he had never been proud of the switch he had made.

He found her in a group of officers who were slightly drunk, highly merry and showing off boisterously in a preening way like the young cockerels they were. Although she was laughing at some quip, he saw an unmistakable flicker of relief in her eyes at his approach.

"I thought it must be time to leave, Tom." She had given him no chance to suggest supper. "I have my shawl. Good night, everybody."

The young officers were reluctant to let her go, spreading their arms and jostling each other in noisy, good-humoured horseplay. She was amused but determined. She slid her hand firmly into the crook of Tom's arm and half steered him out of the room. "Aren't you hungry?" he asked her, thinking with regret of the supper table he had glimpsed through open double doors in an adjoining room. There had been cold roast pork and pink ham and red cabbage and salami and apple strudel among dishes of other good victuals.

"I had a bite with Astrid before I came." The sight of the table had sickened her; that abundance of food had shocked her more than being plunged into that unrelieved mass of enemy uniforms. She thought of the hours her own people spent in food queues for almost nothing. Astrid never complained, except in a joking way, and yet was often exhausted by it, frequently reaching a shop door after a long wait as the last loaf or scrap of meat was sold. The most galling sight on the supper table had been a centrepiece of an enormous bowl of oranges. Norwegian children had forgotten the taste of an orange, and some born after the invasion had never known it. She halted abruptly as she and Tom were about to go down the steps of the building into the courtyard. "I would like one of those oranges." She had thought of a youthful recipient.

"I'll get you a couple," he said at once.

Her request saved his life and hers. As he turned back

into the mansion she followed to wait in the hallway, and in the same instant an enormous explosion split the air as an ammunition dump went sky-high. The blast swept across the courtyard, killing the sentries and lifting the parked cars like toys to hurl them into an untidy mass of wreckage. Windows disintegrated as Johanna and Tom were thrown down across the hall floor that heaved under them, while overhead the wooden balusters of the gallery gave way, falling in a chain reaction like hurled ninepins. A mirror smashed down from the wall, its glittering shards missing Johanna's face by a hair's breadth as she lay sprawled on the stairs where she had landed. There were shouts and running feet and screams from the women left floundering in the shattered remains of the party. The air smelt of dust and cordite, acrid in the throat and nostrils.

"Johanna! Are you all right?" Tom's voice was no more than a croak.

Dazedly she lifted her head. "I think so." Awkwardly she sat up and then saw that he, leaning over her, had blood running down the side of his face. "You're hurt!"

"I think one of the balusters grazed me. It's nothing to worry about. Here. Let me give you a hand. We'll go and see if there's anything we can do to help." He pulled her to her feet. Together they stepped over the debris and went back into the officers' mess. The place was wrecked and there were several casualties. One of the women was hysterical but unharmed; Johanna silenced her with a hard slap and then went to assist Tom. She had some knowledge of first aid and he was thoroughly experienced. Individually they stemmed serious blood flows until stretcher bearers took charge and the medical officer appeared. He had been asleep in bed and arrived with a white coat thrown over his pyjamas, his hair on end. Tom found an unbroken bottle of cognac and gave it to Johanna to swig.

"That's Napoleon brandy," she gulped breathlessly, handing it back to him.

"Trust me to find the best." Grinning, he began handing it around to the minor casualties who were on their feet again, suffering more from shock than from their cuts and grazes.

When there was nothing more they could do, he steered her by the elbow back through the rubble into the open

air. A black cloud of smoke had risen high into the air and
blotted out the stars almost as far as the eye could see.
Soldiers were running purposefully in various directions
and yet gave the impression of still greater confusion.
Whistles were being blown and orders shouted. Tom took
one look at the mangled wreckage of his car.

"It's a long walk home. We had better get started."

It did not suit Tom's bulk to walk, especially as the road
had a steep gradient before dipping down again. Johanna
had lost a shoe in the explosion and walked barefoot on the
grass verge. There were soldiers everywhere, put on an
alert by the act of sabotage, and identity cards were demanded at the checkpoints. Tom's Nazi party membership
card and their bedraggled appearance as survivors of the
blast let them through without too much questioning. He
saw her to the foot of the winding road leading up to
Astrid's house. Just as she was about to leave, he dived a
hand into his pocket and drew out an orange.

"The supper table was a shambles. I managed to find this
one without any glass in it when I got hold of the brandy."

"Oh, Tom." She took it from him, wondering how he
could be such a mixture of what she liked and what she
abhorred. "Thanks for remembering."

Slowly she followed the winding road, holding up the
orange to inhale its aromatic perfume as though it were a
pomander. At the house she let herself in. The landing
light was on and Astrid's shadow heeded her arrival on the
stairs in a silk dressing-gown.

"You have to go straight to the cellar, Johanna," she
whispered. Then she gasped when she saw the girl's bedraggled appearance in a patch of light, the torn evening
dress, the lack of shoes and the upturned face streaked
with dirt. "Were you near the explosion I heard?"

Johanna nodded wearily. Reaction was setting in and
suddenly she felt exhausted. "I have an orange for the
neighbour's boy," she said, putting it aside, "and I'm afraid
your lovely dress is ruined."

"Nothing matters as long as you're unharmed. Go to the
cellar now and tell me what happened in the morning. You
look ready to drop."

"Who's in the cellar. Do you know?"

"It was Gunnar who asked for you. I don't know if anyone else is with him."

Suppressing a sigh, she made her way through the stairway door and tapped the signal on the panel. Until it slid back for her from the inside, she had never realised that animosity and suspicion had its own animal smell. It seemed to engulf her as she was seized roughly on either side and borne forward into the beam of a flashlight shining into her face, her feet not touching the ground. As she shouted a protest she was thrust unceremoniously into a chair. Gunnar's voice burst wrathfully from the darkness behind the circle of light.

"Where the hell have you been? You've kept us waiting."

She answered him in the same fierce tone, blinking against the glare. "Dancing with the Wehrmacht on behalf of the Resistance, almost getting killed by an explosion ignited by my own side in the conflict, and walking barefoot all the way home. Is that reason enough for being late? Especially when I didn't know you'd be here. Who else is with you?" She tried to shade her eyes and found it impossible to detect anything beyond the white eye of the flashlight.

"What double game are you playing? You were planted in Ryen's office to seek out information, not to fraternise. It was your being sighted in his car this evening and again going into the garrison headquarters that sparked off this long overdue investigation."

Foreboding suddenly gripped her. "Investigation?"

"We want the truth out of you and we're going to get it!"

It did not seem possible to her that this could be happening. Too late she remembered her instructions never to make a move on her own initiative outside her allotted realm unless her life or those of her fellow Resistance fighters were in danger. Her role was a sedentary one, no less valuable in its own way, but to emerge from it without notifying anybody had been sheer thoughtlessness on her part. The Resistance was in a hypersensitive state, having suffered too much from informers and double agents, and its position had never been more precarious. The seriousness of her situation was acute.

"I'll tell you how it happened." She attempted to shade

her eyes from the light with her forearm only to have it jerked down to her side and her face pulled upwards again by a tug on her hair. "Maybe I shouldn't have gone to the enemy headquarters this evening without getting it okayed. It was thrust on me. It appears that I've refused dates with the Germans too often. Tom hinted that doubts were starting as to whether I was the right person for his office."

She could hear the faint echo of her own voice bouncing back in the same quiet, constrained tones from the stone walls. Although she could not see anybody or anything in the beam directed into her eyes, she sensed that several men were present, some seated at the table on either side of Gunnar and more lounging in the blackness. She guessed they had been involved in the night's great coup and were taking shelter from the hunt that was on for them after this latest act of sabotage. There would be those among them prepared to silence her permanently if she failed to convince her interrogator that she was innocent of their suspicions.

When her explanations came to an end, Gunnar's questions came at her in a barrage. "Is it not true that when you were taken in for questioning in Oslo you were released almost at once? Is that when your sympathies for the enemy were first enlisted? Freedom in exchange for collaboration? Is it not strange that German intervention should have prevented the arrest of your father? Who put you up to the story you've just given us?"

Her horror of the situation grew with every passing minute and yet she kept her head, thinking carefully before she gave back her answers, determined not to be unnerved or inadvertently tricked into words that could be misinterpreted. As her ordeal continued she became more and more exhausted, keeping her head up with physical difficulty, only a very real fear keeping a yearning for sleep at bay. She was allowed no respite. A sip of water would have helped her dry throat, which had been affected by the dust from the blast, but since it was not offered she would not ask for it. Still the questions came.

"No! Tom did not speak to me of collaboration when we met on the fjord steamship. I can't remember what we talked about."

"Don't make that excuse. He invited you to his office, didn't he?"

"No! If he had, I might well have agreed to go because I didn't know then that he was working for the Nazis."

"I accuse you of working it out with Ryen how much useless information should be filtered through to us."

She had had the fingers of both hands pressed to her temples to support her head and aid her thoughts. Now she raised her face again and lowered her hands to her lap. Her voice, rasping from its dryness, came with renewed force from her throat, her eyes hard and glittering with triumph in the harsh light. "I've just recalled an item of that so-called useless information that I handed on to you, Gunnar. I didn't realise its significance at the time, but I do now. If it hadn't been for me none of you here tonight would have known that the Germans planned to shift the bulk of that ammunition north to Narvik in two days' time. Some of the German-conscripted labour force was to be involved in the loading."

She felt the atmosphere change. There was movement as people stirred; the interrogation was at an end. Gunnar's voice spoke to her on an entirely different note.

"Some of us knew that and some of us didn't. It makes a fitting end to this investigation. You acquitted yourself well. Stay where you are in that chair for the moment. People you don't know will be leaving now." He had averted the flashlight beam from her and if she had had the strength to look up she might have seen their shadowy shapes leaving the cellar. Instead she slumped forward where she sat, completely exhausted, her head down. Gunnar came round the table and touched her on the shoulder. She did not move.

"There's a new ruling from the Resistance. If you are arrested, try to hold back the names of those known to you for twenty-four hours. More can't be expected of anyone under the kind of torture the Gestapo has introduced. It would give everybody else the chance to go into hiding."

"I'll remember," she promised.

"How are you feeling? Everyone could see when you arrived that you'd already been through one ordeal. It made your resilience under my questioning all the more commendable. You've dispelled the doubts of those who had speculated whether you could stand up to Gestapo interrogation."

"I'm relieved to hear it. I wouldn't want you to put me through that again." She did not seem able to move as yet. "Did you know the Waffen S.S. is in the district?"

"We know. They're part of new reinforcements in transit. The Third Reich is anticipating an Allied invasion in northern Norway."

"Do you think it's likely?"

"It's what we're all hoping for. The explosion tonight served a double purpose. It hid the amount of arms we were able to get out for ourselves and destroyed the rest. Now sleep well when you get to bed. You've earned a good rest."

She heard him speak to someone before leaving in the wake of the others, taking the flashlight with him. A match scratched and the lamp on the table was lit, its glow reaching beyond its globe to where she sat. She thought that at least two hours must have gone by since she was pushed into the chair. Wearily she straightened her back and drew her heels together in preparation for rising to her feet. Only then did she raise her head and see Steffen standing on the opposite side of the table, his eyes on her solicitously, the planes of his face highlighted by the lamp. With a sharp intake of breath she clenched her fists and sprang hotly to her feet, her expression contorted.

"You! Here! And you didn't speak up once for me!" She seized the edge of the table and tilted it hard against him, forgetting the lamp, which smashed to the floor and went out, plunging the cellar into inky blackness. She swung blindly in the direction of the panel, trying to locate the steps up to it. Before she could discover them a match flared long enough for Steffen to sight her. She saw the flight and rushed to reach it. As the blackness returned he grabbed her and she struggled violently against him.

"I did speak for you," he gasped, tightening his hold, "before you came. Gunnar had no doubts about you, but he had to go through with it. How do you think I felt when I heard you had been in the headquarters when the explosion took place? You could have been killed. Stop fighting me!"

He found her mouth and her response was avid and wild

until she found the strength to break loose from him. "Light a match," she demanded furiously, her face turned resolutely away from him in the blackness. "I will go from here."

With reluctance he felt in his pocket for a box of matches and struck one. The lamp was almost at his feet and he thought the wick looked undamaged in spite of the smashed glass. The watery light of the flickering flame illumined the main section of the cellar as he carried the lamp to the table, which he set back on its legs again. She stayed propped against the wall, slumped forward with her hands resting on her knees like a sprinter at the end of a race, drawing in breath. Tiredness had caught up with her. Wearily she raised herself up again, letting her head rest once more against the wall and closing her eyes in exhaustion. With effort she swung herself towards the steps and began to mount them slowly. She did not know he had come to the side of the flight until he grabbed her by the hips to swivel her around and press his face against her flat stomach, crushing her to him by the buttocks.

"When are you going to realise that you mean more to me than life?" His voice was hoarse and muffled, his fervent breath warm through the thin fabric that covered her. "Let me share your bed tonight. Don't turn away from me now."

She looked down at him almost in bewilderment, still dazed by all that had happened in the past hours, and unaccountably she experienced a wrenching pang of loneliness, as if given a glimpse of how life would be without him. Her hands hovered like pale birds in the curious light for a few moments about his head before she buried her fingers in his thick hair and pressed him to her with a cry that was close to pain.

He reached up his arms, raising his face to look into hers, and took her by the waist to slide her down into his embrace.

Chapter 10

When Johanna reached her place of work at her usual time, her identity card and her special pass for admission to a military building were checked and double-checked. There were even army dog-handlers by the doorway with the savage brutes used in hunting down escapees and often to guard property. They were kept in cages in a side courtyard when not on duty, showing their fangs and leaping ferociously at the bars whenever anybody came near. Giving a pair of them a wide berth, even though they were on chains, she entered the hallway and, going up the stairs as usual, she found plenty of activity going on, with men of all ranks coming and going. The previous night's act of sabotage appeared to have stirred them up like a stick in a hornets' nest. She realised she would have to be extra cautious for a while, for at times she had risked taking out actual copies of papers she had thought might be of interest to the Resistance.

Sitting down at her desk, she glanced at the mail and then put it aside. Tom was late and she was glad of the delay, appreciating a few quiet minutes to herself in which to think over everything that had happened since she had left her desk yesterday morning. It took a little while before she began work.

She paused in her typing when Tom arrived. He had the buoyant tread common to many overweight men, which somehow added to his air of geniality. There was a wad of dressing secured to his head by a bandage about which he appeared to be somewhat self-conscious. "The gash was a bit worse than I realised. I had to have some stitches put in it this morning at the hospital before coming here. You look fine. Fresh as paint. Not at all as if you had been through a bomb blast experience last night."

"I have your mail ready," she said, gathering it up.

* * *

It was over a month before Tom received a replacement
car. He could have had his choice of several offered to him,
but he rejected each one, determined to hang on until he
gained one up to the standard of the vehicle he had lost.

Eventually he was satisfied and the following weekend
he drove Johanna out to see his house. She had been there
once in childhood and had told him she remembered it as a
grand residence. He would always have welcomed her
branch of the family if Gina had not shown open disapproval of him and his wife and their way of life, putting a
barrier between an interchange of visits, which was why
the relationship had dwindled down to his calling at the
farm occasionally to see Edvard and the children. Even in
his widowerhood Gina had not relented. It meant much to
him that Johanna had become part of his life.

He glanced at her as they drove along. She was often
pensive and lost in thought. When she had heard of the
reprisals by firing squads, and of deportations to foreign
concentration camps for the arms explosion she had
blanched to the lips. He shared her feelings, even though
he considered it politic not to voice them. In his opinion
such tactics strengthened active opposition or antagonised
those prepared to meet the Germans half-way. In many
ways the Germans were their own worst enemy.

"When do you expect Rolf home?" he asked her. The
imprisoned teachers in the Arctic were finally being released. There was no point in keeping them there any
longer when the Teachers' Nazi Association and its accompanying Youth Movement had fizzled out. They were
badly needed in their schools. Many graduate teachers had
escaped to England, adding to the shortage.

"I've no idea." She turned her head to answer him.
"From what I read it seems they are to be let out a few at a
time. None of that matters as long as he comes home again.
He'll have to find another school. The teacher who took his
place can't be thrown out on his ear just because Rolf is to
be freed." She was quietly enjoying the drive. The countryside was steeped in late autumn hues, the wild cranberries still there for the picking, lying like rubies amid
gnarled tree roots, while the wild and barren mountains
lay under a cloud-streaked sky. "Why do you have an

apartment in Ålesund when you could live out here all the week?"

"I took the apartment when I had no car. The wood-burner was too much like hard work for daily travel. No, it suits me to be in town all the week. I wouldn't want my house to become a permanent residence for my German acquaintances. They might start staying on if I were there all the time. I want to keep things the way they are."

She could have said that nothing stayed the same for long during a war. Everything changed constantly, from the prices that continued to soar for every commodity to the people themselves. Many were adapting to the new regime, not always through choice, merely wanting to call a halt to the German reprisals against their communities and to the shedding of blood. Some were against the Resistance for that reason only, even to the point of believing it was their moral duty not to hide what they knew when questioned. Such honesty was as deadly in its own way as vindictive betrayals by collaborators.

Tom's voice broke into her thoughts. "We're nearly there."

She had expected the house to look smaller than she remembered it, knowing that in childhood memories proportions were invariably exaggerated. At the first sight of it she was surprised to discover it in no way diminished. Built in the late eighteenth century by a Trondheim-born ancestor of Tom's late wife, it was reputed to be a copy of a house in the cathedral city that had won a competition among three rich women as to which of them could build the most beautiful residence. From a distance it might have been carved from ivory, with its filigreed ornamentation over windows and doorways and the graceful sweep of the horseshoe flight of steps to the entrance. When the car drew up outside, the fact that it was timber-built was much in evidence and made it at home with its setting of forest slope and water.

"It's as if it were yesterday that I was here," she exclaimed, getting out of the car and looking up at the house. "It's still like something out of a fairy tale."

"Come on in." He took her overnight bag and his own from the back seat. Purposely he had managed to avoid having anyone else come this weekend, for he wanted her to have time to look around and decide what should be done.

She paused on the horseshoe flight to look at the view of the fjord's inlet and the slopes beyond. A wooded island lay offshore and a sailing boat was moored alongside a couple of rowing boats. The house could not have been located in a more idyllic setting. Indoors she found that much of the furniture was of the same period as the house and kept to the rooms where time-faded murals enhanced the walls with pastoral scenes or simply white clouds floating against a shaded sky. Chests, cupboards and chairs were painted and decorated with the old patterns known as rose-painting; the ceiling of one room was entirely covered with these designs, while the floors were of white pine with the knots gleaming like pieces of embedded amber. The rooms led one into another like stage settings for *Hedda Gabler.* Tom went ahead of Johanna, throwing open double doors, pleased by her appreciation of all she saw. The most lived-in part of the house was furnished comfortably in a style fashionable in the early thirties when Tom's wife had still been alive.

"I use the old rooms for parties," Tom told her.

"I can tell that. There are wine and grease stains on those lovely floors."

He spread his hands expressively. "That's what I told you. This place needs proper supervision."

"Where's your housekeeper?"

"In the kitchen, I expect. I let her know we were coming."

There was no one in the well-appointed kitchen, which was far from clean. Johanna went out through the kitchen porch. The housekeeper was in a sun chair in a sheltered corner, her eyes closed, her skirts to her thighs as she attempted to deepen the tan of her legs in the last rays of the late September sun. Her age was no more than nineteen or twenty. Johanna set her arms akimbo and looked over her shoulder at Tom with a wry glance.

"Did you appoint her for her cooking or her legs?"

He grinned, unabashed. "Her mother does the cooking at the weekends."

"Go and give her a week's wages in lieu of notice. I'll see

what I can rustle up for us to eat after I've taken a look upstairs."

From a bedroom window she watched the girl depart, irate and red-faced, a bulging suitcase in one hand and a carrier bag full of belongings in the other. Johanna's inspection of the upper floor ended in the housekeeper's bedroom. Holding her breath at the stale atmosphere, she went to the windows and opened them wide. As she came out again, closing the door behind her on the littered room, she met Tom coming up the stairs with his hand luggage and hers. "Have you chosen your bedroom?" he asked her.

She gave a nod. "The one at the end."

He dropped his hand baggage outside the door of his own room and carried hers along to her choice of accommodation. She had selected it because it had access to a balcony above a verandah and in an emergency she could climb down. Her whole outlook had become geared to observing and thinking ahead, an awareness of danger always with her.

"It's not very large," he said doubtfully. "I'm hoping you will be here often, so I want you to be happy with it."

"It's fine."

In the kitchen she had no difficulty in finding the ingredients for a good meal. Tom had told her he received extra rations for the entertaining of his German guests and the evidence was there in abundance. It went against her whole nature to be extravagant in any way in present times and she made a simple and economical meal. Tom praised it highly.

"I still wish I could persuade you to run this place."

She shook her head, smiling. "I told you, that's out."

"Then you'll have to find me someone as practical as yourself." His ultimatum, given in jovial tones, was nevertheless on a serious level. He knew there had been hopeless mismanagement in the kitchen and it was inevitable that in time the extra rations for collaborating personnel in his position would be reduced. From his Wehrmacht friends he had learned that Hitler was convinced the Allies would attempt to invade Norway sooner or later and reinforcements had brought the number of troops stationed on Norwegian soil to two hundred and fifty thousand. It was

likely that more would come. There would have to be cut-
backs, and the Wehrmacht would be the last to feel the
pinch.

"I'll see you get a good housekeeper, don't worry about
that." She knew Gunnar was looking out for a woman with
Resistance sympathies willing to wait on Germans. He was
being selective about his choice, for he had to be sure of
getting one prepared to support her in an emergency.

After they had eaten, Tom lit a log fire in the open
corner hearth of the sitting room against the chill of the
evening. The birch logs, set vertically, blazed and crackled
cheerfully. She browsed through his collection of books
while listening to the radio. As a collaborator he was allowed to have as many radios as he wished.

The next morning she went for a walk on her own. By
following the inlet she came within sight of a fishing village
reflected in the water of the cove. She could just discern
the German sentry on the jetty. That uniform was everywhere.

At her suggestion, Tom agreed that nobody should be
invited to the house during the renovations and redecora-
tions she deemed necessary. Through his authority it was
not difficult to organise army transport for the gang of
cleaning women from the office buildings to be driven out
to the house daily after their earlier work was done. Gradually the nicotine film was wiped away from the wall
murals and splendidly decorated ceilings, and every stain
removed from the ancient floors. One weekend, armed
with some special paints she had unearthed from a store
cupboard, Johanna herself obliterated the cigarette burns
in the old painted furniture with painstaking care, following the twirls of leaves and roses with the fine tip of a
brush. She was doing it out of love for the house and its
beautiful, time-aged furnishings, not for Tom. Such things
were part of the heritage that was freedom to her.

Her restoration work was left in abeyance on the weekend she went home to see Rolf. He was among the last of
the imprisoned teachers to be released and she had already spoken to him on the telephone. Tom, who had
come to expect her to be with him every weekend for the
time being, was magnanimous about her absence. "I'll give

you a bottle of champagne for the family celebration," he said generously.

Her eyes told him he had blundered. "I'm afraid it wouldn't be accepted, Tom."

He shrugged uncomfortably, still able to feel a twinge of humiliation at being rejected by his own kin. "I wish Rolf well, anyway. I don't bear grudges."

To Karen the homecoming of Erik's brother was particularly poignant. He was thin, having lost a great deal of weight, even though rations for the teachers had improved during their wait for transport home, and prison conditions had eased, making life bearable if still far from pleasant. Seeing him again after such a long absence, she caught expressions across his eyes and in his broad smiles that reminded her searingly of Erik. The fact that Rolf was leaner in the face heightened a likeness she had never noticed before, and her eyes were ever on him for the will-o'-the-wisp resemblance that came and went elusively.

She was happy to witness the reunion between him and his sister. It was as if they had reverted to childhood, hugging each other and laughing and teasing. Her opinion had always been that all three Ryen offspring had inherited the warmth in their nature from Edvard. His good humour had been restored since he had begun carrying out a few light tasks, and he was full of talk about all he would do on the farm when spring came again. There was none of that liveliness in Gina's make-up, although she was smiling one of her shy smiles at the general exuberance.

"What happens now, Rolf?" Johanna asked him when the initial excitement was over and they were gathered around the coffee table.

"I've been offered a school in Ålesund. I start after the Christmas holiday."

"Then I'll be seeing something of you."

"You certainly will."

In the midst of the exchange of talk, Gina, refilling coffee cups, happened to see from the window that Carl Müller was approaching the house. When he noticed her, he came patiently to a standstill to await Karen's coming. Gina turned and gave the girl a nod and a look that had become the only communication necessary between them to announce that he was there again. Obediently Karen went from the room, quietly and unobtrusively. Both she and Gina tried to keep the frequency of the visits away from Edvard, who was alternately enraged and saddened by the liaison which he could neither understand nor accept. He did not miss the closing of the door behind her, his powers of observation restored with his improving health.

"That Nazi is here again, isn't he? It strikes me increasingly that there's more to her keeping company with him than meets the eye. She's not in love with him. Even I can see that."

Gina moved quickly to press a hand on his shoulder. "Don't start imagining things. Remember what I've always said. We'll overlook everything for the unselfish way she nursed you through your illness and for being responsible for saving your life."

Johanna, who had already taken a chance to talk to Rolf about the matter, spoke to her brother in a mutter. "He's bound to guess sooner or later."

"Maybe he should have been told as soon as he was well enough. Surely Karen could have persuaded him not to take any action."

"That's been my opinion ever since I knew the truth."

In the hallway, Karen put on her coat and pulled a knitted hat down over her head as she went outside. The valley itself was still green in spite of its now being deep into December, a trick played by the Gulf Stream, defying the snow flurries that attempted to take hold. It was different on the heights where the winter snows had come to stay, lying like ermine cloaks down through the forests. Carl was wearing his helmet, which she hated, and was fully kitted out with his rifle, his greatcoat making him look twice as broad. One look at his face showed her that something was wrong. "What's happened?" she asked as she reached him, her eyes alarmed.

"I've been posted. I go today."

She stared at him, letting the marvellous news sink into her. Her nightmare was ending. He was going away and with luck she would never see him again. She had a great urge to shriek out her relief, to dance like a madwoman, to throw back her head and laugh until the valley echoed with her happiness. To hide her reaction she was forced to cover her face with her hands. He misunderstood.

"Don't be upset, Karen. I'm being moved somewhere else on the coast. There's some alert on. I think it's due to this invasion we're expecting any day. We'll keep the British out, there's no fear of their landing. Do you know what we call your country? 'Fortress Norway.' How's that for a guarantee of defence?"

She lowered her hands, having regained her composure. "So you've come to say goodbye."

"I'm afraid so. Walk with me. No, not down the valley today where everyone can see us. Let's go in the other direction where we can be alone. We've a lot of talking to do in a short time. You know I'm not one for letter-writing, but I would like to hear from you sometimes."

She listened and said nothing, strolling at his side. He would wait in vain for letters from her. Surely he must realise there had been tyranny in his keeping her under compulsory obligation to him. He had compelled her company and through it she had had to be amiable towards him and to his friends. She had suffered his kisses and his squeezing hands. Only with difficulty had she kept his touch from her flesh, her own natural modesty a resolute barrier that had helped to keep him at bay. Now all that misery was practically over. As the lane dwindled to a mere path between the trees, she felt blissfully buoyant as if her feet were not touching the damp, lush ground.

"These past months have been good ones for me," he continued, holding back overhanging branches for her. His eyes were searching the forest on either side of the path. "I can't tell you what it meant to me to find you again after all those years. What the—!" A hare had burst out of the undergrowth to cross their path and automatically he switched into a defensive stance, instantly slipping back the safety catch of his rifle.

"Don't shoot!" she cried. The hare was white, its coat turned to winter colouring ahead of the snows, making it an easy target as it bounded away.

He laughed, lowering his rifle and shouldering it again. "For you I'll let it go, even though it came out of those ferns like a bullet from an ambush." His arm went around her as they walked on. "It's a reflex action to be constantly alert."

"There is nothing for you to fear here. There's usually nobody around in this quiet spot."

"That's what I thought until the hare appeared." His fingers caressed her arm through her sleeve. "I'm going to miss you. It was a lucky day for me when I was sent to Ryen Farm." Ahead he glimpsed what he had been looking out for. "That brings me to what I want to talk about."

"Yes?" In her euphoric state she was smiling contentedly, reiterating to herself the miraculous fact that he would soon be gone. Ahead was a small wooden hut.

"An army clerk looked up the hostage file for me, and according to the entry Edvard Ryen is deceased as far as the military is concerned." He had slowed her to a standstill and she turned within his encircling arm, her face blooming into sanguine joy.

"Do you mean there's nothing more to worry about?"

He laughed quietly at her excitement. "Nothing at all. That's the army for you. If the files say he's a goner, that's how it is. Nobody is going to query it."

She shut her eyes blissfully and shook her head at the happiness within her. "I don't know how to thank you for telling me this. I'll always be grateful."

"How grateful?"

She saw how he was looking at her, his slewed gaze holding a contained glitter that she did not at first comprehend. "I've told you," she said nervously, "you've proved that what you have always said about friendship towards me is true."

"That's right. Now it's your turn to show an equal strength of friendship towards me." Keeping his gaze steadily on her, he lifted his chin-strap and removed his helmet. Casually he turned to the hut by which they were now standing and put it inside with his rifle. It was a place where spare hay was stored. Now she shook her head for an entirely different reason, fear of him seeping into the marrow of her bones, her eyes dilating, her lips tremulous. He drew her to him gently when she would have backed away, using his hold over her for the last time.

"You wouldn't want me to report to my commanding officer before I leave that there's an error in the files, would you?"

Her throat became tight and dry. She could not find

voice to speak out of the abyss of despair into which she was sinking. To resist him was to lose everything for which she had striven, worked and endured over many months. His inexorable expression showed her there was no escape. The whisper broke from her pale lips.

"No, I wouldn't."

As he guided her into the hut he knew it was not as he had wanted it to be between them. He had known from the day of first going to Ryen Farm that Edvard Ryen had been eliminated as a hostage. The medical officer had stamped and signed the necessary papers upon their return to headquarters and handed them to him to see into the files. He had known that the matter was closed. Afterwards it had never once been his intention to give the old farmer away. There was death enough in war without dragging it in to no purpose. He did not know if he would be killed himself when the Allied invasion came. That was why he had to love Karen just once before he left her and there was no longer any time to wait and hope. He had come to think of her as the sweetest girl he had ever known.

When he was finished with her she drew away bleakly and lay huddled, her clothes still in some disarray, her long pale hair spread out like cobwebs over the hay. Ready to leave, he crouched down and tenderly stroked her face. She jerked away from his touch, shuddering. With a sigh he stepped back, gazing at her and reluctant to part without a last word from her. He spoke coaxingly, trying to get her to look towards him. When he failed to get the least acknowledgement, he accepted that it was useless to wait any longer. Stepping out of the hut, he looked back at her lingeringly. Then abruptly he glanced alertly into the surrounding trees, releasing the safety catch of his rifle again, certain he had heard a rustling. Nothing stirred. Remembering the hare, he shook his head and shouldered his rifle again. He lit a cigarette as he retraced his steps along the narrow track back to the lane.

She could not stop shivering. Neither could she seem able to think. All that did come through to her was that Edvard was safe. And somehow that meant that Erik would be safe too. Just as in childhood there had been the game of not stepping on the lines of cobbles to keep trolls at bay, so keeping Edvard alive had had a double purpose. Her fingers were in her mouth and she was dribbling. She must have done that after Carl had gone. Was she trying to wipe the taste of his kisses away?

The sound of someone entering the hut made her sit bolt upright, convulsed with fear that Carl had returned. Instead she saw a youth from one of the neighbouring farms and crowding into the hut behind him were two brothers of the same age whom she knew well. Their faces were wrathful and full of loathing. The first one spoke in a tone of contempt.

"You dirty Nazi-loving whore!"

She saw he had a pair of sheep-shearer clippers in his hand. "No!" she whimpered, scrambling to her feet and sinking down into the hay as she tried to edge away. "Please. No."

All three of them seized her. She screamed out and a large hand covered her mouth and nose, half smothering her. Her struggling was in vain, for they were strong and muscular. Her wide, dilated eyes saw the long strands of her hair falling from her head as the shears did their brutal work, nicking her scalp agonisingly, the warm blood trickling down her face and neck. When her head was completely shaved they let her go.

She bolted out of the hut, her coat flying and her arms straight out behind her like broken wings, sobbing as she ran. Her instinct was to lose herself in the clean greenness of the forest, only to hear with renewed terror the youths thudding after her. Their pace outstripped hers as she tried to evade them. Spreading out, they herded her like a panic-stricken animal back into the direction of the path. Once on it, they continued to drive her before them back towards the lane and the valley where she would be seen in her branded state from the farmsteads. Her mind seemed to snap and she began to scream, the piercing sound ringing far as the enclosing trees were left behind. Her pursuers fell back, their purpose accomplished.

Not knowing she ran alone, she kept up her hurtling speed, beyond comprehending anything in the grip of hysteria. She neither saw nor heard those who came running out of Ryen farmhouse to stare in disbelief and then dash to halt her headlong flight. At the impact of Rolf's arms she

reeled and collapsed with a suddenness that almost unbal-
anced him, Johanna helping to hold her up by grabbing a
sleeve. He carried her into the house.

Gina and Johanna took charge. In the warm kitchen a
shawl was wrapped around her where they had seated her
on the kitchen bench. Her violent shivering was making
her limbs twitch uncontrollably. Comforting elderberry
tea was trickled through her chattering teeth. When the
cuts on her head were bathed and treated the sting of the
iodine made her eyes water. Her silence was as intense as
her screaming had been.

She did not speak until the next day. Then, with a col-
oured scarf bound about her head, the bandages discarded, she came downstairs at midmorning. Johanna had
just come in from a walk with her brother and Gina was
writing letters. All three of them looked towards her. It
was to Gina that she spoke quite calmly.

"Your husband is safe. Officially his name has gone from
the records. There is nothing more to fear and Carl has
been posted away."

Gina's face crumpled grotesquely into tears of thankful-
ness. She put down her pen and pressed fingertips to her
tremulous mouth. "I never wanted you to be branded in
this terrible way."

"I know that. My hair will grow again. In the meantime I
want to go home. It shouldn't be difficult to get a permit to
leave my place of work here for elsewhere. The Germans
are sympathetic to women who have been treated like
me."

Johanna moved towards her compassionately. "How will
you be received at home?"

"I'll take a chance."

"When shall you be back?"

"I won't be back. I'm sorry to leave, but I have to get
away."

Gina rose slowly from her chair, her elbows at her sides,
her hands clasped tightly together in front of her waist.
"What of Erik?"

Johanna, looking from one to the other of them, sensed
the empathy between the younger and the older woman
as Karen gave a curiously direct answer that was accepted
as if anticipated.

"I hope he forgets me while he's away. That's all I can say."

If Gina had needed confirmation of what she suspected she had it then. Sad in her own thoughts for the girl, she went to find Edvard who was out in the woodshed. The previous day he had sawed a good number of logs for the house stoves and he was looking them over, well pleased with the strength that was coming back into his arms and shoulders.

"Sit down, Edvard," Gina said to him. "I've something to tell you."

She sat down beside him on a wooden bench by the woodshed. When he had heard all she had to say he broke down completely, a hand over his eyes, tears trickling through his fingers. She had only seen him in that state once before. It evoked painful memories for her of an early estrangement in their marriage and she could make no move to comfort him.

"That poor child," he kept reiterating.

After a while Gina went back into the house and sent Karen out to him. When she went out onto the kitchen porch later she saw them sitting quietly together, both Karen's arms about him, his head still bowed, his hands dropped into a loose clasp between his knees.

Shortly before Johanna returned to town early that evening, she went into the bedroom where Karen was packing. "I've a suggestion." She was confident of Gunnar's agreement. "I can offer you a job. After what you've been through you may feel that the last thing you want is to be with Germans at close quarters and I'll understand if you refuse. Tom Ryen needs a housekeeper at his weekend place. It's not all that far from your own village. You'd be on your own in the house most of the time."

Karen closed the lid of the suitcase and fastened the clasps. "Is that where you go?"

"It's part of my job to be civil to the enemy."

"Nobody can say I'm not experienced in that." Her faint smile was chill.

"Well? What do you think?"

Karen went to the door and closed it. Leaning against it, she looked assessingly at Johanna. "I think you have as much good reason as I did for being civil to the Nazis, or

else Rolf wouldn't be on such good terms with you. I know
Gina, too. She doesn't have any proof, but she accepts that
you're leading your life the way you are to a purpose. I'll
take the job. When my hair has grown again I'll go home
and see my family. I didn't want them to see me like this,
but I had to get away from everything that reminded me
of Erik."

"Then that's settled. I'll fix everything with Tom and get
travel and work permits into the post for you tomorrow.
When you receive them on Tuesday come to the office in
Ålesund. I'll see you get transport out to the house that
same day."

"Thank you."

"No thanks are necessary. I can't tell you what it will
mean to me to have a friend I can trust in the house."

Rolf went with Johanna for most of the way into town
before cycling back. After what had happened to Karen,
he was afraid she might be similarly attacked and branded.
He asked her if she had ever been worried by the possibility.

"Up until now I haven't lost any sleep over it. Now I
have to admit that I wouldn't care to walk alone in the
forests and in the mountains where I've always felt free
and safe. That is a great deprivation. It also hurts deeply
that friends and neighbours whom we've known all our
lives no longer speak to me." She smiled at him, hiding her
own pain. "You're a local hero. I think you should have
something better to ride than a bicycle without tires." He
shrugged cheerfully. It was impossible to replace worn-out
inner tubes or even to obtain puncture kits, so hoops of
wood had replaced tires. "It's not comfortable riding, I can
tell you that. It's as well I'll not be needing it much longer."

Something in his tone alerted her. "Are you thinking of
escaping to England?"

He nodded seriously. "After Christmas. I feel I owe that
much to our parents after all they've been through."

"I thought you were keen on your appointment to the
Ålesund school."

"I was, until Karen's announcement that Father has
been removed once and for all from the marked list. That
leaves me free to do what I've wanted ever since we defeated Quisling over the Teachers' Nazi Association. Now I

can join the Free Norwegian forces. My first choice will be to become a fighter pilot."

"Christmas is almost here and I'm spending it with Astrid, who would otherwise be on her own. Does that mean I'll not see you again before you go?"

"It looks like it."

"I wish you all the luck in the world. Maybe you'll meet Erik in England."

"That's what I'm hoping."

She did not ask him any details of how he would escape or from which place. On their walk that morning she had told him that Steffen had taken the transmitter from the schoolhouse and she had disposed of the radio after being instructed by the Resistance to do nothing that might involve her in minor trouble. He was immensely interested in her job at Tom Ryen's office and did not have to be told her reason for being there.

"Don't do anything rash," he advised her when they said goodbye.

"I'll try to remember that, teacher Ryen," she joked bravely. "I'll think of you and Erik having a pint of beer together in an English pub."

Along the coast, less than twenty kilometres from where Johanna and her brother were parting, Steffen was aboard a fishing boat of the Shetland Bus route, about to set sail. Ahead lay consultations in London. Behind him lay many arduous and lonely weeks dogged by misfortune. "Operation Freshman," which had involved intricate planning, had come to nothing. Highly experienced British sappers being flown in by gliders for an attack on the heavy-water plant in Telemark had met with an unprecedented disaster. One glider had crashed into a mountainside and the other mislanded, killing almost everybody. The survivors had been captured and shot by a firing squad. On more than one occasion he himself had been shot at and narrowly escaped capture.

Ahead lay his first trip to Great Britain since he had been trained for service with the S.O.E. at the Company Linge base in Scotland. He would not be seeing Delia this time as he had before. She had done courageous work in Norway, transmitting vital naval information back to British Intelli-

gence, never staying long in one place and carrying out
her work in hazardous and frequently uncomfortable loca-
tions. From the start and on their few subsequent meetings
during her time in the country, he had had the impression
more than once that she had been about to say something
of importance and then changed her mind. When she had
left on the Shetland Bus, as he was doing now, she had
made it clear that it was a final parting.

"Goodbye, Englishman," she had said to him. "I don't
know why you made that your code name in the Resistance. Your heart has never been anywhere else but in this
rugged land."

Into the cabin of the fishing boat came two new arrivals
for the voyage across the North Sea. Steffen guessed they
were Norwegian commandos returning from a reconnais-
sance sortie somewhere along the coast. They exchanged
conventional greetings as if there were nothing unusual
about the circumstances. One of them was carrying a short
fir tree axed off above the roots. There were melting snowflakes on it that had come from a whirling flurry blowing in
from the sea and these sparkled in the cabin's light.

"It's going to London," the bearer said in explanation.

"The King's tree, is it?" Steffen asked.

"That's right. He hasn't had a Christmas in exile yet
without a tree from home."

"How many more to go, I wonder?"

"God knows. All that's certain is that a Norwegian tree
will be crossing the North Sea at Christmastime for as long
as there's need for it."

In the first week of the New Year of 1943, a quiet Christmas at Ryen Farm behind him, Rolf was ready for escape,
his preparations entirely complete. The escapees going
together numbered six. Two of them were fellow teachers
of his own age with whom he had been imprisoned, and
the others were friends from the district who had been
forced, owing to their engineering skills, to work for the
Occupation forces. They gathered as if for a party at one of
the homes, and at dawn slipped down into a previously
selected fishing smack that was in from a night's fishing
with the nets aboard and the catch unloaded. It was going
to be a long wait until nightfall, when they intended to be

the first of the local fleet to set sail before the boat's owner arrived to take out his vessel. The advantage of taking a boat from this area was that the routine of the fishermen could be relied upon and clearly timed, which was why the number of boats taken in this way from all along the west coast went into the thousands.

They passed the time of waiting by reading or dozing. One of the teachers was not allowed to sleep since he proved to be a loud snorer, and they had to maintain absolute silence in order not to be heard from the jetty and suspicions aroused. They were quite a distance from the spot where the sentry chose to stand, but he patrolled once an hour and no risks could be taken.

Towards dusk they packed up their books and papers. Each one continually glanced at his watch as the last hour dragged by, no longer able to concentrate on anything except the moment ahead when Rolf would go into the wheelhouse, a peaked skipper's cap pulled well down over his eyebrows, and start up the engine.

"Only another five minutes," one of them had just remarked when they heard voices approaching the mooring. The atmosphere in the cabin became electric as they all froze, listening intently. It became clear that the German sentry was in quite jovial conversation with a local man.

"Rather you than me on the seas tonight. It's a cold job keeping guard here, but I wouldn't change it for yours at any price."

There was a guffaw. "That's what land folk always say. The sea has never scared me and I tell you I've seen waves as high as mountains in my time. This is good fishing weather. I'll see you get a good-sized cod tomorrow morning if you're on duty."

"I change duties in a couple of hours. My pal will be here. You can give it to him, and a few herrings if you have them."

"It's as good as done. The usual price and the best of the catch."

A pair of heavy feet landed on the deck. The escapees groaned under their breath. They had had the ill luck to choose the one occasion when the skipper had broken with routine. Rolf signalled with quietening hands that nobody should move as yet.

"There's a slim chance he's only come to fetch something and will go again," he murmured. "If the worst happens, you know what to do. None of us is armed and the only way any of us will get out of this mess is to scatter widely."

There came the sound of snow being brushed off the deck. The sentry was still there talking with the skipper about the vessel itself. The owner was proud of it, as these individualistic men always were of their boats and their means of livelihood.

"I'll show you something from the cabin that should interest you," his voice boomed.

Rolf gave the final order: "Don't move until he's in the cabin and we can get him down. Otherwise the doorway will be blocked."

The door banged open and the skipper's bulk filled the space as he took the two steps down the companionway. Although there was no light in the cabin there was enough glimmer from outside for him to see that he had uninvited passengers and he halted abruptly, still at a vantage point from which he could withdraw. He gave a low whistle of surprise.

"Keep calm, boys. I'll come to England with you. Give me time to get rid of the Kraut on the jetty and fetch my wife." With that he reached for a carved wooden ship on the shelf and went out again, shutting the door behind him.

The tension did not ease. "Can we trust him?" was the first question.

"Maybe he's telling the sentry to get reinforcements."

Rolf settled the issue. "We'll trust him. Any other move means that we've lost our chance of getting to England now, and for some of us there'll never be another."

Outside, the voices of the skipper and the sentry faded as they moved away, good-humoured haggling over the price of the hand-carved model taking place. Then there was nothing except the lap and slap of the water against the hull. After half an hour the skipper returned on his own. He opened the door briefly, sticking his head inside.

"My wife wouldn't come. She was too nervous to take the risk. I do a trade in hand-carving. You might as well benefit from my most recent transaction. Don't light up until we're out at sea." He tossed in a couple of packets of German cigarettes.

The familiar tonk-tonk of the engine brought the ship to life. There were a few more minutes of delay with the skipper moving about on deck and then they were moving. Before long they were able to light their cigarettes.

Due to bad weather, the crossing took almost forty-eight hours. It was nighttime again when the vessel put in to the Shetlands. British soldiers came on board to mount guard over them until morning. The escapees slept like logs.

In the morning the skipper woke everyone in the cabin with a roar of rage. First up, he had completed an inspection of his boat only to find it had been practically stripped of everything that could be lifted or unscrewed by thieving hands. He had noticed first that the remaining oil drums were gone. Then he discovered that his tools, which he had had all his seafaring life, were also missing, together with his charts, his spare waterproofs, his ropes and his nets. Since he spoke no English the colourful abuse he hurled at the British sentries missed its mark. They, in any case, had only taken over their duty half an hour before.

At his interrogation by Norwegian and British officials he was informed that the culprits would be traced and his possessions returned to him. It was explained that it was not often the skippers came in with their own boats; mostly the escapees had no idea what was aboard the boats borrowed indefinitely to get away; hence military pilfering rarely came to light. By the time Rolf and the others left him with his boat, he had had some of his tools returned to him. It had not affected his mood. He was still ready to do murder if ever he met the soldiers concerned.

Rolf went through the same screening procedure as his brother and thousands of other escapees before him. His selection by the Free Royal Norwegian Air Force board went through quickly. Within a short time he was at "Little Norway" in Canada, training to be a fighter pilot. Local hospitality was almost overwhelming towards those at the base.

It was a great day for him when he gained his wings. All the Norwegian wings, he learned later, were embroidered by the Royal School of Needlework in London, and it seemed an apt link since his King and government were

settled in that courageous, blitz-stricken city. After the
Wings Parade he was posted to 331 Squadron in England,
just a year having gone by since his escape from Norway.
The squadron was stationed at North Weald, not far from
London. His first sight of the aerodrome was the Norwegian flag flying against an English sky. He wore the top
button of his tunic undone in the tradition of fighter pilots
and, with silent apologies to the ladies of the Royal School
of Needlework, he had rubbed a little dirt into the silver
threads of his wings to take away the bright new look of
them.

He was soon a veteran of many sorties across the Chan-
nel. The day a swastika was painted as his score on the side
of his Spitfire he saw it as the first real blow against the
Nazis at a personal level. He lived every minute of his
hectic life to the full, whether in the air or off duty. On one
leave in London, merry after a party, he and two of his
fellow pilots had an unexpected lift in King Haakon's car,
the monarch being elsewhere, and the driver a former
member of the squadron ground staff. The King was an
avid attender of newsreel theatres, and would take the
driver with him into the inexpensive seats, buying the
tickets himself. Rolf only went to a newsreel theatre when
he had a long wait for a train back to base. There were far
more enjoyable things to do in London. He had tried to
trace Erik, only to draw a blank each time. His hope was
that one day his brother would walk into the County Hotel
or the Shaftsbury, which were centres for Norwegian ser-
vicemen in London, and they would meet that way. For all
he knew, Erik might be on a battleship anywhere in the
world.

On the day a third swastika was painted on the side of his
plane, his life changed. He fell in love with an English girl.
His blond looks, his accent, his blue uniform with "Norway" on the shoulder-flashes, and his wings on his broad
chest had mowed down women for him. When he saw her
across a dance hall in Epping, a village near the aerodrome, her vivacious presence and the rich sheen of her
red-gold hair eclipsed all the rest. She, seeing him come
purposefully across the floor towards her, had a feeling of
destiny.

"May I have this dance?" He saw her eyes were beautiful, a flawless green.

"Yes, of course."

She liked the way he had bowed to her. The Scandinavians did that, whatever their rank. He was a flight-lieutenant. Softly she went into his arms, light as a butterfly. There was a look of discovery on his face as he drew her out onto the floor.

"I'm Rolf Ryen. What's your name?"

"Wendy Townsend."

It had begun.

Chapter 11

For Johanna the first weekend party at Tom's house was nerve-racking. At the office she had comparatively little to do in connection with the military there, apart from the exchange of messages, documents and so forth. Even the party she had attended at the officers' mess had been bearable by being of short duration. With Tom's house parties some of the guests arrived on Friday evenings, shortly after she and Tom got there from the office, and from then until Sunday evening she had to smile, be sociable and hide her hatred of their Nazism, which was rampant among the younger officers, less marked among some of the older men. She thought she would never forget her initiation when, alerted by a car drawing up outside, she had come down the stairs to see a man she had hoped never to see again among the three guests who had arrived together. Standing with two army officers was Axel Werner in his black uniform of the general S.S., promoted in rank since their last meeting. He was regarding her with astonishment.

"Johanna Ryen! I had not connected the surname of our host with you, and yet I was told by Major Ryen that a charming relative was his hostess here. I haven't seen you since you came to my office in Oslo. What a pleasant surprise."

It was anything but that for her. Apart from not wanting to come into contact with his unpleasant personality again, there was the devastating reality of his knowing that she had been under suspicion for anti-Nazi activities while in the capital. Her involvement with Tom and her whole project was in jeopardy. The muscles of her face stiffened to a point where she felt it must splinter like glass as she returned his smile with the biggest bluff she could bring to her aid.

"This should be a big moment for you, Axel. You can see that your kindly advice did not go amiss."

His conceit swelled. Thoroughly egotistical, he was totally prepared to believe he had won her over during what he looked back on as a heart-to-heart talk. This belief was fed by the attitude persistently held by the Third Reich that the Norwegians were blood-brother Aryans still misguided by out-of-date ideas of democracy that would be dispelled with time. Until the country was subservient, the torture of individuals and the savage reprisals for sabotage were necessary measures to bring the people to heel. As for the scarcity of food and commodities, that was the natural outcome of war, particularly when a large army of occupation had to be fed and those at home in Germany were not to go without the privileges of conquest. Axel, biased already by the links of childhood, saw again in Johanna the perfect Aryan woman; that she was now converted to his own ideology was attested to by her presence in the house of a prominent collaborator. "Well done, my dear girl. I'm proud of you."

The taller of the two army officers raised interested, inquiring eyebrows. "What's all this, then?"

Axel chuckled, going forward to meet her and take her hand. "A little secret between us, is it not, Johanna?"

She was able to project some warmth into her reply on the wave of his unwittingly helpful cooperation. "I agree." Half leaning towards him, she added mock-conspiratorially, "I think there's one secret we can disclose." Her smile turned on the other guests. "Axel and I knew each other as children."

"How fortunate for S.S. Obersturmbannführer Werner."

"Some people get all the luck," the second man commented, grinning at her. Axel's smug smile showed that he agreed with them. "Naturally I was practically in my adolescence when Johanna was born," he said with gallantry.

Both men spoke the same thought with laughter. "You don't need to tell us that."

Tom beamed as he carried out the introductions. Johanna was getting off to a flying start, just as he had anticipated. Moreover she looked stunning, wearing a simple dinner gown of creamy velvet with a string of unusual pearly stones linked by gold which seemed a reflection of

her shining hair. If she had appeared in a potato sack she
would have imbued it with her own particular flair, although it was far more satisfactory that she had access to a
fine wardrobe lent by the woman in whose house she lived.
He had managed to get her some French silk stockings and
intended to keep her supplied with them as long as he
could, although they were getting harder to come by. She
had looked as if she was on the point of refusing them, and
probably would have done so if he had not made it clear
that he considered it part of her role as hostess to be as
elegant in appearance as possible.

"Now, gentlemen," he said when the clicking of heels
had subsided. "Frøken Hallsted will show you to your
rooms. Then please join us for a drink before dinner."

Karen, waiting in the background, stepped forward. Johanna had made her a stylish turban-like head covering
out of a piece of silk donated by Astrid. Her hair was
growing again into soft curly strands, but she was too self-
conscious as yet to display it. She failed completely to see it
gave a piquant charm to her face, only conscious of its
unfeminine boyish look, for fashion prevailed even during
the Occupation and almost shoulder-length hair was the
favoured style.

While waiting for his guests to reappear, Tom poured
Johanna a drink and handed it to her. They were in the
room with the rose-painted ceiling, the firelight from the
open corner hearth dancing over the centuries-old designs
and flickering across the pine-white floor.

"What a coincidence that you should know the S.S.
Obersturmbannführer, Johanna."

"Where is he stationed?"

"He's in a commandeered house in Ålesund with several
other officers of the security service at the present time.
This district is to be his—in fact, the whole of the Molde
Fjord and Romsdal Fjord area will be under his command
for his own particular duties. He's here to rout out the
remnants of the Resistance in the area."

"Oh, is he?" Her face was straight as she looked into the
fire, the glass winking in her hand. "That sounds as if he
will be around for a long time."

Tom kept a wary look on the open doorway and lowered
his voice. "I agree with you. He is under the impression

that he can accomplish the task in a matter of weeks, coming in like a new broom, so to speak. It was the arms explosion that brought about his posting here. I hear that Reichskommissar Terboven thinks highly of him. He's a dangerous man. His methods have been ruthless to date."

"That I can believe."

A rumble of voices sounded from the direction of the stairs. "They're coming." Tom went to the bottles on the side table in readiness to deal with his guests' liquid requirements.

It was a very civilised dinner party that evening. Tom sat at the head of the table and Johanna was opposite him. Karen waited on them all, quick and efficient in a white frilled apron, the simple food well cooked by her and attractively garnished. Axel was in high good humour, appreciating the food and the wine and liking the fact that he had known Johanna as long as Tom had. Somehow he seemed to think it gave him an advantage over the other two guests, and that in itself encouraged his mood. Too often the security S.S. was treated with lordly condescension by the more senior services, who were inclined to view them as a jumped-up brigade without traditions. His attitude towards her was similar to Tom's in the role of the benevolent and protective member of the family or, in his case, of old acquaintance.

The army officers made no secret between themselves that they found him a bore. He certainly liked the sound of his own voice, his anecdotes becoming lengthier and more tedious as the wine took a greater hold on him. They themselves were lively company, witty and intelligent and enjoying the presence of a young and beautiful woman. When the opportunity presented itself, both in turn made classic passes at her, just as many more were to do in the time ahead, some with more finesse than others. They accepted her firm and cordial turn-down with singular good grace. On their subsequent visits, until they were posted away from the area, she could easily have come close to friendship with them, something that would never have been possible with Axel. Neither of them was a fanatical Nazi; both were liberal-minded men serving their country to the best of their ability in political circumstances that had run amok. She was deeply grieved when one of them was killed in a British commando raid along the coast.

Johanna kept to the policy she had decided upon in the beginning, of never asking questions about anyone's war role or leaning towards anything that might suggest she was more interested in military matters than she should be as an apparent collaborator. With time she learned much to pass on to Gunnar for Resistance Intelligence, simply by sitting quietly in the after-dinner firelight and listening while the company relaxed and occasionally forgot she was there. No secrets were given away, but she was able to deduce military and naval movements, this information frequently substantiating that already known to the Resistance, who welcomed confirmation from any source. Long after the Resistance knew there would be no Allied invasion of northern Norway after all, the Germans continued to believe that it would come, a belief kept on the boil by subversive activities to suggest aid was being gathered undercover to assist the Allies when they came. Time and again Johanna was able to report German reactions to staged events that were keeping undiminished the vast number of troops stationed in the country when they might have been deployed elsewhere, particularly after the grave losses suffered by the Wehrmacht through the defeat of the Sixth Army at Stalingrad.

There was always plenty of general discussion going on about the war. There was much talk among the officers as to whether timely reinforcements would have saved the North African campaign, which had ended disastrously for Rommel's army. The Allied attack on Italy had also caused much vigorous discussion, their violently voiced opinions of their Italian ally in the Axis partnership anything but complimentary. Their confidence in the German Army as the best fighting force ever seen was still totally undiminished. They continued to see themselves as the master race, destined to dominate the world, and viewed these setbacks as only temporary.

"If it has to be a hundred-year war we'll still come out on top," Axel said one evening when dinner was over and some of the officers had gathered in basket chairs on the verandah in the warm June evening, he himself leaning a shoulder casually against one of the wooden columns. "As

Goebbels said, 'Nobody has to love us, but we'll make sure they damn well fear us!' "

Johanna had heard the quotation before and knew it had originated as a declaration against her own country. She went on refilling coffee cups, something she did while Karen cleared the table in the dining room and dealt with the washing up.

"It won't take a hundred years," drawled somebody else who was present. Johanna did not turn her head, but she recognised the drink-thickened voice of an officer on his first visit to the house, a loose-lipped, brutish-looking man who had tried to seduce Karen forcibly when she had shown him to his room. It was the first incident of its kind and was due mainly to his being half drunk upon arrival. His unsteadiness on his feet had enabled her to escape unscathed—pale, shaken and angry.

"What makes you so sure, Oberleutenant?" Axel's stance became hostile and defensive. It was the Army trying again to take the S.S. down a peg.

"The sweet little product in Telemark that's going to help us quell the world and bring it under the Führer's heel." The speaker lifted up and crashed down his own jackbooted metal heel, making a gash in the verandah floorboard that would be there forever, guffawing at his own demonstrative action.

"Shut your damn mouth," another officer growled from the next chair. Conversations continued as though uninterrupted. Even Axel turned away, putting an end to anything further. It was obvious to Johanna that, although a security gaffe had not been made, the drunken officer had come close to it in the opinion of present company. It was the heavy-water plant at Vemork of present to which he had referred. When an Allied air raid in January had failed to put it out of order, a small band of exceptionally courageous Norwegian saboteurs had entered it in February and blown up vital sections of the plant under the most hazardous conditions. To the Resistance it had been a great boost to morale. So much of what the armed section did was mere harassment with no decisive effect on the war. This action at Vemork was different. The delaying effect on the production by the Germans of the dangerous weapon they were calling the atomic bomb was invaluable. The lieuten-

ant's drunken remark suggested to Johanna that something was still in the wind. She would pass it on for what it
was worth.

When she did, Gunnar received the snippet phlegmati-
cally. "There have been extensive repairs carried out at
the plant over recent months and a shipment of heavy
water was dispatched to Germany a few days ago. I daresay the lieutenant had something to do with the transit en
route. You did right to tell me what you heard. As it happens, it is nothing new. Our Telemark people have the
matter in hand, I'm sure. I think we can leave things to
them."

It was only on rare occasions that he gave back something in return for what she passed on. Usually he was
completely noncommittal. For all she knew, nothing she
had supplied over many months from the office or the
house had been more than confirmation of information
Intelligence already had and which would be drawn in
from other sources anyway. At times it was frustrating to
be so much in the dark, and yet she accepted that security
came before all else.

As she was about to leave, Gunnar dived into his pocket
and brought out a letter. "This is for you. Don't ask me how
I received it or where the sender is, because I can't tell
you." He gave her a grin. "Just be glad it reached you."

It was from Steffen. She read it later alone in her room at
Astrid's house. There was no date and it contained no
news, gave no hint of his whereabouts, and there was no
indication of how long it had been in transit. It was a love
letter. Unashamedly and richly and poignantly a love letter, deserving of a bow of blue ribbon and lavender to keep
it in until it was fragile with age. Instead she put it among
her own everyday possessions and read it over and over
again at intervals until it took on the appearance of being a
delicate artefact and she had to keep it in another envelope to stop it from falling apart.

Karen's hair grew to a length about which she was no
longer self-conscious. She had no wish for it to be as long as
before, never wanting to be reminded of the day she had
seen it slipping in strands like silver-gilt snakes to the hay-
strewn floor of the hut. At last she felt able to visit her

home. Her village was near enough for her to row there in one of the boats in good weather, for she had rowed since childhood, a normal attribute for those who grew up at the fjord's edge, just as it was to swim and fish. Going by boat cut out several kilometres by the road, which followed a sharp inlet where a fishing hamlet was located. There were many such communities in this area and her own village reaped its livelihood as much from the sea as from the surrounding farmland. It had a central gravelled street running up from a cove where fishing boats were moored, a few shops standing at some distance from each other, orchards and gardens and habitations in between. Her married sister Marthe and her husband Raold lived above their bakery and the bakehouse, the grass at the rear reaching down to end in rocks and boulders at the fjord's edge. Karen had lived with them since losing her parents in the winter of 1935. Being childless, they had made her their child and much as she loved them, she found that their protectiveness stifled her liberty, which was why she had left eventually to work at Ryen Farm. She would not have expected to be rejected by her sister if she had come home with a branded head, certain that Marthe would forgive her anything, but she had not known how Raold, a staunch patriot, would receive her. On the day she returned to their doorstep, she arrived by way of the rowboat, tying it up on the rocks below their property and stepping from there up onto the grass. She went almost shyly in the direction of the bakehouse door. Marthe happened to be in there with Raold, saw her coming and ran to meet her.

"You're home!"

They laughed and cried together. Raold, a reserved, serious man, had shaken her hand gladly, covering it with flour. She need not have worried. Gina had sent them a long letter telling them the whole story and advising that they wait until Karen made the first move to return home. They welcomed her like a prodigal daughter.

Later that day Raold offered her the old job she had had with him previously behind the counter in his bakery. She had half expected the offer, although present sales could not possibly warrant her assistance to Marthe in the serving, for rationing had cut his previously thriving business to the bone. The real reason was given as she anticipated.

"There's been talk for a long time about Tom Ryen and the Nazi company he keeps," he said, his thin, bony face extremely grave. "I don't like the thought of your being at that house of his with the carryings-on that take place there." Considerably older than his wife, he felt a keen and undiminished responsibility towards his young sister-in-law.

Marthe, emotional and outgoing, comfortably built as if shaped by nature for a dozen children that she had never had, added her persuasion to try and entice Karen back under their roof. "Come home for good. It upsets me not to see you. Your letters would have puzzled me if Gina Ryen had not told us what was wrong."

Before Karen could make any answer, Raold spoke again. "However, I must be fair with you and put you in possession of the facts of what living with us again would mean to you." It was one of his principles always to be fair with those he dealt with. Until the Germans were stopped from buying food in civilian shops by their own command, there being little enough left over for the population in any case, he had never, in fairness, given them short weight or stale goods. His own table had no more bread than he allowed his customers on their ration cards. "I do what I can to aid those taking a more active part in the eventual liberation of our country. Do you follow me?"

"I do." She thought it was typical of him to do what he considered to be his duty without thought for personal safety. In spite of his being dogmatic in attitude and high-handed in his direction of domestic matters, she had always liked him for his honesty. Marthe, although she appeared docile, had her own way of managing affairs. She slipped extra rolls into customers' baskets and always had a loaf in reserve that he knew nothing about, giving slices to those who needed it or putting some on his plate to keep him better fed when she could be sure he would not raise questions.

"With the cover of the islands and skerries around here near the mouth of the fjord," Raold continued, "our village is often a first port of call and sometimes a departure point for small boats that come in from across the North Sea. You

would not be involved in any of it. On nights when I say I'll
be working alone in the bakehouse, you'll go to bed as
Marthe does and pull the quilt over your ears. Is that understood?"

"Perfectly, except that I'll remain where I am at Tom
Ryen's house and come to see you often on visits as I have
done today."

Nothing more that they could say was able to make her
relent her decision not to accept their kindly and well-
meant offer. She had grown to like her new life. The weekends were hard work, as was the preparation necessary
beforehand, particularly when a large party was to be
held, and it frequently took a couple of days to get the
house in order again afterwards. It was the quietness of
being on her own in between times that was full of balm.
There were moments when she thought fancifully that the
atmosphere of the old house, where the lives of previous
generations had been absorbed into the walls, was in itself
filled with a healing power. In spite of the riotous influx at
some weekends, it was a convent-like retreat for her, and
in it she aimed to sublimate the love and loving desires she
had felt for Erik. The emotional shock of Carl's usage of
her, followed immediately by the shame of her branding,
had ended completely her trust in a future with Erik. All
that was left to her now was to hope that one day she would
feel clean again.

Johanna needed some new shoes. It was not for a whim
of fashion but a simple and basic need for something to
cover her feet out of doors. Leather in any shape or form
had vanished completely from the shops. Shoes were repaired with compressed paper, which did not last long.
Everybody was turning to wooden-soled shoes with uppers
of thick paper or preserved fish skins when their old footwear finally fell apart. Shoe shops did not get supplies of
these very often, and when stocks came in people lined up
immediately all along the street to await their turn to
purchase. On her way to the office one morning Johanna, a
purse of dyed red fish skin under her arm, a smart croco-
dile look to its texture, spotted one of these queues and
joined the end of it. She would be late for work for the first

time, but Tom would not be difficult about it when he heard the reason.

The line moved slowly. Word went back down the queue that in addition to shoes there were summer sandals made of plaited paper string, and purses of the same material. A ripple of excitement went through the female section of the line. Johanna had been waiting nearly an hour when a German major she knew came along. Upon seeing her he stopped and saluted, smart in his well-cut uniform with shining jackboots and the iron cross at the meeting of his high collar.

"*Guten Morgen,* Fräulein Ryen. What are you doing here?"

"Waiting for shoes."

"Waiting? We can't have that. Come with me."

"No," she protested firmly, keeping to her place in the line. Hostile glances were already digging into her like knives. The friendly atmosphere that had previously prevailed would be turning against her now. People would believe they had a collaborator in their midst. To her anger and dismay the officer refused to accept her answer.

"Major Ryen would never forgive me if I allowed you to remain here for hours on end. Shall I send those in front of you back to the end of this lengthy line-up or will you accompany me into the shop?"

She knew he would do as he had said. In fact he had taken a pace or two towards the head of the queue as if prepared to give the order there and then. Hastily she stepped out of the line. "I'm late for work already. I'll take a turn another day."

It was no use. He shepherded her into the shop and waited while she tried on what was available in her size, the designs all the same, the only difference being in a choice of black or brown. It was one pair per customer. The major would have commandeered more for her if he had suspected that she had hoped for a pair of sandals as well. As she carried the shoes out of the shop in the crook of her arm, no wrapping paper being available any more, there came some low booing from further back in the line. It was a humiliating experience, made more so by the major's escorting her all the way to the office. This was one of the times when she felt it would never be possible to settle her personal score against the arrogance of the enemy.

At Tom's large parties there was never really a chance for Johanna to glean anything of interest to her secret work. The officers came to get drunk, to have sex with the women provided for them or whom they had brought along as partners, and to forget for a while everything to do with discipline and army work. She always booked a band, who sweated it out until the company was too drunk or otherwise engaged to dance any more. With Karen's aid she saw that food and drink remained in ample supply, removed smashed glasses before the shards were ground in to cause permanent damage, tried to ensure that those about to vomit got outside or reached the bathroom in time, and generally kept guard over the well-being of the house against its present offenders, ready for the time when they would be gone and forgotten in the better and more peaceful years for which she yearned.

The office continued to be more rewarding in the items she came across. Johanna went straight from there on the day she was to meet Gunnar to hand over a paper she had copied and secluded in a folded newspaper, which she had bought in readiness that morning. The headlines were of a raid by Allied planes on a target near Oslo, the loss of civilian life emphasised in harrowing detail. She knew the destruction of the target was of vital importance to the Allied cause, but she also knew the Milorg of the Resistance was bitterly against these air raids, which were on the increase. Too many innocent lives were lost, and there was often the complete destruction of machinery and facilities essential to an economic recovery when the war was finally over. Sabotage, in spite of the reprisals, saved unnecessary damage and spared far more lives.

Instead of Gunnar at the sheltered corner table of the café she found to her joy that Steffen was waiting for her. It had been a long time since their last meeting and she hurried across to sit down with him, placing her purse and the newspaper on the spare chair. By the brilliance of his smiling eyes directed on her she could tell that his excitement was equal to hers. His mundane opening remarks served to emphasise the current leaping and dancing invisibly between them.

"Nice day."

"Agreed. I had expected Gunnar."

"Instead you have received this pleasant surprise."

Her mouth slipped into reciprocal amusement, her eyes dancing. "You said it, not I."

"Would you like something to eat? I have coupons." He kept himself supplied with coupons and anything else he needed. In his pockets he had half a dozen cards that provided means of sustenance to match those stamped passes that would facilitate escape in a tight corner.

She was hungry; "Yes, I would." After studying the menu, which listed only a few items for those prepared to sacrifice ordinary rations for equal portions with restaurant coupons, she gave him some advice. "Avoid the fish sausage. That's a culinary abomination that has been created out of sheer necessity from fish, oats and black bread. Astrid serves it sometimes when there's literally nothing else to be had. She fries it in cod liver oil."

"My God!" Words failed him as he imagined the taste.

"She does something with the oil first. There's a way of steaming it to get the really objectionable taste away. And I'd never belittle it. When there's only that to fry with, it also represents hours in a food queue." Johanna's glance returned to the menu. "Remember when there used to be meat in butchers' shops and on menus? It's vanished everywhere. Just like milk. If I didn't go home to the farm sometimes and see it being taken away via the dairy to the German barracks, I'd think all the cows had dried up." She made her choice. "I'm going to have boiled cod."

"I'll have the same."

They both knew they were taking a chance on its being fresh, as with any other fish dish on the menu. The best of the sea catch went to the occupation forces. When Steffen gave the order to the waitress, Johanna produced a raw potato from Astrid's kitchen garden to hand over to her. It was only by handing in a raw potato that customers were served a cooked one in exchange. As with meat, dairy products and fish, the potato crop went to feed the enemy in control, and it was the same with carrots and other vegetables, commercial growers being forbidden to place their products elsewhere. Only the rubbish reached the shops. Civilians also grew their own or bought on the black market if desperate enough and able to pay the exorbitant black market prices. If not, they went without. The days when Norway had one of the highest standards of living in the world had become a dream of the past. Hunger had become part of everyday living.

When the cooked potato came steaming on her plate, Johanna was humourously jubilant. "We're in luck! Not only is this cod quite fresh, but this potato is larger than the one I handed in."

"Hurrah," he joked, laughing with her. Meticulously she divided it in half and shared it with him.

They ate with wooden utensils, locally made. It had come to that in most cafés and restaurants as normal cutlery had been hoarded, broken, mislaid or filched by soldiers who had lost their own army issue. The tablecloths were of paper, for the small soap ration made laundry on a large scale difficult. In any case, after three years of Occupation, worn-out tablecloths were impossible to replace.

"I stayed in an Oslo hotel recently," Steffen told her after remarking that when the war was over he was never going to eat fish again. "The bedsheets were paper. I woke up in the morning with ribbons of paper everywhere."

"You must be a restless sleeper."

He gave her a straightforward look. "It depends."

She ignored his remark. "What were you doing in Oslo?"

"Working in a certain good cause."

"That reminds me." She took up the newspaper and passed it across to him. "As arranged, here's something for you to read."

"I'll look forward to studying it." He slipped it vertically into the pocket of his jacket.

"Maybe it's of interest, maybe not." She made a sideways rocking movement with her hand. "I never know."

"You're not meant to. You do your job and we'll do ours. That brings me to something that is on the cards for you. Does Tom ever go to Oslo?"

"Not often. Once in three or four months perhaps. Why?"

"We could do with a regular courier. One with legitimate business in the city. It was hoped you might be able to persuade him to take you along—in the capacity of your work, I hasten to add—if he travelled there fairly often."

"No dice, I'm afraid."

"It's a link that's not needed yet awhile, so keep your eyes and ears open. You never know. It's possible something will come up if he gets a promotion or changes his routine."

"I'll remember."

He stared with a broadening grin at her fast emptying plate. "When did you last eat?"

She was unabashed. "I told you I was hungry."

"Half starved is more like it."

"That's the price of being young and healthy on inadequate rations. It's only when I'm home on the farm or at Tom's for the weekend that I get sufficient food. I always take some back for Astrid, although she has a small appetite." She laid her wooden fork down across her plate. "Why do wooden utensils seem to need a troll's mouth to accommodate them? The Vikings made spoons of polished horn. That must have been much better."

"I'll make you one next time I meet a reindeer."

She laughed softly, her eyes merry. "That's a promise."

His eyes were full of love. "I want to marry you, Jo."

Startled, she drew back slowly in her chair. "Don't say that."

"I mean it. For the first time in my life I want to put a wedding ring on a woman's finger and it can't be done. At least, not here in our own country where officially I don't exist. Come back to England with me the next time I go. We can be married in London."

Spreading her hand down one side of her face, she shielded her expression from anyone glancing across at their secluded corner table and spoke in a fierce whisper. "We're not supposed to make ourselves conspicuous and you put something like that to me with the chance of a dozen or more people looking on!"

His expression remained unconcerned. "You forget I'm facing a mirror. I'm watching the door and the rest of the place all the time. Nobody is interested in us. What do you say?"

"When we first made love it was a commitment to each other, even if we did lose ourselves for a while along the way. Marriage is something that has to wait until life is normal again. Nothing has changed for us yet."

"Yes, it has, now that I've asked you to come to London with me."

She shook her head vigorously. "In the early days of the Occupation I would have gone with you from Oslo if it had been possible. As I mentioned before, maybe I've done nothing of real importance in my underground work so far, but the chance remains that I'll come across something vital at some time, whether I ever know the outcome or not. There isn't anything I could do in exile that would make me feel that much of use in the cause of freedom." Moving back her chair in readiness to leave, she had a chuckle in her throat. "Thanks for suggesting marriage. I had begun to think you'd never ask!"

He grinned at her. "I meant to have you since I first saw you looking out of the Alsteens' window in Oslo at the Nazi bombers on invasion day."

She raised an eyebrow comically. "Now you tell me!"

"I love you."

That made it hard to go from him then, both of them hit by a wave of seriousness, not knowing when they would see each other again. She had to tear her eyes away from the gaze in which he held her and force herself to get up from the chair to leave the café. It would have been all too easy to change her mind and say she would go with him to England, whenever that might be.

Far from clearing up the Resistance in his extensive district, Axel was finding that pockets persisted that he could neither locate nor subdue. He knew that small boats came and went on matters hostile to the Third Reich, that illegal transmitters provided London with vital information and that sabotage plots were hatched in the most commonplace surroundings. It was the secret agents he most wanted to ensnare, and it was galling to suspect he passed them by in the street from the comfort of his large car, for there would be nothing to distinguish them from their fellow citizens.

At least he had made himself feared in the district. Spot checks had increased at his orders, people were brought in for questioning on the slightest cause and every trick in the book used to get information out of those likely to know something merely by observation of others' change of rou-

tine. He did not hesitate to inflict torture on an obstinate
suspect caught in a subversive situation, and when a man
was finally broken it led to the arrest of those named, if
they had not already gone into hiding upon hearing that
their confederate had been taken into custody. The constant challenge excited and stimulated him. There was not
a morning when he did not wake in anticipation of the day,
even when things were swinging temporarily against him.

Although his successes had been moderate, approval of
his thorough and ruthless methods had been voiced by
Reichskommissar Terboven, who was known to be increasingly exasperated that subversive activities should persist
after all the reprisals and punishments meted out during
three and a half years of occupation. Axel foresaw further
promotion and commendation if he could just land a big
fish in the nets that he set wider and wider in his personal
battle against the Resistance.

He had nothing to do with minor matters such as hoarding and black marketeering unless it had a bearing on
security. These matters were dealt with by the quisling
police. It was the suspicion that arms were hidden in an old
warehouse that took him to the scene, only to discover that
the crates held tinned food stolen from the army and other
stores which were not in his field at all. Annoyed, he was
about to leave when a crate was prised open with contents
that caught his attention. Wrapped in protective covering
were a number of silver fox skins. They could not have
been recently produced, for luxury trades had been eliminated everywhere by the war. Without hesitation, he
snapped an order at the sergeant in charge.

"Deliver that crate to my quarters."

It duly arrived and his batman stored it in a cupboard.
For a while he thought no more about it, his instinct never
to let pass any spoils of war having been satisfied. He had
more pressing matters on his mind. An informer had given
him a tip-off that promised to be particularly fruitful.

When catering for the weekends at Tom Ryen's house,
Karen always took an order of bread from her brother-in-
law. Previously she had made the bread herself, but she
saw no reason why Raold should not have the benefit of the
business, particularly as it eased the work-load at the time

of the week when she had much to prepare. Her sister usually made the delivery with a horse and wagonette, using the excuse to see Karen and have a chat. Throughout the summer there had been none of the secret comings and goings to which Raold had referred, but with the arrival of the darker nights of autumn the stage was set once more. Marthe's agitation was noticeable when she brought the bread into the house one Friday afternoon. Twice she dropped loaves as she was helping to unload them from the basket.

"What's the matter with you?" Karen inquired considerately.

Marthe feigned surprise. "There's nothing wrong with me."

Karen smiled at her. "Come on. I know you better than that. Aren't you well?"

The reply came almost irritably. "If you must know, I do get nervous when we get important company after a break from having to watch for Germans night and day."

"Oh." Comprehending, Karen paused in putting the bread away. "I wouldn't have asked if I'd known."

"That's all right." Marthe took the last loaf from the basket. "There's no harm in your knowing. Our visitor came in the middle of the night and tomorrow night he changes places with someone arriving by boat. I never like change-overs. It's a double danger for everyone concerned. I'll be glad when it's all over." She forced a smile. "I expect it will be weeks before anyone else comes and I'll have time to calm down again."

After Marthe had left, Karen finished what she had to do in the kitchen and then went upstairs to put clean towels in the bedrooms and make sure everything was in order when Tom and Johanna arrived. There were to be three house guests, including Axel Werner, while a number of other people were coming to a party on Saturday night. Tom was becoming less inclined to have large parties or to have more than a small number to stay, for food and drink were no longer as easy for him to come by. Fortunately, most of his guests brought bottles with them, and so far Karen's culinary skills had disguised any major shortages. In her own mind she despised Tom for his boot-licking, being less forgiving than Johanna, who tolerated him for

the weak man that he was, seeing his political aims as
pathetically futile, for the Germans admired strength and
his lack of stamina was easy to discern. To her, Johanna had
expressed the conviction more than once that, with some
exceptions, those who came to the house were simply taking advantage of him, and if the slightest thing went wrong
in his managing of the office he would find himself transported into a compulsory labour force the next day. He
had made no friends among the Wehrmacht, of that she
was sure, even if he did believe otherwise.

On Saturday night the party was in full swing. Johanna
kept the dancing to the newer part of the house and it was
from there that most of the noisy laughter came. Two of
the house guests, older men with no interest in dancing,
wanted a game of bridge and had managed to find a third
player. They asked Johanna if she could locate a fourth to
join them.

"I think so." She knew Axel was a keen bridge player
and she went in search of him. Unable to see him in any of
the rooms, she asked for him and was told he had gone out.
Thinking this meant he was taking a breath of fresh air, she
went outside, but could not find him in the porch or on the
verandah. As it was raining, she thought it hardly likely he
was taking a stroll. Deciding to waste no more time, she
went back indoors, found another player instead, and left
the four men on their own in the rose-ceilinged room
while she took a tray of dirty glasses into the kitchen where
Karen was washing up. As Johanna took up a cloth to dry,
Karen glanced at her and noticed some splashes down her
sleeve and damp on her long skirt.

"What's that on your dress?"

"Raindrops. I took a quick look outside for Axel Werner.
There was a bridge game in the offing and that's right up
his street."

"Did you find him?"

"No. A naval man made up a fourth."

Karen stopped washing the dishes and gripped the edge
of the enamel sink, the suds slipping down her hands, a
look of fright in her face. "Go and find out if he's upstairs or
in the bathroom or anywhere," she implored harshly.

Johanna looked at her in anxious bewilderment, a half-
dried plate still in her hands. "What is it? What's wrong?"

"I don't know. It may be nothing, but he's commandant of security and my brother-in-law has a Resistance fighter in his house tonight with another coming off a boat."

Johanna thrust down the dish and the cloth to dash from the kitchen. Upstairs she checked Axel's bedroom and anywhere else where he might have been. Failing to find him, she hastened downstairs again and went through every room. He was not there. She rushed back into the kitchen.

"Tell me where your brother-in-law lives! I'll change my clothes and get over there!"

"No!" Karen was adamant. "I'll go. Nobody will miss me out here in the kitchen, but people expect you to be around all the time. I can reach Raold's place without being seen if I row there." She left the kitchen to fetch a sweater, slacks and sneakers from the room she occupied at the top of the house and changed into them when she returned, not wanting to be spotted in outdoor clothes. Johanna fetched her one of Tom's flashlights and gave her some last-minute advice.

"Do be careful. The area will be alive with troops if things are as we fear. The two men will surely make for the cover of the mountains. Stay the night at your sister's if you can. That would be safer than trying to get back here. I'll cover your absence somehow, although with luck you won't be missed."

Karen slipped out into the darkness of the wet night. Running swiftly away from the house, she went down to the bank where the row-boats were moored. Within moments she had cast off and was settling the oars into the oarlocks. The rain pattered on the boards of the boat and struck cold through the scarf with which she had covered her hair. She was barely aware of it, gripped by fear of what the outcome would be for Marthe and Raold if they were discovered with freedom fighters in their house. With the rustling of the trees along the shoreline, the rain, and the choppiness of the water, she gained no clue as to whether there were any grounds for her alarm until she caught a glimpse of headlights which, in spite of the narrow chink of light allowed to escape ahead, enabled her to see that there was more than one truck approaching along the road. Her guess was that soldiers were being moved in to close upon the village. Desperately she lent her strength to the oars with renewed effort. Never had it seemed longer to reach the moorings below her old home. Once she thought she heard distant shots and strained her ears. When nothing more happened, she decided she must have been mistaken. Perhaps she was still in time.

In the bakehouse Gunnar was waiting and ready to leave, glancing constantly at his watch and pacing restlessly. It was stiflingly hot, for Raold was continuing with his night's baking, the smell of yeast and dough overpowering. In the darkness of a room upstairs, Marthe was keeping watch on the road.

"My colleague is overdue," Gunnar remarked edgily.

Raold, who had the same thought, was glad of the work to keep him occupied. "He is," he admitted. "How much longer are you going to give him?"

"I must go on waiting. He'll come sooner or later. Sorry I'm acting like a caged lion. If I could be outside I would be calmer."

"You can't go outside until you're told where the boat is waiting. Everything depends on sentries and patrol boats as to where the actual landing is made."

Gunnar gave an impatient nod, unable to check his pacing. He had gone out into the hallway several times to sit on the stairs and smoke a cigarette. Raold's standards of hygiene would not permit the ash even of a secret agent in his bakehouse. It seemed about time for another nerve-soothing drag when a hasty knocking came on the door. Immediately Raold gave a tense nod and Gunnar went quickly through into the hallway, his revolver ready in his hand. Through a crack in the door he watched Raold open the outer door cautiously and then widen it immediately to admit a young woman he had never seen before.

"Karen!" Raold exclaimed. "What are you doing here?"

"I've come to warn you! Are the Resistance men still in the house? They should get away at once."

Gunnar emerged from the doorway. "Who are you?"

Raold spoke for her. "My wife's sister."

"What do you think is wrong?" Gunnar questioned her abruptly, putting his revolver away.

She stepped forward in her frantic anxiety. "I've seen trucks approaching the village. More than that. I work at Tom Ryen's house on the other side of the inlet and the S.S.

security commandant in this area left a party there earlier for no apparent reason."

"The Ryen house? Are you with Johanna?"

"Yes, I am. She knows I'm here." She broke off as there came a tapping. Both men recognised the prearranged signal.

"Come into the hallway with me," Gunnar whispered, grabbing her arm. "Just in case the visitor is not whom we're expecting." Again he waited with his revolver raised. Karen pushed back against the stairs behind him and watched as once more Raold opened the door. It was Steffen.

Re-entering the bakehouse, Gunnar ceased grinning as he saw the ashy pallor of Steffen's face and the way in which he slumped back against the wall. "You're hurt! What's happened?"

"I was nicked in the shoulder."

Gunnar pulled Steffen's jacket aside and saw a red stain seeping through the thick wool of the jersey beneath. "You must have that wound dressed. You're losing a lot of blood."

Steffen pushed him away. "That can wait. You can't. Get out of here. Now! The mountains are your only chance. You'd never reach the fishing boat. That's cut off by a nest of Germans. I went smack into them when I came across towards the village. When they don't find me in the undergrowth, they'll move onto the moored vessels and into the village. I only hope the skipper heard the shots, but it's unlikely."

"We'll try for the mountains together." Gunnar grabbed a wad of clean dough coverings from a bench. "These will hold you together until we can get you medical attention."

"I'd never make it. I told you to clear out." Steffen was becoming angry. "I didn't wrench my guts getting here for you to behave like a fool. Any moment there'll be a house-to-house search throughout the village. You won't have a chance."

Gunnar gave a mocking snort, continuing to make an emergency pad of the linen coverings under the shoulder of Steffen's jacket and binding it around as hard as it could be fastened. "Don't be so bloody pig-headed. It's not only you they're hunting. Raold's sister-in-law here believes the

Gestapo had a tip-off. You and I are both in the cart and that means we leave together."

While he was speaking there was a scurrying of footsteps down the stairs and Marthe appeared, trembling with fright in the doorway. "Germans! Coming down the street in both directions!"

Karen ran forward to Gunnar. "I'll show you where I've left a row-boat. Take it. Take Steffen to Tom Ryen's house. I'll tell you where to put ashore. Johanna will be keeping watch. She'll find a place for you to hide. The house is full of Wehrmacht officers. Nobody would look for you there!"

A groan came from Steffen. "Not Johanna! We don't want to involve her in this mess."

Gunnar ignored him, intent on Karen. "Where's this row-boat?"

"Come with me."

When Steffen thrust himself away from the wall he reeled and would have fallen if he had not been given support, Gunnar pulling his uninjured arm about his own shoulders. Raold switched out the light and held the door for them, having been told to stay where he was and get on with his work, there being nothing more he could do. The two of them went with Karen out into the darkness. The rain had become torrential, stinging their faces as they hurried down to the water's edge. Gunnar got Steffen into the boat first, but when he held out his hand to Karen she hung back.

"I'm not going." She gave him instructions as to where to go ashore. "Tell me the name of the fishing boat you were supposed to take and the signal for the skipper. I might get through to warn him by following the rocks."

"*Fjellpike* is the name of the boat and the password is 'Midgard.'"

Steffen supplied the rest of what she had to know. "There's only one place on the west side of the point where fishing boats can put in. You'll find the *Fjellpike* there."

"I know it. Good luck!"

"And to you."

Gunnar pulled strongly away from the shore and she vanished immediately in the wet blackness. Steffen, slumped in the bow, spoke his thoughts for both of them.

"I hope she makes it. It's likely to be curtains for the whole crew if she doesn't."

After that they kept silent for security reasons, it being automatic to them. The boat bobbed through the fierce little waves, spray showering over them continually and yet impossible to define in the downpour beyond a salty taste on the lips. Once the inlet was crossed Gunnar kept close to the shore, Steffen straining his eyes for the boathouses that were the landmark. They loomed up eventually and Gunnar located a place to moor. Whether it was the right mooring or not he had no idea. All that mattered was to get ashore and into hiding.

After helping Steffen out of the boat and into the boathouse, where he slithered to his knees, his head coming to rest weakly against the wall, Gunnar went to reconnoitre. He kept to the cover of the trees. In spite of the black-out, slivers of a gleam outlined some of the windows in the house, which blended into the night, making it impossible to pick out the roof or its proportions. The sound of music was a good guide as to where the party was centred and eventually he darted across to feel his way along the wall to the rear of the house where the kitchen was likely to be located. As he stepped onto the porch an old board creaked and immediately the kitchen door opened narrowly, flooding him with an arrow of light. There was a gasp of astonishment.

"Gunnar!" Johanna darted out to him, closing the door behind her. "Where's Karen?"

"She stayed behind. I've 'the Englishman' with me. He's wounded."

"How badly?" Her voice shook.

"I don't know yet. Where shall I take him?"

"It's essential you come into the house in case there should be a search of the outbuildings in a general check. There's a storeroom off the kitchen where I can hide you for the time being. I had intended to get whoever came into a room at the top of the house next to Karen's and where only she goes, but that will have to wait. Do you want any help?"

"No. Just be ready to let us in."

Johanna went back indoors. Dodging around the table loaded with dirty glasses, she reached the door into the hall, which she had previously locked as a precaution, and peeped through. Nobody was in the hall or on the stairs. She flew up a flight to the landing where an army first-aid box and spare bandages were kept in readiness in a cupboard. With blankets under her other arm she returned to the kitchen and deposited the items on the stone floor of the storeroom. Then back she went to the linen cupboard. She had taken out some sheets when Tom came up the stairs.

"Hello? Remaking beds at this hour?"

"Somebody has vomited," she replied casually.

"It happens," he remarked philosophically, well under the weather himself, and went into a bathroom. Releasing a sigh of tension, she hastened down the stairs again before he could reappear.

Gunnar, reaching the boathouse, found Steffen still conscious but unable to get to his feet unaided. Hauling him up amid his grunts and stifled groans, Gunnar once more supported him and together they reeled and staggered towards the house, Steffen's legs constantly giving way.

When they reached the kitchen porch there was a brief moment in which Steffen focused on Johanna's face in a haze of light before pain and exhaustion finally overtook him and he blacked out.

Along the rocks and boulders at the fjord's edge Karen scrambled along, making good progress at times, at others slowed down by sections difficult to surmount. The knees of her slacks were torn where she had fallen several times and her sneakers were sopping wet where she had plunged her feet into rock pools hidden in the darkness. Occasionally there was a narrow strip of shingle and she would run that distance. Her route was fraught with the danger of slipping on seaweed that clung to much of the rock mass and breaking or spraining an ankle, and her hands and legs were gashed by rugged surfaces. The conviction that nobody could see or hear her from the land rising away from the fjord encouraged her to speed where at times caution would have prevented a fall. Once she heard a patrol boat approaching and flattened herself on a rock only seconds before its searchlights suddenly switched on, illuminating the whole section where she lay, the rain slashing through the beam in rainbow colours as it passed over her and out again over the surface of the water. Many times the choppy waves splashed up over her when she was forced to follow a lower line of rocks, but she was too soaked through already for that to make any difference. Somewhere along the way she had lost her headscarf and her hair clung to her scalp like a cap.

Then ahead, black against the water, was the crag beyond which she would find the waiting fishing boat. She was compelled to come away from the rocks as the height of the land rose, and she ran through the wet grass, knowing she was on the right side of the point and away from the place where Steffen had barely escaped ambush. Coming level with the little bay she saw the boat below, lying without navigation lights. It was here she was to start giving the password, for someone from the vessel would be waiting near the track that led down to the bay.

"Midgard!" she called in a low voice. The name of a sanctuary created for mortals by the Norse gods was appropriate to the wild night, galloping hoofs in the noise of the waves. "Midgard!"

A figure in black oilskins emerged from the trees almost within touching distance, making her start. "Karen? Is it you, Karen?"

"Erik!" She hurled herself into his arms and their mouths met gloriously. They swayed within their embrace of each other. All the past was wiped out for her. She forgot the misery and self-doubts, the conviction that she was lost to him beyond recall, that Carl had destroyed what might have been. Everything she had ever wanted had returned to her in the loving impact of his kiss. When they drew breath, he laughed softly in his joy at this unexpected reunion until she gasped out why she had come.

"Then you'll be caught if you stay here," he exclaimed. "You're coming with me! I'll take you back to the Shetlands with me."

She thought she was crying with happiness but she could not be sure. He paused only to signal a Morse light to the fishing boat to be alert for departure and then began to run with her towards the track. Below them the vessel's engine had tonk-tonked into life.

"*Achtung!*"

It seemed to her that her heart stopped. A single soldier had appeared, chest heaving from running, to face them, rifle pointing. Erik's reaction was instantaneous. He thrust her behind him and fired a signal-gun that she had not known he was carrying. A single red warning star arched through the blackness down to the water below. If orders had not been given for all captives to be taken alive for interrogation, Erik would have been shot. The soldier ran forward, swearing.

"Hands up! Get your hands up! You too," he added to Karen, who had stumbled down through the impact of Erik's attempt to save her. Then the soldier fired a shot into the air in a summons and more soldiers came swarming out of the woods. He shouted to them and many went pouring down the track, firing their rifles at the fishing boat which was drawing out into the fjord. A sergeant snapped an order, detailing a man to get a radio message through to the coastal patrol. Then he came to have a look at the prisoners, shining a torch into Erik's face and then into Karen's. His voice behind the beam brusquely ordered the seaman to be placed under special arrest. The girl was to be escorted back into the village to join those already arrested.

As Erik was shoved forward by rifles, he strained his head back for a last word with Karen. "We'll find each other again one day."

"I love you," she called to him, helpless with tears. Whether he heard her or not she did not know, soldiers coming between them. Sobs racked her, all the more agonising for being soundless. A rifle gave her a sharp push. Allowed to drop her arms to her sides, she stumbled along, her sneakers slopping uncomfortably on her feet. She was chilled to the bone. Neither of the escorting soldiers spoke to her. The woods had become aflicker with flashlights and she heard the bark of tracker dogs.

She smelt burning before she saw the smoke and then the glow of fire. When the village came into sight she stared in disbelief at the scene of destruction. Soldiers were putting a torch to each house and building in turn, the wood crackling, paintwork spitting. The fishing boats moored by the jetty were also in flames. In the red-gold light she saw the women and children of the village gathered into a group, watching their homes burn down. The menfolk were being shepherded away into waiting trucks, only the very old men being weeded out and sent to join a little group of their own, some with coats over their pyjamas, having been raked out of bed, several blank-faced or completely disorientated. Every person had a dazed look of disbelief. Karen felt it stamped on her own features.

"Why are you doing this?" she cried to her escort.

"By order of the commandant. A just punishment for you and those like you for harbouring secret agents. There's the one we caught." He pointed ahead with his rifle. "We would have taken him alive, but he killed an officer and two men before he was brought down."

The dead Norwegian lay sprawled in his own blood. Karen looked down in grief at his quiet face as she went past. It was neither of the men who had been in Raold's bakehouse. Two plainclothesmen, whom she guessed to be Gestapo, were going through his pockets while Axel Werner, jackbooted feet astride, hands clasped behind his back, stood looking on. She could only conclude that by some devious trick of fate there had been a third agent in the village that night on some purpose of his own. The probable tip-off had been aimed at the two men she had seen and this poor stranger had been accidentally caught in the net.

"Over there!"

The thrust sent her spinning towards the group of women. Some of the babies and the toddlers were crying. Marthe had seen her coming and burst into sobs in her arms. "They've taken Raold away. We don't know what's happening to the men or to us."

Karen held her close. Over her sister's head she saw the gilded sign of the kringler above the door of the bakery turn scorched and brown as the flames licked up the building. The unremitting rain did nothing to quell the fierceness of the fires, and sparks hissed and spat in the puddles.

The razing of the village continued. There were spasmodic shots as pets were destroyed or a horse too old for confiscation was found in a stable. Cackling hens were silenced. It was a disciplined destruction. There was no looting. Everything went to the flames.

After a while more trucks arrived. Now it was the turn of

the women and children to be loaded up. As with the old
men, the women in the same age group were pushed
aside. They wept pathetically, seeing daughters and
grandchildren taken from them. The cries from those in
the trucks were as heart-rending as those from the group
being left behind. Karen, helping with the children, was
the last one up into the truck in which Marthe was waiting
for her.

The trucks began to move off slowly in convoy. Through
the flap of the canvas opening Karen looked out on the
burning village, half hidden now by black clouds of smoke.
A sergeant stepped into the wake of the truck, standing in
the middle of the road, the glow touching his helmet and
the planes of his starkly agonised face. Karen recognised
him and let her eyes dwell on him in silent condemnation
as the distance lengthened between them.

A soldier spoke to him. "What's going to happen to the
villagers?"

Carl spoke dully, watching the disappearing trucks.
"The men are to be sent to concentration camps in Germany. The women and children to the same type of camps
in this country."

"What about the old folk?"

"They're being left, because some of them would probably have died en route." He was uncomfortably aware of
an echo in his own words. Hadn't the medical officer said
similar words on the day he had met Karen again?
Abruptly he turned and snarled at the corporal. "Get back
to the fires. On the double!"

He strode off in the same direction. It was his duty to see
that nothing was left undestroyed. His thoughts followed
Karen. If it had been an officer near at hand instead of
himself at the time of her capture she would have been
taken with the seaman for interrogation by the Gestapo.
At least he had spared her that. Nobody in the heat of the
moment had thought to question his action in sending her
back to the village and now nobody would remember anyway. The memory of her face as she was driven away
would stay with him. He hoped she was strong enough to
survive whatever lay ahead for her.

Chapter 12

In the storeroom Steffen lay unconscious on a bed of blankets. Gunnar knelt on one side of him and Johanna on the other. She handed across whatever was required from the German first-aid box and helped cut away the blood-soaked jersey and the shirt beneath to reach the wound. There proved to be no damage to any major blood vessel. It was a flesh wound that had been greatly aggravated by his efforts to reach the bakehouse. He was suffering from shock, exhaustion and a considerable loss of blood. When the dressing was completed, Gunnar drew up the blankets under his colleague's chin and settled the pillow more comfortably.

"He needs rest. Lots of it. When he comes round we must give him plenty of fluid. That's the only treatment in these circumstances." He sat back, setting his hands across his thighs, elbows jutting, and looked across to Johanna. He thought she made an incongruously beautiful sight in their strange surroundings of flour sacks and bottled preserves and storage pots, the wounded man lying between the two of them. Her silky evening dress fell in folds around her where she knelt, a diamanté strap slipping down off one shoulder, a swing of hair tucked behind one ear. Her expression was transparent as she gazed down at Steffen. There was such intense feeling, so much love.

"Is he in a lot of pain, do you think?" she asked anxiously.

"He's not aware of it at the moment." Gunnar saw the tears spill out of her eyes in two large drops and she half covered her mouth with her hand as if holding back a sob. His tone became gentle. "Hey! He's not going to die. I wouldn't let him. Now or any other time."

She lowered her hand to her lap and forced a watery smile. "I know. I'm crying with relief that his wound isn't worse than it is. He looked in a terrible state when you

271

brought him in." Hastily she dried her eyes with the back
of her hand, blinking over it. "I must return to the party.
You'll be safe enough here. I wish I knew that Karen was all
right. Do you think she could have reached the fishing boat
in time?"

"As I told you, she was confident that she could."

"I won't be easy in my mind until she's back. I hope she
makes it before anyone is up and about in the morning."
She rose to her feet. "I'll get a jug of water in readiness for
Steffen and get rid of his shirt and jersey. Tom's wardrobe
has replacements."

When she had put the discarded emergency dressings
and the garments to burn and had emptied away the bowl
of water with which she had washed the blood from Steffen's chest and arms, she filled a jug from the tap and
handed it with a cup to Gunnar. After shutting the storeroom door she leaned against it, closing her eyes briefly as
she fought against a delayed reaction to the shock that the
sight of Steffen had given her. There had been such a rush
of love in her that she had wanted to hold him, kiss him and
weep over him like a character in a Greek tragedy, terrified that he was going to die. But such primeval behaviour
had come nowhere near the surface. Thoroughly twenti-
eth-century, she had stayed calm, taken on the role of
nurse and kept her head even when the mess of the wound
was exposed, her own flesh feeling pain in empathy. Now,
drawing in a deep breath, she went across to a mirror and
checked that there were no blood streaks on her face, and
released her hair from behind her ear. When she went out
of the kitchen she fully expected to be met by Tom ex-
pressing annoyance over her prolonged absence from the
gathering. To her surprise, the army musicians who had
made up the band that evening were packing up their
instruments in the hall.

"Are you going already?" she queried, glancing at her
watch. "It's barely midnight."

"Nobody wants to dance any more," one of the band
answered her. "Those who aren't outside on the verandah
have gone to the fire. We're taking the—er—ladies back to
town in our truck."

"Fire?" She was alarmed. It was not often that a house

caught fire, but when it did it frequently went up like tinder. "Whose home is it? Does anyone know?"

"It looks like the whole village."

She ran through the deserted party room to the verandah. The glow lit the sky above the trees and tinted the fjord. The officers who had not left the house stood smoking cigarettes and exchanging comments. Half a dozen women, subdued by what they were witnessing while at the same time annoyed at being left high and dry, waited together for their ride back. Johanna spotted Tom and darted to him.

"Whatever is happening there? We should go and join a bucket chain or something. The local fire brigade can't cope with that on its own until other brigades arrive. People will be homeless. There'll be lots we can do."

Tom maintained an uncomfortable silence. The officer next to him half turned to address her. "A sergeant has just reported back to us. It's not that kind of fire, fräulein. This is an elimination of subversion. There'll be no homeless there. The population is to be dispersed into places of correction."

She drew back instinctively, struck by a wave of aversion, and stood as if unable to move in any direction, hands limp at her sides. There was a flurry of movement from the direction of the women as the band members' truck appeared. They jumped down the verandah steps and ran across the wet grass, heads down against the rain, grumbling fiercely amongst themselves. Without exception they had arrived in cars. They were used to being treated with callous indifference on occasion, but the present indignity rankled.

Feeling nauseated, Johanna turned back into the house. Tom, seeing her go, followed her. She had sat down sideways on a chair, her arm resting along the back, and was turned away from him. He hovered uncertainly, twisting a gold ring on his finger.

"It could have been worse, Johanna. You heard what was said. The people are being taken away, not shot."

Her voice came tight and strained. "Are you trying to tell me that mercy has been shown?"

"In a way, yes. So far there are no details. We shall hear more when Axel Werner returns. He told me when he arrived that he had to be on duty for a few hours locally this evening. Naturally the firing of the village has upset you. It has upset me. I've known those village families for years. I'm not made of steel." He balled his fists in agitation and shook them in emphasis, even though she remained facing away from him. "For your sake and for mine, don't show any hostility. The Germans are edgy at times like these. We don't want to get involved in trouble of any kind."

He saw her shake her head despairingly and thought she said, "Oh, Tom." He could not be sure. The company was coming in from the verandah and their voices drowned out her quiet murmur. Switching on a jovial smile, he bounced forward to meet them.

"Now, gentlemen. I'm sure your glasses need replenishing."

When he turned again she was no longer in the room. He thought it was as well. Later, when the house guests had retired and the place was quiet again, he took a last look from the front steps. The glow had gone. There was an acrid smell of smoke hanging in the air. Somewhere along the road a car was approaching. As he expected, the S.S. commandant was returning. The driver jumped out to hold the car door and Axel alighted. He looked tired and less than satisfied.

"We wounded one agent, who escaped in the undergrowth," he informed Tom, mounting the steps, "and killed a second one whom we surprised with a transmitter."

"Is the search still on?"

"The area is being tooth-combed." Axel went ahead into the house, removing his shiny-peaked cap and setting it aside. He smoothed his hair back above his ears with the palms of his hands, eradicating the indentation caused by the inner cap band. "A hard night. Not one that I relish."

"We had a report."

"Then you know the villagers' fate. I'm not a butcher, Major Ryen."

"Indeed not."

"Only the menfolk of the house that harboured the secret agent will be put to the firing squad tomorrow morning. It means I'll have to return to duty early, cutting my weekend short. A nuisance, but there it is."

"How many are to be shot?" Tom's tone was hollow.

"The husband, three sons between the ages of eighteen and twenty-two, and an uncle who lived with the family. An unpleasant business, but an example has to be made as a deterrent to others."

"Isn't the razing of the village enough?"

Axel gave him a hard look. "There were three fatal casualties among my forces tonight and two wounded. I could have had every person in that village shot. It has happened in other annexed territories where there has been flagrant defiance of the Third Reich. I've been lenient. Don't you agree?"

"Yes, you have," Tom agreed hastily, perjuring himself.

"We also captured a seaman from the fishing vessel involved in tonight's incident."

"Is he from these parts?"

"His papers gave a name and a home address near Bergen, but the information is probably false. These fellows try to protect their families and friends by assuming other identities. We'll learn more from him when he has been persuaded to talk. The Gestapo are taking him to Oslo."

"What about the fishing boat?"

"Sunk. No survivors. It failed to heed a shot across the bows from a patrol boat."

Tom was relieved Johanna was not within earshot. She was not as tough as he had believed when she had first come to work for him. Had she not been a relative and more efficient than any secretary he had ever had before, he would have had to think twice about keeping her in his employ. He had his own future to consider. "The crew brought it on themselves," he commented crisply.

"How right you are." Axel unbuttoned his uniform jacket and eased his tie free. "Yet I'm an optimist, you know. With time, your countrymen will come to see the error of their ways. As I've always said, it's only a question of eradicating the wrong ideals and beliefs."

"My view entirely. Now what about a cognac before you retire?"

Axel grunted acceptance. In any case it was his cognac. He had presented his host with a bottle upon his arrival for the weekend. "Perhaps Johanna or Frøken What's-her-name could make me a sandwich?"

"That shall be done. I'll pour you the drink first."

Massaging a tired shoulder, Axel followed his host into the rose-ceilinged room where earlier a game of bridge had been played. He flung himself down in a chair and stretched his long legs towards the embers on the stone hearth. Setting his elbows on the wooden arms, he pressed the forefinger of each hand against the bridge of his nose. Tension frequently brought on a headache for him. He was churning with sullen anger that one of his quarries had slipped the noose. His only hope was that the wound inflicted had been a bad one and the body would be found before the night was over. As the glass was handed to him, he looked up as he took it. "The garages and boathouse and the grounds around your house will be searched at some time during the night. There's no need to go outside yourself. No damage will be done." He raised his glass in salute. *"Prosit."*

"Skål."

In the kitchen Johanna had washed up everything from the party and Gunnar had dried it for her. Her aim was to cover Karen's absence for as long as possible, her hope being that the girl had been nowhere near the village when the fire started. The spare crockery was kept in the storeroom when not in use and Gunnar had just carried a stack of plates into the room and onto a shelf there when she heard chair legs scrape in the hall. She had placed a chair awkwardly in front of the door into the kitchen to give warning of anyone's approach. To have locked the door would have invoked questions of one kind or another.

"Someone's coming," she whispered to Gunnar. "Switch off the storeroom light."

Tom entered, grumbling about the chair left in the way, just as the storeroom door closed. Johanna set down the stack of plates she had been about to hand through to Gunnar and looked inquiringly at Tom.

"Is there something you want?"

"Axel Werner is back. He'd like a sandwich." He saw her expression change and held up a placating hand. "I'm not asking you. Karen can do it."

She swallowed hard. "She's finished with chores here this evening. Leave it to me."

He could see what it cost her to oblige him and took it as a sign that, in spite of her emotional traits, she was basically realistic after all. Axel Werner and his ilk were a part of life and would remain so, perhaps for centuries to come. Making him a sandwich was tantamount to acceptance of that fact, all the tragedy of the village put aside as it had to be. Genuinely fond of her, Tom noted the shadows under her eyes. She looked exhausted, almost brittle with stress. The village fire had been as hard on her in its own way as it had been on Axel Werner in another.

"I'll give you some help since Karen has gone to bed. You make the sandwiches and I'll put that heavy crockery away for you."

"No!" She spoke with unusual sharpness, surprising him. Then she smiled, making an apologetic gesture to amend her retort. "I mean, there's no need. It can wait until the morning, for that matter."

"Karen needs the space to prepare breakfast. I know you. You'll do it anyway to get the place tidy for her." He picked up the stack of plates she had put down.

She moved swiftly in front of him, blocking the storeroom door. "Go back to Axel. He's your guest and you're leaving him on his own."

"He'll be all right. It's you I'm worried about." He reached her with the plates. "Step aside now. Nothing is going to make me leave this kitchen until I've put every piece of crockery away."

"Tom!" It was a desperate cry of appeal. "Please do as I say."

"My dear girl. What is it? What's the matter?"

While standing in front of the storeroom door, she had inadvertently touched it with her heel. Not completely closed, it began to swing open slowly behind her until stopped by Gunnar in the triangular space behind it where he had taken up a precautionary position, gun in hand. Steffen might still have remained undiscovered if at that moment he had not begun to regain consciousness, emitting a groan. Further concealment of him was impossible. Tom, his whole face a mask of apprehension, thrust the plates he was holding into Johanna's arms and shoved her aside to stare in appalled disbelief at the wounded man rolling his head from one side to the other on the pillow of the makeshift bed.

"Who is he?" In panic Tom seized Johanna by the shoulders and shook her, his voice frenzied. "Who have you brought into my house?"

She was struggling to keep the plates from sliding out of her grasp. "You must let him stay! I love him, Tom. He was wounded this evening and there was nowhere else for him to go."

"Do you realise what you've done to me?" He shook a fist under her nose as if he could have battered her to pulp, his colour purple, sweat starting in beads from his forehead and upper lip. "Werner has troops combing the district for him and you dare to ask me to let him stay! You might as well ask me to cut my own throat! I'm denouncing him now!"

She swung herself in front of him as he would have made for the hall, defying him with vehemence, she as forgetful as he of the plates that were causing her to bend over them as they slid about in her arms. "I'll swear you were in it as much as I! I'll tell the Nazi that this house is a Resistance hide-out during the week when there's nobody here, and your hospitality to the Wehrmacht is a cover-up. I'll boast that you're related as I am to the Ryen brothers fighting for freedom. I'll say that my lover isn't the first secret agent we've sheltered together. Some of the lies I'll tell them will stick sufficiently to ruin all those hopes you have of any political future. There is even a chance that you'll end up in a concentration camp with me!"

The plates finally defeated her, slithering down out of her arms to smash onto the floor and bounce in pieces about their feet, the noise as terrifying to their taut nerves as if a bomb had exploded between them, no less to Gunnar, out of sight and geared to equal pitch. Axel, who had been on his way to the kitchen, opened the door at that moment and grimaced at the pain that the noise shot through his aching temples.

"What's going on here? I came to tell you that the soldiers are around the house now, Major Ryen. As they're here already I'm going outside to hear if there's any fresh news. Perhaps you would like to come with me." He went straight past the open storeroom door without a glance and reached the back door, which he swung open, and paused to glance back over his shoulder at Tom. "Well?" Then his head snapped back with impatience. "What the hell is the matter with you? It was only a load of plates. You look as if you've just faced the end of the world."

Tom, feeling himself to be in that very position, opened his mouth and closed it again. Out of the corner of his eye he saw Johanna move swiftly to reach into the storeroom and bring the door shut with a click, hiding the secret within.

"I'll join you," he said woodenly to Axel, following after him. His thoughts began to twist and turn. Maybe there was still a means by which he could bring the soldiers into the house and hand the wounded man over to them. Unfortunately for him, no loophole came to mind.

Gunnar raised both hands expressively when Johanna re-entered the storeroom. "Well done! You were fantastic."

"Don't praise me. I worked out long ago that I should have to put pressure on Tom in that manner if he ever caught me taking information from the files. I never thought it would be used in circumstances like this. Luckily he doesn't suspect that you're here, too." She knelt down beside Steffen, taking the hand he held out to her and leaning forward to kiss him lovingly.

"You are here then." His voice was blurred with weakness, a smile catching up one corner of his mouth. "I thought I'd been dreaming."

"I'm here and it's no dream. You just have to be as quiet as you can."

"Where are we? Is it Tom Ryen's place?"

She nodded. "It's safe as long as nobody hears us talking. Gunnar will tell you everything later. Drink some water for me now and then sleep. We want you to rest and get your strength back."

The effort of being slightly raised to drink from the cup made his head swim. He slept as soon as he was returned to the pillow. She slid her arm away from under his neck and stood up, gazing down at him. Gunnar took the cup from her and set it on a shelf. "So far, so good," he remarked.

"I feel as if I'm surrounded by live grenades that might go off at any minute," she confessed. "We can't trust Tom yet. Karen hasn't returned. Upstairs there are three sleeping Nazis with a fourth prowling around outside the house like a stalking leopard." She turned to leave the storeroom.

Gunnar chuckled. "At least we're not lacking excitement."

His cheerful attitude helped to raise her spirits. In the kitchen she made a plate of food for him, cleared up the broken china and prepared sandwiches for Axel. These she carried through to the rose-ceilinged room to await his return. Switching off the light, she held back the black-out curtain to look out, but it was impossible to see anything.

As she had hoped, Tom brought Axel back into the house by the front door. She felt enervated by relief. It meant that Tom had been unable to devise any ruse by which to wriggle off the hook, something that had kept fear high in her. He gave her a murderous look as he came into the room behind Axel. Like most even-tempered people, when he did get in a rage the aftermath made him physically ill and completely upset his metabolism.

"Have the soldiers gone?" she asked Axel.

"Yes. There should be no more disturbances tonight unless a capture is made and that possibility seems to be diminishing with every minute." He flung himself down in a chair and took a sandwich from the tray put beside him. Seeing she was about to leave, he beckoned her back and indicated with a wagging finger that she should sit down in a chair set almost at right angles to him. "There's something I want to ask you."

Her fear increased again. Was he going to play some trick? She saw that Tom, who had sunk down on a wooden-backed sofa on the other side of the room, appeared to have the same misgivings. His drawn face looked old and scared, the jowls hanging, and even his shoulders had taken on a rounded look.

"What did you want to know?" She sat on the edge of the chair, hands linked tightly together.

"It was the colder temperature outside that reminded me. Several times when I've been with you it has slipped my mind. I need some advice about furs and I know you worked in the fur trade."

It was such a totally unexpected topic that she could only look at him speechlessly. Tom, still wary, not entirely sure that he and Johanna and the wounded man were out of the woods yet, made some kind of endorsement. "You couldn't ask anyone better. Johanna knows a lot about furs."

Axel ignored him. "Some silver fox skins came into my possession a few weeks ago. They look good to me and I thought how much my wife would like a new fur coat. It's not altogether easy for those at home in Germany these days, and I think she would appreciate something warm to wear in the winter ahead."

At any other time she might have smiled at his unimaginative attitude. Few women wore a beautiful fur coat for its warmth. As for its not being easy in Germany, several officers had talked to her about conditions at home, either quoting from family letters or describing an uncomfortable leave there. The hardships of war had begun to creep up on their fatherland, much of it due to Allied air raids.

"What did you want to know?" Her question was abrupt.

"If there are enough skins for a coat and whether they're of good enough quality to be made up."

"I'm not an expert, but I could tell you that."

"Then I'll bring them along next time I'm here." He stretched his neck forward to glance across at Tom. "Would you fix that? I wouldn't want to find Johanna had gone home that particular weekend."

Twice Tom struggled to choke up his voice. "Johanna will be here." His gaze switched to meet hers, his murderous look for her unabated. "We can arrange that, can't we?"

"Easily." She felt almost sorry for him.

She sat by Steffen and kept watch most of the night. It was her choice. Then Gunnar woke from among the extra blankets she had supplied him with and took over from her. Steffen was restless and in a lot of pain, but took the fluids they kept pouring into him. In the morning she was up early and her anxiety increased because Karen had not returned. She and Gunnar discussed the possibility, which was becoming more probable with every minute, that she had returned to the village and been transported away from it with her sister and brother-in-law.

Axel was up by seven o'clock and away from the house half an hour later. By midafternoon the other three house guests had departed. Johanna went into the rose-ceilinged

room where she knew Tom would be awaiting her. He sat
with his head in his hands, elbows on his knees. His wrath
of the previous night had gone, but together with the
dreadful suspense in which he had been kept for a night
and best part of the next day, a toll had been taken on him.
He was as lacking in energy as if he had come through a
serious illness. If he had looked in the mirror that morning
and seen that his hair had turned completely white, he
would not have been in the least surprised. As her step
sounded across the pinewood floor he spoke without looking up.

"You said something last night about being in love with
the fellow in the storeroom."

She went to the window and looked out. The autumnal
sun made a pattern through the filmy curtains and veiled
her face. "I do love him. All I want is that we should be able
to spend the rest of our lives together."

"Didn't you think of the risk you were putting on me by
taking him in?"

She turned slowly and rested her hands behind her on
the sill, leaning against them. "I thought only of him."

"Have you known him long?"

"Since the day of the invasion. We met at the Alsteens'.
He used to stay there whenever he was in Oslo."

"Are you involved in his work?" It was the big question
and he dreaded her honest answer.

"I can swear to you that I don't know anything about his
life away from me."

"How is he today?"

"Very weak and in a lot of pain. He shouldn't be moved
yet."

"Does Karen know he's hidden there? And can she be
trusted to keep silent? That's another anxiety that kept me
awake in the night."

"Karen isn't here. I let her go home to her sister yesterday evening and she hasn't returned."

He lowered his big hands and let them droop over his
knees as he lifted his tired-looking face to her. "Then she'll
have been taken away with the rest."

Her eyes darkened on the final, painful acceptance of
the fact. "I've been hoping in vain that she would have
stayed free."

Wearily his head dipped again, jowls hanging. "This is a bad time."

"Would you let me remain here for the rest of the week, Tom?"

He understood her. "He would have to be gone before next Friday."

"He will."

"Could we get him up to one of the beds, do you think?" A catch came in her throat. "Oh, Tom."

"It can't help for him to be lying in his present uncomfortable quarters. Since he means so much to you, the sooner he recovers the better. I also want him well and on his way."

"It would be best if I made up a bed for him on the divan in the small sitting-room. He's sleeping now. When he wakes we can move him."

When Tom bore the brunt of Steffen's weight in helping him from the storeroom and onto the divan, Gunnar remained in concealment. Tom departed later in his car without the least idea that a second agent was sheltering in his house. The sight of the burnt-out village deepened his gloom when he drove past. There was also the prospect of finding a new housekeeper. This time he would not leave the choice to Johanna. He would appoint a fellow collaborator's wife of such dedicated Nazi principles that Johanna would never again dare to bring her Resistance lover under his roof.

All that week Gunnar, except when acting as male nurse and taking his share of night watch, kept tactfully away from Johanna and Steffen as much as possible. She sat for hours holding his hand and when he was awake they talked in low and loving tones, laughed softly at private jokes and had eyes only for each other. Once when Gunnar came into the room unexpectedly, Steffen's hand was on her breast. He decided the patient was well on the way to recovery.

At dawn on Friday morning he and Steffen prepared to leave. They were taking one of the row-boats. Once they were farther up the fjord there were contacts ashore where they could get long-delayed medical attention for Steffen, who was still unable to walk without support. He and Johanna shared a long farewell kiss while Gunnar ostentatiously busied himself with the boat.

She stood on the bank and watched the boat with their two silhouettes disappear into the mist that lay like a veil over the cold bright water.

For a while in the office Johanna was more cautious than ever before, not knowing how far Tom's suspicions were aroused. Then gradually she saw he did not suspect her of engaging in subversive work herself, simply because it had not occurred to him that the simple facts recorded through his office could matter in the least to the Resistance. That she should be supplying tiny and important sections of an all-over pattern put together by Intelligence slipped by him completely. He had accepted that her meeting with Steffen had been inevitable in the circumstances and hoped she would never see him again.

Tom flatly refused to find out where Karen had been taken. Any reference to that weekend made him brusque. "It's an army matter. Nothing to do with me. It's not healthy to show interest in those incarcerated in punishment camps."

Later, by chance, he did discover Karen's fate. A baby farm had been started in a converted domestic science building not far from Oslo. Golden-haired, blue-eyed girls were being mated there with young soldiers of Aryan looks and colouring in the furtherance of Hitler's aim towards a master race. Karen had been selected and Tom thought her fortunate to have escaped the conditions of the concentration camps, for she would be well looked after as a surrogate mother for the Third Reich. Nevertheless he chose not to tell Johanna. He did not think she would view the girl's fate in the same light as himself, for Karen would have had no choice in the matter.

Johanna did not like the new housekeeper, who did not like her. She found herself barred from the kitchen and projected completely into the role of social hostess, which suited her since Karen was no longer there to chat and laugh with while they shared the chores. In conversation with Astrid she had mentioned the silver fox skins that Axel was to bring for her inspection.

Excitedly, Astrid put the palms of her hands lightly together. "Why haven't I thought about it before? I have a fur coat that you can wear. Since you are to give advice on furs you must look the part."

She had three splendid fur coats. The fourth had not seen the light of day since the winter before the invasion, for she had kept it for special occasions. It was blue fox with a huge "Greta Garbo" collar deep enough to drown in. Wrapped in it, Johanna crossed her arms and stroked the sleeves sensuously, her chin tilted, her eyes half closed. "I feel like purring. Mm! What a glorious coat."

She looked beautiful in it. Astrid, watching her as she twirled about in it, decided that she herself would never wear the coat again. It had always been too young for her. It belonged to youth and beauty. "It's yours. Keep it. No arguments. It never suited me. Wear it to Oslo when you go, like a banner for times to come."

Johanna wore it for the first time when the snows came, the flakes softly powdering the fur, her hair and her lashes. Not for the first time Tom thought what a waste it was that she should be pining for a man likely to end up before a firing squad when she could have had her choice among the top ranks of the Wehrmacht.

The following weekend at Tom's she learned from Axel that the lieutenant who had upset Karen and annoyed his fellow officers with his drunken talk had been killed in an Allied bombing raid on the Vemork hydro plant in Telemark. The air raid indicated to her that the Allies had become concerned again with the plant's heavy water production. There was talk about the raid among the other military present until Axel removed the lid from the box of furs he had brought with him. Then everyone gathered around to watch.

Taking the skins out in turn, Johanna held each one by the head and smoothed it down to the tail before blowing on it lightly to divide the fur, checking for colour and quality. Many a time she had watched Leif Moen examine skins and knew what to look for in a good one. These would never have made his salon in the days of luxuriance, but they would pass muster for her purpose.

"You have enough skins here," she said, putting one over each shoulder to display them to him. "They're not top quality, but as you can see for yourself they'll still make up into a nice coat. What about measurements?"

"I'll send for them."

"And the design?"

"I'd like to leave that with you. Could it be made locally?"

"Not as far as I know. If you are going to let me see to everything for you, I should like to take them to my former boss in Oslo. He's a genius with furs."

From the start Axel had had a bargain in mind. The furs had cost him nothing and the making up would be a mere pittance compared with the price of such a coat from a rack, even if such a garment had still been available. He would not have considered having the coat made otherwise. It was not his custom to indulge the women in his life.

"There's no difficulty there," he assured her. "I'll ask Major Ryen to let you have a couple of days away from the office to do this for me."

She was quick to seize her chance. "It would take more than one trip."

He gestured nonchalantly. "There's no problem. I'll give you an open travel permit valid for three months with my personal stamp and endorsement."

Once she had not wanted a permit signed by him. Now, in different circumstances, it was hard not to catch her breath at her swift success. "Then your wife shall have a coat to please her."

Someone on the outskirts of those standing around edged his way to the front. "Is there any chance that this man you're going to see will have any skins tucked away somewhere? My fiancée would go crazy over a fur coat."

"So would mine," said somebody else.

She sank her chin into the soft fur she had drawn across her neck, her thoughts busy. Her original aim had been to establish three or four legitimate trips to Oslo in order to act as courier for the Resistance. Since Steffen had first asked her if she ever got the chance to travel with Tom, she had remembered all he had said and watched for such an opportunity. Now she saw that these trips might be stretched out indefinitely. It would depend on whether she could persuade Leif Moen to part with the precious furs he had in his vault.

"I can't make any promises. All I can say is that if it's possible to locate any furs for you when I get to Oslo, I shall do so."

Throughout the rest of the weekend she had more inquiries. All the officers had accumulated funds, there being nothing to spend money on beyond mess bills and minor expenses, the shops being totally bare of anything worth purchasing. The chance of furs interested every one of them.

When she met Gunnar in the cellar to pass on the news of this development, he gave her some rare praise for what she had arranged and hoped to organise. "Well done! Let me know when you've fixed the first journey." He thought there was something else she wanted to say, although she already knew that Steffen had made a good recovery. "Yes?"

She shook her head. "Nothing. That's all." There was no point in saying that she hated more and more her enforced association with the enemy. It had come to a point, at times, when her flesh crawled at the duplicity she was compelled to use, the smiles she had to return. All that stabilised her was the hope that through it she contributed, no matter how indirectly, to the saving of life somewhere, whether it was that of a sailor on a British ship or a Resistance fighter evading an area into which more troops had been posted. Maybe Gunnar saw something in her eyes of what she was feeling at that moment.

"I believe the new year will be an important one for us, Johanna—1944 has to be a turning point. Since the Allied invasion didn't come to Norway last year when we had high hopes for it, it can only mean that their forces are being saved for a main attack somewhere along the French coast. That's where it has to come now."

"I hope it comes soon," she exclaimed vehemently. "I'm tired of being patient."

"We all are. And we're not alone. Every other occupied country must be as sickened as we are of the Nazis and their brutality." Knowing she was under immense strain, he did not add that the great fear of the Resistance was that the Germans, having made Norway into a fortress, might hold out against the Allies long after other occupied lands were liberated.

When Johanna arrived in Oslo early in the new year of
1944 she could have wept for the city where she had
known so much happiness in the past. It had been stricken
by privation on her last visit, but now a war weariness lay
like a cloud over it, dragging at the faces of the people. As
in Ålesund and elsewhere, she saw civilian pedestrians
thrust off the pavements by sauntering soldiers who
savoured this petty and arrogant display of power. Owing
to restrictions on the use of electricity, there was no heating in the shops. The assistants were wrapped in coats and
mufflers and the people waiting outside food shops became
white as snowmen in the thickly falling snow. The shabbi-
ness of everyone's clothing after four years of occupation
was apparent everywhere. She had become accustomed to
the same conditions in her own part of the country, but
somehow seeing Oslo gripped by them tore at her anew.
On her journey her fur coat had drawn no envy, only angry
eyes. She had felt shame at travelling first class in the
company of Nazis instead of taking a place with the civilians herded together into a few coaches at the rear of the
train. At Østbane station a military car organised by Axel
was waiting to take her and the box of furs to the fur shop.
When she alighted she saw there was nothing in the windows. Leif was waiting for her, for she had telephoned him
in advance. He was wearing his overcoat as a protection
against the bitter chill of the unheated premises, and for
this reason he did not offer to take her coat from her.

"It's good to see you, Johanna." He was thinner and
greyer than when she had last seen him. When the driver
had put down the box of furs and she had told him at what
time to return, Leif bolted the door and took her into his
office. "What a splendid coat! When you came into the
shop I thought the clock had turned back to the days when
my customers bought such garments from me."

"If only that could be." She made an unhappy grimace.
"Everyone thinks I'm a Nazi collaborator. If looks could
kill, I would never have reached here."

His face was full of sympathy as he pulled up a chair to sit
opposite to her. "One day the truth will come out."

"Not before we're free, I hope," she joked uneasily. "I
hardly go home any more. Local people cut me. As a precaution my father, who is in much better health by the

way, always meets me and sees me on my way again. For my parents' sake, it's really better if I stay away." She switched from the subject, inquiring about his wife, people they both knew, and finally how he was able to keep the shop open with nothing for sale in the windows.

"It's surprising how much work comes my way, and you would be even more amazed at the skins that are brought in to be made up in the sewing room. Calf skins, plenty of reindeer skins, some seal from time to time, and there's quite a black market trade in rabbit skins, particularly white ones. I have nothing to do with that side of it. Racketeering is not for me."

"Then fur coats of any kind are greatly in demand?"

"Never more so. With fuel and heating so hard to come by, people will wear anything to keep warm. If it's possible to give the finished product some style, I see that it is done. Mostly, I'm afraid, it's a question of simply trying to get enough out of the skins provided to get a finished garment."

"I've brought you some work. You won't like making a coat for the enemy, but it's enabling me to travel to Oslo in the cause we both support and I'm hoping you will enable me to make further trips in time to come."

"How may I do that?"

"By releasing some of the lovely furs that you have in storage. On the pretext of getting them designed and made, I'll be able to extend my courier work indefinitely."

His expression of regret told her at once that her hopes would come to nothing. "You should have had them if they had still been here. Let me show you what happened." Leading the way, he took her down to the saferoom below the shop. The door had been broken open at some time and the vault was completely empty. "Black marketeers stole every garment. I had brought in a man I thought I could trust to build a brick wall across the door and wall to seal the furs away until the end of the war. Maybe he talked about what he believed to be inside the saferoom, because I hadn't shown him. When I arrived the next morning, everything had gone."

"Were the thieves never traced?"

He gave a wry smile, turning to lead her back up the steps to the shop again. "I did not report the theft. This

would have been a matter for the quisling police and I
should have found myself in dire trouble for hoarding
goods. They would have judged me by their own standards
and believed that I had kept the furs back to charge in-
flated prices at a time of my own choosing. If the furs had
been recovered they would have been confiscated. Either
way I'd have been the loser by being the one to serve the
longest sentence."

"I'm so sorry."

"My chief regret now is that they're not here to be of use
to you. Let me see the skins you've brought to be made up.
I promise to make as many visits as possible for you out of
them."

There proved to be more than he would need for one
coat if a simple design was decided upon. He thought he
could get two short capes from the remainder.

"Knowing Axel, I should think he would be prepared to
sell those skins," Johanna said. "Then if you said you had to
finish the coat before making a start on the capes, that
would extend my visits still further."

"That's how it shall be done."

Together they settled on the style and he promised to
deliver a pen sketch of the coat and one of each proposed
cape at her hotel before she left Oslo again by the morning
train. Never before in his career had it been necessary for
him to skimp on silver fox skins and he had nothing in his
books of designs to represent what he would now be making.

Johanna's hotel was a well established one. In peacetime
it had been popular with British and American tourists.
There were some civilians staying there, including a party
of the Swiss Red Cross, who were probably in the country
to view whatever the Germans had prepared for them to
see and no more. Mostly the guests were German officers
of all three services, either in transit on leave to Germany
or making the most of shorter passes allowing them a few
days in the city. For this reason some heating was allowed
in the hotel. Johanna had not been long in her room when
there was a knock on the door and a chambermaid entered
with paper towels for the bathroom. Johanna had already
noticed there were paper sheets and pillowcases on the
bed, the paper quilt cover even embossed with a simple

design. She hoped she would not prove to be a restless sleeper.

"Is there anything else you require, frøken?" the chambermaid asked her.

Johanna, seated in front of the dressing-table, looked at the woman's reflection in the mirror and knew with some sixth sense that this was the contact she had been told to expect. "I would like to know where I can buy a flower to wear this evening."

"You would like a bloom that never fades." Prearranged words.

"I would indeed."

"I can recommend a red carnation." Symbol of the Royal House and the coded message.

"Then I think we understand each other." Johanna left the dressing-table and went to the fur coat in the wardrobe. From a secret pocket that she had sewn herself, she took out the paper she had to deliver. "What is the name of this carnation?"

The woman completed the message. *"Alt for Norge."*

All for Norway. Johanna handed over the paper. Her courier assignment for this time had been fulfilled.

While Johanna was sleeping in her paper sheets, Steffen was far away in Telemark, spending the night in a dug-out in the snow. He was south of Lake Tinnsjø where the forested slopes closed in upon the single railway track. North of the lake the Germans were moving a vitally important shipment of the remaining supplies of heavy water produced at the Vemork plant. The entire production of their new atomic weapon depended on it. Never had they used greater security. From the time it left the plant the day before, there had been troops riding with it and around it, guarding its slow and important progress by rail to the ferry where it would be shunted aboard for transit down the long lake.

At dawn Steffen had seen a second train chug up from the distant port of Porsgrunn in readiness to meet the ferry and take on the load of heavy water for the final stage of its journey through the Norwegian countryside before shipment to Germany. As soon as it had gone past him he gave a signal. Down out of the forest came half a dozen men.

Silently and swiftly they ran to allotted places along the track and began to fix explosives to the rails in readiness for the train's return with its newly collected load. Theirs was the second stage of a three-point plan to prevent the heavy water from reaching Germany. During the night explosives should have been placed on the ferry. If that ruse was foiled there would be the charges on the rail track. Should those explosives be detected, the Royal Air Force would bomb the ship bearing the heavy water en route to Germany. All stops had been pulled out for this last great attempt to beat the Germans in the race for the new powerful bomb.

"It's done!" one of the men had reported to him.

"Good. Now comes the worst part. We have to wait. If the ferry blows up as planned, we remove the charges to save unnecessary loss of life."

Strapping on his skis again, he set off to reach a vantage point that gave him a view of the greater part of the lake. There he settled to watch with binoculars for first sight of the ferry with its dangerous cargo, his white camouflage clothing making him blend with his snowy surroundings. It was a long wait before he finally detected the distant speck that was the ferry. On and on it came, making steady and untroubled progress. Had the two Resistance fighters detailed to set the delayed action charges been caught before they could carry out their work? If the charges did not work now, it would be too late. He could hear the engines quietly chugging in the still air. Nothing was happening. Nothing.

The explosion came with a force and a roar that sent echoes far and wide. Holding his breath, he saw the bow dip. People had been thrown from the deck into the icy water. Down and down went the ferry, the lake churning around and over it as the waters bore the container of heavy water down to the dark, deep depths from which it could never be retrieved.

He lowered his binoculars and still gazed towards the place where the ferry had vanished. Row-boats were pulling out from the shore to rescue those struggling to keep afloat. He hoped the loss of life was small. The tragedy was that there had been ordinary people aboard going about their daily business, getting to work or to the shops. To have forewarned them would have jeopardized the whole success of the mission. They had died that countless others might live. It did not ease their sacrifice for him.

With a thrust of his ski sticks Steffen crossed to a place where he could signal success to the next man, who was a mere speck on the white landscape. There was an enthusiastic wave in return before the man disappeared to alert others along the track that the job was done and the explosives could be removed.

Although he kept a sharp lookout automatically as he skied down to his own section of the line, his thoughts were already turning to Johanna. Now that this present project was completed he would get back to the Ålesund area. He was hoping there would be a brief respite from duty that he could spend entirely with her. Swiftly he removed the charges and explosives, replacing them in his knapsack. He felt that this had been one of the greatest days for the Resistance. Free people everywhere had been saved from a Nazi atom bomb.

Axel Werner was not a frequent visitor at Tom's office, but he did call in occasionally, usually when visiting the building from his own headquarters to oversee some security matter in the military section. "I see you're hard at work," he greeted Johanna. "I'll not disturb you because it's Major Ryen I've come to see. However, I received your message about the surplus silver fox skins and I'm prepared to sell them at their market value. Major von Clausen and Oberleutenant Hendrich are both interested. Perhaps you would like to discuss the matter of design with them at some time."

"I will." Johanna smiled to herself. It was extremely satisfying that Axel's greed should aid her Resistance work.

While he was in with Tom and after she had served them coffee, she returned to her task at hand, which was copying a letter that had reached Tom from Oslo that day. It was from one of the most treacherous and dangerous ministers in the Quisling government, and gave instructions for a special registration for labour service by all males between the ages of eighteen and twenty-five. Tom was to be in charge of it in his area. She was puzzled as to why only those of a prime age group should be required to register,

and decided to pass on the information, for what it was
worth, to Gunnar without delay. It suddenly occurred to
her that perhaps this was what Axel was talking over with
Tom at that very moment. He had had a leather folder
under his arm, but then he usually did when he came.
Many a time she had wished she could get access to it.

The copy finished, she folded it and slipped it into the
secret pocket under the waistband of her skirt. She had
sewn these secret pockets into all her office clothes. The
door of the inner office opened and Tom escorted Axel out
as he always did. Again Axel paused at her desk.

"My wife's letters are full of this fur coat she's going to
receive. Can you give me a progress report to pass on to
her when I write later today?"

"All I know is that it is in the fur shop's sewing room and
the lining is to be of heavy satin, some left from a prewar
stock. Her initials will be embroidered on an inside
pocket."

"Splendid!" He strolled towards the outer door, which
Tom opened for him. "*Auf Wiedersehen,* Major Ryen." His
right hand came up smartly in the Nazi salute. "Heil
Hitler."

"Heil Hitler," Tom replied, sheeplike.

Johanna had no chance to discuss the copy of the minis-
ter's letter with Gunnar, simply leaving it for him under a
loose slab of stone in the cellar floor, after letting him know
by secret message that something important would be
there. His arrival late at night coincided with Steffen's
return from Telemark. Gunnar made a gleeful fist of victory upon hearing how thoroughly successful the sinking
of the ferry had been.

"There's new and urgent work for us here," he said,
banishing Steffen's hopes of a day or two alone in Johanna's
company. "Before I go into details, I'll see what has been
left for me." He took the paper from under the stone and
read it through in the lamplight. With satisfaction he gave
a low whistle and slapped the sheet of paper with the back
of his fingers. "Here's something. It couldn't have come at
a better time. Intelligence was notified by a vigilant
woman typist in the Ministry of Justice as to what was in
the wind some weeks ago. Now Johanna has given us a
detailed report on the local moves that will be taken in a

compulsory registration. It's what I was going to tell you about. Everything has accelerated in your absence."

"What registration is this?" Steffen took the paper and perused it, resting his weight on the edge of the table.

"Officially it's for labour service. In reality it's Quisling's camouflage for conscription. He has offered the Third Reich seventy-five thousand young Norwegians in an allotted age group as cannon-fodder for the Russian Front."

Steffen's eyes narrowed incredulously. Then he derided the idea. "He can offer them, but how does he imagine he will get them to fight for Nazism?"

"They are not to know what is expected of them until after they have registered."

"It still won't work. Weapons are what they have been wanting. Put guns into their hands and they'll turn against the Germans."

"That flaw must have been pointed out. So no arms will be issued to them until they reach the front. Then they'll have to face the full force of the Russians bearing down on them, with the Germans ready to shoot them from the back if they fail to make a stand. Coded instructions came through only an hour ago on the BBC from London. Nobody is to register for labour service."

Steffen moved restlessly away from the table. "We must get to work at once. Warnings must not be delayed. The men concerned must disappear into the mountains and the forests, get into Sweden or across to England. It's the only way. For us there'll be the sabotage of offices where registration is to take place, which Johanna's paper gives us, and we must destroy the punch-card machines and generally foil this scheme from every angle."

The next half hour was taken up in drafting plans and alloting tasks to those who would be awaiting orders. Then Gunnar left to start putting the operations in motion, Steffen's part to begin at dawn. Alone, he went through the panel and into the quiet house that had been his home from boyhood. Silently he went up the stairs and opened the door into Johanna's room. She had drawn the black-out curtains before getting into bed and the white moonlight shone through the canopy of icicles outside the window, turning them to crystal. He could see her form moulded by the quilt and looked down on her sleeping face. Without a

sound he undressed. Then he remembered to turn the key
in the lock. The click disturbed her. She stirred and rolled
over without waking. He spoke her name softly, sitting
down on the bed to lean over her and smooth a strand of
hair back from her brow. "My love. I'm here."

She opened her eyes lazily and smiled without the least
surprise, as though he were a natural extension of her
dream. She reached out her arms to him. He turned back
the quilt and slid in beside her, drawing her warmth to him
in passionate tenderness.

Chapter 13

On the morning of June 6 Johanna was returning to Tom's office after mailing a batch of letters when she overheard a conversation between two German naval officers going down the stairs.

"It happened early this morning. An Allied invasion of Normandy. Didn't you hear the news?"

"No. I only came ashore ten minutes ago. Normandy! That's crazy. They'll never gain a foothold. They'll be back in the sea by now."

"We're strafing them right and left, by all accounts. A Norwegian battleship has been sunk already. The beaches are thick with bodies."

"There you are. What did I say?" Their voices faded as they went out of the building.

Johanna went into her office and sat down at her desk in a daze. After more than four years of brutal occupation, of fear and persecution, a sense of isolation had been dispelled. At last there was light at the end of the tunnel. Her heart went out to those fighting on the beaches. Did they have any inkling of what their courage was doing for people like herself, of the hopes they were raising, of the never-ending gratitude they were bringing upon themselves? She would never forget this moment, or this day, or those men, particularly those who had already given their lives and would never know the outcome. Something splashed down on her hands folded in her lap and she saw it was a tear. Her face was wet with tears and she had not realised it.

By the time she arrived home that evening Astrid had a copy of Eisenhower's message to the people of occupied lands. It had been rushed out by the underground press. "Be patient. Don't take up arms until a given time. Liberation is on its way!"

"I think it's going to be harder to be patient now than ever before," Astrid remarked with a sigh. "The advice is most apt. My first instinct was to take a stick and drive those hussies beyond the dividing door out of my house."

"Wait till the day of liberation," Johanna said with a chuckle, enjoying the image that Astrid had conjured up. "It's a sight I wouldn't want to miss."

The following Saturday she went home to stay overnight. All the time she had been travelling to and fro from Oslo during the making of the fur garments she had had no chance and, as she had once said to Leif Moen, it was better in any case for her parents if she stayed away. She had completed several courier missions before the excuse for her journeys came to an end. During that time she twice saw Germans in an uproar over acts of sabotage, armoured cars racing through the streets. She had heard from Gunnar of the "Oslo gang," a daring group of Resistance fighters who operated in that area and had put out of action several important factories and other sites vital to the German war machine. As she sometimes collected a sealed paper instead of delivering one, she had wondered if she carried reports of these exploits through to Intelligence. She was almost certain that at one time she had taken to Oslo a special message concerning those still evading registration for service at the Russian Front. Thanks to the Resistance, which had now amalgamated its branches into the new name of "Home Front," thousands of young men had escaped that fate. They were camping out in many isolated mountain hiding places, often in great hardship, surviving on such food as could be got through to them and whatever wildlife could be trapped. The few who had registered, either not heeding the warning or receiving it too late, had been shipped out immediately. Nobody knew how they had fared before the Russian advance.

"I've missed you," Edvard greeted her warmly upon her arrival at the farmstead. He was remarkably fit and, in spite of some stiffness remaining in his hip and knee joints, a seemingly permanent after-state of his illness, he was able to do a full day's work on his land, of which he was justly proud. No other house helper had taken Karen's place. Instead a widow from the hamlet came daily to assist with the chores. She did, however, refuse to come when her employers' daughter was at home, not wanting to associate with a collaborator. So Johanna, who had always known her, never saw her on these occasions.

Gina was waiting with the Red Cross letter from Durban, South Africa, that had brought about this visit. It had come from someone unknown to them and upon receiving it she had gone flying to the telephone to ask Johanna to come home and see it for herself. "Here it is. Read it. Then tell us what you think."

Johanna, although it had been read twice to her over the telephone, obediently read through the pencilled message on the Red Cross letter form, which had stringently kept to the limit of words allowed. *All Well. Rolf and Wendy married. Greetings to everyone.*

"Well?" Gina was hovering eagerly. "Give us your opinion. The address is definitely ours, so there's no mistake there, but why should Rolf—if it is our Rolf—be as far away as South Africa?"

Johanna smiled at her parents in turn. "I don't think he's anywhere near that country. He was too set on being a fighter pilot in the heat of battle when he left Norway. My guess is that he devised a clever way of letting you know about his marriage without putting you in danger by it. For all the Germans know, this message has come from a Norwegian relative in South Africa. He could never have sent this letter from England, and if he had been in Durban he would have sent it himself. That's proof enough. Perhaps the sender is a relative of his wife who lives there." She took hold of her mother by the shoulders and smiled wider. "Wendy . . . she must be English. You and Father have an English daughter-in-law. Congratulations!"

Gina clasped a hand to her brow. "Great world! An English girl. I won't be able to talk to her."

Johanna and Edvard exchanged a smiling glance. He patted his wife on the shoulder. "When the day comes, just say '*Velkommen*' to her as you do to anyone else you welcome to our home. It has the same sound in every language."

That evening the three of them listened to the news in Norwegian from the BBC. Progress was being made by the Allies in Normandy and the heaviest fighting was around

Caen. More details were given about the actual invasion day, and the magnitude of the operation almost defied comprehension. It was impossible not to worry as to whether Erik had been on the Norwegian ship that had been sunk on D-Day.

Before leaving home again after her brief visit, Johanna helped her mother fill in the Red Cross reply form that had been attached to the letter. They tried to get as much family goodwill as possible into the few words permitted in a message that would travel many thousands of miles in a roundabout route before it reached the newly married couple for whom it was intended.

It was not long before Tom's weekend parties all but faded out. Restricted rations could no longer be subsidised freely for him from army quarters, and the only drink easily available was beer and a raw German wine bottled too soon and dispatched hastily to meet the vast thirst of a quarter of a million men in a land that produced no wine of its own. Duties had also been extended. Hitler had been caught off guard in Normandy, but he still retained his quirky determination not to be similarly surprised in Norway. The iron fist had never been tighter on the Norwegians than it was in the summer of 1944. The least diversion resulted in arrest. The firing squad took up its position almost daily in the small courtyard of Akershus Castle in Oslo. Often the condemned patriots, broken physically and mentally by the Gestapo, could not walk unaided, or stand for their last moments. Erik did manage to shuffle ahead of his guards, although his whole body was a mass of pain. He no longer thought about it. Before coming out into the sun for the last time he had had Karen to dwell on, childhood memories of the farm and his parents, the good times he had had in his life and throughout his years at sea. In his mind he was at peace. He had given nothing away. In spite of all they had done to him he had told them nothing of value.

He came to a standstill. The seafaring sounds of the harbour reached him in the clear early morning air. His last sight was of a sea gull wheeling against the Oslo sky.

Daily the Germans received news of the Allied advance on the continent, and equally worrying for them was the relentless pressure of the Russians to the east of their homeland. The news was not all black—they were cheered when battles went in their favour and were jubilant over the devastating effect that their V-1 and V-2 flying bombs were having on London, where the damage and loss of life were enormous. Ironically, lying like a cloud over them all, officers and ranks alike, was anxiety about their own families exposed to the heavy Allied bombing raids, and they scanned their own army press and the newspapers sent from home for whatever they could glean of situations local to them. When the soldiers marched they still sang lustily, but "We March Against England" was no longer the prime favourite. They met with too much derision from civilian bystanders.

Those who did still visit Tom were as arrogant and confident as ever about their own position in Norway. They had made it into a stronghold fit to withstand any onslaught, defences burrowed deep into the mountains and new roads built for the swift deployment of troops and armed vehicles. Among themselves, they were highly critical of their own forces that had fallen back before the Allies. "It won't happen here" was the confident opinion voiced many times over.

To Johanna it was like a minor liberation not to have to associate socially with the Wehrmacht any more. Some still dropped in to see her in the office when they were in town and she kept up a surface appearance for the sake of any future subversive work, but the relief of weekends free to do as she wished was enormous. She swam in a small cove and sunbathed at every available opportunity, rolling her swimsuit down to her hips when she knew she was alone and there was no chance of intrusion. Her body and limbs became golden brown. The sensuous basking frequently aroused memories of another kind of warmth.

She had seen Steffen only once since the night she had awakened to find him in her room. In the company of Gunnar, whom she saw frequently, they had met briefly in the cellar. Steffen had had time only to hand her the package she was to take to Oslo, a delivery Gunnar usually made. Neither she nor Astrid had had any word since. All Gunnar said was that "the Englishman" had important work in hand. She could guess what it was. A new and

intensive wave of sabotage actions had hit the occupation
forces, hindering the production and shipping of materials
essential to the Nazi war machine in its defence of Germany against the advancing Allies. Ships in Oslo harbour,
including a notorious prison ship, had been blown up, as
had fuel and ammunition dumps, railways and bridges and
selected factories. She thought Steffen had made a point of
seeing her for those few minutes, not knowing when he
would get the chance again.

The hard truth of the Allied advance continued to ham-
mer through. Late in July came the news of a group of
German generals' attempt to assassinate Hitler. She had
met one of them, a distinguished grey-haired man of the
old German tradition. Axel took an almost fiendish pleasure in the foiling of this attempt on the life of the Führer,
taking it as proof of the unreliability of the army in comparison with the unquestioned loyalty of his own S.S. security force.

"If I had been there, I'd have hanged the lot on the
spot," he declared on the Friday morning when he strut-
ted through Johanna's office, already in conversation with
Tom, whom he had met on the stairs. The generals had
recently been condemned to that method of execution,
their request to be shot as soldiers refused. The whole
affair had a sobering effect on the officers whom Johanna
knew. She suspected that two or three less avidly Nazi
than the majority had more sympathy with the rebels than
they would ever admit.

Judging the moment to be right to make coffee, Johanna
put the cups on a tray and when it was ready took it in to
Tom's office. Axel had his leather folder on the desk and
although it was open he was referring to a top paper without showing it to Tom, who was swinging to and fro in his
swivel chair, listening intently. They stopped talking when
she entered, Axel taking the cup she had poured for him
with a nod of thanks. She left the door just on the latch
when she returned to her own office, but the remarks they
made were only concluding ones, holding no substance of
interest, and she gave up straining her ears from the vicinity of her desk.

Her curiosity persisted. She decided to fetch the tray.
The door, still as she had left it, pushed open as she en-

tered. Axel and Tom were by the window, looking out at some military activity in the street below. On the desk by the chair where he had been sitting was Axel's folder, half zipped up again, but with the top paper projecting from it. Her action was almost a reflex one. She simply took a corner of the paper and whipped it out, at the same time stepping back out of the office. Outside the open door she held her breath, expecting a shout. They had not noticed anything, and were still talking about what was happening outside. She snatched a glance at the paper. It looked interesting. Then, looking around for a hiding place, she slipped it behind a picture on the wall.

Now she returned again to the doorway of Tom's office, reaching out to grip the door handle as if she had just opened it. "May I remove the tray?"

They both turned. Tom answered her. "Yes, of course."

She collected everything and carried it out. Axel came after her. "I'm going to Major Ryen's this weekend. Shall you be there this time?"

She paused in the middle of her office floor and faced him. "Yes, I'm driving out with him this evening after work." It was not something she was looking forward to, but Tom had asked her particularly. A Quisling Nazi party leader was to be a weekend guest, and with Tom's hopes rising towards a political future, he wanted the man to have the best of service and attention. The replacement housekeeper was not as efficient as Karen had been. Axel looked pleased.

"Good. I have a photograph to bring along that my wife sent me. She is wearing the silver fox coat. I'd like to show it to you."

"I'll be interested to see it."

He smiled and turned back into Tom's office. She was still taut with suspense. As he emerged with the folder under his arm, he saluted her cheerily. The paper had not been missed. With luck he would not discover where it had been "mislaid."

In her lunch-break she went to a public telephone booth and her short, blandly worded message covered an announcement of a matter of utmost urgency. She had the paper folded into her secret pocket when she went from the building at the end of the working day. Unable to wait

for Gunnar, she left the paper under the cellar stone and
was ready at the gate when Tom arrived in his car to pick
her up.

"The weather promises to be good," he said in an attempt at conversation.

"I hope for a swim tomorrow," she gave back in reply.

He no longer found it easy to talk to her, nor she to him.
It was as if he pretended to himself that he had never
discovered a wounded man in his storeroom, and yet his
attitude towards her had changed. His fondness for her
had waned. It was as if he had come to hate her, whether
he realised it or not, for having exposed him to the kind of
dangers he had gone out of his way to avoid. The sacrifice
he had made of his self-respect and his patriotism had
almost come to nothing through what he regarded as her
foolhardy action. Now more than ever his allegiance to his
German masters was all-important to him. He did not like
the turn the war had taken, but he was convinced that
Norway would remain under German control and that the
Germans would hold their own borders even if everything
else went from them under the advance of the Allied
tanks.

The weekend was as dreary as Johanna had expected it
to be. The quisling party leader was pompous and objectionable, and it made her despair to see how obsequious
Tom was to him. Axel, whose company she always chose to
avoid, took an instant dislike to Tom's guest of honour and
tacked on to her, going for a swim with her and then
inviting her for a row in the boat, which she declined. The
photograph of his wife had been a surprise. She was not the
hefty German frau that Johanna had expected from her
measurements. Instead she was plump and pretty with a
smile shy with pride over the fur coat, which suited her. It
was probably the first nice present she had ever received
from Axel.

The weekend was moving towards its close when the
housekeeper informed Johanna that Frøken Larsen
wished to speak to her on the telephone. Johanna was filled
with misgivings. Astrid never telephoned her at Tom's
house. She took the receiver. "Hello, Astrid."

"You must get tomorrow off from work. I'm not well."

"What's the matter? Have you had the doctor?" Johanna was concerned.

"Yes. It's a chill. He's coming again tomorrow. I must stay in bed. *Farvel.*"

Johanna replaced the receiver, thinking that Astrid had sounded quite strange. She went back to the verandah where she had been sitting with Tom and his guests and at the first opportunity told him about the call. Tom was immediately annoyed. Monday was always busy. He granted her the time off with reluctance. Gone was the good humour towards her that he would have shown in the past.

When he dropped her at the gate she ran up the path and into the house. Halfway up the stairs she was surprised to see Astrid looking over the baluster and not seeming in the least ill in spite of being in night clothes.

"There's nothing wrong with me," she announced at once. "I took the precaution of getting undressed for bed in case anyone came with you to see how I was. Steffen was here. He says you must meet him in the cellar at four o'clock tomorrow morning. Wear your office clothes and sensible shoes in case you have to run." She raised both hands to ward off enquiry. "Don't ask me what it's about, because I don't know. I've simply done my part as requested."

Johanna set her alarm clock but woke before it rang, excitement priming her. At five minutes before four she went down to the cellar. Steffen was waiting for her. They wrapped their arms about each other, relishing the sheer physical pleasure of being together.

"Hey," he said, drawing his head back, "how are you?"

"All the better for seeing you. Why am I here at this unearthly hour?"

He frowned seriously. "In brief, that paper you took for us revealed the latest Quisling move to get Norwegians into service at the Russian Front and the consequences that await them. There's no time to tell you everything now. It's enough to say I've never read anything more inhuman. Gunnar is waiting for us with a farm truck. I'll tell you the rest later." His hand took hers. "I have to ask you if you're willing to play a risky part in today's events?"

"You don't have to. Let's go."

He took her out by the tunnel entrance of the cellar. She
had never been along that route before and was amazed to
find that it wound like a snake. When they emerged into
the rosy daylight, he had to hold back a thick bush that hid
the entrance completely. They were deep in the forest. He
led her to a lane where the farm truck was waiting, Gunnar at the wheel. Steffen helped her into the back where
she was concealed behind boxes of vegetables. He could
talk to her by holding back the dividing canvas behind the
driver's seat as they drove along.

"As you know, shortly everyone in the country has to
register again for new ration cards. That German document told us that only those who apply personally will
receive a card, which automatically cuts out those in hiding. Keeping those thousands fed in their widely scattered
camps is difficult enough as it is, and without use of their
ration cards it would be impossible to get enough food to
them. The Germans are hoping to force them out of hiding
by starvation. We're out today to help ourselves to a sufficient number of ration cards on delivery from the printers.
The Home Front in Oslo is hijacking a larger load at the
same time. Nobody is going to starve after this venture, I
promise you."

She raised her eyebrows admiringly. "You've been busy
over the weekend, haven't you? It's a good scheme. Simple
and effective. Where do I come in?"

"During the morning the packaged boxes of cards that
we're after will be delivered to a small depot. You'll be in
the office to sign for them. We shall have removed the girl
who is normally there, and she'll be tied up somewhere
until we're safely away. The same applies to the caretaker,
who would normally help with the unloading. You'll see
Gunnar and me taking over that task. The whole operation
shouldn't take more than twenty minutes. Then Gunnar
will leave with the goods reloaded in this truck, and you
and I will depart in a van that will be waiting for us."

"What if other people come in to the office in the meantime?"

"That's up to you. You'll have to bluff your way through
somehow. It shouldn't be difficult. We'll be there in plenty
of time for you to look through the files and get a grasp of
what goes on there. It's mostly signing in and out. It will be

simple stuff compared with the work you've been used to."
He lowered his voice. "We're approaching the ferry now.
Sorry you have to make the fjord crossing out of sight."

The canvas screen dropped back into place. She heard
the German guard ask for papers and another came to the
back of the truck to check the load. Being slim, she occupied a narrow space behind one of the crates and there
would be nothing to suggest to an outside observer that
anyone was concealed there. One of the Germans must
have signalled the truck through. It rolled forward and
there was a noisy clatter as it went up the ramp and onto
the ferry.

Gunnar got out to stretch his legs as the ferry started to
move. Steffen remained in the driving cab, his arms resting on the back of the seat to be near her. The crossing
took twenty-five minutes. Then Gunnar returned to the
driver's seat and they went clattering off the ferry onto a
country road.

Their destination was a small town that was typical in its
layout, with woodland taking over the outskirts to shield
ugly workshops and commercial properties. Next to the
depot to which they had come was a dairy building where
several farm trucks were parked. Gunnar drew up in line
with them. It was perfect cover for the vehicle, which
would appear to be part of normal activity around the
dairy. Parked deeper and more inconspicuously under the
trees was the van in which she and Steffen would leave
again. They alighted, Gunnar going first to make sure they
would be unobserved. Due to the still early hour there
were few people about. They reached the rear of the depot, a sturdy wooden structure in need of a coat of paint, as
were so many buildings since such materials had become
scarce during the Occupation. Steffen opened the door
silently from a ring of master keys.

Upon entering, Johanna noted it was a depot of some
security. There were stout doors with padlocks. It was
from here that the new ration cards would be issued in
bulk to district civic officials, who would in turn distribute
them to those registering at their own centres. She waited
in silence just inside the door as Steffen and Gunnar surprised the caretaker. There was a scuffling sound before he
was bound and gagged and put behind a locked door.

Steffen took her through to the office at the front of the
building. It led off a small entrance hall illuminated by a
glass panel in the street door. He left her there to look
around and it was not long before she felt she could have
taken over the simple work there in full capacity. Steffen
locked up the office again when it was time for her to go
into hiding, and she waited in the caretaker's vacated
quarters while the two men kept watch.

The office girl arrived on time at eight-thirty, but did not
enter for a nerve-racking ten minutes while she chatted
and giggled outside with a couple of soldiers on normal
patrol. They departed when she let herself in. She sang to
herself as she busied herself hanging up her jacket and
tidying her appearance before a mirror. Her eyes went
wide in her reflection as Gunnar clapped a hand over her
mouth and carried her bodily out of the office and into one
of the strongholds. Johanna went to take the girl's place
behind the counter-desk. She lifted the telephone receiver
off the hook to avoid any incoming calls. Then there was
nothing to do except wait. Quite a number of people went
past the building as the town came to life. A postman
brought in a parcel and some mail. "Where's Christina
today then?" he inquired.

"She's having some time off."

After that there were no further interruptions. The expected truck slowed down outside at midmorning and
drew round to the rear of the building. She saw that there
was an armed soldier sitting beside the driver to oversee
the goods into safe storage. Ration cards were valuable
commodities, far more so at the present time than the
soldier could ever suspect. Knowing she would have to
check the delivery and put her signature to the receipt
forms, she left the office to go through the building to
where the unloading was taking place. The soldier was
leaning against the doorjamb, watching idly as Gunnar
trundled the first batch through on a trolley. Outside, the
driver, a thickset fellow with a ruddy face and straw-col-
oured hair, was in the back of the truck, swinging the
packages down to Steffen, who was stacking a second trolley. As the last package changed hands, the driver leaped
down from the truck and refastened the back. Then he
came strolling into the building, mopping his sweaty brow

and neck with a dark blue handkerchief, in time to see Johanna padlock the door where the packages had been placed. For the second time that day she was asked the same question.

"Here! Where's Christina? Who are you?"

Johanna experienced a qualm. Neither Steffen nor Gunnar had expected the driver to know the office girl, since he had come from Trondheim. Obviously Christina was a girl who had made her mark on him during his delivery of ration cards the preceding year. She made the same reply as she had made to the postman, looking bored by it, and took the clipboard from him with the papers she had to sign, using a signature she had invented for herself at the bottom of each sheet. "There you are," she said, handing the clipboard back to him. "I'll tell Christina you asked about her."

The man looked as if he might have said something more. The moment of hesitation passed. "Yes, do that. Bjorn is the name. She'll know me all right." He stuck his pencil back behind his ear and went back to clamber up into the truck, the soldier following to get in by the far door. As he drew away, he glanced back in his side mirror as if seeking some clue to the mystery of Christina's absence. "That was odd," he remarked, as much to himself as to his companion, drawing out onto the main road for the return journey north.

"What was?"

"Christina not being in the office. I spoke to her on the phone last week and said I'd be here today. She said nothing about having time off."

"Your girlfriend, is she?"

"No. She's my sister-in-law. My wife's going to be really disappointed that I didn't see her." There was a lapse of time while he watched the road ahead, the heat shimmering up from the dusty surface. Traffic was sparse. His thoughts churned over. At his side the soldier settled more comfortably with his head back and eyes closed, helmet under the seat since there was nothing more to guard. Then the driver spoke out again, giving the wheel a thump with his fist, "I tell you there was something fishy going on at the depot today. Those fellows who unloaded were strangers to me. Where had they come from? Why wasn't

the caretaker giving a hand? I've been to that place three
times this year and the caretaker is always there."

The soldier had begun to listen sharply, relinquishing his
original idea of a doze. "What could be wrong, do you
think?"

"I don't know, but I'm going to turn back and find out."
He began to strain his neck, looking for a place where he
could turn.

The soldier sat forward. "Keep going. There's an army
pillbox a little way ahead. I'll make a report there. Maybe
that trio were black marketeers after those ration cards."

The driver put his foot down on the accelerator. He was
worried about Christina. His interest in her was not wholly
that of a concerned relative. She could be a lot of fun.
Beside him the soldier retrieved his helmet from under
the seat and put it on.

At the depot, Johanna helped with the loading into the
farm truck which had been brought to the door, the crates
of vegetables removed until a few could be piled back to
hide what lay behind them. It was swift and desperate
work, for all three had been left with the impression that
the driver was far from satisfied with the explanation for
the office girl's absence. To leave without enough cards
would be disastrous. The whole action had to be completed before card-issuing began the following week and
there would be no chance to gain extra stock once the
Germans discovered what had taken place. Johanna was
glad she had chosen to wear sneakers. She ran easily in
them. It was her shoulders and back that were feeling the
strain of the heavy packages, every muscle aching, the
sweat running down inside her dress.

"That's it!" Steffen proclaimed the truck full. "We've
enough and some to spare. In with the vegetable crates
now."

When that was done, Gunnar took the wheel again and
waved to Johanna and Steffen before he turned into the
road. Steffen finished shutting the depot doors. Then he
and Johanna ran for the van under the trees, she taking the
passenger seat. As he backed out he saw an army truck
approaching in the distance. Gunnar had met and passed
it, which was a good sign. Steffen turned the van in the
opposite direction to go back through the town and take

the road beyond that would lead him to the ferry. A last
look as he turned the corner showed him the army truck
drawing up outside the depot.

"We must get moving," he said with dry understate-
ment. "It looks as if they're on to us. At least Gunnar has
slipped through, thank God. That's what matters. That and
your safety. I'm going to make sure of that now."

He drove. The gravel road was rough and pitted, making
the van leap where the surface rose and fell like a roller-
coaster, owing to the casual disregard for the levelling of
country routes. Johanna, bounding on the old leather seat,
held on tightly. She had no illusions about the danger they
were in. When the Germans discovered two people tied
up and the packages missing it would not take them long to
learn from passersby that a van had been seen in the vicinity, even allowing for the number who automatically held
their tongues when questioned about anything by the enemy. S.S. security would be notified, soldiers dispatched
and quayside guards alerted. She and Steffen had become
far more of a quarry than Gunnar ambling past military
traffic at a farmer's pace to allay suspicion. In the back of
the van the remainder of the vegetable crates danced and
fell about like dice in a box, sufficient camouflage for a
guard at a road-block or on a jetty making a routine check,
but nothing to stand up to close scrutiny and merciless
questions if suspicions were fully aroused.

The road took them to a brow of a hill and the sudden
and beautiful view of the wide fjord lying below. A ferry
was drawing close in to shore. "We must catch that ferry
before it leaves again!" Steffen exclaimed. He gave her
instructions as the van charged down the winding road,
scooping gravel up under the wheels with every bend. "I'll
slow down just before we get within sight of the jetty.
Then you'll get out and run to catch it. You can't risk
remaining in the van with me. I'll time the driving to get
on board just behind you, but you must not speak to me or
acknowledge me in any way from the moment you leave
the van. Your life could depend upon it. Once you're the
other side of the fjord, catch the bus into town and go back
to Astrid, or you could go in to work. Try to make the rest
of the day as normal as possible."

"Why don't you dump the van and run with me?"

"I don't want to leave it this side of the fjord. The longer
I can make the Germans think I may have the packages in
the back of this van, the better chance Gunnar has of
getting clear away." He observed how quiet she became,
and knew she did not want to make the break and yet
understood that it was necessary. Below them military and
civilian vehicles had begun to roll off the ferry. As a precaution he drew into a side track, having spotted a truckload of soldiers who might easily have been dispatched to
search for him. There would be guards to question him on
the jetty, but he planned to take a chance and rush them as
the ferry was on the point of departure. He put an arm
around her, gathering her to him. "It's time for you to go
now."

She clung to him, kissing him back with all of herself.
Then he leaned across to open the van door for her and she
jumped out. As she ran towards the road, she saw an open
staff car bearing past at full speed, Axel and another S.S.
officer sitting in the back seat. Although she jerked her face
away, she could not be sure that Axel had not glimpsed
her. There was no sense in waiting to find out and at least
the car was driving away from the ferry. Thankful for all
her efforts to keep trained in running, she began to race
down the last slope to the fjord, keeping to the grass verge
until it gave way to the open parking area. Her hair
streamed out, her legs flew. The ferry was on the point of
departure. She waved frantically in a plea to wait and saw
the ferryhand let the half-lifted ramp fall back for her and
the van that was following behind. A guard stepped forward. "Papers! Papers!"

She had her identity card ready and he perused it at a
glance so as not to delay her. Almost leaping on board she
swung round as Steffen began to drive full speed for the
ferry, ignoring the guard who was shouting at him. It was
only then she saw Axel's car coming up in the rear. The
driver must have turned round after Axel's sighting of her
and was coming after them. The ferryhand, with the blank
look on his face that people chose to adopt in the pretence
of not understanding anything, shouted at them in German, prepared to wind up the ramp the moment the van
was aboard. Then he hesitated. The junior officer beside
the driver had stood up, one hand gripping the top of the

windscreen, the other raised in imperious command that the ferry should be delayed for them. Johanna stood numbed by a sense of disaster as the ferryhand obediently kept the ramp in position after Steffen had shot past her in the van and braked to a halt, the only vehicle on board. Axel could only have come onto the scene in the first place through having been notified by telephone of what had occurred at the depot. Now he was about to make a personal arrest. She and Steffen together. The car was close enough now for her to see Axel's iron face clamp into full recognition as he stared directly at her.

The front wheels of the large car rolled onto the ramp. Johanna stared in horrified disbelief, seeing that, although the ramp had been kept in position, the ferryhand had not signalled through to the skipper at the wheel. The ferry was moving. As she watched, the whole sequence was seemingly almost in slow motion, and yet it took place in a matter of seconds. The back of the car began to dip. She saw Axel's expression change. Then, like a child's toy, the car was completely upended as the gap between the quay and the ferry widened swiftly. Amid the Germans' terrified shouts, the whole vehicle plunged down under the swirling water. Johanna covered her eyes with her hands.

When she looked again, the ferry was several metres out into the fjord on its unhalted way. People on shore had rushed to the scene. Row-boats were already gathering. The officer who had been standing in the front of the car had escaped and was being hauled out of the water, but of Axel and the two other occupants there was no sign. Johanna could guess at the depths of the water there. Trapped under the upended car against the rocks, they would have had no chance. Slowly she turned her head and looked towards the ferryhand. Their eyes met. His were totally without expression and deliberately he looked away from her towards Steffen, who had got out of the van. She saw the ferryhand give him the same steady glance before turning that expressionless gaze shorewards again. He had saved them. He had seen the pursuit and he had saved them.

Shakily she went to the saloon and sat down on one of the seats. Nobody else was there. The few passengers on board were civilian and they were all on deck, watching events. Steffen seized the opportunity to come in search of her. He slid onto the neighbouring seat and put an arm around her.

"Listen to me," he said urgently. "All hell is going to be let loose after this. That officer who escaped drowning is going to be on a telephone at this moment and I expect a full military reception committee when I get to the other side. You should be perfectly safe. There's no reason for anyone to suspect you were with me, which is why I mustn't stay with you much longer."

"That was Axel Werner in the car. He recognised me."

"Can you be sure of that?"

"I thought he glimpsed me when I came out of the sidetrack. His expression was terrible when he stared at me on the ferry."

"I expect he was beginning to connect the disappearance of his secret paper with his visit to your office. Probably he looked back to see if it was you he had glimpsed just as I pulled out into the road. The van would have sent him turning back immediately. Did you know either of the officers with him?"

"No. I'd never seen either of them before."

"Then there's a chance he said nothing about you to them, because the sight of the van would have been an important development. Was he talking to his fellow officers when he stared at you?"

She shook her head. "I think it was only in those last moments that he was entirely sure that it was me he had seen."

"Good. When the ferry arrives, simply walk off with the other passengers and take the bus into town. Axel is the only person who could have named you as being connected with today's events and he has gone."

"But what will you do?"

He gave her a smile. "I'm going to swim for it. Now, when everybody's attention is elsewhere."

He would not let her watch him go, for it would have involved her in an unnecessary risk. On deck, he slipped off his sneakers, stuck them into his belt, clambered up onto the rails and dived. The sun-shot water was so clear that when he cleaved through it and began to rise for air he could see the hull of the ferry and the churning of the propeller, the shoals of darting fish and starfish floating in the blue-green light like diaphanous decorations adrift from a Christmas tree. When he broke the sparkling surface and gulped in air, there was no shout from the ferry. His escape had been unobserved. He struck out strongly, knowing himself protected from observation by the sun-diamonds lifting the surface of the fjord. His aim was to put as great a distance as possible between himself and the two landing stages of the ferry where his pursuers would gather.

When Johanna came out on deck again she glanced around at the water and could not see him anywhere. On the approaching shore, army vehicles made a blockade and there were soldiers with rifles on the quay. The moment the ramp was lowered they rushed on board to surround the van and start herding the passengers and crew into the saloon for questioning while a thorough search was made of the ferry, the Germans going down into the engine-room and into the lavatories and the equipment lockers to make sure no one was in hiding. All papers were checked. When it became obvious that the driver of the van was not among those present, the soldiers made a second search. A child's remark that he had seen a man go for a swim solved the mystery for the officer in charge. In exasperation he permitted the passengers to leave, keeping the skipper and the ferryhand in the saloon for further interrogation. All on board had vouched for its having been an accident. He was of the same opinion. The ferryhand was a simple country lout and too stupid to have planned anything.

Johanna took her place in the bus. When asked why she had been on the other side of the fjord, she had said she had heard there was knitting wool on sale that day in one of the shops and she had gone to wait in line for it without success. It was a reasonable explanation. Women went everywhere within an area in which travel was allowed to get anything that was in short supply. The bus began to move. Her thoughts were with Steffen. He had promised to contact her and let her know he was safe, even if he was not able to come himself.

The delay had made it too late to go to work. She would go home to Astrid's house and hope for news that evening.

Steffen had chosen to come ashore where boulders from an ancient avalanche had made easy access out of the water. He had disturbed a pair of otters, who stared at him, droplets glittering on their whiskers before diving out of sight under the water with barely a ripple. When he threw himself down on the soft grass and fir cones beneath the trees, red squirrels bounded away at his intrusion. As he lay gasping to get his breath back he could hear them in the branches overhead.

He was almost rested when there came other sounds, a crackling of twigs underfoot that made him freeze through to the marrow of his spine. Scrambling to his feet, he stood poised for flight. On the sun-patched slope between the trees were a dozen soldiers with rifles pointing directly at him. He took a step backwards in the direction of the water.

"Achtung! Hands up!"

Every rifle had slipped its safety catch with an ominous click. There was no chance. He would be dead before he could dive from the rocks. Inwardly a surge of wrath overcame fear. He saw everything sliding away from him. His liberty to help his country; his strong physical strength through what they would do to his body to try and extract information from him; his future with the woman he loved. Her name was a silent shout in his mind, a last link with hope and sanity. Johanna!

No word came that evening. When Johanna went to work next morning she was surprised as time went by and Tom did not appear. One of the letters she opened was on an urgent matter. When she telephoned his Ålesund apartment, hoping to contact him, there was no reply. She went down to the reception area in the hall and asked the soldier on duty if Major Ryen had left any message for her.

"No, fräulein. I have heard he is under arrest."

"On what charge?" she demanded incredulously.

"I don't know. It was said that S.S. Obersturmbannführer Werner made the charge early yesterday morning before being called away on an urgent matter. Did you hear that he was drowned in an accident with the car later in the day? A sad business."

"I heard." She returned to the office and went to Tom's

desk, opening drawers. It looked as though papers had been removed for inspection. Yet there was nothing that Tom handled that could be remotely incriminating. Then she remembered the paper she had removed from Axel's folder. Had Tom been accused of that? Leaving the office again, she went downstairs to the military department and asked to see one of the young officers she knew there. He was able to answer her questions.

"Ryen was arrested after Werner discovered an important paper was missing from his files yesterday morning. The folder had been in a safe since he had placed it there after leaving Ryen's office. Nobody else could have taken it. Ryen was the only one to be left alone with the folder at any time. Werner's drowning has delayed the questioning. Somebody else will deal with it in a day or two."

"May I see Major Ryen?"

"He's allowed no visitors."

It was always the same. To be accused was tantamount to being found guilty already. Justice was a travesty when the Third Reich made its interrogations. There was nothing she could do until she had consulted with a Resistance leader. Her hope was that they might help her think of a loophole through which to extract Tom from the charge. With Axel gone there would be no one to deny it was the truth if she said she saw him crumple the paper into the wastepaper basket or tear it across, or otherwise dispose of it. Better still, if she could get the original paper back she could leave it somewhere in the building to be discovered by chance and Tom would be cleared.

Two nights later Gunnar came to the cellar. It was after midnight. Sliding back the panel, he entered the house. A fan of light shone from the kitchen and he saw Astrid in a silken robe seated at the kitchen table. He spoke her name quietly, not wanting to alarm her. She gave a start, rising to her feet and opening the door wider. Seeing him, she drew her fingers lightly across her brow.

"It's you, Gunnar. I never seem to get used to one section of my house being occupied by strangers while the cellar is reserved for my friends. Come into the kitchen." She gestured to a chair. "Would you like a cup of elderberry tea? I made the tea myself by drying the petals last summer. It's an old recipe of my grandmother's." Her voice faltered. "Why am I talking so quickly? Is it because I believe you have something to tell me?"

"I'm afraid so."

Her mouth was working. There was a shaking in her that made the hand she reached to him for support flutter like a bird within his. "That must be why I couldn't sleep, because the house is quiet enough tonight. Is Steffen dead?"

"No. He's been taken prisoner."

Her eyes were enormous with the tears she could not shed. "Should I thank God for that?"

"Steffen is a fighter."

"The Gestapo will torture him." She swallowed a thin wail, keeping it trapped within her throat.

"They won't break his spirit."

She moved unsteadily to the door. He would have assisted her up the stairs, but she held herself erect. "I can manage. Please tell Johanna for me. I would like to be on my own for a little while."

Slowly she went up the stairs, holding on to the baluster rail, her silk robe trailing after her like a geisha skirt. On the landing she tapped on Johanna's door until there was a response. Then she went to her own room.

Johanna came out on the landing sleepily, tying the ribbons of a striped robe. When she saw Gunnar in the well of light at the foot of the stairs a tremor went through her. "How did it go?"

"The sortie was a complete success. The ration cards are already in the right hands. The national press has been forbidden by Reichskommissar Terboven to mention either the Oslo hijack or our little venture. That's a good sign. It shows that the last thing he wants is for their trickery to come to light. Werner's drowning has received full coverage as you've probably seen. Even that has been classed as an accident. But that's not why I'm here."

"I know. I can see it in your face and I don't think I have the strength to bear it."

"The Gestapo have Steffen."

She sank down on the top tread as if the power to stand had deserted her. Her head bowed to her knees, her arms encompassing them. He went up the stairs to sit beside her. She wasn't crying. She was shuddering violently.

"Don't," he muttered helplessly, putting his big hand on

her shoulder. She did not hear him, locked in anguish and despair. He sat with her in silent commiseration and did not leave her side until he remembered the elderberry tea and went to fetch a cup of it. He pulled her head up to put it to her lips. It quieted her.

"Thank you for coming to tell me," she said in little more than a whisper.

"I don't know when I'll see you again. As you'll remember, the rules are for freedom fighters to go to ground when a close contact is captured. As for you, don't go down to the cellar any more. I've smashed the table to make it appear as if it's been in disuse for years and brought the lamp, matches and a few other odds and ends into the cupboard under the stairs. Disperse them around the house tomorrow. It's simply a precaution."

"Before you go I must ask you if you still have that paper from Axel Werner's folder." She explained why, her voice sounding stilted to her own ears, her face stiff and dry.

"A copy was made and the original paper should have been returned to you by now with the suggestion it should be found in a gutter as if it had fallen out of Ryen's window while he and Werner were watching events below, but the agent bringing it was forced into hiding when almost trapped by the increased security forces. Then Werner's death made its return appear less urgent. The paper was invaluable to Intelligence, as it refers to other matters besides the ration book ruse. They were listed on the same sheet and will need the Resistance's investigation and disruption. I can guess at the furor its disappearance caused in the German military department. You are bound to be questioned, although it will be simply routine in your case. I know you'll keep your head. If you want to help Ryen— well, that's up to you. Be vague about thinking you saw Werner sorting out papers and discarding them. You mustn't be pinned down. If you are, you won't do Ryen or yourself any good."

She nodded that she understood. He gripped her shoulder again in sympathy and encouragement before leaving her. How long she was there on the stairs she did not know. With her head leaning against the bannisters she finally slept in exhaustion and awoke in the morning to find the nightmare of what had happened still with her. Astrid, courageous as always, strengthened her by example.

She went to work as usual. The golden rule of the Resistance was always to carry on a normal routine. It was often the best protection. At midmorning two S.S. security guards in their hated black uniforms marched into her office.

"S.S. Oberführer Richter wants to see you at headquarters. If you have a coat here, bring it."

It was Axel's successor who had summoned her, a man new to the district whom she had yet to meet. The instruction to take a coat was not a good sign. It was always an indication that the questioning would be long. For those with no hope it was always the first announcement that their fate was sealed. She put on her coat, the weather having turned cooler the previous day, and went with the guards downstairs and outside to a waiting vehicle. At the headquarters where she had first attended a Wehrmacht party with Tom she was taken to Richter's office. He was not alone. A bald-headed, middle-aged man in civilian clothes stood by the window smoking a cigarette. She knew him for what he was. Gestapo. Richter was a sharp-faced man with closely cropped grey hair and gold-rimmed spectacles. He did not rise when she entered, merely indicating that she take the chair set before his desk.

"*Guten Morgen, Fräulein Ryen.* I'm informed that your German is fluent. Therefore I shall address you in my own language. You will answer my questions truthfully and without deviousness. You were well acquainted with the late Axel Werner, I believe."

"We knew each other as children."

"How would you define your relationship with him?"

"It was an acquaintanceship with roots in the past."

"Were you lovers?"

"No!" The suggestion was so objectionably ludicrous that the answer burst from her.

"Major Ryen has suggested to me that you were."

She stared incredulously. "You must have misunderstood him. He knows there was never anything between Axel Werner and me."

"You arranged to have some silver fox skins acquired by

Werner made up into a coat. I put it to you that he wished you to be the recipient of the finished garment, but due to an error of measurements the coat didn't fit and so he sent it to his wife instead."

"I've never heard anything more absurd. His wife was as short as I am tall. No furrier of repute would make that sort of error."

Richter cleared his throat, changing his line of questioning. "You and Werner were often together at Major Ryen's weekend parties. Do you remember the night a neighbouring village was the scene of a hunt for two wanted men?"

"I do." She was deeply alarmed at the way the interview was going. Tom's treachery was getting through to her. Unable to shift the blame for the missing paper onto anyone else through the report that Axel had made on its disappearance, he was trying to cast doubts on Axel's integrity as a Nazi and had used her name to further that end. It was a cunning defence, for the case of the rebel generals was still in everybody's mind, suspicions swift to flare at any hint of insubordination. When unable to trust each other, the Nazis could be as ruthless to their own kind as to any beneath their heel. Tom had used his wits to the full.

"One of the wanted men was killed attempting to escape. The second was never found, although believed to have been wounded. He must have been given shelter, wouldn't you say?"

"Not if he was able to reach the mountains."

"That did not happen. He came to Major Ryen's house. You let him in and nursed him until he was fit to leave."

She bluffed fiercely, determined to fight Tom's betrayal. "You can't be in possession of the facts of the situation that night. No fugitive in his right mind would have come to a house full of Wehrmacht officers with soldiers thick as ants over the whole area."

"Let us have no more pretence, fräulein. You took that man in. Major Ryen discovered you and reported to Werner, whose infatuation for you stopped him from making an arrest." His accusing finger shot out at her across the desk. "You were Werner's downfall! He threatened Major Ryen with immediate imprisonment on a trumped-up

charge if he gave you away. His last act was to make Major
Ryen a scapegoat for his own carelessness in mislaying an
important document." He thrust his face towards her, his
spectacles glinting. "Now I'll have from you the name of
the wounded man you took into the house that night!"

The time had come for the stock answer she had been
instructed to use if ever finding herself in such a situation.
"I know nothing."

She was to repeat those words all the time she had the
physical strength to say them. Fainting gave her some
respite from pain. They burned her breasts with cigarettes
and pulled out her fingernails. "I know nothing," became
her litany. They extracted nothing from her.

Chapter 14

In Grini concentration camp a grapevine kept the several thousand prisoners informed of outside affairs. Johanna, in the women's section, had been in the camp for over seven months by April 1945 when she heard of the death of President Roosevelt. It saddened her. He had been a good friend to Norway. When the Crown Princess and the royal children had taken refuge in Sweden at the time of the Occupation, he had sent a warship specially to transport them to the safety of American soil. Later he had held up Norway as an example to the world of what human courage could do in the face of adversity. She wished he could have lived to see the end of the war.

Although almost every other occupied country had been liberated in the Allies' advance towards Berlin, Russians to the east, the British and Americans to the west, Norway was still as isolated as ever within the Nazi grip. In the far north the Russians had crossed Finland to break through the German defences in northern Norway. In the retreat, during the bitter Arctic winter, the Germans had put the whole area to the torch, leaving people without food and shelter. Their plight had been disastrous and many had died of exposure. It was still the boast of the Nazis in Norway that they were equipped to fight on indefinitely, no matter how many other annexed territories were lost.

Every morning Johanna took her mop, scrubbing brush and bucket to carry out the domestic chores allotted to her and other women in her group. There were twenty-five long grey accommodation huts in the camp, plus administrative buildings, the commandant's quarters, the guards' barracks and eight watch-towers with searchlights and machine-guns set above the high encompassing barbed-wire fence, which in turn was surrounded by an electrified fence and a minefield. Whenever it was possible, Johanna

stood by the fence to gaze out at the wooded countryside
backed by rolling hills. Beyond that undulating horizon lay
Oslo and life that was normal, despite all the hazards of
Occupation, in comparison with the wretched existence of
those imprisoned within Grini's confines. The commandant was a cruel and brutal man who ruled the camp with
an iron fist. The women were not spared through physical
weakness or any ailment that did not take them off their
feet from the many hard tasks to which they were set.
They wore wooden shoes that were made by the male
prisoners, and throughout the camp in both the men's and
women's sections the rattle of this footwear was a constant
sound.

Johanna's nails had grown again and her burns healed,
although the scars remained, flawing flesh that had always
been smooth and blemish-free. Without doubt she had
escaped further torture through convincing her interro-
gators by her silence that although she might have sheltered a secret agent, she simply had not known his name.
That was perfectly logical to the Germans, since they
knew that Resistance fighters kept their names to themselves. Clearly Richter and his Gestapo colleague had not
believed it possible for her not to confess what she knew
during all they had done to her. After it was over she had
been herded into a cattle truck with other prisoners and
taken south to Oslo and to Grini.

She was always hungry. Her stomach had curved inward
between her hip-bones. The food was abysmal, often the
smell of it so revolting that in spite of hunger she would
barter her small bowl of victuals if someone had a needle
and a length of thread to exchange for it. Sewing helped to
pass the time and any small scrap of material could be
utilised. Small toys were a favourite product with many of
the women, some of whom had children they had not seen
for a long time. Sometimes Johanna bartered a finished
article for a stub of pencil or a sheet of paper on which to
write her continuous love-letter to Steffen. Through it she
felt in constant touch with him. At times he filled her
dreams to such an extent that when she awoke with a start
to the loneliness of her threadbare blanket, she was unable
to believe for a few moments that she was not in his arms.
Although she chose to keep her distress at these times to

herself, it was a common sight in the mornings to see women weeping after dreams of home and those they loved. On a more mundane level many were plagued by dreams of food, particularly when rations were worse than usual.

Even if Johanna had known where Steffen was she could not have sent a letter to him. Mail was not allowed to be sent or received. She simply knew in her heart that he was alive and she set down her loving thoughts on the paper that she kept hidden behind a loose board at the side of her bunk, which was the top one in a tier of four in one of the long rows that stretched the length of the hut.

Her fellow internees were mostly Norwegian. There were half a dozen French prostitutes who had rebelled against working on one of the coastal brothel ships, for they had been seasick all the time, even in harbour, and had staged a strike. As a result, they found themselves in Grini. Although they were a lively lot, they were also slovenly in their habits. There was conflict when they met the national trait of Scandinavians for cleanliness of almost fetish proportions, but after a while they conformed and followed the example set for them by airing their blankets outside every day and taking their turn in scrubbing the hut to keep it as spotless as possible.

All the huts were locked by the guards at night, and on one occasion the youngest of the Frenchwomen, having forgotten her blanket was still on the line, slipped out of the window to retrieve it. She had to dodge the searchlight fanning the compound, and upon returning to the hut, she threw in her blanket and then found the window too high for her to climb back, although Johanna and two more inmates tried to haul her up. The searchlight was approaching. If she was seen, there would be an immediate burst of machine-gun fire from the nearest watch-tower. She was completely panic-stricken.

"Take a dive through the door panel!" Johanna cried. The girl obeyed the authority in her voice and sprang up the steps to dive head first through the glass. The others caught her. Seconds later the searchlight reached the broken pane. The sirens began to wail and guards appeared at a run. Within the hut, everyone dived for her bed and pulled the blanket over her head. Johanna stayed just long

enough to throw a few pieces of glass outside to confuse
the issue. The guards did not investigate the hut until they
had searched the compound in vain for whoever had broken out of the locked quarters. Only then did they count
the inmates and find that nobody was missing. The broken
pane remained a mystery. It never occurred to them that
someone had broken in instead of out. When the guards
were out of hearing everyone became nearly hysterical
with mirth.

It was not often that there was cause for laughter. Sorrow was more the order of the day. Women fell sick and
died. Under the commandant's direction the guards also
played a horrible trick of occasionally bringing a white
sock into the hut and throwing it to a woman to put on. At a
roll-call later she would be called out and led away. No one
knew what happened to those women. They were never
seen again. The white sock became the most dreaded sight
in the camp.

The women were divided off from the men's section and
although contact was strictly forbidden, at times they
could see them through the fencing, black-jacketed,
stripe-trousered figures, some with specially marked trian-
gles on their jackets so that they could be picked out by the
guards for harsher treatment. Occasionally work parties
passed nearby. Then the Frenchwomen would try to
dodge past the guards to shout volubly to them in French,
never having mastered the Norwegian language. Even
those men who did not understand what was being said
could comprehend the meaning and were cheered by the
cheeky encounter, grins on their emaciated faces.

If life was bleak for the women it was worse for the men,
who suffered the most merciless punishment drills and
were driven to the limit of their endurance. The saddest
task for Johanna was when she had to clean out the hut
with its iron-barred windows in which those condemned to
death spent their last hours. The walls were tragically covered with last messages, sometimes in pencil, more often
scratched with the point of a fragment of sharp rock or the
edge of a tin food bowl. *Please tell my wife . . . Let my
parents know . . . My loving thoughts are with . . . Last
greetings to . . .*
From the first she decided to do what she could to help

fulfil those last requests. Each time she went there she recorded messages and names on whatever paper came into her possession either by barter or from sympathetic inmates who wanted to help. There were always means by which messages could be smuggled out of a camp, even though it sometimes meant waiting weeks before it could be done. By the time she heard of the passing of President Roosevelt, she had smuggled over forty last messages out of the camp. They were concealed in cavities in the corner parts of a fish crate during the regular delivery of fish to the kitchens, one of the ways in which communications were passed in and out of Grini.

Now everything in the camp began to change. The guards were restless, some making overtures of friendship, others more aggressive in the resolve that a last stand should be made in Norway. Rumours circulated as much between the Germans in the camp as among the internees, but the truth emerged strongly that the Wehrmacht in Europe had turned into a retreating rabble, surrendering at all points. On the first day of May, word flew around the camp that Hitler was dead. Upon the news being confirmed, one of the guards committed suicide and the next day another followed suit.

The vicious hold of Grini's commandant did not lessen. If anything, punishments became more frequent and too often for scarcely any reason at all. Dread, unspoken, was in everyone as to how the commandant would deal with them when a total German defeat was secured by the Allies.

Johanna was sent again to the condemned cell where the previous night a man had been held before being taken at dawn to his place of execution. Upon entering she set down her mop and bucket to look for his signature. Each wall was like a familiar map to her and she could usually spot a new message straight away. It was the same with this one, except that it sent waves of shock washing over her, his name going straight to her heart. She went stumbling towards it with hands outstretched, reading what was there. *To Johanna of Ryendal my love into eternity. Steffen Larsen. 5th May, 1945.*

She uttered a sharp cry on the grief that burst agonisingly within her and threw herself against the wall, pressing her cheek against the writing while the huge and terrible sobs tore out of her body in her utter desolation. He had been in Grini all this time and she had not known. He had been in this hut and breathed this air and walked this floor and she had not known. Everything he must have suffered over the past months had not saved him. In the end the Nazis had murdered him.

One of the Frenchwomen found her there. Although not knowing the reason for Johanna's terrible grief she managed to get her away before any questions could be asked by the guard. It was the Frenchwoman's opinion that the Germans in their present nervous state were likely to see rebellion even in a weeping woman's failure to mop a floor. She had always hated the Boche.

Shock made it impossible for Johanna to sleep. That night she lay awake under her blanket staring upwards in the darkness, and the next day she went around in a daze to face a similar terrible night. She collapsed on the morning of the seventh of May while at a laundry tub. Other women carried her to her bunk where the Frenchwoman cradled her until she slept.

Not yet recovered from her exhaustion, she was the last in the hut to wake during the night when there was a disturbance in the camp. She sat up in her bunk to see all the women huddled together in terror. Swiftly she swung her feet to the floor and went to join them; no need to ask what was happening. As the guards unlocked the door of the hut and ordered everyone outside, she shared the same thought with all the rest of the women: now it was to be their turn. It was as each one of them had feared at the back of her mind. When the last day came, the Germans would turn on their prisoners and shoot them down.

"Out! All of you! Move!" The guards were in a savage mood.

Some of the women began to cry. Johanna put her arm around one who had an injured leg and helped her down the steps. All the camp lights were on. They and the rest of the women trailing out of the other huts made a curious sight in their variety of makeshift nightclothes, some clutching blankets around them, a few bravely holding up heads full of curling rags, for all had clung to routine as a means of sustaining morale. Many were barefoot as they gathered close together in the compound. Searchlights, adding to the blaze on them, showed their stricken faces. Yet there was no panic. They simply drew still nearer one another for support and comfort when, from the direction of the barracks, there was the dreaded sound of military footsteps approaching at a sharp pace.

"They're coming," one woman exclaimed tremulously. A catching of breath and a suppressed sob or two went through the crowd of frightened women like a soft breeze. Johanna steeled herself for whatever was to come, her arm still steadying her injured companion. Briefly she closed her eyes to summon up courage.

A man in a uniform that neither she nor the other women immediately recognised came striding into the compound, followed by several others. Quickly he mounted some steps in front of a building and turned to address them in a loud, strong voice, throwing his arms wide.

"Ladies! We are the Swedish Red Cross and we have come to take care of you. The war is over. Germany has surrendered to the Allies. You are free!"

There was such a long silence that the Red Cross commander began to wonder if his Swedish accent had made his announcement unintelligible to his listeners. Then there came a spontaneous outburst of joy. The women began to dance and laugh and hug each other, every one of them crying with happiness. A few, unable to bear such momentous news after so much despair, sat down on the ground and rocked with the wonder of it. Johanna stood motionless, hands dropped to her side, while the weeping and embracing and prancing went on around her as if she were in the eye of a hurricane. She was thinking of Steffen. If only he could have been allowed another forty-eight hours he would have been rejoicing in the men's compound where a great shout had gone up that must have been heard far across the neighbouring hills.

Returning to their huts, the women dressed and began gathering together their few possessions. The Red Cross had transport waiting at the gates. Those living within the Oslo region would be taken home. The rest would be housed overnight in schools and hospitals in the capital where the hotels were prepared to feed them, food having

been secretly moved in over the past weeks by the Resistance in preparation for the liberation of those in the concentration camps. Johanna collected up the small treasures
that had kept her mind occupied through many dreary
hours; a small rag doll she had sewn, a patchwork scarf
made from scraps, and a plaited belt. Last of all she took
her letter to Steffen from behind the panel. It had been her
link with him during the last months of his life and she
could not discard it now.

"Are you ready?" A Red Cross woman was at her side.
"Good. Where is your home?"

"On the west coast, but I'd like to be taken to a house in
Grefsen. That was my second home for a long time."

"Will anyone be there to look after you?"

"I'll be all right."

Johanna joined the rest of the women leaving the hut.
When they came near the open gates that were standing
wide, they broke spontaneously into a run, laughing and
shrieking and shouting with joy. Johanna ran with them
and once outside the gates she stopped to breathe free air
deep into her lungs. Many others did the same. In the
distance there was the sweet sound of a church bell chim-
ing in freedom. It was a deeply moving moment.

Then the women were assisted up into the waiting
buses, sitting jammed together to make room for as many
as possible, all wanting to get away from Grini without any
delay. There was a sea of released people everywhere, a
disciplined crowd in spite of the exuberance of mood and
occasionally wild bursts of cheering and singing of the
national anthem and happy embracing.

In the bus Johanna sat looking out at the landscape revealed by the dawn light. When the bus drove through
Oslo, dropping women off at their homes, there were
many reunions, with people rushing out of houses in their
nightclothes and whole families hugging each other in a
group, the returned member laughing and crying in the
middle. In the city itself the Norwegian flag had appeared
everywhere, as if there had been a sudden blossoming of
red, white and blue. Swastikas were being pulled down
and two men on ladders were already chipping away at a
plaster German eagle spread across the entrance of a
building. All government buildings and former military

headquarters were being guarded by members of the Resistance in white armbands. Their aim was to keep the peace and prevent any uprising in vengeance against the enemy. Johanna guessed the situation was still extremely delicate. The Germans in Norway, unlike their comrades elsewhere in rabble-like disintegration, were still in top form and fully equipped, and had yet to lay down their weapons. A twist of mood by Reichskommissar Terboven and a rescinded decision to follow in the wake of the rest of the defeated Wehrmacht could be catastrophic. Johanna had her own personal battle waiting for her in the Alsteens' house. She intended to drive out the German officer who was there.

She was the last passenger in the bus and was dropped at the gate. The front door was open and there were lights in the house. As the bus drew away she waved to her rescuers; then she went up the path, memories flooding in on her. As soon as she entered, she realised that the Nazi occupant had departed in haste. Going from room to room she saw where he had gathered up possessions from bureaus, cupboards and drawers. In the kitchen the coffeepot was still warm and on the table a patch of crumbs, remnants of a hasty snack. Upstairs it was the same. The bed was rumpled and the quilt thrown back as he must have left it upon hearing of his country's surrender from the telephone at the bedside—a new extension. He had forgotten a leather greatcoat in the clothes closet. In a sudden surge of ungovernable rage she tore it from the hanger, threw it on the floor and kicked it frenziedly all the way down the stairs as if its owner were in it. When she had kicked it outside she slammed the front door shut and leaned against it, feeling quite unsteady.

After getting her breath back, she lifted the telephone receiver in the hall and rang home. Her father, up for the milking, answered.

"Hello, Father," she said huskily. "It's Johanna. I'm free."

It was the most emotional call she had ever made, speaking to her parents in turn, all three of them overwhelmed. Afterwards came the saddest. She rang Astrid and they spoke quietly together for several minutes. Astrid was

brave and did not give way. "Come and see me as soon as
you can, my dear."

"I will."

Johanna was less brave. As soon as she had replaced the
receiver she sat bowed over with sorrow in the hall chair
for a considerable time. When she did move it was to
switch off the lights that had been left burning and go
listlessly upstairs to run a hot bath. The Nazi officer had left
soap and shampoo. For the first time in months she saw her
naked body in a mirror. She was so thin that all her bones
stood out and there were sores on her arms from malnutrition. It was therapeutic to immerse herself completely in
the steaming water. For months she had had only cold
showers, standing on wooden slats in a chill bathhouse with
hundreds of other naked women as thin as herself, many
prisoners of long standing being positively skeletal. She
washed her hair into a luxurious lather, never again to
have it raked viciously through by a toothcomb wielded by
a hard-handed Nazi nurse in the disinfection hut. When
she stepped out of the bath there were soft towels to wrap
around her. Nothing seemed quite real.

Still in the towel, she wondered if there was anything in
the house she could wear until she had laundered her
clothes from the camp. She opened drawers and found
nothing. It was when she was coming out of her old room
that she remembered leaving a box of clothes in the cellar.
Was it possible they were still under the cupboard where
she had hidden them?

In her bare feet she hurried down there. At first glance
she thought there was no hope. All the treasured things
Anna had stored there were gone. The old cupboard was
still bolted to the wall, the doors removed, probably for
firewood. Kneeling down, she stretched her hand underneath through a mass of clinging cobwebs. Just when she
was thinking the box was no longer there, she felt the
corner of it and pulled it forward. She had some difficulty
in getting it through the aperture, and the box split. When
she lifted the lid it was like discovering a treasure trove.
On top of some evening dresses were some items of satin
lingerie, a couple of dresses, skirts, jackets and a pair of
evening sandals.

While dressing in her old room she thought she heard a

vehicle draw up in the lane and depart again, but paid no attention. When her dress was fastened she sat down on a chair to put on the evening sandals, vaguely thankful to be rid of the wooden clogs that had often rubbed her toes. A numbness within her still remained, a combination of grief and a certain bewilderment at all that had happened with such speed. She had just finished putting the straps through the buckles when she heard the front door open. Had the Alsteens returned home already? Uncertainly she went out onto the landing.

A tall man stood in the hall, a borrowed raincoat over black prison garb with the special triangle for harsh treatment on his chest, a package under his arm. At the sound of her approach he looked up, his face lighting up in welcome and joy. He was far thinner and paler than when she had last seen him, his temple and cheeks hollow, his bones sharp. She could only gasp his name rapturously: "Steffen!"

"Jo, darling!"

She flew down to meet him as he flung aside the package to hold out his arms to her. He seized her in an impact of kissing that melded them together and they stayed in their embrace, unable to speak or even to think beyond this mind-dazzling moment of reunion.

"Tell me I'm not dreaming," she implored frantically, her fingertips running over his face as he still held her within the tight circle of his arms.

"As you once said to me, this is no dream. We're together, Jo. No more partings."

Her voice was choked. "I saw your last message to me in Grini. We must ring Astrid. She thinks—"

"I've already done that. It's how I knew you were here. She had just spoken to you when I rang."

"How did you escape being shot?"

"It was more than a firing squad that was meant for me. Hundreds of special prisoners like me, who had failed to talk or against whom the Nazis had a particular grudge, were hurriedly transferred to Mysen, a camp near the Swedish border. The whole area had been laid with explosives. At the moment of liberation we were to be blown up in our huts. Fortunately the commandant in charge of the camp was absent with eye trouble and his deputy got cold feet at the last minute. He was suddenly afraid for his own

skin. Local Resistance freed us and issued each one with a
package of new clothes, which I've yet to put on, and
brought me into Oslo by bus. My only thought was to find
you."

She was filled with wonderment that so much happiness
could come at once. Still more happiness came to them in
the hours that followed, hours that were completely theirs.

Away in the city a kind of joyous madness had taken
over. The German commander-in-chief had formally surrendered to the Resistance. Every shop and place of business was shut in a public holiday. After Steffen had burned
his prison uniform and Johanna's camp clothes, he deposited the Nazi's leather greatcoat in the garbage bin for
collection. Then they went to see and join in the celebrations. Oslo was alive with flags. Everyone carried one or
wore one or cheered the unfurling of yet another on a
flagpole. Every street fluttered with the Union Jack and
the Stars and Stripes with the Norwegian flag hanging
from balconies and roofs. A placard in one of the store
windows summed up the atmosphere of the day: *Closed
because of Joy!*

Policemen who had refused to collaborate, or had
worked secretly within the quisling ranks as Resistance
contacts, had donned their dark blue uniforms again and
were hailed enthusiastically as they directed traffic and
controlled the rejoicing crowds with grins and laughter.
Bands played, people sang and danced and young children
were wide-eyed at the jollifications, having no memory of
anything but fear on the streets. Members of the Resistance, in the open at last and on duty as Johanna had seen
earlier, had flowers thrust into their lapels and pockets.
There had been some minor incidents that they had been
unable to prevent. The windows of several Nazi headquarters had been smashed. In the suburbs, as elsewhere in the
country, quislings had had their windows smashed and
their property taken out of their houses and burned in
bonfires. Yet few, if any, suffered personal attacks. In the
hour of liberation the people were remarkably tolerant. It
was a national characteristic to forgive but never to forget.
Each quisling was destined to live with the stigma of traitor to the end of his or her days.

Steffen reported for duty at a Resistance mobilisation

centre. The Milorg officer with the armband on his tweed jacket regarded Steffen's thin face and hands observantly. "You're right out of camp, aren't you? Which one?"

"Grini."

The officer whistled through his teeth. "Are you! This isn't the place for you. You're entitled to a full spell of recuperation. We'll be guarding every main building until the government returns from London and we hand over our emergency rule. The Crown Prince is on his way. The King will follow next month. In the meantime enjoy yourself for a while. You've earned it."

The celebrations went on all through the night, but Steffen and Johanna returned home to the peace and quiet of the house. Bonfires of black-out material burned everywhere, the glow flickering across the ceiling of the room where they slept in each other's arms.

Behind the festivities in the city and elsewhere, much was going on. Quisling had been arrested. Reichskommissar Terboven had committed suicide. The prisons were filling up with collaborators, black market racketeers, former secret police and Nazi informers. All the Gestapo had fled from their headquarters in Victoria Terrasse, disguising themselves as ordinary officers of the Wehrmacht, but they were known to too many and found themselves rounded up into their own cells where they had tortured and mentally destroyed so many in their power. The Gestapo chief was in the cell where Steffen had suffered the most cruelly devised violence that had left permanent scars on his body and which was to haunt him in nightmares for many years to come.

The telephone awoke Johanna in the morning. With Steffen still sleeping she left the narrow bed they had shared in her old room and padded through to the new telephone the Nazi had installed. It was her mother, excitedly ringing to say a cable from Rolf had arrived.

"It says: *'Safe and well. Coming home soon. Wendy and your new grandson will follow shortly. Fond greetings to all, Rolf.'*"

"That's wonderful news! There's nothing from Erik yet?"

"Nothing."

Johanna and Steffen decided to have a week on their

own together before going home. They needed the time, not only to make the most of being with each other again, but to adjust to life away from camp routine. They both had to report to the hospital for medical care and to receive extra vitamins provided by the International Red Cross to rebuild their strength. Johanna's menstrual cycle had almost ceased during imprisonment on the inadequate diet and through stress, and she was afraid she had been deprived of the chance to have children. The doctors were reassuring and told her that with time all should be well.

Together they saw the exuberant return of Crown Prince Olav in a sea of flags, and watched British-trained Free Norwegian troops who had served from D-Day right through to victory in Germany march with other Allied troops down Karl Johans Gate. Garlanded with flowers, the men were cheered until they were surely deafened by the joyous noise. Overhead Norwegian squadrons came home. Rolf flew his Spitfire into Gardermoen aerodrome near Oslo. When he jumped from it onto Norwegian soil he felt himself take root again.

Johanna had cleared away all evidence of a Nazi officer's ever having been in the Alsteens' home by the last day before she and Steffen planned to leave for the west coast. She was sitting in the flower garden writing a letter to Anna and Viktor, which she intended to leave in the house for them, when she heard a taxi. Putting the pen and the writing paper down on the slatted seat beside her, she sprang up and hurried to see who had come. A small woman on her own was paying the taxi driver, who had placed her suitcases on the front porch. It was Anna. When she saw Johanna she exclaimed with delighted surprise. They rushed to hug each other joyfully.

"Let me look at you." Anna held her back to study her face. "You're too thin. I must cook you some good meals. I have a crate of food coming from Sweden. No rationing there, you know. Lights on all through the war and no black-out." Then she saw the question in Johanna's eyes and smiled sadly. "My dear Viktor died over four years ago on the way into Sweden. He never knew that we reached safety."

"I'm so sorry. That dear man."

Anna looked nostalgically towards the house, her voice softening. "It's good to be home again. I've always loved this house. All this time I've longed to be back here."

"There's somebody indoors whom you know. He's putting new doors on a cupboard in the cellar."

"Is it Steffen?"

"That's right. The man I'm going to marry."

Anna's face bloomed anew at this announcement and she embraced Johanna again. "That's marvellous! I always wanted you to meet each other. I remember not telling him that Viktor and I would be away on holiday when he telephoned the day before we left to say he planned to come to Oslo very shortly."

Johanna laughed quietly. "I admit I have wondered about that. A lot has happened since then. Let's go inside. I'll tell you all about it."

In the house, after an exuberant greeting with Steffen, who swung her off her feet, Anna was like a child in her joy at being home again. She ran in and out of the rooms, relieved to find the house much as she had left it and wasting no tears over the ornaments and silver that were missing. Before Johanna and Steffen departed for the railway station in the morning she was full of plans to convert the upper floor into an apartment for them after they were married, for warning had been given in the press that the housing shortage was going to be acute throughout the country. The situation would be aggravated by the number of war brides coming from Britain and Canada. There was also urgent need to house those from northern Norway, as hundreds were still homeless from the devastation caused by the Germans in their retreat before the Russians, who had returned to the other side of the Finnish border, which was now their territory.

"I don't even know yet if I'll be doing the same job as before the invasion," Steffen pointed out, not wanting to build up Anna's hopes. "You mustn't bank on our being here."

For the first time since her return, some of the happiness dulled in Anna's eyes. Johanna, watching her, saw that she dreaded the loneliness of the house without Viktor.

Rolf was at home on the farm when Johanna and Steffen arrived. A flag was flying at every farmstead in the valley in

honour of her brother's safe return. The local brass band
had come the first morning to play patriotic tunes under
his window, a tribute he missed by sleeping right through
it due to a party in the mess on the eve of his homecoming!
Johanna met with smiles again. Neighbours came running
to their gate to wave to her and, when the chance presented itself, apologise for not having guessed she had
been engaged in secret work. The pleasure of being home
again was overshadowed by a new sorrow. Rolf broke the
news to her, one look at her parents' faces having prepared
her.

"Erik is dead. He served with the Shetland Bus, risking
his life many times over before he was caught and shot at
Akershus Castle. I hear there is to be a memorial stone in
the courtyard where so many of our men faced the firing
squad. At least we can pay our last respects to him there.
The Germans used communal, unmarked graves. We may
never know where he lies."

When Johanna was able to accept what had happened,
she was thankful that her parents would have a grandchild
to bring them some comfort in the years ahead. Nobody
could ever take her late brother's place, but the newest
member of the family, when Wendy arrived with him,
would give them a new and healing interest.

At Astrid's home Johanna and Steffen found her in full
possession of the whole house again, which she had
scrubbed from cellar to attic. Bonfires had disposed of everything soiled during its tenancy.

"I did what I always said I would do when liberation
came," she said. "I drove those women out with a broom
and threw a bucket of water over one who had always
been impudent to me. The Resistance weren't much help.
Mostly they stood and laughed. It was the same when the
police turned up. In the end the women were taken away
in police vans and I invited everyone else in to drink up
the wine in the cellars. We had a wonderful liberation
party!"

They stayed several days with her. During that time
they heard that Tom Ryen had been arrested and could
expect a long prison sentence when brought to trial. There
was talk of the firing squad for Vidkun Quisling when he
was called upon to account for his crimes, but capital pun-

ishment had been abolished for many years under Norwegian law and people were against its being restored under any circumstances, even for the traitor who had endowed all traitors with his own name for the rest of time.

While still at Astrid's Johanna received a letter that had been forwarded from the farm. Karen had phoned Gina and learned of Erik's death. Afterwards she had penned a courageous letter. She had had one baby at the child farm that had been taken from her and sent to Germany. There was no way of tracing her son. Then she had been impregnated again and given birth to a daughter before the liberation. If Erik had lived she believed he would have adopted the child, loving her as he did. In that respect nothing had changed, for she intended to keep the baby and bring her daughter up on her own. Her brother-in-law had returned with other prisoners from Germany and her sister had come through safely. They wanted her to live with them when they reopened their bakery in new premises, but she needed to be independent and build up a new life for herself and her child. Did Johanna know of any accommodation that might be open to her as an unmarried mother?

"I do!" Johanna exclaimed aloud. She knew what it would mean for Anna to have a baby in the house to love and care for. It would be the answer to everything. Karen could find herself a job in Oslo and have no worries during the day about the baby's being well looked after. Knowing both women—Anna with her generous heart and Karen with her sweet nature—Johanna foresaw a most satisfactory outcome to their individual problems. Meanwhile she had her marriage to look forward to and the forthcoming meeting with Rolf's wife, her English sister-in-law.

Thanks to Wendy's having an influential uncle in the diplomatic service, she was able to arrive in Norway ahead of the rest of the war brides, actually travelling with a party returning to the embassy in Oslo. She was up at four o'clock in the morning, the sun having risen long before her in the everlasting summer light, to get her first glimpse of Oslo Fjord from the deck of the ship. Its beauty astounded her. Skerries and islands floating jewel-like to set off rocky shores where matchbox houses in muted primary

colours perched on lush green against woodland and dense
forest. Every house on shore and every summer cabin
tucked into island scenery had a flagpole, spattering red,
white and blue like confetti amid the trees. Sailing din-
ghies skimmed the surface; everyone was up with the sun
and fishing boats tonk-tonked out to sea. Overhead the sea
gulls made an ever-changing pattern of white and grey
against the blue sky. This was her new land. She loved it
already.

She stood at the rails with her baby in her arms as the
ship sailed into harbour. The city seemed to smile at her.
She could see a reception pavilion surrounded by flowers
on the quayside and was told it had been erected for the
homecoming of King Haakon in a few days' time. The
royal arms glinted from the City Hall, which dominated
the harbour and was hung with bunting. The ancient Akershus Castle loomed up from the water. Amid those gathered on the quayside she could see Rolf in uniform, a
bouquet of red roses in his hand. She waved excitedly to
him and he waved back.

"We're here, Paul," she said softly to her son, still waving. "I've brought you home."

It was a daunting prospect to learn later that she was to
meet her in-laws all on the same day at the wedding of
Rolf's sister. She need not have worried, for when the time
came she had never felt more welcome, and the valley and
the farmstead seemed like a missing part of the pattern of
her life, put together at last.

Johanna and Steffen were married in the local church by
the fjord. In the congregation Wendy saw national cos-
tumes for the first time, worn naturally as best wear on
special occasions. She was as intrigued by the embroidery
and gold ornaments as she was by the interior of the ancient church with its pine fragrance and rich decorations
painted by the hands of valley craftsmen who had been
gone two hundred years and more. Johanna wore a white
gown previously worn by Astrid's grandmother—a high-
necked, long-sleeved garment of lace and silk that had
simple lines and suited her slender figure. When the bride
and groom emerged into the sunshine there was no chim-
ing of the church bell, for it had been rung with such

enthusiasm on liberation day that it had cracked, the fate
of several old bells throughout the land.

The weather being warm, the wedding feast was set out
on long tables in the shade of trees by the farmhouse. The
traditional wedding cake, which had not been seen
throughout the Occupation, being made of ground al-
monds and sugar, rose in a tall pyramid of rings, the ingredients having been sent from Sweden and baked by Anna,
who had brought it with her from Oslo. Throughout the
meal there was a programme of songs dedicated to the
bridal couple and those close to them, sung to familiar
tunes, the words written by friends and family. There
were also plenty of speeches. Gunnar, who was best man,
spoke of the time he had known the bride and groom
during their Resistance days, but did not refer to any spe-
cific venture. That was to become the accepted rule
among those of the home front. Without any discussion,
there was a spontaneous, unspoken decision among them
all that since they had each played a part with many others, none holding himself or herself to be more important
than the rest, there should be a veil drawn over individual
achievements. Many members of the Resistance were to
receive decorations from the King, Steffen included, but
he never spoke of what he had done, not even to Johanna,
and she respected his reserve.

They returned to Oslo to see the King come home. It
was June 7, exactly five years to the day since he had sailed
into exile. Again the city burst into rejoicing on a scale that
surpassed in many respects even that of liberation day.
After rain in the morning, the sun came out to greet the
King in naval uniform and the Crown Princess and the
three royal children, who had returned home with him. In
an open car the King rode up banner-hung Karl Johans
Gate to the palace. On the balcony he took the salute as
those of the Resistance marched past him in their thousands, in the weatherproof jackets and rucksacks that had
been their everyday wear throughout five years of hiding
in mountains and in secret work. Steffen and Johanna were
among their number. With them marched brass bands
leading armed forces, released prisoners from the camps
and, miraculously, a Jewish boy, one of only twenty-four
Norwegian Jews to survive the extermination camps in

Germany and come home again. It was the greatest procession the city had ever seen and a day Johanna was to
remember all her life. The cheering in the exhilaration of
freedom regained was to echo in her heart down the years.

In 1984 she was in London shortly before Christmas.
Steffen, who had substantial interests in a Norwegian oil
company, had had a business meeting with his British
counterpart. She had accompanied him from their home
in Oslo, seizing the opportunity to do her seasonal shopping in her favourite London store. Both their sons were
married with three children each and she had a long list to
fill. At the end of a busy day she was relaxing in a taxi on
her way back to the hotel when it turned into Trafalgar
Square. Suddenly she leaned forward and tapped urgently
on the glass to the driver.

"Stop here, please."

"Your hotel isn't around here."

"I know. I've changed my mind for the moment."

With a Harrods green plastic bag full of festively
wrapped gifts on her arm, she got out and paid him. As he
drove away into the rush hour traffic, she turned to look
across at the Norwegian Christmas tree by the fountains in
the lee of Nelson's column. Casually and expensively
dressed, her elegance could still turn heads as she walked
slowly across the square until she came within a few yards
of the tree, which a short while ago had been felled in the
forests around Oslo. Her gaze travelled slowly up its great
height of forty feet or more to the crowning star. Its thickly
foliaged branches sparkled with white lights and swayed in
the chill breeze as if vibrating with life, an aura of brilliance hanging about it. The glow fell full on her upturned
face, whose beauty had defied the passage of time.

Every year a Norwegian tree came to London at Christmastime, just as it had during the war to remind an exiled
king of his homeland and of the people who awaited him
there. It came nowadays as a link between the friendship
of the past and the friendship of the future. Many memories stirred within her. Beloved faces long since gone
passed again before her eyes. She was deeply moved, just
as when she had visited the Resistance Museum in Akershus Castle for the first time and viewed the history that

had been hers and that of forty thousand others of the home front. By that long-ago agreement there were no names, not even of those whose exceptional courage had changed the course of history.

A young choir had filed into place by the tree, boys of a cathedral school, looking well brushed and neat for the occasion. There was some shifting of feet, a fluttering of song sheets, and then the choirmaster raised his arms, demanding full attention. They opened with "Silent Night," the music of their clear, high voices rising against a backcloth of the National Gallery and St. Martin-in-the-Fields. She lost track of time as she listened to them.

Somewhere a clock struck, reminding her that Steffen would be back at the hotel and looking for her. They were still lovers. There had never been anyone else for either of them. Leaving the Christmas tree, she hailed another taxi and it drew up for her. She paused for a moment before getting into it, looking back over her shoulder. The tree was a beautiful sight, the lights as white as the snows of Norway.

ABOUT THE AUTHOR

Rosalind Laker's many credits include *Banners of Silk*, *This Shining Land*, and *The Silver Touch*, about which Belva Plain said, "Richly packed with information, it gleams like fine silver itself." Her most recent novel, *To Dance With Kings*, was a Dual Main Selection of the Literary Guild. Ms. Laker lives in Sussex, England, with her husband.

DON'T MISS
THESE CURRENT
Bantam Bestsellers

☐ 26807	**THE BEET QUEEN** Louise Edrich	$4.50
☐ 26808	**LOVE MEDICINE** Louise Edrich	$4.50
☐ 25800	**THE CIDER HOUSE RULES** John Irving	$4.95
☐ 26554	**HOLD THE DREAM** Barbara Taylor Bradford	$4.95
☐ 26253	**VOICE OF THE HEART** Barbara Taylor Bradford	$4.95
☐ 26322	**THE BOURNE SUPREMACY** Robert Ludlum	$4.95
☐ 26888	**THE PRINCE OF TIDES** Pat Conroy	$4.95
☐ 26892	**THE GREAT SANTINI** Pat Conroy	$4.95
☐ 26574	**SACRED SINS** Nora Roberts	$3.95
☐ 26798	**THE SCREAM** Jonathan Skipp and Craig Spector	$3.95
☐ 27018	**DESTINY** Sally Beauman	$4.95
☐ 27032	**FIRST BORN** Doris Mortman	$4.95
☐ 27458	**NEW MEXICO—WAGONS WEST #22** Dana Fuller Ross	$4.50
☐ 27300	**OMAMORI** Richard McGill	$4.95
☐ 27248	**'TIL THE REAL THING COMES ALONG** Iris Rainer Dart	$4.50
☐ 27261	**THE UNLOVED** John Saul	$4.50

Prices and availability subject to change without notice.

Buy them at your local bookstore or use this page to order.

- -

Bantam Books, Dept. FB, 414 East Golf Road, Des Plaines, IL 60016

Please send me the books I have checked above. I am enclosing $_____
(please add $2.00 to cover postage and handling). Send check or money order
—no cash or C.O.D.s please.

Mr/Ms _____

Address _____

City/State _____ Zip _____

FB—2/89

Please allow four to six weeks for delivery. This offer expires 8/89.